*I did it. At the age of ten, I killed my father.*
*It was an accident, but it was still my fault.*
*Nothing I do can ever make up for the heinous mistake.*
*But I will spend the rest of my life trying . . .*

The canopy blew away from the flyer. A spring-loaded mechanism punched her out into open air.

Brooke plunged and spun out of control. Rushing air pummeled her in the face. Gravity shoved the terror-stricken screams back down her throat.

The automatic parachute blew open, jerking her body upward. Her orientation righted, and her descent slowed.

*The Little Angel* disappeared over the nearest mountain, but she couldn't locate her father's chute anywhere in the sky.

*Where is he? Didn't he jump out? Did his seat malfunction?*

The wind whipped through her hair. Water trickled through a stream far below her hanging feet. A flock of birds glided past her.

A thunderclap jolted her heart.

An explosion mushroomed upward from behind the mountain, burning the image into her memory forever.

"Daddy!"

**Books in the Beyond Saga**

Beyond Cloud Nine
Beyond the Horizon
Beyond Yesterday
Beyond Existence

**Other books by Greg Spry**

Destalis

**Short stories by Greg Spry**

Bears in Space
Goodbye, Mars

# BEYOND CLOUD NINE

GREG SPRY

www.beyondcloudnine.com

This is a work of fiction. Names, characters, places, and incidents either are the product of the author's imagination or are used fictitiously. Any resemblance to actual events, locales, business establishments, or persons, living or dead, is entirely coincidental. The publisher does not have any control over and assumes no responsibility for third-party websites or their content.

ISBN-10: 0990822400
ISBN-13: 978-0-9908224-0-0

Written and published by Greg Spry

www.gregspry.com
author@gregspry.com

www.beyondcloudnine.com
author@beyondcloudnine.com

Edited by Rose Jasper Fox ~ The Copymancer, www.copymancer.com
Proofread by Sophie Logan of Sharper Editing, www.sharperediting.com
Overall book cover design by Tobias Roetsch, www.gtgraphics.de
Character designs by Aaron Page, aaronpage.deviantart.com
Fighter plane designs by Chi-Chun Liu, pvtskwerl.deviantart.com

Printed by CreateSpace, an Amazon Company
Printed in the United States of America
Published September 2014
First Paperback Edition

## One—Coup de Main
## Jupiter Orbit, March 2247 AD

Stars twinkled below Lieutenant Brooke Davis's dangling feet. Resting her forearms on the railing, she gazed through the floor of a seldom-visited observation deck aboard the UN spacecraft carrier *Terminus*. The pinpoints of light seemed to orbit around her as the carrier rotated.

*Alone at last, away from everyone and everything*, she mused while almost cracking a smile. She'd chosen this hideaway near the aft engine block because the crew and her fellow pilots almost never came back here. *I'm not near them, they're not near me, and everybody's happy.* She'd given up trying to relate to people. Was it her genetic disorder that had caused this rift? Did her mixed heritage leave her stranded between Japanese and American cultures, without a people to call her own?

She wrinkled her nose at the thought. The reasons didn't really matter, and she didn't much care.

Her surroundings brightened. Brooke leaned over the railing and watched the brown belts and white zones of the planet Jupiter rising up from beneath her boots. Over the next few minutes, the gas giant's ring system scrolled into view, followed by its two Great Red Spots. Storm clouds churned and lightning crackled within the two oversized hurricanes, which stared back at her like a pair of angry eyes. The thought of how each one could swallow the Earth three times over put the insignificance of her life into perspective.

She craned her neck upward and looked along the hull of the carrier. The observation deck hung from a curved artificial horizon like the gondola of an antique blimp. To the rear of the carrier, she could see three of its six cylindrical antimatter nacelles. Each nacelle possessed twice the size of the ancient Saturn V rocket, the vehicle that had carried the first astronauts to Earth's moon almost three centuries ago. *We're much more advanced now, but not nearly enough to get me where I want to go.* She sighed.

Jupiter rose above and behind her head before disappearing.

Vibrations reverberated through the carrier, shaking her seat. The pulsations undulated through her toes, shook her body, and chattered her teeth.

An SF-522 Starthroat launched from the flight deck and blended into the backdrop of space. The sleek black star fighter's running lights blinked, its thrusters burned, and its fuselage blotted out the occasional star.

The Starthroat ignited its afterburners, flaring like a supernova. Automatically, the deck tinted near-opaque, dimming the flare of the fighter's plasma exhaust. Still, she had to squint and turn her head away.

A second later, the blinding light faded. The Starthroat rocketed away toward the planet, on course to defend one of the atmospheric particle collector balloons that provided the Jovian system with its chief source of power.

Watching a launch never got old, but she preferred the rush of the firsthand experience. Few things in life compared to pushing hundreds of gees in the fastest spacecraft known to exist.

She reached for the travel box of Fruity Planets cereal on the seat next to her, pulled out a piece, and tossed it into the air. The blinking, Saturn-shaped marshmallow wafted up and drifted down in slow motion, thanks to the quarter-gee rotational force that pulled everything to the interior of the outer hull.

The marshmallow settled onto her tongue, and she chewed and swallowed the sweetest bliss in the universe. After two more pieces, she tapped the top of the box, which morphed into a bowl, filled with milk, and produced a spoon.

While crunching away, she magnified a nearby constellation. Supposedly, three habitable exoplanets existed in the region—none with life as complex as that on Earth, but amazing nonetheless. Her skin tingled when she thought of how the UN's Project Luminosity might make it possible to reach these worlds in her lifetime. Her career as an Aerospace Defense pilot meant everything to her—she'd left Earth six years ago to pursue that dream—yet she'd give it up in a second to be selected as the first human to fly faster than light.

Her chest burned when she thought of the idiots who threatened the project.

Two of the hovering displays in the observation deck showed the divided nations and colonies of humanity fighting among themselves and each other. Skirmishes on and near the Earth, Luna, Mars, Ceres, and Jupiter dominated the news feeds. Pundits criticized the UN for its waning ability to keep the peace, and questioned whether its leaders should reassess the project.

One screen carried the South American Space Network, which broadcast a speech by a separatist group leader. "As of this day, March third, 2247, Minas Gerais secedes from Brazil under the direction of the Neoconservative Party." The smart-suited man palmed a fist. "We seek to gain equal footing through the procurement of antimatter and phase technology. The UN has implemented faster-than-light communications among its elitist nations and colonies without doing the same for the less fortunate. And now, the imminent arrival of FTL ships and fighters threatens to create an imbalance of power from which the solar system may never recover. We secede in the hope that others will follow and force the UN's hand."

Similar statements resounded from factions once part of the Chinese Solar Republic, the African Star Union, and the Russian Planetary Federation. Brooke had lost track of the number of new governments and territorial realignments. They seemed to change by the hour.

The voice of the UN secretary-general Danuwa Ajunwa boomed from the IntraSolar News channel. "The UN implores all nations and colonies to leverage diplomacy to settle these disputes—but let me make one thing clear." Her low, direct tone made every hair on Brooke's neck stand on end. "Acts of terrorism won't be tolerated. Everyone must trust that the UN has the long-term best interests of the solar system at heart. Efforts on the scale of Project Luminosity take time, but in the end, each and every human being will reap the benefits of phase technology. Therefore, I request your patience and understanding."

An image of the president of the UN Security Council, Edward Collins, replaced the secretary-general. "I'm pleased to announce Project Luminosity is progressing on schedule," he said from behind a podium. "The communication systems rollout to UN installations and testing of unmanned spacecraft is now underway, and the first manned flights should happen within a year. Qualified pilots may submit applications to the Luminosity Candidacy Training Program."

Chills surged through Brooke's limbs. She visualized herself at the controls of a superluminal fighter, hopping from star to star, feeling the theorized rush of hyperspace.

Putting on her net specs, she summoned Project Luminosity's SolNet presence, only to dismiss it right away. *You've signed, sealed, and transmitted your application. There's no way they've responded yet, so stop checking every five minutes.* She tried not to think about how every pilot in the solar system had likely applied.

"Attention all hands," the flight controller's voice squawked, cutting off Collins mid-sentence. "Separatist forces have been detected over the northeast hemisphere. All units are ordered to scramble immediately. This is not a drill. Attention all hands—"

Brooke hopped up and sprinted for the flight deck.

♦

Brooke's weightless body, clad in flight armor, floated down into the cockpit of her Starthroat. Fuel and coolant tubes slithered up the plane's fuselage, connecting to nozzle entry points.

As she settled into her seat, her arm twitched and she felt a twinge of anxiety that had nothing to do with mission jitters. *The sparks must be wearing off.* She clamped her fingers around her wrist. Even as she thought *I shouldn't take them*, she reached beneath her seat and pulled out an injector. Holding her ponytail to the side, she jabbed the auto-syringe into her neck. Nanorobotic narcotics flooded her nervous system, jolting her spine.

Clarity of thought soothed the brain freeze, and the quivering of her limbs subsided. *Nothing to worry about.*

She fastened her helmet to her armor and sealed her face shield, feeling like a futuristic knight. After the safety harness clamped down around her shoulders, locking her in place, the canopy closed. Gravity gel rose up above her boots, legs, torso, and helmet until it filled the cockpit. The gel buoyed up her body, soothing her as if she'd crawled back into the womb.

The neurotronic padding inside her helmet induced a tingle in her scalp, and her mental control systems flashed to life.

Her AI's voice intruded upon her thoughts. *<Gravgel immersion complete, ma'am. I've validated all subsystems, and flight control reports a green light. Ready for launch.>*

*Sounds good, Bob. Let's go.*

The flight elevator lifted her Starthroat up the launch tube and into the flight airlock. As the overhead bay doors slid aside, starlight brightened the cockpit, and the lift platform rose until it locked flush with the exterior hull.

Her fighter emerged like a mighty beast after a long slumber, ready to hunt for its prey. Latches released, and pneumatics catapulted it away from *Terminus*.

Lieutenant Jeff Braxton, her assigned wing mate, maneuvered his Starthroat into formation alongside her fighter.

"Control's assigned us collector 59-A," she said over the comm net. "I'm sending you the rendezvous trajectory."

"Whatever you say, Angel." Jeff's slow, monotone drawl over-enunciated her call sign. "I'll take point, if you don't mind."

"Actually, I do mind, Cobra. I'm the assigned flight leader for this sortie, so you'll follow my lead."

"Yes, ma'am." The inflection in his voice told her he didn't respect her authority or approve of his assignment as her dash-two. *What else is new?*

Brooke ignited her Starthroat's afterburners. Plasma erupted from the rear exhaust nozzles. She struggled to breathe as the gel squeezed her, protecting her from the crushing acceleration. The digits multiplied on her mental speed gauge, which toggled from kilometers per hour to kilometers per second.

The exhilaration helped to subdue the pangs of rejection.

Jupiter ballooned until it swallowed her surroundings. On Bob's signal, she cut the main rockets and coasted above a sea of swirling shades of brown. Ice crystals shimmered within the clouds, reflecting the faint sunlight.

She burned her fighter's retrorockets and decelerated, descending into the upper atmosphere. Her mental displays indicated the position of collector 59-A, currently engaged in its offloading ascent. Her cameras zoomed in on the oblong balloon.

Bob matched her Starthroat to the collector's orbit and she settled into a defensive posture a kilometer away. Jeff's fighter took up position nearby.

*<I've detected two bogeys at one hundred thousand kilometers' distance, ma'am.>*

An additional display popped into her field of vision. Shades of violet and crimson highlighted the bandits' armaments and weak points. UN Aerospace Defense identified the fighters as belonging to one of the separatist groups on Ganymede. They were patchwork spacecraft cobbled together from decades-old Chinese, Russian, Brazilian, and American star fighters—no threat to her sleek

Starthroat.

*<The bandits appear to be on an intercept course, ma'am. T-minus four minutes, thirty-two seconds until they reach the collector.>*

*Any other bogeys in the area?*

*<None that my sensors can detect, ma'am.>*

"Do you have them on your scope, Cobra?" she asked.

"I see 'em, Angel. There're only two. I reckon we oughta intercept before they make a run at the collector."

"Negative. That'd leave it vulnerable." She thought about it. "You go. I'll stay."

"Yes, ma'am." He burned his Starthroat's rockets and shot away.

She tracked his progress on her instruments. Pixels blinked, indicating weapons fire.

*<Ma'am, three more bandits are closing on Cobra's position,>* Bob warned.

*Where'd they come from? I thought you said—*

*<They were hiding lower in the atmosphere, ma'am. The turbulence must have shielded them from detection.>*

*Lower? They'd risk getting crushed to gain an extra few seconds of surprise?* She shook off her disbelief and leapt away, intending to back up her wingman.

A burst of silent light flashed up ahead.

*<Cobra has destroyed one of the first two bandits, ma'am. We should reach him in twenty-eight seconds, eleven seconds before the other three enemy spacecraft.>*

*Okay, target—*

*<Ma'am, two more bogies have appeared twenty thousand kilometers from the collector.>*

*What?!* She cursed, spun her fighter, and fired her afterburners, cutting her backward momentum. Once it hit zero, her Starthroat reversed direction and rocketed back toward the collector.

*<Ma'am, bandit six is coming toward us. Number seven remains on course for the—incoming warheads.>*

Bob sprayed anti-missile countermeasures from slots in the Starthroat's fuselage. Each deterrent emitted hyper-frequency jamming signals designed to confuse the projectiles.

Two of the three seekers lost target lock. Their thrusters fired at random, sending them on unpredictable paths. The first seeker shot past her fighter, descended into Jupiter's upper atmosphere, and detonated amid the halo-shaped clouds. The second seeker followed a stair-step trajectory off into space.

Brooke zigzagged her Starthroat, grunting. The third seeker buzzed her canopy, missing by meters. It exploded just past her starboard wing.

Her field of vision filled with data and graphic symbols. A red icon blinked in the star field, representing the enemy fighter. Neutrino radar tracked its position and flight path.

When the targeting bracket locked on, Brooke discharged the particle cannons. Blue-white death struck the bandit, popping its force field like a bubble.

Her Starthroat rocketed straight through the exploding craft. Searing heat and shards of metal almost overloaded her fighter's shielding.

Brooke got a fix on the seventh bandit and gasped. Pangs of dread coursed through her every appendage.

*<Ma'am, the bandit is on a collision course with the collector. We won't enter weapons range in time. Pull away at once.>*

Gritting her teeth, she darted away and throttled her afterburners to maximum output. Thin atmosphere scraped against her fighter's force field. A red glow shrouded the canopy.

Rear cameras showed the bandit slam into the collector. Flame and shrapnel burgeoned in all directions, obscuring the turbulent troposphere below.

The cockpit shuddered when the blast caught up to her Starthroat. Debris pummeled the fighter's shielding from behind.

She clamped her eyelids shut. The arteries in her neck throbbed with blood and adrenaline. She gulped air, hearing a whine as the life support system struggled to keep up with her hyperventilation.

Her seat and harness vibrated like a tuning fork, and the gravgel wavered, refracting starlight in rainbow patterns.

The explosion dissipated. Her fighter rocketed up and out of the atmosphere, and she blew out a long-winded breath.

After cutting speed, she asked, *Bob, where's Cobra?*

*<The other bandits retreated once the collector was destroyed. I show your wingman on a rendezvous trajectory.>*

*Thank the stars.*

Her Starthroat passed above the first of Jupiter's rings. Fine dust particles flowed like a river within the glittering inner halo ring.

Brooke stared back at the planet. Nothing remained of the particle collector. Dense clouds of amber and beige swirled beneath the dissipating blast.

Both her shoulders slumped.

"Y'know they'd rather die than accept the march of progress," Jeff said as his craft matched her course and speed.

Brooke scrunched her nose. *How did I miss that the first few fighters were decoys? Still, I should've been able to recover in time to stop that last one.*

"I'll say one thing, though. You're quick. I couldn't have reacted fast enough to escape those fireworks."

She wiggled her gloved fingers within the gravgel. *Was that a compliment?*

"I reckon nobody else could've, actually. You've got some kind of gene thing that makes you so fast, right?"

"My prenatal gene therapy had complications," she snarled, "but the doctors fixed them."

Jeff coughed, apparently realizing he'd overstepped. "At any rate, it's stupid we're all even out here. These dang terrorists can't hope to stop the project."

"I'll take them all on myself before I let that happen."

He sighed. "All I want is to be back on Callisto with my wife and baby girl."

Her Starthroat cleared the rings, bringing *Terminus* into view. Shaped like a fat metal rod, the carrier measured a kilometer in length and a quarter-kilometer in diameter. Particle beam turrets, missile launch racks, and remote sensing antennae protruded from its exterior.

Bob synchronized the Starthroat's orientation and velocity with the rotating carrier until its curved hull became her horizon. Her fighter descended and docked, followed by Jeff's fighter.

Dread burned within her chest. Once inside, she'd have to explain how she failed to prevent a group of overmatched terrorist fighters from destroying a collector. She'd face the scorn of her superiors and pitying stares of her fellow officers. *And what if my application gets denied because I screwed up?*

The voice of *Terminus*'s flight controller yammered from the speakers in Brooke's helmet. "We've intercepted a distress call from a civilian facility. Now altering course to respond. All fighter groups remain at ready status."

*Now what?* Brooke longed to return to her quarters. *This day can't end quickly enough.*

"Here's what we received before the signal terminated," the controller said.

The voice of a frantic woman usurped the comm net. "This is the Artemis Water Treatment Plant on Europa. We're under attack. They're trying to force their way into the control room. Requesting immediate UN assist—" A throat-scraping shriek cut off the woman's words.

Brooke winced.

"Single fighter craft on approach toward *Terminus*," the controller said. "Its triangular configuration conforms to no known design."

Shock laced the neudar operator's voice in the background. "The bogey's exceeding known speed thresholds and still accelerating."

"All units—"

The spacecraft carrier lurched, jarred by an impact. The force almost wrenched Brooke out of her seat harness. Pain knifed into her collar bone.

*<Ma'am, the command deck of* Terminus *has sustained a direct hit.>*

A mind screen replayed an explosion bursting forth from the bridge near the bow of the carrier. The turrets mounted along the hull ceased firing.

The comm net erupted with requests for orders and every curse word in the dictionary. Pleas begging the bridge to respond went unanswered.

The bright blue exhaust of tens of Starthroats leapt away from *Terminus*.

A white blur streaked past the carrier above her head.

She replayed the flyby in slow motion. The white isosceles triangle compared in size to her Starthroat. The tri-fighter's sleek fuselage gleamed in the distant sunlight. Aft exhaust ports whited out her mental display screen.

The UN's space superiority fighters darted about like dazed mosquitoes, fleeing the tri-fighter.

"Something's frying my neurotronics," a pilot yelled.

"I've lost control," another pilot shouted. "Propulsion systems nonfunctional."

Without engines or attitude control, Starthroats coasted on straight-line trajectories. Gurgling death screeches pierced her eardrums. Blue flames winked out of existence one by one. She shuddered.

*<Networked sensor data from operational units indicates the unidentified craft has destroyed twelve—correction, thirteen—friendlies, ma'am.>*

*Thirteen?!*

Her Starthroat's auxiliary consoles flashed.

*<A quantum jamming virus is interfering with onboard systems, ma'am.>*

Her scalp smoldered. Static electricity zapped her brain.

*Networked data*, Brooke realized, grimacing. *Firewall all external data ports!*

*<Done, ma'am.>*

The consoles ceased flickering, and the inside of her helmet cooled. She blinked the moisture out of her eyes.

*<Ma'am, we cannot receive telemetry in standalone mode.>*

*We'll have to do without it. Let's go.*

Her Starthroat broke away from *Terminus*.

Dialogue over the comm net confirmed the remaining pilots had figured out how to block the virus.

Jeff cursed. "My launch struts won't release."

Brooke executed a series of thruster burns, positioning her fighter above Jeff's Starthroat, covering him.

Her heads-up display showed the tri-fighter on a return approach to *Terminus*. The craft blasted launching Starthroats as it accelerated toward her.

*<Incoming particle discharges, ma'am.>*

She rolled her fighter, dodging a series of bright white pulses.

A pulse struck one of her Starthroat's wings. The impact spun her fighter counterclockwise. Brooke suppressed shudders of fright and trusted Bob to stabilize her craft.

With even breaths, she focused and anticipated. Her perception of time and the tri-fighter's movements slowed to a crawl.

She launched a pair of seekers, waited a fraction of a second, and fired a third. The bandit avoided the first two but couldn't avoid number three. The last seeker exploded against the tri-fighter's force field, knocking the craft away from *Terminus*.

*<Damage to port wing assessed as negligible on SF-522 performance, ma'am. Dispatching nanorepair bots.>*

"The release protocols are busted up," Jeff said. "I'm going to have to spacewalk."

Brooke's displays showed the recovered tri-fighter streaking toward them.

*Tactical assessment, Bob. Evaluate my ability to protect Cobra.*

*<Based on the maneuverability and armament precision of the unidentified spacecraft, the chances of preventing a positive hit on your wingman's craft are miniscule, ma'am. Cobra will avoid destruction only if the bogey refrains from targeting him.>*

*So, the only way to protect Cobra is to give the bandit a different target.* She plotted an intercept trajectory and fired the Starthroat's afterburners.

"Where're you going, Angel?" Jeff yelled. "I've got one foot out of the cockpit here. You're supposed to cover me."

*I am.*

Her Starthroat rocketed toward the tri-fighter. Jupiter engulfed her forward view.

*<Entering weapons range, ma'am.>*

Her heart thumped in her chest, but she held off the mental trigger.

White lightning lashed out from the tri-fighter. Brooke kept her Starthroat's nose pointed straight ahead and executed a series of minute thruster burns. The bolts missed her craft by centimeters.

She launched six seekers at the tri-fighter. It avoided them as she expected, but their dispersal pattern forced the bandit into her path.

*Route all power to the shield generator and reverse polarity, Bob.* She devoted her faculties to anticipating her enemy's movements.

*<Ma'am, collision imminent—>*

She wailed.

Her Starthroat's force field bashed into the tri-fighter's protective barrier. Discharges crackled around both spacecraft, bleeding more power than terrestrial lightning strikes.

Every mental display flickered out. The gravgel prevented the current from electrocuting her but failed to absorb the full force of impact.

Whiplash. Something snapped in her chest. She cried out through clenched teeth.

*<You've fractured two ribs, ma'am. >*

Electromagnetism repulsed. The two spacecraft ricocheted off each other in opposite directions. The tri-fighter sailed off into space. Brooke's fighter plunged toward the gas giant's turbulent atmosphere, spinning like a gyroscope.

*Bob!*

*<Propulsion and neurotronic control systems failing, ma'am. Working to correct the issues.>*

A blaze of crimson engulfed the Starthroat. Temperature gauges shot into the red, and sweat soaked her flight suit. Rear cameras showed a flaming wake trailing her fighter.

Warning icons blinked within her mind-vision.

*Got to stay awake.* She swallowed hard. *Not gonna power puke.* Her eyeballs squeezed and compressed.

*<The fuselage has exceeded structural limitations, ma'am.>*

The gravgel blurred. Extreme g-force pressed in on her like a trash compactor. The skin on her face pulled and stretched.

Brooke blacked out.

## Two—Polemology
## Chicago, March 2247 AD

Marie donned a no-nonsense frown and marched toward the new Stateway Gardens Revitalization Center.

A UN security guard blocked the gate. “Press pass?” A respirator muffled his deep voice.

She pulled the breather off her mouth and held up her news agency card. “My name is Marie Davis, correspondent for the Chicago VidStreamer.”

The guard turned his visor toward the bar code on her card. “I don’t see your name or organization on the list of approved media reps.”

“I applied for admittance but received no response.” Marie folded her arms. “UN press policy states that any representative of a credentialed journalistic entity has the right to attend any UN-sponsored event in said entity’s coverage area.”

His brow lifted. “It says here the Chicago VidStreamer serves four neighborhoods. It’s not much more than a community flyer.”

“If you do more than two seconds of research, you’ll see my organization and I have the necessary qualifications.”

“This event is being broadcast across the solar system. The secretary-general is making a personal appearance.” The guard smirked. “Only real news agencies have been granted access.”

“Local e-media has the same rights as the big boys. Or doesn’t the UN obey its own laws?”

The solar-collecting asphalt of the parking lot radiated heat despite the clouds of smog hanging overhead. Marie fanned her neck with her ID card while straightening her blouse and skirt. Nanofabric sensed her irritation and tinted red.

“No pass, no entry,” he said. “It’s that simple.”

She smiled her most patient smile. “You can’t legally deny me access. Now, if you don’t mind, I have a ribbon-cutting ceremony to cover.” She wiggled around the man’s seven-foot stature.

The guard clamped his hand around her arm and she winced. His grip felt like it might snap her thin limb.

*Bio-augmented strength?* She yanked her arm away, jumped back, and rubbed the bruise.

“I’m sorry, ma’am. I can’t admit you.”

Marie placed her hands on her hips. “Let me see if I’ve got this straight. Despite purporting equality and togetherness, the UN is playing favorites. Not only is this discrimination, it’s a violation of the UN Charter and basic freedom of the press.” She reached into her purse, whipped out an eyecam, and affixed it to her hair. The cam’s targeting display flipped down over her right eye. “Well, if you won’t let me through”—she winked, enabling record mode.—“you’re going to be the centerpiece of my next story.” She held out a tiny wireless mike. “Creating a center to serve the underprivileged while denying the little guy an audience makes the secretary-general look like a hypocrite, if not a criminal. Care to comment? Inquiring viewers in all four neighborhoods want to know.”

The man leaned forward, ready to pounce. Marie stifled a gasp.

A woman in a supervisor’s uniform came up behind him and put a hand on his shoulder. “Excuse me, ma’am, what was your name and affiliation?” she asked.

Exhaling, Marie said, “Marie Davis. Chicago VidStreamer.”

The supervisor ran her fingers across her e-slip. “Ah, yes. I see the problem. Apparently, your application got caught in an AI filter.”

*AI filter? Right . . . Somebody higher up took notice and doesn’t want a PR debacle. The VidStreamer may not be ISN, but something like this could go viral in a hurry.*

“Please issue Ms. Davis a press pass,” the supervisor said.

The guard nodded. “Yes, ma’am.” To Marie, he said, “My apologies, Ms. Davis. I’ll need to run a security sweep first before you enter.”

Marie straightened her grin.

After the guard completed his scan, Marie strutted through the gate. The revitalization center cast its shadow over the courtyard. At eighty-two stories tall, the structure qualified as a speed bump compared to the stratoscrapers of the downtown area. Holographic wrapping paper shrouded the new building, complete with a gigantic flickering bow.

While resisting the urge to pump a triumphant fist, Marie caught sight of the ISN logo flickering on the tie of a middle-aged reporter. The stocky man reminded Marie of her editor and the lack of faith he had shown in her that morning.

"If you want to waste your time, be my guest," Daniel Kern had said.

"They can't legally keep me out," Marie yelled across the leased office space. "I'm on the side of right, and the forces of good always prevail."

"Marie, you and I live in very different universes."

"You think so? Okay, then. Five thousand bucks says I not only finesse my way in but get Ajunwa to answer one of my questions."

Kern laughed. "Five K?" He plopped his girth down behind his desk. "You can't even get a burger for that these days. Make it six figures, a month's salary."

"You're on—no, forget the money. If I win, I want you to send me to—"

"We've been over this, Marie. We're a local feed. I can't afford to fly you to the West Coast to report on the project."

"Whatever." She scooped up her purse and stomped toward the exit. "You'll see."

"I was once a gung-ho college grad too, you know. Want my advice? Stick to local convenience store robberies."

*Well,* Marie thought. She pulled her breather up over her mouth and worked her way into the crowd. *I won the first part of the bet. Now on to the second.*

She couldn't push past the third-to-last row. Reporters knocked elbows. Hundreds of journalists boasting more impressive credentials than Marie fought for position in front of the portable stage.

*How am I going to get close enough to ask anything?*

A pair of tall metal cylinders, each with a ten-foot diameter, stood on either side of the stage. The crowd noise didn't quite drown out the humming the cylinders emitted.

*Military force-field generators? Guess the secretary-general is taking those death threats seriously.*

Conversations waned. Ajunwa's aides, the center director, and the mayor of Chicago stepped up onto the stage. The suits shuffled over to the seats behind the podium but remained standing.

Danuwa Ajunwa, the UN secretary-general, strode up onto the stage. Marie thought she looked both serious and stylish in her green and yellow gele and matching patterned mask. Two bodyguards flanked her.

The hum of the force field generators intensified. A shimmering effect obscured the figures behind the field.

Little red lights blinked on hundreds of eyecams, transmitting the secretary-general's image to the thirty-five billion people living throughout the solar system.

Three spherecams hovered above the crowd. Only major networks such as IntraSolar News could afford the expensive floating cameras.

Ajunwa lowered the mask from her mouth. "Welcome, everyone. I hope you and your families are in good health." Her dark brown eyes and the creases surrounding them conveyed great empathy. "On behalf of the United Nations, the city of Chicago, and innumerable benefactors, it's my pleasure to announce the opening of the new Stateway Gardens Revitalization Center."

Marie stood on tiptoe, angling her eyecam to get a better view. *Why couldn't I have grown another two inches?* She sighed, resigned to the presence of a woman's orange hairdo at the bottom of the footage.

"It has long been a dream of mankind—as well as a key objective of the One Humanity initiative—to end poverty, hunger, and crime. Cynics claim this isn't possible. In our modern era, however, such feats are within our grasp. We need only lay down arms and come together to attain these goals." Ajunwa radiated conviction. "This part of Chicago has long been one of the most impoverished in the American Colonies, a fitting place to erect this institution."

A tall reporter standing to Marie's right coughed behind his mask. "There are a bazillion places needier than here." He coughed again. Marie edged away slightly.

"Obviously," said the woman on the other side of him, "she wasn't about to do this little PR stunt in a country or colony engaged in civil war."

"The center behind me will provide services aimed at revitalizing the community," Ajunwa continued. "Prenatal gene therapy will be administered to infants of parents in low income brackets, resulting in fewer birth defects. The center's staff will find employment for every last jobless worker, increase the number of community service occupations, feed the hungry, raise funding for education and local law enforcement, offer mental pathway reconfiguration, and coordinate after-school activities for youths. My plan is to construct centers in countries free of hostilities."

Marie's toes fatigued. She dropped back down onto her heels.

A man wearing a visor-like pair of net specs shoved his way into the crowded space to her left and tinkered with a spherecam. When he caught Marie staring at him, his mouth contorted into a crooked smirk.

*Why do I feel like I've seen your mug shot on a low-budget crime drama?* She pried her glance away and stood as tall as possible.

Ajunwa gripped the podium with two hands. "Of course, this center and others to follow cannot solve society's problems alone. Only the full breadth of the One Humanity Act can do this."

"Here comes the sales pitch," said the coughing reporter. "Ajunwa's magical fix to everything."

Ajunwa paced atop the stage. "The One Humanity Act aims to achieve unparalleled cooperation and coordination while maintaining the freedoms of member nation-states. Funds will be shifted to areas of greatest need. Oversight committees will exercise authority over matters such as agriculture, health, and science. We have the technology to feed everyone and counter the pollution forcing us to wear these on bad days." Ajunwa tapped the mask hanging around her neck. "The only barrier is the selfish shortsightedness driving the current political climate."

"You can't force policy on us like a communist dictator," someone shouted from the middle of the crowd.

The secretary-general nodded and returned to the podium. "Contrary to propaganda spread by separatist groups, the UN isn't trying to impose a communist dictatorship. We're here to serve as an intrasolar arbitrator. One Humanity combines the most effective elements of historical government structures, those which yield equality and prosperity for every human being. I championed the cause, but the battles being waged throughout the solar system belie my ability to force policy on anyone. Unsubstantiated fears drive the killing going on around us."

"What about Project Luminosity, Madam Secretary?" a reporter near the stage blurted out. "How do you respond to claims that only the privileged few stand to benefit from a potentially dangerous new technology?"

"Quite frankly, I'm surprised by such reactions. We're entering an exciting new era, one in which the distance between family members will soon drop from weeks to minutes—one which will allow the human race to explore the galaxy. There will always be those who remind us to heed caution, and I thank them for keeping us honest. A healthy fear of the atomic bomb prevented its use beyond the mid-twentieth century and led to nuclear power generators. In a similar manner, antimatter should do nothing but benefit mankind under the direction of the UN. I won't allow a handful of malcontents to stand in the way of a better tomorrow for everyone. "

A group of inner-city youth filed toward one side of the stage.

Ajunwa held out an open palm, indicating the youth group. "These children will be the first to benefit from the center's services. They are our tomorrow. I can think of no more appropriate act than to allow them to 'unwrap' the building."

The podium slid to the side. A platform with a big green button rose out of the stage.

The pushy newcomer held up his spherecam. The device rose from his palms, levitated above everyone's heads, and drifted closer to the stage. "For tomorrow," he whispered.

The man tapped his net specs, turned, and elbowed his way out of the crowd.

Marie watched the spherecam. Its height dipped, rose, and dipped again.

*Seems heavier than the others.* A bad feeling pierced her gut. *What's wrong with this scene? Some creep launches a device he shouldn't be able to afford from the back of the crowd right when . . .*

The hum of the force field generators dissipated. The shimmering in front of the stage vanished, allowing the children to ascend the stairs.

The spherecam shot toward them.

## Three—Outbrave
## Jupiter Orbit, March 2247 AD

Memories of the first time Brooke pushed a plane beyond the limit flooded her subconscious.

"Ready, Brooke?" her father asked.

She whipped her chin up and down like a bobblehead doll. "Ready, Daddy."

Robert Davis helped his ten-year-old daughter crawl up into his ion flyer. "Parachute fastened?"

Brooke plopped down into the front seat and tugged on her shoulder straps. "Cutting off my circulation."

Her father smiled, smoothed his mustache, and hopped into the rear seat. One palm caressed the fuselage of the century-old family heirloom. His fingers traced the flyer's name, *The Little Angel*, written in cursive.

After securing his parachute, he leaned over Brooke's shoulder and ran her through the pre-flight ritual his grandfather had once performed. "Here, we have the altimeter, speedometer, climb—"

"Climb-descent, artificial horizon, flap, and fuel gauges. You've explained them a hundred times, Daddy."

"Well, then." Father settled back into his seat. "Take us up."

"Okay." Goosebumps tickled her arms. *I'm really going to fly it!*

She pressed the ignition switch. The engine hummed. Vibrations shook the cramped cockpit and heightened her anxiety.

She waved to her mother and twin sister.

"Bye!" Marie jumped up and down in front of the hangar.

Worry creased the wrinkles on her mother's forehead. A breeze blew down from the Colorado Rockies, ruffling her blouse.

Brooke tapped on the old touchscreen interface. The bubble canopy descended over both seats, latching with a click. Then she slipped on a pair of aviator goggles, a gift from her father. The vintage eyewear made her feel like a pilot from one of those ancient black-and-white feeds.

Her intestines knotted in anticipation. She twisted the throttle, nudging the plane forward.

*The Little Angel* picked up speed. The engine buzzed louder. Grass blurred to a sheet of green.

She pulled the control stick toward her lap, lifting the flyer's nose. Her stomach sank while the plane soared up and away into the blue yonder. "See what I can do, Daddy?" She gripped the stick with both hands, whipped it to the right, and attempted a barrel roll.

The flyer spun sideways faster than she anticipated, throwing her to the side. In response, she yanked the stick back the other way. The engine coughed. Torque stressed the flyer's thin fuselage.

"Whoa, easy," Father said. "*The Little Angel* responds to slow, gradual adjustments."

"I know," Brooke grumbled. She spent a few minutes feeling out how the flyer responded. She worked the flaps, steered the plane toward Denver, and circled back around in the direction of the Rockies.

"Why don't you take us up higher?"

"Okay." She pulled the stick back as far as it would go. The digital altimeter climbed. She fell back into her seat.

The early-morning sun peeked its way up over the mountains. Vehicles, roads, fields, and rocky hills shrank until they resembled a model train set.

Brooke swallowed, equalizing the pressure in her ears.

Thick clouds swallowed the flyer. Mist sprayed the front of the canopy. Brooke imagined her body drifting out among the gentle, rolling puffs.

The plane poked its way up into the clear, breaching the stratosphere.

Her father leaned forward. "We're approaching our atmospheric service ceiling."

"I know, Daddy. It's the highest we can go." She throttled back, leveled out the flyer, and flipped it upside down. Gravity tugged her out of her seat. Her shoulders dug into her harness, which prevented her from falling toward the canopy bubble.

Snow-drenched mountains poked through the glowing cloud cover below. The horizon line sloped in a majestic blue streak. Azure shades faded to the blackness of the great beyond.

Her mouth hung open. She felt like the most powerful ten-year-old girl in the solar system.

After rotating the flyer right-side-up, she craned her neck toward the fading stars in the brightening sky. "I want to fly up into space and explore other galaxies, Daddy."

Her father chuckled. "So do I, but maybe we should start with this one." He leaned over her and pointed to a group of stars. "Do you recognize that constellation?"

"Um . . . Orion, right?"

"Yes, good job. Scientists have discovered at least one habitable exoplanet in that stellar nursery. They say it's a lot like Earth but the plant life and sky are different colors."

"Wow. Can we go and see?"

He stroked his mustache, grinned, and sat back. "It's my dream to do that someday. I don't know if I'll get the chance, but I hope you will."

"Me, too, Daddy. I can't wait to get far away from here."

"You mean from Earth? Why would you say that?"

"The kids at school are mean. They make fun of me because I'm different."

"Because of your disorder?"

"And because I'm half Japanese." She squeezed the control stick. "I get so mad, I want to hurt them all."

"I see. Well, kids—people—can be cruel sometimes."

"Will it stop when I get older?"

Her father sighed. "It might, but it never stops completely. The adult world can be far crueler than a child's sometimes."

"Mom says I should think happy thoughts and pretend they're not making fun of me, but I can't do that."

"That does sound like your mother. I won't contradict her, but I do understand your feelings." After further mustache-stroking, he said, "Personally, I'd rather be miserable knowing the truth than happy living a lie, but not everyone feels that way. There isn't a right or easy answer to the question. Everyone has to make their own decision."

"I don't think I understand, Daddy."

"You will someday."

A warning light flashed. The flyer's computer tracked two craft on the radar screen.

Miles away, a pair of bright blue specks pierced the clouds and ascended toward low Earth orbit.

"Oh, wow." Pangs of giddiness undulated through her body. "Star fighters." She turned her head partway around. "UN SF-515 Cormorants, right?"

"You got it."

She faced forward. The canopy darkened, shielding her vision from the glare of the Cormorants' exhaust.

Gripping the throttle, she said, "I want to get a closer look."

"All right, but maintain a safe distance."

The ion flyer picked up speed. Brooke closed in on the Cormorants enough to discern their shapes. The fat metallic birds' wings retracted as they left the atmosphere behind.

Brooke pushed the flyer to max velocity and lifted it higher, following them. She imagined sitting in the cockpit of one of those fighters, rocketing toward the stars.

Her father lurched forward in his seat. "Brooke, you're getting too close. Cut speed and turn around before—"

The flyer's console flashed and beeped.

Superheated air rushed into the cockpit, blasting her in the face. Brooke clamped both eyelids shut, closed her mouth, and whipped her head to the side. Her lungs felt like they had inhaled fire. Searing heat stung but didn't quite burn her skin.

The engine sputtered and shut off.

The sweltering feeling dissipated as quickly as it had washed over her.

"We flew through their exhaust vortex," her father said. "The flyer's intake manifolds can't handle the plasma backwash." He hunched over her, reached for the emergency ignition switch, and pressed it. "I should've been paying closer—" The starter clicked and droned. "The propellant won't ionize." His face paled. "The couplers must be oversaturated. It won't restart."

The flyer's nose dipped. Brooke felt her stomach drop.

She peered back at her father, trembling. "I'm sorry." Tears streamed down her cheeks.

The flyer plunged toward the Earth. The digits on the altimeter cycled downward. Brooke couldn't budge the control stick.

"We have to eject," her father yelled.

Her heart pounded. She tried to recall the lectures he had given her on what to do in such an event, but her mind wouldn't focus.

"Ready?" he shouted.

A whimper escaped Brooke's lips.

"Now!"

She reached down and yanked the lever beneath her seat.

The canopy blew away from the flyer. A spring-loaded mechanism punched her out into open air.

Brooke plunged and spun out of control. Rushing air pummeled her in the face. Gravity shoved the terror-stricken screams back down her throat.

The automatic parachute blew open, jerking her body upward. Her orientation righted, and her descent slowed.

*The Little Angel* disappeared over the nearest mountain, but she couldn't locate her father's chute anywhere in the sky.

*Where is he? Didn't he jump out? Did his seat malfunction?*

The wind whipped through her hair. Water trickled through a stream far below her hanging feet. A flock of birds glided past her.

A thunderclap jolted her heart.

An explosion mushroomed upward from behind the mountain, burning the image into her memory forever.

"Daddy!"

Shock jolted Brooke back into the present. Her eyes burst open.

The Starthroat leapt clear of Jupiter's atmosphere.

Bob's voice echoed throughout her head. *<All systems have been restored, ma'am. Increasing oxygen levels to aid in respiration.>*

Her lungs sucked in air. Pain pierced her chest. Brooke recoiled.

*<Two of your ribs are broken, ma'am. Releasing medical nanites.>*

A short needle formed inside her flight armor and pricked her inner elbow. Cool liquid rushed beneath her flesh, flooding her bloodstream with thousands of tiny healing robots.

*<The discomfort should subside within a few seconds, ma'am. You'll require one to two additional injections to completely correct the skeletal damage.>*

The stabbing sensation lessened to an uncomfortable scraping within her ribcage.

She forced the discomfort from her mind. *How long was I out?*

*<You lost consciousness for twelve-point-three seconds, ma'am.>*

*What happened to that bogey?*

*<The damaged spacecraft has righted its trajectory and is headed for Europa under reduced power, ma'am.>*

*Europa? That can't be a coincidence.*

*<The enemy craft's approach toward* Terminus *indicated Europa as its most probable point of origin, ma'am. Therefore, I project a seventy-nine percent likelihood the craft was involved in the attack on the Artemis Water Treatment Plant.>*

*Can we catch the bandit before it reaches Europa?*

*<Ma'am, Europan space has been designated as a restricted zone by Command.>*

*What? A major moon with multiple colonies and bases? That makes no sense.*

*<I cannot offer an explanation, ma'am, but I recommend ceasing pursuit.>*

*Negative. I want to intercept that craft and figure out where it came from. Command needs to know.*

*<We must decelerate for orbital insertion and moonfall, ma'am. Therefore, we will reach the surface thirty seconds after the bandit.>*

*What if we don't slow down?*

*<Ma'am, we need to begin decelerating in three minutes, or we'll slam into the moon's surface.>*

*That's not what I asked.* Brooke bit her lower lip. *If we wait to cut speed, we should be able to catch up.*

*<We can intercept the bandit's trajectory by delaying our deceleration burn by forty-nine seconds, ma'am. However, doing so will require us to veer away from the moon.>*

*Exactly. Calculate a swing-by to help us slow down the rest of the way.*

*<Ma'am, I don't recommend—>*

*Just do it, Bob.*

Europa grew from a pinpoint of light to a ball of ice the size of Brooke's fist. She tuned out the automated message warning her away from the moon.

On Bob's mark, Brooke twirled her fighter around and fired its afterburners. She didn't like charging toward an enemy—or a big ball of rock—backwards, but the Starthroat's forward retrorockets couldn't provide the necessary braking thrust.

Europa's cold, bright face ballooned to engulf her forward view. The crisscrossing cracks and dark streaks in the surface ice resembled living veins and arteries.

Brooke's augmented mentality identified the tri-fighter's position. It remained on approach toward Europa and had begun cutting speed. Her instruments showed fluctuations in the bandit's power signature. The underside of the craft's fuselage vented crystalizing smoke.

*<We now lack sufficient time to achieve a capture orbit or surface*

*landing, ma'am. Weapons range in fifty-eight seconds.>*

The Starthroat closed the distance to the tri-fighter. Her face shield tinted, dimming the craft's flaring white exhaust.

*<Now, ma'am.>*

Brooke aimed in front of the tri-fighter's approach path and launched six seekers.

The bandit struggled to avoid the higher velocity projectiles. Two of the seekers detonated against its shielding before the craft disappeared behind Europa.

Her Starthroat shot around the opposite side of the moon, nose still pointing backwards. Mountains and canyons of water ice whipped past meters above the canopy.

Europa flew by and shrank away.

The tri-fighter reappeared on the other the side of the moon and unleashed a barrage of white energy pulses. One struck the Starthroat's force field, rocking the craft.

Her fighter's backward velocity hit zero, slowing to a stop relative to the moon. She kept the afterburners engaged and barreled back in the direction of Europa.

The Starthroat descended toward the surface and soared over frozen buttes and ravines. A faint blue haze hung over the curving horizon. Jupiter dominated the sky.

*<We're now passing above the geological terrain known as Conamara Chaos, ma'am.>*

*Isn't that the location of the water plant?*

*<Correct, ma'am.>*

Three-dimensional blueprints of the Artemis Water Treatment Plant appeared in her mind's eye. The facility consisted of ten cylindrical tanks the size of UN spacecraft carriers. Domes, communications towers, laser drilling rigs, and radiation shield generators huddled around them.

*<Incoming bogey, ma'am. It's launched eight warheads.>*

Brooke dove into the nearest canyon. Walls of rock and ice towered overhead. Missiles rained down like a hailstorm, detonating against the chasm floor. Flame and ice spewed from the impact points, spraying the Starthroat's shielding. Shock waves thudded against the fuselage. Even with its wings retracted, her fighter came within meters of knocking into the canyon walls on each juke.

After reversing thrust, she backed her fighter up against a wall. Bob calculated the trajectories for each remaining missile, allowing her to blast them.

She launched her Starthroat up out of the chasm.

The tri-fighter peppered the space around her craft with bursts of white lightning. No matter what maneuver she pulled, she couldn't shake the bandit.

*What does it take to knock this guy out?*

Particle discharges struck her force field. Displays flickered. The rumbling of her engines waned but her pulse quickened.

Brooke gasped as the tri-fighter narrowed the gap between them.

## Four—Cabal
## Europa, March 2247 AD

Sapphire bursts of light pelted the tri-fighter from overhead. Its force field sustained multiple hits before the craft veered away from her.

*<Single friendly approaching from three o'clock high, ma'am.>*

Jeff Braxton's Starthroat descended toward the moon's surface.

Elation coursed through her, and she launched all her remaining seekers. The kinetic energy-packed warheads spun away from the Starthroat's undercarriage, trailing coils of exhaust.

The tri-fighter dodged the first four seekers, but the fifth, sixth, and seventh hit home. The craft's force field burned crimson, overloading. Secondary explosions erupted all around it.

With engines flickering, the tri-fighter fled toward the water distillation plant.

Brooke exhaled. The prodding in her chest returned, and she grimaced.

♦

Jeff maneuvered his Starthroat into the water plant's pressurized hangar bay. After setting his fighter down next to Brooke's craft, he instructed his AI matrix to seal the interior bay doors.

Once the bay had repressurized, the cockpit drained of gravgel. He flipped open the canopy, stood, stretched, and pulled off his helmet. The ceiling's plasma strips cast a soft glow over the bay, which appeared big enough for maybe half a dozen craft. Nearby, two other unoccupied Starthroats sat parked next to the tri-fighter that had attacked *Terminus*.

He folded his arms, considering the scene. UN reinforcements could've arrived ahead of him and Brooke, and the tri-fighter had retreated here for whatever reason, but the presence of two friendlies together with the enemy craft made little sense.

*Why in blazes did I follow her here?* Jeff asked himself. After completing his spacewalk and manually releasing the launch struts from his Starthroat, he'd flown off in search of Brooke, following his AI's prediction that the tri-fighter had attacked the plant.

He grabbed his particle rifle, jumped out of the cockpit, and drifted down to the deck in Europa's thirteen percent Earth-nominal gravity.

Brooke stumbled out of her fighter and floated down. The moment her boots contacted with the floor plating, her body recoiled. She dropped her rifle, clutched her chest, and collapsed.

He helped her sit up and decoupled her helmet from her flight armor. Strands of lavender-streaked black hair strayed from her ponytail. Every muscle in her round face contorted in pain. The pores in her forehead and cheeks glistened with sweat. She glared at him, irises tinted violet by military-issue ocular implants.

"What did you do to yourself?" Jeff rushed back to his Starthroat and returned with its med kit. He pulled an auto-syringe out of the kit and jabbed it in her neck.

Brooke hissed. She clutched her upper torso.

"I shot you full of medites." He shook his head. "They should heal your ribs in a few hours, but I reckon we should get you back to Callisto."

"No."

He folded his arms and peered around the hangar. "We should raise Command before doing anything."

The external speakers on Brooke's Starthroat amplified the voice of its intelligence matrix. <All frequencies are being jammed, sir. I've been unable to send or receive transmissions since we made moonfall.>

Brooke thrust her chin at the abandoned Starthroats. "Bob, pull registry data for both of those rides."

Jeff raised an eyebrow. " 'Bob'?"

She scowled and pushed to her feet. He tried to help her, but she shrugged him off.

<Ma’am, I cannot locate serial numbers for either SF-522 Starthroat. According to the Defense inventory manifest, these spacecraft were never manufactured.>

“That don’t make a lick of sense,” Jeff said.

She directed her gaze at the tri-fighter. “And this thing?”

<Ma’am, the unidentified spacecraft’s fuselage shows damage consistent with weapons impacts. I calculate a ninety-nine-point-eight percent probability this is the craft we engaged.>

“What’s it doing here, saddled up next to two of ours?” Jeff asked.

<I have insufficient data with which to formulate a hypothesis, sir.>

Brooke leaned against the nose of her fighter and faced the triangular craft. Her lithe body blocked part of the inscription of her call sign, Angel.

The tri-fighter’s fuselage possessed the smoothness of porcelain with rounded edges and corners. Faint grooves connected sections of white composite plating.

Jeff squinted, zooming in on the tri-fighter’s hull. “She’s gussied up prettier than one of our babies.”

<My scans show its engineering tolerances to be more precise than those of a Starthroat, sir.>

Holes from high-velocity particle and warhead impacts sealed in slow motion. Charred sections of paneling whitened, prompting Jeff to whistle. “She’s got some advanced repair systems, too.”

“Bob,” Brooke asked, “what’s the situation inside the plant?”

<The facility’s control center has failed to respond to repeated hails, and its intelligence matrix is offline. Much of the plant has depressurized. I detect no structural breaches, which suggests intentional shutdown of the environmental systems. My infrared scanners detect three heat sources of probable biological origin.>

“Only three?” Jeff asked.

<Affirmative, sir.>

He folded his arms. “I thought this plant was manned by a couple hundred folks.”

<Last registered personnel complement was two hundred and fourteen, sir.>

“All dead . . .” He shuddered, then shook it off and peered across the bay. “Should we do something to sabotage those fighters?”

Brooke’s hawk-like stare shifted in that direction. “Two of those rides are still ours, and that strange craft might be booby-trapped. Let’s concentrate on tracking down those three heat signs and getting some answers.” She jammed the power clip into her particle rifle.

After donning their helmets, Jeff and Brooke took position on opposite sides of the airlock leading to the plant's interior.

"You feeling okay, Angel?" he asked over a direct comm net channel.

She turned to face him. The bay's dim illumination and her angular visor hid her expression. "Override the lock, Bob." She glanced at Jeff. "And tune in Cobra."

The AI's voice echoed in Jeff's head. *<Opening now, ma'am.>* Its clipped tones made it sound as tight-assed as Brooke. Jeff shook his head at the thought.

The airlock spiraled open. He braced for a particle beam assault, but nothing happened.

"What do you see, Bob?" she asked.

*<Nothing on infrared in the adjacent corridor, ma'am. The three heat signatures must be further inside, possibly underground. It should be safe to enter.>*

"Reckon the separatists are here to wrestle the place from the UN?" Jeff asked. "This plant provides most of our water."

She shrugged.

*<This is the only facility with the infrastructure to pipe up water from the underground ocean, sir. Whoever controls this place holds significant leverage over the Jovian system.>*

Brooke entered the corridor with her weapon raised, top-mounted flashlight slicing through the darkness.

Jeff followed. The hallway stretched as far as he could see without his eye-zoom enabled. The ceiling rose to a height of four meters. Not one door stood between him and the far end. Bodies lay motionless across the floor. A floating blue screen flickered within the wall like a strobe light, giving the hallway the feel of a haunted house.

Brooke bent down to inspect a corpse. The man wore a gray jumpsuit.

"Looks like a plant engineer," Jeff said. "I wonder whether the poor bastard suffocated or froze to death."

She nudged the man over onto his back. His skin had swollen. Frozen blood jutted out from his inner ear. Two stiff hands clenched his neck, and his mouth hung agape.

Jeff forced down a gag.

"His saliva must've boiled when the facility lost pressure." Brooke rose to her feet, bounded over to the wall screen, and poked a distorted icon with her gloved finger. The screen flashed red. "Bob, any luck interfacing?"

*<Negative, ma'am. My attempts to bring the facility's AI online*

*have failed.>*

"Let's head for the control room," Jeff said. "I'll take point." He expected Brooke to argue, but she nodded and let him go first.

Jeff worked his way through the plant's corridors, strides long and slow in the reduced gravity. He passed through a mess hall, workout room, laboratory, and office space. Bodies littered the hallways and hunched over workstations. He shivered at the sight of each one.

*<I'm encountering difficulty tracking the heat sources, ma'am. Something's interfering with my infrared.>*

As Jeff entered yet another passageway, he kept one eye on a holographic layout of the facility. A red dot appeared and disappeared ten meters from his current position.

A volley of white energy bolts shot toward him from the darkness. One struck him in the chest. The force of the blast drove him back and knocked the rifle out of his hands.

He peered down and whimpered. His armor's ultra-strong carbon nanotube plating could stop a bullet or low-intensity particle beam, but before his eyes, it was beginning to evaporate. In moments a hole exposed the fabric of his flight suit. He stared in horror as the fabric also melted away, revealing bare skin. Red icons flashed decompression warnings in his mental vision. Light-headed, he fell back against the corridor wall and slid to the floor.

♦

Brooke dove into a nearby doorway.

She glanced back at Jeff out in the passageway in shock. Nozzles on the inside of his suit sprayed foam across his chest. The sealant hardened within seconds, patching the breach. He managed to drag himself into a room across from her. His gasps hissed over the comm net.

She checked her displays. No heat sources registered, but her gut insisted that one was looming close to them.

Another barrage bombarded their position. A section of the metal wall dissolved, giving her an unobstructed window out into the corridor.

"Can you walk?" Brooke asked.

"I reckon so."

"That foam won't hold for long. Get out of here."

"What about you?"

"I'll cover you and follow when I can."

"That ain't right, Angel. We oughta leave together."

"And get shot in the back as we flee?"

"Well—"

"That's an order."

A third light show flashed between them.

"Dang it all, Angel."

She stuck her rifle out into the hallway and fired a rapid succession of bursts. "Go!"

Jeff stumbled to his feet and lumbered back down the corridor in the direction they had come.

Brooke pulled back. Another volley tore through the hallway and struck a load-bearing beam, caving in the ceiling. She rolled further into the room. Machinery massive enough to crush her drifted down from above. Europa's low gravity saved her from being flattened.

"Cobra?"

The comm net hissed with interference. She thought she heard one brief syllable in his voice but couldn't tell for certain.

"Bob? Bob, can you hear me?"

More static.

*What the hell's going on? Separatists aren't capable of this!* She surveyed the dim room she had entered, noting the outlines of desks, chairs, and tables in the auxiliary lighting. She found another exit on the opposite side of the room, hopped to her feet, and darted through it.

Her infrared registered a heat source around the upcoming corner.

It disappeared again.

A flexible tube as thin as a human hair extended from her rifle and bent around the corner. Its camera showed her a three-meter-tall intruder in a white spacesuit standing at the far end of the corridor. She couldn't discern a face behind the black, bowl-shaped face shield, but she took notice of the sleek rifle aimed in her direction.

White energy bolts disintegrated the corner, nearly frying the tube.

Yelling into her helmet mic, she broadcast her voice over all frequencies. "You're trespassing in a facility under the jurisdiction of the United Nations! Drop your weapon and get down on the floor, now."

Seventeen seconds passed according to her chronometer.

Her mental displays flashed, indicating an incoming communications signal.

"It honors me to face you again," said a very articulate voice. It sounded like a man, yet his pitch wavered in synthesized fashion.

Her brow dipped. "Again?"

"You're the first adversary I've had the pleasure of failing against."

"You're the pilot of the tri-fighter."

The orange-red smudge of his heat signature returned to her mental map.

The smudge turned to leave.

She jumped out into the corridor, raised her rifle, and sighted the back of his slim spacesuit. “Stop. Don’t force me to shoot you.”

He halted. “Discharge your weapon if you feel so inclined.” His head twisted around. “It shall make no difference.”

Brooke squeezed the trigger. Blue pulses of light leapt from the muzzle.

Lightning crackled around a sphere of shielding enveloping his suit. A fuzzy haze absorbed and dissipated her pulses, leaving him unscathed.

“A personal force field?” She jumped back behind the corner. “Who is this guy?” she mumbled.

“I’m a part of that which will save you from yourself.”

“What?”

She re-extended the camera around the bend. The intruder was stepping through the hatch at the end of the corridor. “Until we meet again, Lieutenant Brooke Davis.” The hatch slid shut behind him.

*<Ma’am.>* Bob’s voice cut through the static. *<I’ve triangulated the location of the three heat sources. Two are located six levels below your position, inside the underground ITER fusion reactor chamber. The third is moving away from your position, headed for a probable rendezvous with the others.>*

Her stomach dropped straight down to Europa’s metallic core. *Bob, stand by for takeoff.* Returning to her Starthroat and getting the hell out of there seemed prudent, but she couldn’t turn tail, not if she had the slimmest chance of stopping what she assumed the intruders intended to do. *I’ve come this far . . . I’m going in after him. Keep an eye on me if you can, and if I get into trouble, get me out.*

Bob’s directions led her down a sloping, twisting corridor that led deep underground.

The hallway widened, giving way to towering walls of ice and rock. The faint humming that had begun at the mouth of the corridor grew to a loud rumbling.

*<Ma’am, I’m losing your sig—>*

*Bob?* Interference crackled. *Bob!* She stomped a booted foot.

The tunnel dead-ended at a concrete wall. Her map indicated that the wall made up one side of the subterranean structure housing the plant’s massive fusion reactor.

Brooke crept toward the structure’s airlock. Her suit sensors failed to distinguish anything from the noise generated by the reactor.

After swallowing hard, she pressed the holopad next to the airlock.

The pad blinked red with the text "I-Matrix Offline. Manual Override Required."

She ran a search through her data on the facility. The instructions she located required her to open an access panel in the wall near the ground.

Brooke bent down and reached for the toolkit affixed to her left hip. She stopped when she noticed the panel propped up against the wall.

Someone had removed it.

With her index finger, she pushed an orange Decompress button inside the open compartment. A red light blinked. When it ceased flashing and turned green, she pulled the lever next to it.

The airlock's outer hatch swished open.

Brooke stepped into a chamber large enough to accommodate three or four people. The outer door closed, followed by the hiss of oxygen rushing to fill the vacuum. She tapped her boot against the floor, waiting. Five seconds felt like an eternity.

The inner hatch parted.

She entered the reactor hold, leading with her rifle.

Her surroundings opened up into a chamber fifty meters tall and wide. Rows of thick viewports lined the central concrete cylinder housing the reactor, protecting outsiders from the excess heat and radiation the internal force fields failed to contain. Field coils spun behind the windows, emitting every color in the rainbow. The chamber vibrated.

Her suit displays confirmed the presence of breathable atmosphere. She pressed a button on the side of her helmet. Her face shield retracted. Cool air wafted over her face.

Voices echoed throughout the reactor hold. Her suit's acoustic software traced the points of origin to behind the central reactor tower, filtered out background noise, and amplified the conversation.

"I've set the antimatter charge," a man said. "T-minus fifteen minutes."

The words froze Brooke in place halfway to the reactor. *How do they have antimatter?* She set her mental chronometer to count down from fifteen minutes. *And where have I heard that voice before?*

"Do we really want to do this?" a second man asked.

"With phase technology coming, we have to set the plan in motion now or risk discovery," the first responded.

"Such action may seem extreme, but it's the only method by which to ensure your tomorrow." The third voice belonged to the white-suited intruder. "This is in service of the greater good."

"C'mon, let's get the hell out of here," the first man said.

Footsteps clanged against metal flooring.

Brooke backpedaled.

The three men emerged around the side of the reactor.

She recognized the two UN Aerospace Defense pilots. *Sterling and Hunter?*

Each pilot wore the same flight armor as her, standard Defense-issue. They slung their particle rifles over their shoulders and carried their helmets in their hands.

She had served with these two men up until about a year ago. One day, they had disappeared without warning. Scuttlebutt claimed Command had reassigned them to Titan, but none of their buddies on Callisto had heard from them since the transfer.

The tall intruder trailed the pilots, also carrying his helmet. The shoulders of his white space suit towered over their heads. His elongated face possessed an anemic tint, as if his blood lacked oxygen. He seemed human enough, yet he didn't look like someone who had grown up on any known world or colony.

The two pilots lurched to a halt, blinking in disbelief. The tall man stopped short of bumping into them.

"Who the—?" Sterling murmured.

"Hey," Hunter said, "if it isn't—don't help me—Officer Candidate Brooke Davis, right?" His jovial tone grated on Brooke's nerves.

"It's first lieutenant now."

"That so?" Hunter shot Sterling a look. "Guess we've all moved up in the universe."

"Why have you rigged the reactor to blow?" She thrust her chin in the tall man's direction. "Who's this guy?"

"There are things you don't know anything about, lieutenant," Hunter said. "Big things. We may look rather suspect, but what we're doing is in everyone's best interest. Trust me on that."

"I'm not the trusting type."

"Okay." The lines in Hunter's forehead creased. "If you don't believe me, I'll prove it." He twisted, reaching behind his back. "I've got all the evidence you need right here." He grabbed his rifle and whipped it forward.

Brooke fired before he could get off a shot.

The intruder's force field deflected her attack. Electrical discharges crackled across the surface of the flashing sphere, which had grown to encompass the three of them.

She unloaded her particle rifle at their feet. The men flinched backward as shrapnel, dust, and shards of rock pummeled the intruder's shield. Plumes of dust and smoke shrouded the area around the reactor.

Brooke spun and sprinted for the airlock.

After sealing her helmet visor, she set her rifle to its highest power setting and bombarded the inner hatch. Her initial salvo bored a chest-sized hole. A second discharge tore a breach big enough for her to lunge through.

The outer hatch possessed five times the thickness of the inner hatch, so she concentrated her fire on the locking mechanism. One pulse tore the latch apart. A second blew the door open by five or six centimeters. She gripped the edge of the hatch with both hands and yanked, breathing heavy. It budged just enough to allow her to squeeze out.

Particle beams shattered rock and ice behind her while she dashed up the winding corridor. She stayed close to the curvature of the wall. Leaping steps kept her ahead of the intruders' direct line of fire. Somehow, she made it back up to ground level unscathed.

Her chronometer indicated eleven minutes, twenty-eight seconds.

Viewing the map of the facility, she determined the only unobstructed way back to the hangar. Her pursuers would use the same route, her knotting stomach reminded her, but she hadn't time for detours.

Eight minutes, forty-seven seconds.

Brooke tore down a far-stretching hallway. *Almost there.* The hatch at the end came into view.

The hatch spiraled open. Sterling leapt out of it and blocked her path, weapon raised.

The soles of her boots sparked against the floor plating as she skidded to a stop. *How'd he manage to cut me off?*

Footsteps clanged toward her from behind. She whirled to find Hunter obstructing any hope of retreat.

She lifted her rifle. Moisture clouded her vision despite her best efforts.

A voice entered her mind. *<Drop to the floor, ma'am.>*

Brooke dove down.

Heavy particle beams tore through one of the corridor walls. The thundering pulses ripped Sterling and Hunter apart. Tiny spheres of blood sprayed in all directions.

Brooke slid toward the breach and collided with the wall. The thud jarred her ribs and she winced.

Three minutes, nine seconds.

Calm settled over the corridor.

*<All clear, ma'am.>*

Brooke heaved her aching body to its feet and gazed out of the breach. Her Starthroat hovered outside, its engines shaking everything around her. A quarter-crescent Jupiter peeked up above the icy terrain in the background.

Bob poked the nose of the fighter inside the corridor.

She hopped on and crawled up to the canopy. It popped open, and she hopped into the cockpit.

One minute, thirty-nine seconds.

Her harness clamped into place the moment she settled into her seat. Gravgel poured over her boots and legs.

Twenty-three seconds.

She stood the fighter on end and burned thrusters. The Starthroat rose up from Europa, but not quickly enough.

The gravgel submerged her helmet. *C'mon, c'mon! Fill already!*

Five seconds.

Her mental scope registered the tri-fighter launching from the facility.

*<Gravgel immersion complete, ma'am.>*

The chronometer hit zero.

Brooke pushed the engine to max thrust. Fusion afterburners scorched the Europan ice. Intense acceleration pinned her back while the Starthroat hurtled away from the moon.

Mental displays showed cracks zigzagging away from the water distillation plant, propagating out for hundreds of kilometers. Ripples radiated through the surrounding ice as if someone had tossed a stone into a cream sea. Trillions of gallons of water spewed upward from the epicenter. The erupting geyser swallowed the facility and neighboring colony.

Bright light mushroomed upward and overtook her fighter. A yellow-white canvas vanquished the stars.

## Five—Tenacity
## Chicago, March 2247 AD

Marie barged into her editor's office and limped over to his desk.

Daniel leaned back in his chair and stared up at her. "Marie, what are you still doing here? I told you to take the rest of the day off."

"Check my latest submission," she said.

With a heavy sigh, Daniel swiped a finger through the screen hovering in front of him. A window containing Marie's image expanded. He flicked an oversized green arrow below the window, streaming her report on the revitalization center assassination attempt.

Marie bowed her head. In her mind, she relived the horrific event while a recording of her voice summarized what happened.

The shimmer of the force field reappeared to protect the stage. Marie dropped to her knees in the crowd and covered her head. A nanosecond later, the rogue spherecam slammed into the field and detonated. She clamped her eyelids shut in response to the blinding flash. Sweltering heat washed over her. Shrill screams pierced her ears. Someone trampled her ankle. She yelped.

Marie huddled in the fetal position until everything stopped shaking.

She lifted her head to take a peek. Smoke stung her eyes. Her breathing mask saved her lungs from the fits of coughing all around her.

Charred bodies lay near the stage. The unlucky souls in the front rows had borne the brunt of the explosion.

She sprang to her feet. *The children.*

Reporters picked themselves up in the back rows. She limped her way around them toward the empty stage. The secretary-general and other delegates had retreated to safety behind the force field.

Marie picked up stray masks and fitted them onto the mouths of the wounded. Lacerations covered foreheads, cheeks, necks, and arms. Broken bones and third-degree burns gave way to corpses the closer she drew to the front.

Marie retched.

After sucking in a breath, she enabled her eyecam's record mode. *How can I use the plight of these people for my latest scoop?* A pang of guilt stirred in her gut, but she shook it off. *No, it's my duty to show what happened here*.

She focused the cam on the foot of the stage. The unmoving bodies of boys and girls lay sprawled over the steps. She couldn't begin to process the degree of dismemberment. None of the children had reached double digits in age, and now, none of them ever would.

Her overactive imagination placed her daughter, Maya, among them.

"Marie?" her editor asked.

She lifted her gaze to find Daniel leaning over his desk.

"Are you all right, Marie?"

She tensed her muscles to keep from trembling and nodded.

"Well, then." He settled back into his chair. "Don't let the compliment go to your head, but this some of the best work I've seen. I'll upload it to the front page in a few minutes."

"Thank you." She pulled her specs down from the top of her head. "Before I forget . . ." She glanced at her personal finance program. "I owe you a hundred thousand dollars."

"No, you won the bet by getting into the ceremony."

"Yeah, but I also claimed I would get Ajunwa to answer at least one question."

"Take those things off, Marie." Daniel heaved to his feet and rounded the desk. "I owe you." The VidStreamer logo on his holotie danced and flashed. "I won't hear of anything to the contrary."

Marie took off her specs, placed the tip of the earpiece on her lower lip, and cracked a smile for the first time since the incident. "In that case, I believe we changed the wager from money to—"

"Don't think I'll send you to Dryden because you're a little banged up. My sympathy runs far deeper than the company expense account."

"You said my piece was some of the best stuff you've seen." She struck a defiant pose. "I've worked here long enough to know the VidStreamer doesn't publish stories like this one. The front page of our local feed is about to feature the same report as all the solar networks. Ratings will be high enough for us to expand clear across Chicago. The increased sales should allow you to send out the reporter who brought about that success to scoop the next big story. Don't you see? This is an investment in the future of your organization."

"Your powers of persuasion need work."

"Hey, my debate team at the University of Colorado won nationals two years in a row. I know how to drive a point home. Was that not why you hired me?"

Kern folded his arms across a healthy gut and grumbled. "The issue of money aside, you would still need a press badge. Sending you to the Advanced Propulsion Research Center is a moot point if they won't let you inside." He tapped the graying stubble on his chin. "Although I could call in a favor with an old friend at *L.A. Daily* . . ."

"Sounds like I'm good to go."

He shook his head. "What am I saying? No, Marie. This is too much. You need to come back down from Mars, accept that you work for a local feed, and concentrate on stories in this community."

"But sir, I—"

"Enough, Marie. My decision is final."

The fatigue of the day's events caught up with her. Her shoulders slumped, and her arms fell limp at her sides.

She wanted to collapse on the worn office carpeting. Instead, she straightened her posture. "In that case, you leave me with little choice." She dropped down on her knees. The scrapes on her legs stung. She ignored the pain, crawled forward, and clamped a bear hug around her editor's left leg.

Daniel stared down at her, eyes bulging. "What do you think you're doing?"

She whipped her hair out of her face and twisted her neck to view his expression. "I'm not letting go until you send me."

"Get up now, Marie." Daniel tried to shake her off and lost his footing. His gut jiggled. One hand caught the edge of his desk, saving him from toppling over. "If you think this immature stunt will convince me to reconsider—"

"We'll see what you're willing to consider come four o'clock in the morning." She squeezed his calf tighter.

"You have three seconds to release me, or you're fired."

"Then go ahead and fire me."

A half-growl, half-sigh rumbled up from Daniel's chest. "This is that important to you?"

"Yes." She let go and hopped to her feet. "Love for flying and space exploration has been in my family for generations. My father was a UN Defense pilot, and my sis—"

She bit off the word and shook her head. "Please, sir, I've been waiting for this moment all my life."

Daniel dipped his chin. His head swayed back and forth. The lines on his forehead squeezed closer together.

Marie hung on his every twitch. The tick of the office's antique clock counted the seconds.

He sighed. "If this were purely a matter of principle, Marie, I would, but the money just isn't there. I'm sorry."

After a zombie-like shuffle back to her cubicle, Marie collapsed into her swivel chair. She sat hunched over and let her arms go limp at her sides.

The solid partition separating her cubicle from its neighbor dissolved and entertainment reporter Denise Stevens peeked through.

"Are you okay? You look even worse than before."

The clashing colors and patterns of the worn carpeting looked hideous. "He said no," Marie whispered.

"I see. I guess playing the poor, helpless victim wasn't even enough."

"I was certain today's incident would tip the scale in my favor."

Denise's blue-streaked beehive hairdo bobbed up and down. "Well, whenever I'm upset, I eat something sweet. Have a cookie." She held up a box of gingersnap delights.

Marie stared at the box for a moment, grabbed a cookie, and nibbled.

"Do you want to grab a drink, maybe vent a little?" Denise asked. "Happy hour starts in fifteen minutes."

Marie's frown upturned slightly. "Thanks for the offer, but all I want to do is go home and see my daughter."

"Maya is an adorable one, isn't she?" Denise clasped both palms together. "I remember when my children were that age." The nostalgia drained from her face. "Back before they started stealing from my purse and swearing their little heads off."

"I hope I never live to see Maya turn out like that." She swiveled her chair partway around. "Put the wall back up, would you? I need to finish a couple things before I head home."

"Always the overachiever." Denise lifted her hand to reactivate the wall but pulled her palm back. "Oh, by the way, I found a couple of ISN feeds I thought might interest you."

Marie rolled over to her holotouch screen and worked her fingers through it. "Jupiter exclusive: UN maintains control of atmospheric particle collectors despite heavy casualties." She skimmed the text for highlights. "Three aerostat particle collectors destroyed, two UN Aerospace Defense Force pilots killed . . ."

Her stomach wound into knots at the next headline. "Fifty Thousand Perish in Explosion on Europa." The vid showed a simulated reenactment of the incredible eruption. Europa pulsated and spewed a water geyser. It looked like someone had squeezed an off-white orange, squirting juice everywhere. "Artemis colony and water distillation plant destroyed . . . Chinese separatist group claims responsibility . . . UN evacuating all other Europan colonies . . ."

The last feed showed a poll in which public approval of the separatist movement plummeted due to the incident. Analysts asserted the terrorists had crossed a line by destroying a defenseless civilian outpost. Separatist leaders issued public statements expressing their regrets and reaffirming that their grievances were only with the UN government and military infrastructure.

"Isn't it horrible?" Denise said. "All those people . . ."

Marie forced herself to take a deep breath.

"I sent you the feeds because I thought you had family out near Jupiter." Denise tapped her chin, light glinting off her prosthetic hand. "A sister, right?"

Marie sprang up out of her seat and limped over to a window.

Outside, a bright sun shone down from a blue sky filled with fluffy white clouds. Marie swiped her hand through the window, disabling the pseudo-beautiful day. Now an overcast sky loomed over hundreds of stratoscrapers, zeniths obscured by a brown haze. Streets wound around the lower sections of buildings like concrete vines. Tens of thousands of vehicles—autonomously driven and human-operated, running on charge and hydrogen and petroleum—raced along Chicago's multi-tiered freeway system. Lake Michigan's murky waters sloshed about. The digital readout in the bottom corner of the window reported the temperature at ninety-two degrees Fahrenheit with a moderately unhealthy Air Quality Index.

*Maya better have worn her breather today*, she thought.

Marie re-enabled Sunny Day Mode and returned to her desk.

Denise's voice was muffled as she chewed on a cookie. "At least, I thought you had somebody close out there."

Marie faced her screen, stuck in a pair of wireless ear buds, and blasted the most uplifting song she could stream. “Close?” she muttered. “No, no one close.”

## Six—Relegated
## Base HOPE, Callisto, March 2247 AD

The spacecraft elevator lowered Brooke's Starthroat underground. Once the canopy had retracted, she stood within the cockpit and stretched. The frozen, cratered landscape of Jupiter's eighth moon shimmered beyond the radiation shielding surrounding New Galilei. Domes and towers jutted up from the colony. *Terminus*, crippled and barely functioning, descended from the lambent star field overhead, on course for the shipyard.

Her mind rehashed the explosion from the water distillation plant. Thousands of degrees of searing heat lashed out to smite her fighter, and she resigned herself to incineration by the antimatter-induced inferno. A second before the Starthroat's force field overloaded, her fighter leapt clear of the blast radius.

Brooke exhaled, releasing the tension gnawing at her innards. The knots in her stomach wouldn't unravel. She felt hot and cold at the same time. *Withdrawal symptoms? No, that's what happens to spark addicts, not me. I'm just a little on edge.* Thoughts of the tri-fighter, the tall intruder, the two UN pilots, and her escape from Europa exacerbated her angst. *Fifty thousand colonists died, and I couldn't stop it.* She forced down a pang of regret.

*<Our efforts helped to protect the remaining three-point-two*

*million inhabitants of the Jovian community, ma'am.>*

*That doesn't make me feel any better, Bob, but thanks for trying.*

The elevator platform thudded to a halt, jarring the fighter and cockpit.

She pressed her hand to her chest. When she twisted her torso, she felt only slight stiffness thanks to the medites.

The overhead doors closed and latched, vanquishing the stars. After the compartment pressurized, the spacecraft elevator resumed its subterranean trek.

The elevator emerged from the shaft into an arena-sized hangar bay. The bay stood over fifty meters tall, measured two hundred wide, and stretched for a kilometer. Row after row of spacecraft lined the deck. State-of-the-art SF-522 Starthroats sat perched next to their more elongated predecessors, SF-515 Cormorants. Rovers, fuel tankers, and utility vehicles navigated the aisles. Technicians and repair bots scurried between military machines, patching them up for the next sortie. Clanking and drilling played in concert with the low whine of idling fusion rockets, like music to her ears.

The elevator platform settled flush with the deck paneling.

A graying, unshaven little man in soiled coveralls rushed over to her fighter. "Mother of Christ, what did you do to my sweet little girl?" The old-timer pulled at his hair.

His assistant, a male technician in his late teens, stepped over to the plane. "Paint's burnt right off." He reached out, touched the fuselage, and recoiled. "Ah! She's still hot."

Brooke hurdled the side of the cockpit and jumped down. She floated to the deck in Callisto's one-eighth gee, inspecting her Starthroat while she fell.

Explosive backwash had scorched the lettering off the nose of her fighter. Extreme heat turned its smooth black finish the color of burnt charcoal. Ridges and grooves covered the melted exterior. Her inadvertent plunge into Jupiter's atmosphere had warped the fighter's moldable wings. The multi-trillion-dollar star fighter looked like some kid's amateur ceramic creation, straight out of the shop class kiln.

She scrunched her nose at the mess. *How am I even still alive?*

The old-timer swore under his breath. "How many times have I told you not to push these ladies beyond spec?" He waived an autowrench as big as his forearm in the air. "There must be ten or twenty trillion worth of damage. We might even have to scrap her."

Brooke's boots touched down.

She thrust her helmet into the young tech's arms. He gasped.

Brooke marched away. "If you can't salvage the plane," she called back over her shoulder, "download Bob's matrix into my next ride."

"Bob?" the tech asked.

The old-timer grunted.

A group of officers approached her as she strode across the hangar deck. The dozen or so men and women in glossy navy and black uniforms crowded around her, led by Jeff Braxton.

Knowing Jeff made it back alive eased her weariness, but that didn't mean she wanted to deal with him—or anyone else—right now. *All I want right now is to shower, crawl into my bunk—check my application status—and forget about everything that happened.*

"They're saying Artemis went up like a Fourth of July festival." Jeff's southern drawl exaggerated every vowel. "That so?"

Brooke stared up at his freckled, country-boy face. Bright red hair dye amplified his hickness.

Jeff cocked his head. "Thousands die, I almost meet my maker, and you got nothing to say. What happened after I left? How'd you get out?"

She shrugged.

"Damn it, Angel. It's like pulling shrapnel with you."

"I got out in time." She stepped around him. "Just leave me alone."

He blocked her path. His two-meter frame cast a shadow over her, blocking out the floodlight from the plasma strips high above.

She tried scooting around him without success.

"I heard you submitted your test pilot application." He peered back at the others. "So did everybody else here. The way I see it, you've got an ice cube's chance in hell."

Brooke scowled. *Let it go*, she pleaded with herself. *You're exhausted and not thinking straight*. She opened her mouth to order Jeff to back off, but the fury coursing through her coaxed a different set of words out of her. "I hope they pick me soon. I'm getting sick of babysitting you out there."

His fists clenched. A vein in his forehead bulged.

The surrounding techs, desk jockeys, and pilots gasped. Everyone huddled closer, forming a tight circle around them.

Jeff gnashed his teeth. "If you weren't my superior . . . if you weren't a woman . . ."

She backpedaled and bumped into someone—the old-timer, her peripheral vision identified. His wrench knocked into the back of her upper leg. "Good thing. You wouldn't want to get your ass kicked by a girl."

Jeff lunged forward, throwing a right hook. To Brooke, his fist lagged in slow motion.

She jerked her body left. His knuckles sailed clear of her cheek.

While he teetered off balance, she swung and connected. A splattering thud muffled a clang. The crunch of snapping cartilage silenced the crowd.

Jeff squealed in pain. He dropped to his knees, clutching his bleeding nose. Blood oozed from between his fingers.

"Call the medics!" an officer shouted.

Brooke stared at the wrench in her hand.

Her father had once told her a pilot only had one life to lose, so she should leverage any advantage she could find.

The thought flashed her back to an incident that had occurred on the playground at age twelve. She had wrapped her jump rope around a boy's neck because he'd called Marie "squinty-eyed." His face had turned bright purple, and he might have suffocated if her sister hadn't loosened the rope in time. Guilt pierced her abdomen when she thought of how close she had come to killing him, but she dismissed it. The idiot had deserved the scare for making fun of their heritage—and for hurting her one and only immediate family member.

Brooke dangled the wrench by the handle and offered it back to the old-timer. "Sorry about the blood. Hopefully, it'll be easier to clean up than the fighter."

She resumed her trek toward the barracks. Everyone in the crowd took a good three steps back, letting her pass.

♦

General Frederick Douglas sat at the desk in his office in Base HOPE, staring out the window. Transparent biodomes, each a kilometer or more in diameter, bubbled up from Callisto's cratered surface, shielding the inhabitants beneath them. The tops of the domes rose only meters above the surface. The majority of the structures existed underground. Each dome looked like a sporting arena that had sunk into the ground.

The destruction of the water plant and adjoining colony weighed heavily on the general. His abdomen had constricted when the president of the UN Security Council had ordered him to suspend military operations on Europa, but Douglas had ignored his misgivings in the name of following orders. Now he grew lightheaded at the notion he might have played a part in the death of fifty thousand people. Had an accident occurred, or had the commander-in-chief of the UN's armed forces intended for the tragedy to happen? It didn't seem possible.

He clasped both hands over the belly his wife insisted he work off and sighed. "Matrix, establish a secure channel to UN Headquarters in

New York. Patch me through to President Collins."

A screen materialized above the smooth marble desk. The transparent rectangle displayed the UN emblem. <Voice pattern recognized as General Frederick C. Douglas,> said the matrix's articulate female voice. <One moment please, sir.>

Only in the last year had phase tunneling allowed Douglas to speak with Earth in real time. This groundbreaking advance in communications technology, implemented during the first tier of Project Luminosity, gave the UN a significant advantage over the separatists. More importantly, it put people in touch with their loved ones.

Three minutes later, security president Edward Collins's thin face and shaved scalp replaced the loading graphic.

"Sir," Douglas said.

"Douglas. I was expecting you to ring."

Douglas hesitated, unsure of how to begin. "I suspended operations near Europa under protest, sir. This incident shouldn't have happened."

"Indeed. It's a deplorable tragedy."

"Sir, the Jovian system falls within my jurisdiction, and I have a right to know what's going on within it. Why did you order me to declare Europa off-limits?"

"The matter remains classified."

"Classified? Still? Please tell me that blowing a hole in Europa and killing thousands of people wasn't part of any 'classified' plan. The UN would never sanction such a thing."

"The latest intelligence suggests the destruction of the plant was a separatist attack, and a full investigation is under way."

"Still, my forces should've remained in place to protect the facility."

Collins interlaced his fingers on his desk and leaned forward. "The presence of your forces might very well have provoked the situation."

Douglas's chest deflated. Of course, the Security Council president already knew.

"It seems two of your fighters violated the restricted space," Collins said.

"Yes, that's correct. Tracking and sensor data show that the first pilot entered the water plant but retreated soon after. The second reached the reactor, made contact with three trespassers, and somehow got out before the place went up. Two of the intruders wore Defense-issue garb. Were these your officers?"

Collins sat back from the screen. "You need only be concerned with officers under your command."

Douglas suppressed a growl. "What would you like me to do, sir?"

"The first man doesn't concern me, but the second man—"

"The second was a woman—my best pilot, actually. She chased the unidentified craft away from *Terminus* when the carrier responded to the plant's distress call."

Collins adjusted the cuff of the pressed shirt beneath his blazer. "General, I'm worried your subordinates might have played a role in the destruction of the plant, so here are your orders. Instruct both pilots not to discuss what they witnessed with anyone. Then relieve the woman of duty and make sure she finds her way to Earth on leave. I want to meet this lass, after which time I'll determine what to do with her." He cracked a faint smile. "Skilled pilots are hard to come by these days, and I've got a project to implement."

"Why not assign her to UN Headquarters, sir?"

"I want her close, but not that close. Simply order her to undergo a physical before she leaves Callisto. Tell your chief flight surgeon to tap the neurofeeds to her implants. I want to see and hear everything she does." He stood up from his desk and straightened his tailored suit coat. "Now, if that's all, I'm off to catch a game of footy."

♦

Brooke knocked her forehead against the cold shower wall. Warm mist swirled around her body, caressing her from head to toe, but she didn't deserve to feel good right now. *How could I have been so stupid? I've not only jeopardized my career but any shot I had at the candidacy program!* She pounded a fist against the tile and fought the urge to sob.

The next time her forehead bumped the wall, the shower stall seemed to spin. Her stomach cramped, and bile bubbled up into her throat. Unable to keep her balance, she dropped to her knees. Both hands flew to her head. When she ran her fingers over her scalp, strands of hair pulled loose, complete with follicles. *Side effects of the sparks? But I haven't been taking them that long!*

She'd sparked for the first time four months ago by sheer chance. On one of her rare excursions into New Galilei, she'd wandered into a small shop called Virtual Vik's, searching for games to occupy her off-duty solitude. The owner, a scrawny Indian with spiked orange hair, had declared her the best-looking girl to ever grace his establishment and invited her to game with him and a friend in the back storeroom.

While settling onto a crate and donning a pair of interface specs, she'd caught Vik pressing some sort of injector to his neck. "What're you doing?" she'd asked.

"A little something to provide a spark," he'd explained.

She'd declined to try it at first, but after being blown to smithereens umpteen times, and after hearing Vik attribute his marksmanship to the sparks, she'd decided to give it a shot.

Pricking her neck with an injector had induced a mild static shock. Her skin had tingled. And then it had hit her. A jolt had coursed through her spine, undulated through her limbs, and shot to her head, leaving her with acute brain freeze. She'd collapsed onto the floor amidst discarded fast food wrappers and convulsed.

The unkempt store room had faded in and out, but she'd remained coherent enough to see Vik and his friend hop to their feet.

"Man, I've never seen that happen before," the friend had said. "Should we call the med line?"

Vik had whacked his arm. "You looking to do time?" Then he'd stared down at her. "She'll pull out of it. She has to."

Sure enough, her body had calmed after three or four seconds.

Vik and his pal had helped her up onto the crate, given her water, and asked if she felt okay.

She'd ignored him while cocking her head at the pores opening and closing on Vik's face.

Brooke had insisted she'd felt good enough to return home to rest, so she'd left Vik's as quickly as possible. But the last thing she'd wanted to do was lie down.

In the hours which had followed, she'd sprinted through the streets, laughed for no reason, cartwheeled, eavesdropped on distant conversations, done backflips, spotted insects high above in the imitation sky, hiked up to the dome observation platforms, remembered where she'd lost her doll at age five, and never lacked for energy.

Her enhanced reasoning hadn't taken long to realize what sparking would do for her in the cockpit, so she'd returned to see Vik. The price had proven steep—two weeks' pay for a month's supply—but worth it. The first sortie she'd flown under the influence, the sparks had enhanced her neurotronic interface with her Starthroat. She'd blanked fourteen separatist fighters that day.

With a bit of SolNet research, she'd uncovered studies identifying the nanorobotic medicine as a disappointment. After it'd failed to cure certain neurological diseases in clinical trials, the narcotic had found its way onto the black market. Chat rooms had revealed hardcore gamers sparking to increase their scores but had made no mention of the almost superhuman feats she'd performed. Further digging had led her to believe the sparks had interacted with a gene that her botched prenatal therapy had activated, which explained why sparking had underwhelmed the two other pilots she knew who'd tried it.

And now, as she crouched on the floor of the shower, clinging to the wall for support, her body reeled because of the choice she'd made.

She reached for the cereal bowl she'd set on the shower floor before stepping inside. The sugary flakes no longer crunched, and the soggy marshmallows drooped, but they tasted every bit as divine. If tragedy ever marooned her on a desert planet in a remote star system, and she could only choose one food source on which to survive, it would be Fruity Planets.

Her desktop matrix chimed out in the main section of her quarters. Brooke let it go on for over a minute, dreading what she knew the call would be about.

She engaged the shower's dry cycle. Superheated air currents swirled within the stall, drying her within seconds.

Naked, she hobbled over to the matrix, disabled the visual feed, and answered the call. The voice of an irate colonel demanded she report to Base HOPE's main conference room.

Her temples throbbed and her hands shook, urging her toward the bottom dresser drawer where she kept her sparks. *No, it's not worth sacrificing my health—but I feel like I'm about to die!* She reached out for relief, but a more important realization stopped her. *The candidacy program will almost certainly require med screenings . . .*

To ease her pain, she instead opted for a maximum strength pain reliever and a douse of cold water to the face. The reprieve paled in comparison to sparking, but somehow she found the strength to jam her body into uniform, pull her hair back, and stuff her calluses into her boots.

Brooke dodged around an automated delivery bot on her way to the conference room. When she arrived, she found it unoccupied, so she bounded over to its panoramic window.

Her reflection revealed baggy eyes and a creased uniform. She smoothed her coat's single lapel and zipped up the tight-fitting cardigan beneath it. The proud symbol of the United Nations—two olive branches hugging the planets of the solar system—glimmered above her left breast. With a finger, she polished the silver bar on her collar, which designated her rank as first lieutenant in the UN Aerospace Defense Force.

She twisted her body so she could see her left shoulder and adjusted the Jovian Fighter Wing patch. Her fingers brushed her right arm, which featured the seventy-two stars and thirteen stripes of the American Colonies, with Japan's rising red sun below.

Her gaze drifted past the marginal improvement in her appearance. A moon rover bounced along outside, circling one of the domes, ferrying supplies. A group of six orange construction bots marched past it, robotic feet fashioning mini craters with each lunging step. A passenger shuttle launched from the spaceport runway and headed for a rendezvous with one of the transit liners making the multi-week journeys to Mars or Earth. The shuttle rose up and away toward Jupiter, which measured five times the size of Luna in Earth's sky. The gas giant's two Great Red Spots gazed back at her like ever-watchful eyes.

At the center of the colony, in the middle of the Valhalla crater, sat the Jovian system's most important historical landmark. She squinted and zoomed in, magnifying the antiquated spacecraft. The moon lander rested in a cordoned-off area that marked the first location where humans had set foot almost one hundred and fifty years ago. The craft measured fifteen meters in height and ten in diameter, a horse and buggy by 23rd-century standards. A pole jutted up from the ice near it, displaying the flag of the American Colonies. Additive fabricators had engraved the acronym HOPE into the adjacent memorial, short for Human Outer Planets Exploration, the last mission NASA had launched before UN Aerospace had absorbed it. The monument served as a testament to human collaboration and perseverance, not that she bought into that kind of feel-good crap.

She hated admitting her feebleness. She preferred to believe she didn't need anyone or anything, but if they drummed her out of the service or took away her shot at the candidacy program, she didn't know what she'd do.

Flinching at the swish of the room's automatic doors, she spun around and snapped to attention.

General Douglas, the base commander, strode into the dim room. He worked his way around the far side of the conference table and took a seat at the end.

He flicked through the menus on a paper-thin e-slip. Her backwards picture slid on and off the transparent device.

"First Lieutenant Kishiko 'Brooke' Davis." His deep baritone rumbled like a fusion engine. "Background . . . age twenty-four. Born in Yokohama, Japan. Raised in Colorado Springs of the American Colonies. Psych profile and med history show anti-social behavior along with upper-percentile spatial awareness and reflexes due to a rare genetic disorder." He took his time scanning the slip. "Service record . . . recently promoted to flight leader." His head jerked up. "Do I have this correct, Lieutenant?"

"Yes, sir."

"Well, it's a shame you've chosen to throw all that away."

Her stomach plummeted through to the moon's core.

General Douglas leaned back in his chair and interlocked his fingers atop his stomach. The man possessed a complexion like dark brown leather. "I thought you might like to know that Second Lieutenant Jeff Braxton is recovering in the medical ward. The doctors say you fractured his nasal septum." A thin goatee framed his frown. "Fortunately, that's all you broke. He should be good as new by tomorrow."

Brooke counted the treads in the floor plating and whispered, "Yes, sir."

"In regards to the legalities, Braxton is refusing to press charges. He's the prideful, old-fashioned type, which exonerates you in that area. But the breach in discipline is a different matter." He rose to his feet and approached the window. "I cannot fathom what possessed you to take a wrench to his face," General Douglas said.

"Sir, it started when—"

He silenced her with a piercing glower. "I'm not interested in the story, Lieutenant. Quite frankly, I can't think of a single, justifiable reason for such an act."

Brooke swallowed hard. Her throat felt coarser than regolith.

"By all rights, Lieutenant, you should be facing a court-martial." His gaze remained focused in the direction of the ancient lander. "That said, I can't ignore the brighter points of your record. Your piloting skills are unparalleled, and I won't simply brush aside a soldier who escaped with her life in the line of duty." He shook his head. "Defense doesn't want to lose an officer of your caliber, but you've put me in a difficult position."

"Yes, sir."

The hum of the air circulation system permeated an otherwise uncomfortable silence.

After at least a minute, Brooke said, "Sir, regarding my most recent sortie, I wanted to report—"

"I know full well what you think you encountered, Lieutenant. Consider yourself under direct orders not to discuss any aspect of the incident with anyone."

"Sir? Won't there be a formal debriefing?"

General Douglas dragged his feet back to the conference table and leaned over it. His tired gaze alternated between opposite sides of the room. The baby blue United Nations flag covered the left wall. A portrait of a Starthroat rocketing away from Jupiter hung to the right.

"There won't be a debriefing."

"None, sir?"

He shook his head, and for a moment Brooke thought he looked more glum than grim. Then the general straightened his posture, adjusted the umpteen medals on his blazer, and faced her. "Separatists claimed responsibility for the attacks." His voice cracked like a laser whip. "Is that understood?"

She stiffened her posture. "Sir, yes, sir!"

General Douglas grunted his assent. "Also, you're relieved of active duty until further notice. I want you to go home to Earth and think hard about what your career means to you."

"But sir, I don't, um . . ." Brooke's intestines knotted. "I don't want to—"

"That wasn't a request, Lieutenant." Her superior reached for the e-slip on the table. "Both father and mother are deceased. You have my sympathies." He perused the slip. "However, it appears you have a sister living in Chicago." He peered up at her. "I'd say now's the perfect time for a visit."

She contorted her face.

"Nothing's more important than family, Lieutenant. Dismissed."

Brooke hunched her shoulders as she left, unable to deny the gut-wrenching truth of his statement.

## Seven—Repatriated
## Earth Orbit, April 2247 AD

*Home?* Brooke's nose crinkled at the blue-white ball of bad memories outside the porthole. *No, I don't think of you as home any more.*

Earth dominated the view outside the passenger cabin of Virgin Galactic Flight 3589. The planet's deep blue oceans showed no evidence of contamination from high above. Swirling, puffy white clouds suggested no hint of pollutants. The greens and browns of the continents betrayed no signs of the hunger, greed, and war raging across them.

She'd said good riddance to Earth six years ago. Never once did she regret leaving.

The commercial orbiter disengaged from one of the docking ports on the New International Space Station. Brooke zoomed in on the massive gray ring. Its portholes, airlocks, communication antennae, and solar panels shrank into the distance while the orbiter dove toward the Earth.

NISS provided permanent residence for twenty thousand people. Hundreds of space stations orbited the planet, but only NISS functioned as a full-fledged city. The station served as the primary commercial transport hub between Earth, Luna, and farther destinations. Embassies and military bases maintained presences aboard as well.

Brooke had forgotten how much traffic cluttered low Earth orbit. Space hotels, habitats, research outposts, and other manmade structures circled the planet at altitudes above and below the station. Refueling tugs arrived from Luna, docked with vessels, and delivered materials collected from the lunar surface. In higher orbit, mining bots raced back and forth between automated factories and one of a dozen asteroids captured by mining companies.

The disgruntled separatists considered NISS and all commercial ventures neutral parties. Thus far, private industry had escaped the carnage.

Her father had once asserted the infrastructure was building toward the eventual ability to send mankind beyond the solar system. Thinking of it choked her up a bit. Had she missed her chance to book passage on that flight?

The transit liner that had transported her there from Jupiter rocketed away from NISS, its six exhaust nozzles torching space with blue-white fire. The elongated blimp resembled a smaller and far more underwhelming version of a UN spacecraft carrier. Instead of fighters and particle beam turrets, the transit liner featured gift shops and wet bars. Instead of soldiers and pilots, she had to put up with blabbermouth businessmen, gossiping women, and crying babies. Thank the stars both Earth and Jupiter were on the same side of the sun, or the trip would've lasted over twice as long. Recollections of her time aboard stifled her starry-eyed visions of the future.

The gravity reconditioning therapy had proven almost as bad as the passengers. Regular gravite injections prevented partial muscle atrophy, but she required greater measures to re-acclimate to Earth's stronger gravity, so she'd spent an hour each day undergoing musculo-skeletal shock treatment and another hour in the ship's workout facility. These efforts, plus the gradual acceleration of the transit liner's rotation, had prepared her for the increased strain the planet would put on her body.

At one point, upon growing tired of listening to a kid kick the wall of her cabin, she'd thought of asking the captain to jack up the spin by a few notches. That way, all those hyperactive children might've found their screaming mouths plastered to the deck.

She sank down into her seat and hid behind her net specs. She could contact Marie again, but the thought quickened her pulse. Now that she thought about it, she couldn't remember the last time she placed a call. She used her specs only to surf SolNet, stream music, and check her application, which still had no response.

Resisting the urge to stick out her tongue, she glanced at her message outbox. The text she had written to Marie scrolled across the thin lenses. “Hey, it’s been a while since we talked,” the message read. “I’m returning to Earth, and maybe I’ll drop by for a bit.”

Brooke muffled a whimper. It’d taken hours to work up the nerve to type that much. She’d paced back and forth within her cabin for another hour before sending it.

Her message sounded pathetic. “‘A while since we talked?’” She hadn’t spoken to Marie in six years. Brooke hadn’t even said good-bye before leaving the planet. “‘Maybe I’ll drop by for a bit’?” It read as if she planned on driving into town from the suburbs. She didn’t have anywhere to go or anything else to do. Her sister reserved every right to take insult or not even respond.

But in typical fashion, Marie had replied seconds later. “Do I know you?” she wrote. “Seriously, pilots stationed near Jupiter don’t ‘drop by.’ You’re in obvious need of a place to crash, and as your sister, I can’t refuse, can I? When are you coming? Book a flight to O’Hare when the mothership arrives at NISS, and send me the information.”

The orbiter wobbled as it entered Earth’s atmosphere. Over a hundred passengers sat in the rows surrounding her. Tension contorted their faces.

Their dismay puzzled Brooke. *You people have no idea what scary is.*

She did, however, find her lack of control somewhat unsettling. *What if we were attacked right now? These commercial pilots wouldn’t know what to do.*

Since the separatists had begun seceding, the media had reported the destruction of only two civilian spacecraft. Experts labeled both incidents as accidents. So far, the malcontented separatists refrained from violating the Ninth Geneva Convention, not counting Artemis.

The view outside the porthole flashed orange and red. The light blue haze of the orbiter’s magnetic field kept the heat at bay.

Pain stabbed her forehead. She shifted in her seat and rubbed her temples.

General Douglas had ordered her to undergo a physical before returning to Earth. Doc Gordon, Base HOPE’s chief flight surgeon, had inoculated her when she’d visited the infirmary. “To build your immunity against terrestrial bacteria and viruses,” he’d explained. The shot had cramped her stomach, the room had swayed, and she’d passed out. “A common reaction,” Doc had told her when she’d awoken, her mind clogged by grogginess. “Better now than when you arrive.”

Her eyes and inner ear had felt strained since the inoculation. Sparking might have alleviated the pressure, but she insisted to herself that she had quit.

Thoughts of Callisto brought General Douglas's strange orders back to the forefront of her mind. *Why did he lie? Why would the UN blow up the water plant and kill fifty thousand people? Are they trying to frame the separatists? Make the populace feel they've gone too far?* Her gut insisted Command hadn't expected her to live long enough to pose the question.

The orbiter's retrorockets fired, pressing her stomach up into her throat.

She swallowed and composed herself. *Best keep my mouth shut if I want to get reinstated.* She put it out of her mind. In a few minutes, she'd face a much more unnerving situation.

♦

Brooke stepped out onto concourse S of terminal eight within Chicago O'Hare Intrasolar Spaceport.

The concourse shifted in and out of focus, obscured by the late-day glare. The sun's rays pierced the terminal windows and stabbed her temples. She dragged her legs like lead weights. Thousands of people of all shapes, sizes, and ethnic backgrounds stomped one foot after the other instead of bounding in graceful strides. Travelers sat in rows of cheap plastic chairs. Business professionals marched along like kings and queens, toting the royal luggage behind them. One teenage girl flaunted a pink mohawk and skin-tight leopard jumpsuit. A man had dyed his crew cut neon blue to match his high-collared plastic shirt and sparkling pants.

Compared to the local clientele, Brooke felt awfully mundane.

*So many damn people! I can't believe I'm here . . .*

Her stomach gurgled, urging her toward the ladies room and into a stall. *Earth adaption syndrome is far worse than space sickness.*

Feeling better, she checked her appearance in the restroom mirror. An annoying commercial for a hair care product blocked her reflection; she flicked the ad out of the way. Her irises and lavender highlights radiated at their most vivid. She had redone the latter a couple days ago on the transit liner.

She zipped up her black hooded sweatshirt, picked at the holes in her jeans, and pulled her hair back into a ponytail—not that she cared how she looked.

After exiting the security checkpoint, she passed through the ticketing area and caught sight of Marie near the baggage claim. Her twin sister stood in the center of a sparse crowd, sporting a checkered skirt suit. Her blue irises stared back at Brooke, fill with apprehension. A respirator hung around her neck while the toe of one shoe tapped against the floor.

Looking at her sister felt like gazing into a mirror, almost—a reflection of what Brooke might look like in a parallel universe inhabited by polar opposites. If she chopped her hair chin-length, removed her implants, dressed fashionably, and smiled more often, most people would fail to tell them apart.

*Unlikely,* Brooke mused.

She stood rooted in place, avoiding her sister's gaze. A flood of memories gushed to the surface, which she shoved deep down.

At last, she strolled over her twin and shrugged. "Hey."

Marie nodded, tight-lipped. "Hi."

Brooke gave a start when she peered down at Marie's side. A little girl stood next to Marie, holding her hand. The child looked about four years of age. She had her short black hair styled like Marie's, and she wore a Cyber Girl Super Nova t-shirt underneath pink overalls. Two tiny shoes sported silly monkey faces. Her inquisitive eyes remained locked on the newcomer.

Marie released the girl's hand. "Go say hello to Auntie Brooke, Maya."

The child took five tentative steps toward Brooke and said, "Want to hear me recite the alphabet backwards?"

"Okay," Brooke said.

With a mischievous grin on her face, the girl turned, faced her back to her aunt, and said, "A, B, C, D . . ." She continued until she reached the letter Z.

Maya spun back around, swayed back and forth on the balls of her feet, and giggled.

Marie rolled her eyes and grinned.

Brooke blinked.

The little girl's exuberance devolved to a pout. "Don't you get it? I didn't say the letters in reverse, I—"

"Auntie Brooke understands." Marie's grin widened. "She's laughing on the inside."

Brooke frowned at her sister. "I get it." *Now that she explained it, anyway . . .*

Maya cocked her head at Brooke as if analyzing a lab specimen. "You're strange. Where'd you come from?"

"Well, um . . ." Brooke inspected a hole in her jeans. "I live out in space, pretty far away on Callisto, which is—"

"Jupiter's eighth moon. Everybody lives under big circles in the ground and can jump really, really high."

"That's right, squirt."

Maya scampered back to Marie and latched onto her leg. "I want to go up into space, Mommy." She tugged at her mother's skirt. "I want to visit Mars and Jupiter and Saturn and Uranus and Neptune and Pluto and Eris and every star out there!"

"We're a family of dreamers." Marie stroked the girl's hair.

"Smart kid." Brooke stuck out her lower lip, marveling at her niece. "She's yours?"

Marie pulled Maya toward the baggage claim. "No . . . I just, you know, like to pick up stray children at the spaceport."

♦

Brooke gasped. "Hey, watch out!" She almost ripped the safety handle out of the electrocar's roof.

A luxury autosedan nearly rear-ended their car when Marie merged onto the expressway. She floored the accelerator, squeezing into the narrow space in front of the vehicle. Tires screeched. Horns blared. "Thank you!" She waved back over her shoulder.

Brooke groaned.

"Is the ace star fighter pilot scared of a little traffic?" Marie asked.

"No, your shi—" Brooke thought of Maya sitting in her booster seat in the back and stifled her curse. "Your terrible driving is making me sick." She pulled her mask up over her mouth and sucked in filtered oxygen.

Leaning an elbow against the windowsill, she stared out at the expressway. The multi-tiered concrete highway measured twenty lanes wide. She heard oncoming traffic racing along on the four levels above and five below them.

She donned her net specs and watched a virtual interstate marker crawl past them on the side of the freeway. A pixelated sign followed next as the car slowed to a standstill, hitting bumper-to-bumper traffic. The sign read "Chicago: 15 Miles." A third graphic hovering above read "To Downtown: 137 Minutes."

Brooke's stomach gurgled. Her temples throbbed. "So many people," she muttered.

"Yeah, I'm still waiting for my flying car." Marie honked at the rover in front of her. "Then I'll be able to soar over any jam."

"Flying cars?" Brooke snorted.

"I know, I know. People have been wishing for flying cars for centuries." Marie laced her tone with condescension. "The technology's doable, but giving that kind of power to civilians would be like putting a gun in a child's hands. Every time a car malfunctioned and dropped out of the sky, it'd cause more death and destruction than the separatists." She waved her hand, indicating the tiered concrete freeway. "Plus, highway construction workers would lose their jobs."

Marie gripped the wheel with both hands and stuck out her lower lip. "But no one can stop me from dreaming." A truck blared its horn as she butted in front of it. "The traffic could be a lot worse. Off-world migration has slowed the population increase. People are leaving to escape the fighting and declining conditions."

Brooke coughed and sucked air from her breather. "Like all the smog?" She gazed down at a refueling station, situated at ground level along a street with boarded-up houses. The station's flickering sign promised the lowest prices for hydrogen, liquid nitrogen, ammonia, battery quick-charging, biomass, unleaded gasoline, and diesel.

A light rain broke, pattering against the car. She watched a drop slide down the windshield, leaving a brown trail behind it. Not a cloud had blocked the sky when they left O'Hare.

"You know it snowed in Mexico City this month," Marie said. "It got up over eighty degrees in Antarctica one day, too. Things aren't as bad here in the Midwest, but it stays up over a hundred all summer long now."

*Eighty?* Brooke's mind screamed. *A hundred?* She slapped an imaginary palm to her forehead. *Oh, right. Fahrenheit, not Celsius—and miles, not kilometers. It's been a while.*

"You'll be happy to know we're not going all the way downtown. We're getting off the freeway in a couple miles."

Brooke shut her eyes and pinched the bridge of her nose. "Good."

"I don't see how you can race around in the vacuum of space with no problem, yet you can't even—"

"Could we not talk for a while, please?"

"Fine."

In her peripheral vision, Brooke watched icons shift and flash on Marie's specs.

The radio switched on.

"—and in other news," an anchorwoman announced, "the United Nations has scheduled a press conference regarding tier two of Project Luminosity."

Brooke sat up in her seat. Marie's irises shifted, turning up the volume.

The anchorwoman continued. "At one o'clock Pacific Standard Time on Friday, April twenty-third—one week from tomorrow—the United Nations will hold a press conference at the Dryden Advanced

Propulsion Research Center located near Los Angeles, California. The UN has been elusive about the details, but sources close to ISN have confirmed they'll announce the completion of successful unmanned FTL flights. If that's the case, the implications for both intra- and intersolar travel cannot be overstated, and—"

With a grumble, Brooke whacked the power button on the dash, silencing the radio.

Marie frowned but said nothing, much to Brooke's surprise.

The car inched forward in traffic.

About one mile and ten minutes later, Marie said, "I begged my editor to send me to L.A. to cover the announcement. I was this close to convincing him—you wouldn't believe what I did—but in the end he said no. I've been pretty down about it." She tapped a finger against the wheel. "You must've been the first to apply for the test pilot program, but you're here, so something must've happened. Want to talk about it?"

Brooke pressed her forehead to the window. "Just leave me alone."

"That bad, huh?" When her twin failed to add anything else, Marie said, "Well, you may enjoy the silence, but I'm sick of it."

The voice of a radio DJ blared over the speakers. "You're listening to hits from the twentieth, twenty-first, and twenty-second centuries."

"You still listen to this ancient crap?" Brooke asked.

"Okay, then." Marie snorted and twisted her head around to peer back at Maya. "Something more recent coming right up." A grin stretched her face. "Time for the Happy Fun Sing-Along Song."

"Yay!" Maya's mask muffled her cheers. "Hap-py Song!"

*No!* Brooke's mind begged.

A goofy chipmunk voice filled the car, accompanied by carefree whistling and upbeat drumming. A choir of boisterous children provided backup vocals.

It's happy fun time, dear boys and girls.
It's happy fun time all 'round the world!
So come on everybody, it won't be long.
It's time for the happy fun sing-along song!

Mother and daughter recited the lyrics in unison. Maya squirmed in her seat, going, "La la la" when she didn't know the words.

Marie swayed back and forth to the beat. She wiggled the wheel in rhythm, making the car dance. Nearby motorists laid on their horns.

Brooke slumped down in her seat and cupped her hands over her ears. *I wish I'd died on Europa.*

## Eight—Antipodal
## Chicago's North Side, April 2247 AD

The aroma of buttermilk and maple syrup roused Brooke from a fitful slumber.

She lifted one eyelid. Then she opened the other and grunted. Glaring yellow rays peeked their way through the window blinds.

After scooting back on the futon, she propped her head up on a pillow and pulled her arms out from under the blanket. *I don't remember covering up. How did—? Oh, yeah.*

The stop-and-go freeway traffic had lasted over two hours, but the agony hadn't ended there. Weaving through the city streets to Marie's apartment required another thirty minutes. An hour after that, Marie wedged the car into a parking spot. Brooke heaved her body up three flights of creaking stairs and stumbled into the apartment. Bile soured her throat. Marie guided her into the bathroom, where she spent the rest of the evening alternating positions at the toilet. After the dry heaves subsided, she collapsed on the futon in the living room and passed out.

*Why do I feel like I'm hungover?* Brooke studied the activity in the kitchenette on the far side of the apartment. Marie tapped her foot in front of a small stove, humming to a tune in her earpiece while supervising a panbot. The stovetop helper flipped four flapjacks at once, but in the process splattered pancake mix on her boxers and vintage NASA T-shirt. Apparently thinking no one was watching, Marie licked the batter off her shirt.

*That's my shirt!*

Maya waddled into the kitchenette in fuzzy pink pajamas, grabbed a platter, and held it up. Marie danced around her daughter and dropped a pancake onto the plate. In turn, the little girl scurried over to a child's play table, where she dumped the pancake on top of a steadily-growing stack.

The muscles in Brooke's body constricted, and her stomach cramped. She held her hand up. It wouldn't stop shaking.

She grabbed fistfuls of the blanket while questioning the wisdom of quitting the sparks.

The worst of the pain subsided after a few seconds.

When she turned her head, she gasped and sprang to a sitting position.

An egg-shaped robot sat next to the futon, its white-and-green composite body leaning toward her. Its spherical head swiveled two black oval eyes in her direction. <Good morning, Brooke,> its comical machine-voice said. The bot possessed no mouth, but two spherical ears flashed green when it spoke. <Are you feeling better today?>

She leaned back on her palms, glaring at the annoying personal assistant bot. From ads, she knew the thing could vacuum, play music, answer trivia questions, act as a home security system, and perform a bunch of other trivial tasks. The bot possessed a simple AI with the sophistication of an abacus when compared to her Starthroat's matrix.

Marie glanced over at the bot. "Papero," she yelled. "Come here."

<It was a pleasure meeting you, Brooke.> The bot spun and rolled over to the kitchen.

"We bought a different kind of pet since Maya's allergic to dogs and cats," Marie said.

Brooke retreated back under the covers. "The doctors didn't fix that?" she mumbled.

"I wouldn't let them."

Papero stopped near the table.

"Arms." Maya's voice squeaked like a mouse.

Two mechanical limbs extended from the bot. Maya placed a serving tray on top of them. "Delivery."

Papero twirled and rolled back over to Brooke. <Here's your breakfast, ma'am.>

She accepted the tray in Bob's honor. *Ma'am, huh?* She placed it on her lap, dug a fork into a pancake, and took a bite. It tasted pretty good, maybe even better than breakfast in the mess back on Callisto. She swallowed the food in tiny bits, wary of her still-tender stomach. Her breakfast stayed down long enough for her to risk a sip from a Hyperspace Hamster apple juice box. The animated rodent zoomed around the galactic core and accelerated amid rainbow-colored motion lines. *So unrealistic!*

Her attention remained locked on Papero the entire time. The bot stared back.

"Don't you have anything better to do?" she asked.

Papero's head swiveled and cocked to one side. <Blood vessel contraction. Arched eyebrows lower at the medial ends. Tightening of the inner eyelids. My facial recognition program suggests irritation, perhaps anger. Are you angry, Brooke?>

"All the time," Marie said as she approached.

She slid the table in front of the couch, bent down, and cut a pancake into pieces for Maya. Then she plopped down onto the couch with her own food.

Her daughter nudged a chair her size over to the table, sat down, and attacked a chunk of pancake with a spork.

Brooke's utensil protruded from her mouth. The stupid bot continued to intrude upon her personal space.

Papero's head turned upside-down. <Anger, a strong feeling of displeasure or hostility, often regarded as a negative emotion. Why would a human being choose to exist in such a state?>

Marie almost choked on her latest mouthful, laughing.

A swift kick from Brooke toppled the bot over onto its side.

Maya's head whipped toward the bot. "Hey! Be nice to Pappy."

<An act of aggression.> The bot buzzed as its wheels spun in the air. <If Papero was a human being, it might take offense to such action.> An arm extended from its side, pushing the bot upright. Once its wheels found traction, it whirred off behind the futon.

Brooke went back to eating her breakfast.

Maya glared at her aunt while impaling another morsel. The spork caught the edge of the piece, launching it into the air and onto the carpeting.

Marie dug a remote control out from beneath the couch cushions and pointed the device at the opposite wall. A screen fuzzed into existence between four metal joints roughly nailed into the drywall.

An anchorwoman sitting behind a desk appeared on the screen. "Thank you for tuning in to this edition of IntraSolar News for April sixteenth, 2247." Picture-in-picture windows popped up to her left.

displaying images of Mars's terraforming efforts. "While the bold have roamed the Martian surface without environmental suits for the past decade, planetary engineers have officially declared the atmospheric density high enough to eliminate the need for pressure suits. Respirators, however, will still be necessary for at least twenty more years due to carbon dioxide levels." Multiple rows of stock tickers scrolled along beneath her, racing toward a 3D ISN logo.

"I'm happy you showed up on a night when I don't work in the morning." Marie let the fluffy cushions consume her.

Finishing her last bite, Brooke set her tray on the floor.

"Look, I know there's a lot of stuff unsaid between us," Marie said. "Heck, after six years, we don't know each other very well anymore. For what it's worth, though, I'm happy you're here, happy you decided to come back."

Brooke nodded, tight-lipped. She gazed up at the ceiling.

Maya pushed her tray of unfinished food forward on the table. "Mom, can I have Fruity Planets?"

Brooke's brow lifted at the mention of her favorite food.

"No sugary cereal," Marie said. "We only eat Fruity Planets once in a while. Finish your pancakes."

"But the marshmallows flash different colors. Can't I have a little bit for dessert?"

"Dessert after breakfast? Forget it. Eat what's on your plate." Marie peered at her twin. "Kids these days. Where do they get such ideas?"

Brooke wouldn't have minded some dessert, but she let it go.

Maya shoved the tray away and ran off toward her bedroom.

"So, um . . ." Brooke nodded at her sister's hand and then at the girl. "I don't see a ring, so . . . who's the, you know . . ."

The cushions swallowed her sister deeper still. "I spent the summer following my freshman year in college in Yokohama with Obaa-chan."

"You slept with someone while staying with Grandma?"

"Weird, I know. I wasn't looking for it to happen, but I met this nice boy at a friend's party. We had a little to drink, one thing led to another, and . . ." She held a palm out toward her daughter's bedroom.

Maya rushed out of her room and plopped a box down in her aunt's lap. "Will you put it together for me, Auntie?"

Brooke cracked a faint smile at the sight of the toy rocket. "Hey, I used to have one of these." The flashing display on the box showed a cartoon rocket blasting away from a shrinking Earth.

"It shoots super-high into orbit and uses remote sensors to look down so I can see myself."

Auntie Brooke set the box on the futon. “Maybe later, squirt.”

Maya bowed her head. “Okay.” She dragged her feet back to the table and ran an oversized stylus over a coloring e-slip.

“So, where is he now?” Brooke asked her sister.

Marie sighed. “Turns out he wasn’t so nice after all. When I realized I was pregnant, I tried to track him down. Luckily, we recorded a bunch of drunken nonsense with my net specs, thinking we were funny or something. I took the vid to the police and explained my situation. They gave me his address, but when I got there, he didn’t want anything to do with us. He said a kid would derail his lofty career goals. It was never love, anyway, so . . .” She shrugged. “He sends money every month, but that’s all I’ve ever expected.” Her expression hardened. “It’s been tough, but I’ve made it work.”

Brooke almost jumped off the futon and embraced her sister. She wanted to comfort and protect her like she used to so long ago.

Instead, she said, “Well, that was stupid of you.”

Marie sprang to her feet, body shaking. She thrust an index finger toward her daughter’s bedroom. “Maya, go play in your room.”

Her daughter’s wide eyes protested.

The staring contest ending with Maya circling the kitchenette with her head hung, dragging the coloring slip behind her.

As soon as Maya’s door slammed shut, Marie exploded. “I was hoping we could ease into this—maybe talk about it like two adults—but I guess that’s not your style.”

Brooke shrunk back against the futon. “Don’t yell at me.” Her nose scrunched. “It aggravates my—”

“Don’t try to use your ‘disorder’ as an excuse. I don’t care what the doctors say. There’s nothing wrong with you.”

“Marie—”

“Six years!” Marie’s voice sounded like the screeching of a missile launch. “Six years, and in all that time, fewer than half that many messages. Not one call. Not even a ‘sayonara.’” She clenched both fists. “You dropped out of high school, signed up with the military, and left the planet. You’ve no idea how much effort it took to figure that out. I thought you were dead.”

“If I were dead—”

“Now, you message me out of the blue, come here with your bad attitude, and have the nerve to judge me?”

Her sister’s face glowed redder than the Great Red Spots, but Brooke knew the anger served only as a front. “What do you want me to say?”

“How about one simple word—if you’re capable of it?” Marie

placed her hands on her hips, waiting.

Brooke focused on anything and everything but her sister. *It's just a word. Why is it so difficult to say?* A minute later, she blew out a deflated sigh. "Sorry…"

Marie plopped back down on the couch. "It's a start. Next, you can tell me why."

"Do you have to ask? I couldn't take it anymore. I couldn't sit still in school, couldn't stand everyone making fun of me. I grew to hate everything about this stupid planet. And believe me, the rest of the world felt the same way. Plus, flying's all I've ever been good at."

"I don't blame you for following your dream, Kishi, but it still doesn't explain why you couldn't tell me. Why couldn't you have said, 'Oh, by the way, I'm leaving the planet. See you in six years or so'?"

"It was easier that way—and don't call me Kishi. I hate it."

"Why? Kishi's short for your real name. It's what I've always called you." Marie faced her twin. "But back on topic, I know why you left without a word. You didn't want to deal with the guilt of watching me collapse in anguish, which would've given you second thoughts. By avoiding confrontation, you pretended that I'd shrugged and said 'Whatever' like you always do." She snorted. "My sister. She's human, but she wouldn't admit it even if she were tortured by exobeings."

"Sounds like you've figured it all out, so why do we need to talk about it?"

Marie's head vibrated and jerked back. "Oh my God! Your bitch-mass is denser than ever." She grunted in exasperation. "People talk, Brooke. You know? People com-mun-i-cate, especially people who care about each other." She softened her tone. "You're my sister, and I love you, even though I don't like you most of the time."

"You know . . . you know I . . ." Brooke let her words trail off. She wanted to sink through the futon, down to the first floor, and all the way to Earth's molten core. "Why does it need saying?"

"Sometimes it does. Sometimes people don't know. Sometimes they wonder." She rose to her feet and shoved the table away. After leaning over the back of the couch, she found a mat and spread it out on the floor. Sitting pretzel-legged on the mat, she closed her eyes and pressed her palms together.

"What're you doing?" Brooke asked.

Marie sucked in a deep, calming breath. "What does it look like? It's yoga. Is that okay with you?" She didn't wait for an answer. "I don't judge you for jumping in a plane every time you need to feel better about yourself."

Neither of them said a word for minutes. Marie stretched and contorted into various positions. Brooke stared up at the ceiling, sulking. The IntraSolar News network filled the uncomfortable silence.

"I guess I shouldn't expect you to say anything," Marie said. "It doesn't take a psychiatrist to see how emotionally closed off you are. Like Dad." She placed her hands over her heart. "I was Mommy's little princess, and you were Daddy's special girl. Mom and I played with dolls and baked cookies. Meanwhile, Dad took you flying. That's how it was, and that's how we turned out."

Trembling, Brooke said, "Can we please not talk about them?"

Marie whipped her head in her sister's direction. "You're still blaming yourself? Dad's death wasn't your fault. Get over it already."

"How do you know?" Brooke clung to the pain. "Were you up there with us?"

"No, but that doesn't mean I didn't read all the police reports. I studied it from every possible angle, which probably led to my becoming a journalist. Nobody blamed you. It was an accident." Marie rested her back against the couch.

Brooke banged her fist against the futon.

"—investigations continue into the destruction of the Artemis Water Treatment Plant on Europa," the ISN anchorwoman said. "UN officials insist they won't rest until they determine how separatists obtained an antimatter charge with a high enough explosive yield to blast all the way down to the underground ocean."

The screen showed a sim of the explosion on the surface of the icy Jovian moon.

"When I first heard about that," Marie said, "it scared the heck out of me. I thought something might've happened to you."

General Douglas's orders resonated in Brooke's mind. Her fingers squeezed her throbbing temples. "I wasn't anywhere near it."

"Glad to hear it." Marie tapped a cushion with her fingernails. "You know, given how far technology's come, I've never understood why they can't operate fighters remotely or let AIs do the piloting—not that I want to put you out of a job, but it might keep me from worrying."

"It's simple. There's too great a time lag for remote operation, and as smart as AI's have become, they lack intuition and adaptability. AI-operated craft have flown, but a human mind-linked to a support AI beats it every time."

"Oh."

"—and in other news," the screen squawked, "the countdown continues to the United Nation's press conference regarding tier two of—”

“Shut it off, already,” Brooke said.

Marie straightened a grin and cleared her throat. “I thought you’d be in love with Luminosity given your obsession with flying. Why’re you so grumpy about it?”

“I’m not grumpy, I’m just . . .” Brooke wanted to confess everything but instead said, “It’s none of your business.”

Her sister uttered a “tsk tsk,” stood, and strolled toward the kitchenette. “That’s a shame—although it actually works out well. Since you don’t care, you can stay here and watch Maya while I head out to Dryden to report on the press conference.”

“Wait, what?” Brooke teetered on the edge of the futon. “I thought you said—”

Marie swiped a pair of small slips off the island countertop, spun to face her twin, and fanned herself with them. “It’s going to be hot out there in the desert.”

“Marie!”

“My editor called and woke me up early this morning to tell me he changed his mind.” She grinned her widest grin yet but stopped waving the slips. “When I asked why, he told me not to look a gift editor in the mouth. I don’t get it, but by midmorning, these arrived.” She held out the slips. “One’s a plane ticket. The other’s a press badge granting me access to the conference. These’re why I’ve been in such a good mood all morning—at least until you woke up.”

“Oh . . .” Every part of Brooke’s body drooped. “Well, good for you,” she muttered. She fell back onto the futon and stared up at the ceiling. The urge to cry almost overwhelmed her, but she wasn’t about to in front of her sister. *Fate, why must you rub it in my face?*

“You’re not upset, are you?”

Brooke blinked away tears. “Who, me?” She tried to tune everything out. “I couldn’t care less.”

After a minute of lying there, she turned her head and saw Marie still standing in the same spot. Brooke’s gaze traveled up to her sister’s smirk and caught her fanning herself with the slips again, only now Brooke was seeing double.

Pushing to a sitting position, Brooke furrowed her brow. She stared at the quartet of slips long and hard before saying, “Is it my imagination, or are there four now?”

“For a fighter pilot, you sure are slow.” Marie marched up to her, grabbed her hand, and slapped two of the four slips into it.

Brooke ogled the gifts. The first showed a sim of a cartoon airplane hopping over puffy clouds. The text “ORD to LAX” flashed in front of the sim. The second featured a rotating UN emblem, the Luminosity Project patch, and the date of the conference.

A feeling of weightlessness buoyed her up as if she'd been whisked back to Callisto. “Thank you,” she whispered.

“You’re so transparent.” Marie placed a finger on her lower lip. “Now, I still don’t get why my editor sprung for two tickets when he couldn’t afford one before, but . . .” She shrugged. “We fly out middle of next week—I mean, if you’re really interested.”

## Nine—Prodigious
## Dryden Advanced Propulsion Center, April 2247 AD

Professor Kevin Sommerfield dragged both hands through his hair, recoiling at the sight of the crowd. Thousands of reporters, cameramen, politicians, government officials, soldiers, celebrities, and academics crowded around the stage at the center of the arena-sized spacecraft hangar. Did they expect him to give a simple speech? It seemed more like they wanted him to perform the halftime show at the Super Bowl.

He retreated behind an antique F-22 Raptor and scampered past his colleagues like a frightened teen in a horror sim. He fled inside the adjoining office space and slammed the door behind him.

Kevin pulled an inhaler out of his suit coat pocket and sucked in a puff. The thought of thousands of medites scurrying down his trachea increased his hyperventilation until the tightness in his chest vanished and he could breathe again.

The office door swung open. “How are you doing, Kevin?” one of his colleagues asked as she entered.

He shoved the inhaler into his pocket and straightened his posture. “Oh, I’m fine. I just forgot something.”

Dr. Christine Yeager smirked. “I think you’re the worst liar in the solar system.”

The comment eased his tension. “I became a physicist to avoid public speeches." He sat on the edge of a desk. "I should be at my matrix working on enhancements to the drive or back at the quantum collider running sims, not giving speeches. Can't one of these politicians make the announcement?"

"One of them could." Christine placed a hand on his shoulder. "But people don't want to hear the news from a messenger. They want to hear it from the man who did it."

Kevin shook his head. "We all did it. It took hundreds—if not thousands—of minds laboring over the course of centuries. Newton, Einstein, Schwarzschild, and countless others loosened the lid. I was the latest person to twist and it happened to open."

"Mr. Modesty. You lifted the lid all right, and you did it by altering the physical properties of the jar. You're a modern-day Einstein, a guy who's redefined physics and made science fiction a reality." She jabbed a thumb back at the door. "Now, come on. You're not getting out of this. If you don't get going, one of those soldiers will bust in here and escort you out at gunpoint."

Kevin swallowed hard and nodded.

He crept out of the office after Christine, emerging from behind an antique F-22 Raptor. Ignoring the stares of the crowd, he dragged himself up onto the stage and stood with the rest of his research team.

An English accent echoed throughout the hangar's composite foundation. Kevin recognized the voice, which had hounded him every day since he reported the feat to the United Nations.

Security Council President Edward Collins, the man in charge of all UN military operations, stood on the stage behind the podium. "Thank you for joining us in hangar seven-oh-three of the Dryden Advanced Propulsion Research Center." The glow on his face left little doubt that he loved the attention. "This facility has long been home to numerous groundbreaking aerospace advancements, from the ancient Apollo capsules to the first nuclear-powered rockets to the fusion and antimatter drives in use today. Therefore, we felt it appropriate to unveil the next great breakthrough in the project from this location.

"And so," Collins held a hand out toward the professor, "without further ado, I give you the man who's rewritten the physics textbooks and altered the course of human history forever, Professor Kevin Sommerfield."

Eyecams targeted Kevin, who managed a crooked smile. His motions felt mechanical. He forced his mind to envision how his favorite quarterback would handle such a situation while he shook Collins's hand. The defense mechanism helped numb him to his somersaulting stomach and lightheadedness.

He faced the crowd from behind the podium. The murmurs died down, and thousands of unsettling gazes pierced him. Not even the mental removal of garments eased his trembling.

A searing gust of air washed over him. Sweat slicked his forehead and palms. It felt hotter than the sun's corona inside the hangar, which resembled a huge metal tent more than a building with its three mammoth doors slid all the way open.

Kevin found he couldn't recall the speech he had spent hours memorizing. "Hello everyone." His voice cracked. The podium's microphone sent a ringing echo throughout the hangar, and the crowd winced. "Thanks . . . thanks for coming."

Collins gripped the mike with one hand and placed the other on Kevin's shoulder. "Give him a moment, folks. This is a big, emotional discovery, quite possibly the most important breakthrough in human history. You can only imagine what the fellow's going through." He unbuttoned the lapels on his blazer and loosened his tie. "Would someone turn on the air conditioning?"

The crowd chuckled.

"Like this hangar has air conditioning," someone said from the foot of the stage.

Kevin's muscles relaxed. His breathing evened. "As I'm sure you're all aware," he said, gazing beyond the audience at a Starthroat the UN had placed on display, "the rollout of phase tunneling in tier one revolutionized the way we communicate. Because of advancements in quantum gravity, string, and bulk theory, we came to better understand the true nature of the multiverse. During experiments conducted at CERN's Transdimensional Quantum Collider, we succeeded in creating wormholes, punctures in the fabric of space-time, that lead to higher spatial dimensions. We transmitted pulses of data through these wormholes, which arrived at distant destinations in less time than it took a photon of light to travel the physical distance." His gaze landed on a middle-aged man in a business suit. "I named this process of poking holes in space-time 'phase shifting' because it involves shifting to another phase of reality. Within higher spatial dimensions, the laws of physics operate very differently."

The suited man cocked his head. His brow dipped.

"You don't have a clue what he's talking about, do you?" whispered the woman standing next to the man.

The man adjusted his tie. "And you do?"

The woman shrugged.

Kevin peered at Collins, who gave a slight nod.

*Hurry up and get to the point*, Kevin translated. *I get it.*

He directed his attention back toward the offices. "Ladies and gentlemen, I'd like to introduce a very special friend of mine." A zookeeper emerged from behind the Raptor, walking hand-in-hand with a rhesus monkey. "Meet Albert XXI, the first mammal ever to arrive at a destination faster than light."

Eyecams tracked the monkey.

Albert hobbled up on stage and flailed his tongue at everyone.

"In other words, tier two has been an incredible success," Collins said.

Kevin continued. "First, I want to assure everyone that Albert's rights were respected throughout the process. As a matter of fact, we went beyond the UN Animal Ethics Mandate and conducted the flight as if it involved a human pilot. Only after thorough unmanned tests, trials with holopersona dummies, and risk mitigation to within acceptable human rating levels did we make the attempt." He cleared his throat. "Now, during his first space flight, Albert traveled the shortest distance between Earth and Mars—about a hundred-million kilometers—in under five minutes. I'd love to go into more detail about the prototype spacecraft he used—" He glanced at Collins. "—but that's been classified by the UN"

Knowing groans escaped the mouths of multiple audience members.

"With the successful unmanned trials of tier two completed, we've initiated tier three, design and construction of a manned FTL spacecraft. I'll let the Security Council president field questions on that topic. Now, I'll open up the floor to inquiries about the science of transdimensional phase shifting."

The Q&A session descended into a chaotic free-for-all among hundreds of shouting reporters.

*Who do I call on first?* He pointed at a reporter wearing an eyecam with the IntraSolar News logo.

The crowed quieted, allowing the man to ask his question.

"Isn't traveling faster than light the same thing as going back in time?" the reporter asked. "That's what's referred to as causality, right? Does phase shifting violate causality?"

Kevin shook his head. "No, in this case, matter doesn't actually travel faster than light. It takes a shortcut through a higher spatial dimension, like driving through a tunnel dug into a mountain instead of going around it. Excellent question, though. It's theoretically possible to create a wormhole that can not only transport matter to a distant point in space but also to a distant point in time, although the latter is much trickier. Next question."

"What about time dilation?" another reporter blurted out. "Doesn't time pass at a slower pace the closer you get to the speed of light? Did time slow down for Albert during his flights?"

"Good question. Calculations must be precise to ensure that no time discrepancies occur. We want Albert to arrive at his destination before we're all old and gray. Okay, who's next?"

He scanned the faces in the crowd. *These journalists all look like clones of one another. All the same—*

His gaze swept past an attractive young woman and whipped back in her direction.

The reporter waved one arm above her head. Chin-length black hair strayed out from behind her ear. Narrow blue eyes sparkled above a hopeful smile, giving him the impression being called on meant a lot to her.

And if the sight of her failed to entice him, he swore he was seeing double.

He nodded at the young woman. "Yes, you, the reporter from . . . I'm sorry, I'm not sure which organization you represent."

"The Chicago VidStreamer," the woman said. "It's no surprise you haven't heard of us, but thanks for taking the time to answer my question."

*Huh, no one else thanked me.*

"First, I want to put into words what I'm sure everyone here is feeling," she said. "This new technology is mind-blowing, and I can't wait to see where it takes us. But really, I'd like to know more about the emotion surrounding the discovery. How did you feel when Albert emerged alive and well from the far end of that wormhole for the first time?"

He stared at her for a moment, lost in the soft features of an angel. "It felt amazing. It vindicated my life's work."

"Wow." She adjusted her eyecam. "What about Kevin Sommerfield the man, as opposed to Kevin Sommerfield the physicist? Do you have a wife or children? I don't see a ring. How about a fiancée or girlfriend?"

"Unfortunately, my work tends to consume me."

"That's a shame. Tell me you at least got lucky the night of your triumph."

The crowd exploded with laughter.

Kevin's face flushed. *How can I hide the lonely truth?* "Well . . ." The perfect answer hit him like a particle collision. "I'll leave that to your imagination."

♦

"I didn't know the VidStreamer was a tabloid," Brooke said.

The professor turned his attention to another reporter.

Marie flipped up her cam's eyepiece and turned on her sister. "I do my best to report events in a respectful and professional manner, but the news has to entertain to grab people's attention. That's the reality of the industry."

"That doesn't make it right."

"I don't tell you how to do your job. Don't tell me how to do mine." Marie twirled to face the stage.

After a minute, she said, "You know, the professor's not bad-looking. That five o'clock shadow works for him. I could do without the blue highlights, though. Sticking with natural brown would be more flattering."

Brooke frowned.

Professor Sommerfield announced he would answer one last question.

The people huddled behind Brooke pushed forward with raised hands. A beefy man knocked into her. She threw her elbows, fighting for personal space. "Damn it," she muttered. "I feel like I'm caught in a horde of screaming teenyboppers, smitten over a shameless corporate boy band."

"Always the life of the party," Marie said over her shoulder.

Brooke wrinkled her nose, cursing the heat and inconsiderate twits around her.

She fanned herself with the bottom of her t-shirt and yanked on the press badge hanging around her neck. A mild shudder ran down her spine, uncomfortable but nowhere near as bad as the withdrawal symptoms of the previous week.

Reporters shouted at Professor Sommerfield. His shoulders buckled under all the attention.

*I feel you, buddy. You're quite the humble guy for somebody who's just revolutionized the solar system.*

Security president Collins stood to the left of the podium.

*Is it my imagination, or is he staring at me?* Brooke magnified Collins's face, leaving little doubt that his penetrating green eyes were directed at her. *Why is he looking at me like he knows me? Did word of my screw-ups reach him?*

She turned toward the runway and desert landscape outside the hangar.

When she looked back at the stage, he had retaken the podium. "Thank you, Professor Sommerfield. How about a round of applause for the man of the hour?"

The crowd clapped and hooted.

Once quiet settled over the hangar, he spoke. "The professor will be doing one-on-one interviews with select e-media representatives later this afternoon. Now, I'll speak briefly about construction of the first manned faster-than-light spacecraft. Initial designs are already being laid out, and the prototype shuttle should embark on its maiden voyage by the end of the year. The test location has yet to be chosen, and test pilot application screening is still underway."

## Ten—Vis-à-vis
## Dryden Advanced Propulsion Center, April 2247 AD

"It's a pleasure to meet you, Miss Davis." Kevin shook the reporter's hand.

"The pleasure's mine, Professor Sommerfield," she said, "and please call me Marie. I'm flattered you chose me to conduct your first interview."

The bureaucrats had allowed Kevin to determine which e-media groups received first crack at him. Without a second thought, he selected the young woman who stood out from the rest of the crowd.

Security president Collins, the CERN director-general, and the Dryden director had wanted him to limit interviews to the major networks, like ISN. "Don't waste your time with the little guys," they had said. A part of his ego welcomed the widespread recognition the e-media giants would shower upon him, but only a small part. The thought of someone shouting, "Hey, that's the guy!" every time he set foot in a grocery store or movie theater ignited antimatter eruptions within his abdomen.

Instead of taking everyone's advice, he had listened to his desires. *I don't see anything wrong with having a pleasant conversation with an attractive young woman.*

Kevin settled into a director's chair. "Your questions caught people's attention earlier today. I'm sure that's why they picked you for the first interview."

"Yeah, I'm kind of known for my wit." Miss Davis—no, Marie smiled and shrugged.

Her warm joviality eased his stomach grumbling. *This feels like having coffee with an old friend, which is how it should feel.*

Relocating to Dryden's largest conference room had alleviated his tension. Marie sat across from him in another director's chair, wearing a blouse that tinted to a different pastel color every three minutes. Her smooth legs crossed beneath a summer skirt. A green screen hung on the wall behind them.

A borrowed cameraman stood across from the chairs, flanked by an AV technician working an e-slip. Collins loomed behind them.

Multiple screens hovered next to the vidcam, displaying what the viewers at home saw. One of the displays showed Kevin and Marie sitting in the middle of a runway. The sun set behind them against the backdrop of the Mojave Desert.

The only other person in the room, a mysterious young woman, leaned against the far wall behind Marie. She stood with thumbs in her pockets, one leg crossed in front of the other, neither frowning nor smiling. Except for a few stylistic differences, she looked just like the reporter.

"Ready to get started?" Marie asked.

Kevin clasped his hands in his lap. "Sure."

She shot the cameraman a glance.

The red light on the vidcam blinked to life. Its operator jabbed his thumb in the air.

"Hello, everyone," Marie said into the cam. "I'm the Chicago VidStreamer's Marie Davis. Joining me is Professor Kevin Sommerfield, the inventor of the first faster-than-light propulsion system, for an exclusive interview." She turned to Kevin. "Now, Professor, if it's all right with you, I'd like to focus on the personal journey that brought you to this point."

"That's fine," he said, "although I'm not sure how I feel about the personal query you made out in the hangar."

"Don't worry. We'll keep things appropriate for the whole family. Let's start with the basics. Where are you from?"

"Well, I grew up in Green Bay, Wisconsin. It's a small city of a quarter-million people."

"Ya der, a Cheesehead, eh? I live in Chicag-oh, doncha know? Soh, I see dem Cheeseheads all da times."

Kevin failed to stifle a chuckle.

She flipped back to reporter mode. “And did you always have an affinity for science from a young age?”

“Oh, yes. I was never one of the jocks, one of the cool kids. As a matter of fact”— He stroked the stubble covering his chin. —“I remember my reports back in early grade school. The other kids talked about children’s stories, sports—normal stuff. I would bring stacks of slips about science and space to class. I would stand up in front of everyone and explain how there are more than three spatial dimensions and how there used to be nine planets before Pluto got demoted to a dwarf. Everyone stared at me like I was an idiot.” He shivered. “Eventually, the teacher told me I had to report on something else. In retrospect, the ridicule is probably what led me to seeking out an interest like football—American football—that better allows me to relate to people.”

“Sports do have more general appeal.” Marie scribbled notes with a stylus on an e-slip.

She said something else, but Kevin missed it. His attention drifted over to the woman behind her. *She has to be the reporter’s identical twin sister—either that or a clone. No, that’s stupid. They banned human cloning hundreds of years ago.*

He studied the lookalike with intrigue. Her purple irises intoxicated him. *Must be some type of implants*. The woman leaned toward them, hanging on the conversation. Then she caught him looking in her direction and averted her gaze.

For some dumb, testosterone-laden reason, his mind insisted on playing an immature game. *Which twin do I think is cuter?*

He tuned back into the interview and caught Marie’s latest question.

“—and did you graduate early from high school or college, being a genius and all?”

“I wish you wouldn’t use that term. I’m no ‘genius.’ It took me five years to complete my undergraduate physics degree.”

“I see. I’ll avoid using inaccurate labels in the future, and . . .”

In contrast to Marie’s dressier outfit, her sister wore a tight black T-shirt. Her faded blue jeans sported plenty of holes, and her boots looked far too warm for the desert heat. She resembled a punk rocker from the twentieth century, with the lavender highlights in the black strands of her ponytail.

Most people, Kevin figured, would label Marie as the better catch. Her appearance screamed personable and well-mannered. A man could puff out his chest when introducing her to family and friends.

Perhaps that factored into why the doppelgänger fascinated him more so than Marie. *I've always been attracted to tough women. Why is that? Does my subconscious long for some kind of countering force to balance out my lack of manliness? Or maybe it has more to do with raw psychology. They say people are often attracted to the wrong person in the same way the best-tasting foods have the worst nutritional value. People crave the feeling of aliveness, no matter how negative, over comfort and ease.*

After much mental deliberation, he declared a stalemate. *If the twin would smile, it might put her over the top.*

The reporter asked him another question, stealing him from his fantasies.

♦

Brooke pressed her back flat against the drywall while rubbing her bare arms. The hangar had felt like a fusion inferno. Now, the temperature of her skin felt cold as ice, courtesy of the damned air conditioning.

Peering up at the ceiling, she thought, *Was the professor really looking at me, or did I imagine it?* She supposed the whole identical twin thing fascinated him. For some dumb reason, it captivated everyone. "Oh my Gawd!" idiots had babbled far too many times. "I can, like, barely tell you apart. Do you girls, like, go everywhere and do everything together? Finish each other's sentences, and like, wear the same outfits? That would be so cute . . ."

*Ugh.*

She had spent most of the interview pretending the professor and his accomplishments held no interest for her, but deep down, she wanted to grab his coat, shake him, and not let go until he agreed to let her pilot every ship he ever created. He had surprised her with his modesty and with how much he cared, and she couldn't stop thinking about how his invention would at long last bring her father's dream to fruition.

"Incredible, isn't it, Lieutenant?"

Brooke jerked her head right. The president of the UN Security Council, Edward Collins, stood at her side. He faced the interview, hands clasped behind his back. The man stood a half-head taller than her, not a large individual by any means. However, he radiated a confident command authority, giving him an imposing aura.

Out of habit, she stiffened to attention. "Sir."

"At ease, Lieutenant." Collins wore a slight grin. "You're on leave, remember?"

She tried to relax her muscles, but tension gripped her.

Brooke leaned back against the wall, shoved her thumbs in her pockets, and averted her gaze.

"I've been hearing a lot about you lately." He looked her over. "For some reason, I thought you'd be—" He paused, searching for the right words. "—more imposing."

Her brow dipped.

"But I suppose looks aren't everything, are they?" he said. "According to General Douglas, you're the best pilot in the fleet. Did you know you have as many kills as officers twice your age?"

Brooke shrugged.

"The abilities afforded to you by your condition are blinding." His voice took on an eerie softness, accentuating the inflections. "But the fact that you're still alive is a bloody miracle."

A twinge coursed through her. "I don't know what you're talking about, sir."

"Indeed. My mistake." He dipped his narrow chin and leaned in closer to her. "Now, it's come to my attention that you've applied for the candidacy program. I'm sure it'll be a dream come true for whomever the committee selects. Of course, the UN Security Council has to approve the final selection."

Chills of angst and anticipation surged through Brooke's body.

"A new future is coming, Lieutenant, a future so profound it'll make the sum of all mankind's accomplishments look like some lad's crayon masterpiece hung up on Mummy's icebox." The man's nose hovered centimeters away from hers, aftershave overpowering her nostrils. She resisted the urge to slide away along the wall. "As UN officers, it's critical we follow orders and trust our superiors to fulfill that vision. Do you understand what I'm saying?"

Despite her confused scowl, she did her best to nod.

Collins backed away and straightened his blazer, tone reverting to cheery old Brit mode. "I'm pleased we could have this little talk." He took two steps toward the door, stopped, and shook his head at Marie's flirtatious laughter. "You know, you two shouldn't fight. Life's too short. Cheerio." He marched out of the conference room.

Brooke slid down the wall to the floor, unnerved. *What the hell just happened? Was he hinting he'd make me test pilot if I keep my mouth shut? And how does he know what Marie and I do?* She hadn't planned on disobeying orders. She cared far too much about her career and maintaining whatever slim chance she had at acceptance to the candidacy program.

Across the room, the chat between Miss Charismatic and Mr. Genius had engrossed the vidcam crew. It didn't appear as if they'd noticed the other bit of nearby dialogue.

♦

"Forgive me if I'm out of line," Professor Sommerfield said, "but I've told you so much about myself. I'd like to hear a little bit about you."

"Now, now." Marie waved a finger at him. *So far, this assignment is even more fun than I'd hoped.* "This is an interview, not a date." She faced the vidcam crew and drew a line across her neck. "Why don't you guys take a break?"

The crew shrugged, switched off their equipment, and filed out of the room.

"I suppose it can't hurt," Marie said. "What do you want to know?"

"Well," the professor asked, "let's start with the basics. Where are you from?"

Marie tapped the stylus against her lower lip and sank into her chair. "I was born in Yokohama, Japan. There's not much cheese there, but they've got a lot of fish and rice."

"You don't look entirely Japanese, if you don't mind my saying."

"I'm only half Japanese. My father, Robert Davis, was American. He met my mother, Natsumi Hayashi, while stationed at the UN base in Yokohama. We lived there for five years before they transferred Dad to Colorado Springs, at which point he carted us back with him."

"Us?"

"My mom, my sister, and me."

"Sister?"

Marie nodded. "That reminds me." She yelled over her shoulder. "Hey Brooke, come over here." When her sister failed to respond, she called out again, putting emphasis on every syllable of her twin's given name. "Hey Ki-shi-ko . . ."

Kevin dipped his bushy eyebrows. "Kishiko?"

"It means 'child of the seashore' in Japanese." Marie smirked. "You don't dare call her by her real name, though, not if you value your vital organs."

"Seashore . . . water . . . brook. I get it. Kishiko's a beautiful name, though. Why doesn't she like it?"

"Kids made fun of her for it, so Dad came up with the nickname. Brooke worshipped the man, and when he . . ." She closed her eyes.

Kevin held a hand up. "Say no more."

Marie twisted her body around and searched the area behind her chair.

Brooke sat on the floor, leaning against the wall, violet eyes staring off into space. Her face appeared paler and more disgruntled than usual.

"What's with you?" Marie asked.

Brooke shook her head as if emerging from a trance and glared at her sister. The light-year-thick emotional wall Brooke put between herself and everyone else closed around her.

"Nothing." She hopped up and trudged her way onto the set. "What do you want?"

"Well," Marie said, "I thought you might like to meet Professor Sommerfield. Not many people come face-to-face with a modern-day Einstein, Kishi."

"Please don't call me that," both Kevin and Brooke said at the same time.

Kevin laughed.

Brooke squinted at Marie.

"It's Brooke, right?" Kevin asked, staring up at her.

She looked at him without answering. Her face flushed, and she swallowed.

*Now who's the teenybopper?* Stifling a grin, Marie swore she felt something more between them, but knowing her sister—and considering the professor—she found the notion hard to believe. "My sister's a fighter pilot with UN Aerospace Defense."

Brooke smacked her on the shoulder.

"A pilot, huh?" Intrigue laced Kevin's tone.

"That's right." Marie held her arms out to the sides. "And what's this I hear? The candidacy program is looking for test pilots? Where do you suppose we could find a pilot around here?" She stuck her neck out in all directions, shielding her eyes from imaginary brightness, gazing everywhere except at her sister.

"Marie . . ." Brooke hissed.

The professor ran a hand through his disheveled mop of hair. "Well, I'm on the selection committee, but there's a process I have to follow to ensure everyone gets a fair shot. Have you applied?"

"Uh . . . yes, yes I have."

"Okay, I'll take a look at your application the first chance I get." He smiled.

"I tell you, this stuff doesn't just happen." Marie leaned back in her chair and tapped her lip with the stylus. "You could end up flying the ship while I report on it. It must be fate."

"I don't believe in fate," Brooke said.

Kevin nodded. "Sorry to disappoint you, Marie, but neither do I."

"Oh, come on, you two," Marie said. "Have a little more faith."

## Eleven—Encumbrance
## Chicago, May 2247 AD

"Maya, no!" Brooke watched glasses, plates, and bowls fall in seeming slow motion.

The little girl charged down the department store aisle with arms stretched out, imitating a star fighter. The expensive merchandise her hand knocked off the shelf crashed against the floor with all the force of Earth's standard gravity. A domino effect sent more and more dishes careening toward certain doom.

Maya stopped and spun. Her face flushed, and both eyes wavered with guilt.

Dinnerware shattered all around the girl, showering her with broken pieces. She threw both arms up to shield herself.

The nanoplastic disintegrated in a poof, pummeling her with fine granules as harmless as grains of sand.

Maya coughed and spit some out.

"You little . . ." Fuming, Brooke dashed after her niece.

Maya whirled and scurried off to another aisle.

A saleswoman appeared and rushed over to the mess. "Excuse me."

Brooke skidded to a halt, wrinkling her nose and puffing out her cheeks.

“I’m sorry, but you’re going to have to pay for the items your daughter broke,” the woman said.

“She’s not mine,” Brooke stammered. *Why did Marie take a new job that includes travel?* A grunt rumbled up from her chest. *I’m no good with kids!*

“Well, someone has to pay for—”

Brooke flipped her net specs down over her eyes and slid aside the novel-length list of junk Marie had told her to buy. Grumbling, she logged into her personal credit app and interfaced with the store AI matrix.

The saleswoman lifted the e-pad dangling from her belt and swiped a command. “Thank you. The store matrix has confirmed receipt of your payment.”

Brooke took off sprinting. She searched Electronics, Home Improvement, and Women’s Apparel but failed to locate her niece. *Give me a firefight in Jupiter orbit, please!* Brooke felt like she had aged decades in the past couple of weeks while wrestling with the kid’s tantrums. Maya behaved as well as anyone could expect with her mother present, but the girl never listened to her aunt. Shouts, pouts, and stomps had commenced the moment Marie walked out the door.

Thirty minutes later, Brooke had scoured every corner of the department store without success.

She sank deep into the cushions of a couch in Home Furnishings. *Where is she? How will I explain her disappearance to Marie?* “Great going, Kishi,” she’ll say. “Way to kill off another family member.” She tugged at her hair. *I’m going to have to ask the store matrix to announce her name.* Her head flopped into her hands. *This can’t be happening . . .*

Her peripheral vision caught a mound of black hair poking up from behind one side of the couch.

Brooke sprang upright. “Where’ve you been?”

Maya’s words came out in a pouty growl. “I’ve been following you.”

“You mean you let me wander around like an idiot for half an hour?”

“You didn’t even know.”

“Get over here right now.” Searing heat shot up Brooke’s spine. “We’re going home.”

“No!”

“Right now, you little brat, or else—”

Maya whined in high pitch and then exploded into tears.

Brooke recoiled. *I’m treating her exactly how kids used to treat me.*

A pair of shoppers stopped and stared.

She held up a palm, indicating she had everything under control.

Brooke sat down and let Maya cry for a minute.

"I'm sorry," Brooke said. "I shouldn't have yelled or called you a name." She breathed deep and forced her next words out. "I was really scared when I couldn't find you."

Maya's crying subsided to sniffles. "You're mean."

"You're right, I am, but I don't want to be that way." Brooke shook her head. "I suck at this babysitting stuff. I don't know what I'm doing." She bowed her head. "When I was growing up, kids used to put me down all the time, but I don't want to do that to you. I don't want you to turn out as messed up as I am." She sighed. "So again, I'm sorry, and I'd appreciate it if you would please come out."

Brooke waited a few seconds before lifting her chin.

Maya crawled into view around the corner of the couch.

"Thank you," Brooke said.

The little girl lowered her bloodshot eyes and fidgeted with one of the buttons on her shiny pink overalls. Her frown crept upward, morphing into a contemplative squiggle. "Mommy said she was going to buy me Bio Bear. It's super soft and talks and dances and tells jokes and helps with math."

Brooke skimmed Marie's list in her specs. "Hmm, I don't see it." She winked. "Tell you what. If you help me grab all this other stuff for your mom, I'll buy it for you."

Maya beamed.

♦

The Chicago L hovertrain whirred past outside, shaking the dark apartment.

Brooke's eyelids parted, and she squinted. Streetlight pierced the living room's flickering window blinds.

Her lids fluttered and closed.

She tried to roll over on her side, but a small, warm body pinned her arm against the couch.

"Maya?" Brooke mumbled after peering down.

The girl snuggled closer to her, gripping her security blanket. Dancing farm animals fizzled in and out of existence above its projection fibers. "I can't sleep, Auntie. I'm scared. I want Mommy."

"Your mom's in Europe at CERN, interviewing Professor Sommerfield for the *Tribune*. She'll be home tomorrow." Brooke yawned. "Go back to bed." She pulled her arm out from under her niece and flipped over on her side, facing the back of the couch.

Maya lay still for a few seconds before sitting up. Instead of leaving, she climbed over her aunt and wedged her body between Brooke and the cushions. After reeling in her smart blanky, she stuck her thumb in her mouth and shifted around.

Brooke rolled onto her back and groaned. "Maya. Seriously. Go to bed."

"No. I can't sleep."

"Why not?"

"I'm scared."

"Of what?"

"Gamma rays, asteroids, solar flares, and the Earth's magnetic field collapsing."

"What?" Brooke's brow rose clear up to her hairline.

"I read about them on SolNet. The scientists say—"

"None of that's going to hurt you tonight." *If I didn't know better, I'd think this kid had been sparking.* "For the last time, go to your room and go to bed."

"No, there are monsters in there."

Brooke sighed. "There aren't any monsters in your room, not unless you count that stupid robot."

"Pappy's not stupid."

"Right. Sorry." Brooke draped one arm over her forehead. *Here we go again.* She hopped to her feet, bent down, and picked Maya up off the couch. The kid radiated heat like a little fusion reactor. Fuzzy pink pajamas tickled Brooke's hands.

She set her niece down. "Okay, off to bed now."

Maya whipped her head from side to side, clutching her blanky.

Brooke sighed. "All right, I'll come with you." She placed a firm hand on Maya's back and nudged her toward the bedroom.

The dancing clock above the stove in the kitchen read 3:12 AM.

Maya recoiled when she reached the bedroom door.

"I'll go first." Brooke flipped the light switch. The overhead plasma strip flickered, buzzed, and fizzled out. *Of all the times for the light to burn out!* She felt her way forward. Crescent moons, rocket ships, stars, and other animated stickers glowed on the ceiling, giving vague outlines to the furniture. Thick curtains blocked the streetlight.

Her hand reached out and touched the dresser. A couple steps later, a stuffed animal tripped her up, and her knee knocked the footboard of Maya's twin bed. She bit her lip and ran a hand along the mattress. After locating the nightstand, she felt around for the lamp and tapped the base. Soft white light peeked out from beneath the lampshade.

Brooke sat down on the bed, patting the Time Turtle bed sheets with one hand. "Let's go now. Get in here."

Maya tiptoed into the room and searched beneath the bed.

"There's nothing under there except toys collecting dust," Brooke said. "Now, come on."

With a running start, Maya leapt and dove onto her bed. She yanked her feet away from the edge, apparently in case something from below tried to yank her down.

Brooke pulled the covers up over her. "Okay, nighty night now." She patted her niece on the head and stood up.

"Double check under the bed, please. Make sure there are no monsters."

One of Brooke's eyebrows twitched. "There's no such thing as monsters." *At least, none that aren't human.*

"What about Looney the Wacky Moon Monster?"

Brooke's shoulders slumped. *How do I answer that question? Do I explain he's a holopersona, or that none of the characters on any of the shows she watches are real?* "He's too busy hopping from crater to crater on Luna to be under your bed."

"Oh yeah." Maya's brow creased. "Still check. Just in case."

*This'll drag on all night if I don't humor the kid.* Brooke dropped her bare knees to the carpet and peeked beneath the bedframe. Faint light outlined a stuffed dinosaur, a squeeze toy that emitted clichéd animal noises, and a stack of e-slips containing bedtime stories.

She popped her head up. "No monsters."

Maya crouched at the edge of the mattress. Her nose hovered centimeters from her aunt's face. "Why are your eyes purple?"

Brooke blinked. "The implants help me see better when I fly my plane."

"Can I have implants like you?"

"I don't think Mommy would approve."

"Why?"

"You're too young."

"Why?"

"I don't know. Maybe we want you to be normal." Brooke rose to her feet and guided Maya back under the covers. "All right, I certify this room as a monster-free zone. Go to sleep now." She reached for the lamp.

Maya said, "Need Pappy to scan. Just in case."

Brooke bit her lower lip. "I did a human check. That's better than any robot scan."

"What about mike-scop-pick in-viz-bowl monsters?"

*Where does this kid get these crazy ideas?* "The words are

pronounced 'invisible' and 'microscopic,' squirt."

"That's what I said. Have Pappy scan for them, pretty please."

"All right, fine." Brooke raised her voice. "Papero, come here."

Spherical ears flashed green in the corner of the bedroom, accompanied by the soft hum of a motor.

The robot rolled its way around the foot of the bed. <How may I be of service, ma'am?>

Brooke pointed beneath the bed. "Scan for monsters, and make it quick."

<My pleasure, Brooke. Now initiating my trademark Monster Scan.> Two lights on the front of Papero's oblong torso came to life. Per a program Marie had created, it wiggled back and forth in front of the bed, casting soft white illumination beneath it. Ten seconds later, it ceased all motion and shut off its lights. <No monsters detected.>

Maya clapped. "Thank you, Pappy."

<I'm happy to help, Maya. Is there anything else I can do for you?>

"No," Brooke said.

<Have a pleasant night.> Papero wheeled back into the corner, plugged into the wall, and resumed sleep mode.

Brooke tucked the kid in again. "Okay, good night for real this time." She tapped the lamp off and scurried for the door.

About halfway there, she heard, "Auntie?"

She stopped and glared back, masking her welling angst with a grin. "Yes?"

"I'm not sleepy anymore."

Every muscle in Brooke's body gave out. "Well, go to sleep anyway."

"I can't. Can you read me a story?"

"Tomorrow morning. I promise. Now go to sleep."

She stepped through the doorway.

Sniffles echoed from the bedroom behind her.

Brooke blew out a sigh and turned back around. *Well, it's not like I have to get up for anything.* She felt her way back into the room, turned on the lamp, and fetched one of the e-slips from beneath the bed. After climbing underneath the covers next to Maya, she enabled the paper-thin slip. A blue rocket ship with wide grin on its nose hurtled across the screen-page. "My dad used to read this story to me. It was one of the first things that got me interested in flying and space exploration."

"I'm going to be an explorer when I grow up," Maya said matter-of-factly. "I'll have my own ship and travel to distant stars and fight bad guys and fall in love and save the galaxy."

One corner of Brooke's mouth curled upward. "Is that so?"

"Yep, and Mommy says you're going to fly the new super-fast ship. Will you give me a ride, please, Auntie, will you?"

Dread swelled within Brooke's chest. "We'll see, squirt. I might not even get the chance to compete to fly it." She squashed the feeling deep down. "Let's read the story."

Maya grabbed Bio Bear from behind one of her pillows and nuzzled up to her aunt, who tapped the page.

"Once upon a time," an elderly woman's voice narrated, "there was a little ship that said—"

Maya slapped the slip, pausing it. "I want you to read, Auntie."

"But it tells the story for us."

"I like it when you read."

Brooke gave a slow nod and smiled. "Okay." She held up the e-slip, tapped the Disable Narration menu option, and cleared her throat.

Maya swiped a finger over the slip, backing it up to the beginning of the story. Then she fished a crumpled box of Fruity Planets out from beneath a pillow and offered it to her aunt.

Brooke reached into the box and grabbed a handful of cereal. "Once upon a time," she read between munches, "there was a little ship that said, 'I believe in myself, I believe in myself . . .'"

♦

Brooke awoke to the distant chime of her specs. Faint sunlight illuminated the kitchen beyond the doorway.

After rolling Maya away, she slipped out of bed and dragged her feet into the living room.

She pulled the specs out of her duffel bag and put them on. Two messages demanded her attention. The first, from Command, read, "Lieutenant Brooke Davis, you are hereby reinstated to active duty, assignment pending. Further orders to follow." The second stated, "After reviewing your application, the selection committee is pleased to offer you a position in the Luminosity Candidate Training Program."

Her jaw drooped, and she fell to her knees, laughing one moment and screaming the next.

♦

"You're sure this isn't a scheme to ditch me?" Marie asked. "We were getting along so well."

Brooke helped the driver shove her bag into the trunk of the h-rover. As the hatch retracted, she stepped up onto the sidewalk next to her sister. "I showed you my acceptance."

Marie nodded, tight-lipped. “I know, and I’m happy for you.”

Brooke returned an awkward nod. *I’ve never been great at goodbyes, but at least I’m saying one this time.*

Maya pulled away from Marie’s leg and hurried over to her aunt. “I don’t want you to go, Auntie.”

Brooke bent down and rustled the kid’s hair. “I wish I could stay, squirt.” She gave Maya a big hug. “If I win, I’ll take you for that ride.”

“Promise?” Maya insisted.

“I promise.”

After releasing her niece, she stood and turned to Marie. “Thanks for, you know, everything. It wasn’t as bad as I expected.”

Marie chuckled. “Maybe you’ll come back sooner rather than later.”

“Anything’s possible.”

“Then again, I work for the *Tribune* now.” Marie winked. “Chances are good I’ll be seeing you there.”

“I can’t wait . . .” Brooke worked her way over to the rover and opened the front passenger-side door.

Hesitation gripped her.

She slammed the door, hurried back to her sister, and squeezed her tight.

## Twelve—Polytechnic
## Earhart Pilot Training Center, Mars, June 2247 AD

A four-dimensional wire cube rotated on the display screen hovering above Brooke's desk. Depending on how she looked at the tesseract, it resembled a cube within a larger cube, a collection of intersecting parallelograms, or the jungle gym she had played on with Maya last month.

She read the math problem below the cube and scrunched her nose. Swiping her finger through the screen, she skipped ahead to the next exam question.

"A spacecraft enters a traversable wormhole at the following spatial coordinates," she mumbled. "After upshifting to hyperspace, the craft traverses the given set of hypervectors and downshifts after one hour passes within the reference frame of a stationary observer in normal space-time. Assuming negligible gravity fields at the wormhole entry and exit points, calculate the craft's effective velocity and destination coordinates."

Her forehead banged the desk. Thoughts of her struggles in grade school induced twinges of panic.

"Question?"

Brooke sat up straight. Dr. Christine Yeager, the Luminosity hypergeometry instructor, stood beside her desk.

“Probably,” Brooke said, “but first I need to figure out what to ask.”

Christine’s eyelids fluttered. “C’mon, Lieutenant Davis. You know this stuff.”

“I swear . . . all I’ve done since the program began is study math and physics. I’m starting to wonder why you don’t find a scientist to fly the shuttle.”

“We’re not pilots. You are.”

“Well, I’m no number cruncher. The phase drive AI performs all the calculations. What’s the point of learning this stuff?”

Christine folded her arms and stared at her student.

Sighing, Brooke said, “Because I still need a basic grasp of the underlying principles to operate the craft or find my way out of hyperspace if a malfunction occurs.”

The instructor extended a bag of goodies toward her. “Chocolate?”

“No thanks.” Brooke shook one of six travel boxes of Fruity Planets.

Christine shoved the bag back into her coat pocket. “Clock’s ticking, Lieutenant.”

Brooke watched the woman saunter off down the aisle of the lecture hall. A week ago, Brooke had sat in this seat for the first time along with twenty-four other candidates, starry-eyed and bursting with aberrant giddiness. *This is a dream come true. I’ve got a real chance to be the first to fly faster than light, so I need to stick with it.* After taking in the view outside the window—a yellow-orange haze hung over the canyons of Valles Marineris—she inhaled a slow breath and got back to work.

♦

With hands clasped in her lap, Brooke sat in the hot seat in a small interview room. Members of the evaluation board sat across from her on the opposite side of a long table.

“A number of things about you caught our attention during the selection process,” a four-star UN general stated. The aging woman’s augmented irises perused one of many slips on the table in front of her. “I was particularly intrigued by the essay you wrote on what becoming the phase shuttle test pilot would mean to you. You say you’re doing it for your father, whom you literally killed? Tell me more about him and what happened.”

Brooke sucked in her abdomen, stifling the queasiness. Writing about her horrific mistake had proven difficult enough. Talking about it required every last shred of self-discipline to keep from wilting. “My father taught me everything I know about flying. He used to take me up in his flyer, point out the constellations, and tell me all about the wonders of the galaxy."

Mist blurred her vision. She blinked it away and explained how her father had failed to eject after she flew his flyer into the plasma backwash of the Cormorants. "I've spent my life trying to fulfill the dreams he instilled in me, which keeps him alive and with me in some small way. It's the least I can do."

"Very touching," the general said.

"Indeed," the chief flight surgeon said. "Now, your performance as a conventional pilot has rated in the top one percent of all Defense pilots in the last four years. Part of this can be attributed to your father's tutelage from such a young age, I'm sure. But according to your medical records, a genetic disorder introduced by prenatal gene therapy malpractice seems to have heightened your spatial awareness and reflexes. All signs point to these traits being an asset throughout the candidacy program. For all we know, you might be better equipped than anyone to handle the effects of hyperspace. However, I've ordered additional tests during your upcoming medical evaluation to determine whether complications could arise due to your condition."

Brooke nodded. "I understand."

"Another potential concern we have is your proficiency with technical concepts," the CERN director-general said. "Your scores have been below average in preliminary aptitude tests. Most of your fellow candidates graduated from university, but you didn't complete your final year of high school." The white-haired man stared at her, awaiting a response.

"I know I'm starting out at a disadvantage, sir, but I'm intent on putting in the time to make up ground. I understand the basic concepts, but I'm not a great test-taker. I'm committed to improving, though, because of how important this is to me."

Professor Sommerfield ran a hand through his hair and glanced at Dr. Yeager seated next to him. "Both Christine and I are at your disposal should you require additional tutoring."

"Thank you," Brooke said.

After sipping from a mug, the UN general flipped to a different e-slip in her stack. "You were recently relieved of duty due to an incident with a fellow pilot, and then reinstated by General Frederick Douglas. He cites severe combat stress as provoking the confrontation, which he believes won't happen again. Would you agree with that assessment, or should we be concerned about your interactions with fellow candidates?"

Her skin steamed beneath her uniform. "I admit to losing my cool, yes, but I think I've learned from the mistake and matured. I've faced the consequences of my actions and won't let something like that happen again."

"I'll hold you to that. Should this committee select you, you'll be required to interact with a lot of people. Your psychological profile labels you as an introvert, one who withdraws from social situations. Should you be the first to fly faster than light, you'd become an instant celebrity and a spokeswoman for the UN How do you feel about that?"

Brooke shrugged. "I've never been fond of crowds or public speeches, and I don't think that'll ever change. But if I'm doing what I love, I think it'll be easier to talk about it with others."

The board members turned to one another, asking if anyone had any other questions. No one did.

"Thank you, Lieutenant Davis," the UN general said. "You're dismissed."

♦

The medical exam followed. It seemed geared more toward torturing her than running tests. The staff affixed dozens of transmitters to her body and then collected biometric data while she jogged for kilometers or sprinted. Sit-ups, pull-ups, and every weight-lifting machine known to humankind stressed her muscles to the limits. *Thank the stars for the lower Martian gravity,* she thought, although the nurse compensated by loading her up with three times the weight she would've lifted on Earth. Brooke discovered just how close she could come—or not come—to doing the splits, and how much she disliked knowing her body fat percentage. Not since her days as a new Defense recruit had she endured such pain and suffering.

As she lay on an exam table, a machine scanned her body. Lifelike renditions of her musculoskeletal, nervous, and circulatory systems materialized above floor emitters. Dread chilled her real organs as the doctors scrutinized sims of her spine and nerve endings. "I'm seeing some unusual degradation," a physician said to a nurse. "It's as if something's gnawed away her nerve tissue. Forward these scans to my office for further analysis."

*Side effects of the sparks?* Her heart thumped. She could only hope they couldn't connect the symptoms to the cause.

Throughout the following week, her evaluation scores continued to slip even though she threw herself into every challenge. Kevin went out of his way to tutor her in hypergeometry and phase theory, which helped, but she still struggled on the exams. Her brain just wasn't wired that way.

She performed better when sitting in the simulated cabin of the phase shuttle, but the impromptu attack sims killed her. Lee Min-Sung, the main programmer of the phase drive's AI matrix, liked to surprise everyone with virtual separatist raids and other emergency scenarios during control system training.

Engineers planned on constructing the real phase shuttle without weapons. They needed to minimize protrusions and grooves on its sleek fuselage for wormhole entry, having wrestled with the exit hatch design for months. A lack of armaments left the shuttle vulnerable while Brooke waited for its drive to charge, and her attempts at improvisation ended in simulated death. On one occasion, she fled a pursuing spacecraft by following a gravity assist trajectory around a gas giant, but the shuttle's limited maneuvering capability left her to burn up in the atmosphere. Then she tried using the plasma exhaust from the shuttle's fusion rockets to incinerate a not-very-convincing flying saucer, only to collide with an asteroid that came out of nowhere.

With a groan, Brooke pulled off her breather and collapsed onto the bed. An orange-red sunset bathed her hotel suite in crimson light, giving it the feel of an outmoded darkroom.

She knew she'd only torture herself by checking, but she threw on her specs and called up the latest candidate scores anyway. Out of twenty-five pilots, she ranked fourteenth. *I'm not even in the top half anymore!* She whipped off the visor and pressed both palms to her forehead. Her hands shook, along with the rest of her body. *Withdrawal symptoms, still? It's been three months since I sparked.* The doctors' scans and comments made her wonder. *Have I caused permanent damage? Will these relapses never go away?*

Gnarling fistfuls of bedding brought little relief. *What does my health matter? If I lose the competition, my life's basically over . . . so if I did spark, it might give me the edge I need to win.* She rolled over on her stomach. *But the side effects . . . and if anyone finds out . . . there's no way—*

Her specs beeped.

"Who is it?" she asked.

"Incoming call from Marie Davis," the specs said.

Brooke grumbled. The last thing she wanted to endure was her twin's moral support. "Send to voice message."

The beeping ceased, but before she could roll onto her back, the visor chirped again.

She slammed the specs onto her face, almost punching her nose in the process. "What do you want?" she hissed.

"Not to be sent to voicemail." Marie smiled, stretched, and

yawned. Bright yellow sunlight shrouded her image in a glow. “Good morning—or should I say good evening since it’s almost nighttime by you.”

“What do you want, Marie?”

“I want a trillion dollars, but I’ll settle for catching up with my sister. Or should I try again in six more years?”

Brooke grumbled.

“So how’re things going?” Marie asked.

“Fine.”

“That bad, huh?”

“What do you want me to say?”

“You could tell me all about the wonders of candidacy training.”

“It’s wonderful. Anything else?”

“If you want to be a bitch to me, fine, but think about Maya. You’re her hero, you know. Somehow, she got the impression her aunt’s going to give her a ride aboard the fastest ship ever, and she’s going around telling everyone—”

Brooke tapped her specs, ending the call. The pit in her stomach forced a decision.

♦

The chief flight surgeon of the UN Office of Aerospace Medicine at Earhart sat at her desk, enjoying a cup of coffee.

A young physician barged into her office. “Chief, I found something,” he said.

“Oh?” She set her mug down.

The physician tapped the chief’s desk, summoning a floating 3D model of a candidate’s nervous system. “Lieutenant Davis’s initial bioscans showed strange nerve tissue damage, so I ran an electromyogram and nerve conduction test.” With his thumb and middle finger, he magnified a section of her spine down to the cellular level, showing a black, spider-like object not much larger than a cell lodged in the surrounding tissue. “At first, I thought this little guy was a medite that failed to break down after previous treatment, but further analysis showed it’s a nanorobotic narcotic known as a spark.”

“I’m familiar with sparks, doctor.”

“Yes, of course, ma’am. Anyway, this explains the tissue damage. It’s a shame, but I believe this is grounds not only for dismissal from the program and the Defense force but criminal prosecution as well.”

“Thank you, doctor.” The chief flight surgeon picked up her mug, sipped, and reclined in her chair. “Please secure all of the lieutenant’s medical records and transfer them to me. I’ll take it from here.”

The physician dipped his brow. “Chief?”

"In cases such as this, there are more considerations than the medical analysis. For starters, I refuse to make accusations based on a single assessment, so I plan to personally check and recheck your findings. The nanite you found may look like a spark, but are we one hundred percent certain? There're also patient confidentiality, political ramifications, and other, larger issues at stake."

"Larger issues?"

"Please keep this matter to yourself, doctor. Again, I thank you for bringing it to my attention." She stared the young physician down until he shrank back out of her office.

The chief flight surgeon savored each drop of almond coffee until she emptied the mug. Then she placed a call to the office of the president of the UN Security Council.

♦

A series of messages from Vik led Brooke to a club in the downtown district of Red Rock City. "Alex is expecting you," the doorman said.

She stepped inside, checked her heavy coat, and recoiled at the mob packed onto the dance floor. Limbs swayed with a gracefulness not found on Earth but with a level of control impossible on Callisto. Freaks of every persuasion pressed tight-fitting and often-transparent bodysuits against one another. A feline woman bent over backwards and allowed a man with peacock feathers to drag his crotch over her face. Their suits sparked and bodies shuddered.

As if such interactions weren't unsettling enough, the club lacked flashing lights or thumping music. When Brooke blocked the feed to her specs, dim light and grunting filled the place. Masquerade masks fed neurosynth harmonies straight to dancers' minds and virtualized the party. Brooke's specs played conventional audio and revealed holographic strippers working their hips to strobe lights.

She almost bolted for the exit. *No, I won't let down my father or Maya, whatever it takes.*

Her nostril twitched as she pushed through the crowd, and she cringed when slipping between people. Sweat rubbed off on her shirt and arms. The stench of breath triggered her gag reflex. To her relief, no one seemed interested in grinding on someone without a suit.

The sanctity of personal space greeted her on the other side of the dance floor.

Brooke approached the rigid bouncer guarding the exit to the balcony. "I'm here to see Alex."

The man consulted his visor, disabled the force field blocking her path, and waved her past.

After pulling her respirator up over her mouth, she looked around for Vik's supplier. Fashionable VIPs sat on plush lounge sofas, engrossed by the worlds within their visors. Pairs, triples, and quartets of lovers nuzzled together.

The transparent floor of the balcony stretched out over the chasm. Artificial lighting from structures protruding from the cliff wall shined below her feet. Like New Galilei, the majority of Red Rock City existed underground. Only in the last few years had open-air buildings sprouted up above the surface.

"Are you Alex?" she asked a seated man.

The man snorted and raised his neon purple eyebrows. "Not likely."

"Okay, do you know where I can find him?"

A finger poked her in the back.

Brooke turned to find a petite girl of no more than fifteen clinking a six-inch heel against the floor. A micro bikini top and ruffled miniskirt left little to the imagination.

*Isn't she cold?* Brooke wondered until she noticed a slight shimmering obscuring the stars above. *That's why it's so warm out here.*

"Can I help you?" the girl asked.

"Nothing for me, thanks," Brooke said.

The girl strutted away. "If you didn't want them, then why did you come?" she called back over her shoulder.

Brooke's jaw drooped. She looked back at the man.

"That would be Alex, the club owner." His grin almost wrapped around his head.

Cursing, Brooke hurried after her.

Alex's runway strut brought her up a short staircase to an elevated section guarded by two sentry bots. The bots swiveled, tracking Brooke's movements. Red laser light reflected off her torso while she passed.

After plopping down on a couch, Alex sparked an electronic cigarette.

Brooke stood before her and blinked. She had seen old pics of cigarettes on SolNet but never in person.

"I like the lavender highlights in your hair." Alex sucked in a long drag and blew out a ring. "They really bring out those artificial irises."

"I'm sorry about before," Brooke stammered.

"Ha. Sometimes, I think I had all this work done just to mess with people."

*Work done . . .* Brooke zoomed in on the girl's face. The increased magnification revealed shiny skin, miniscule indentations, and other signs of reconstructive nanosurgery, the kind celebrities struggled to afford.

Thick eyelashes followed her visitor's gaze. "Let's just say I can tell you about the days when stepping outside would've killed you in a matter of seconds."

A nod was all Brooke could manage.

"You're Jovian, aren't you? The way you dip when you walk gives it away." The owner thrust her chin out. "And you don't actually need that."

Brooke touched her mask. "The air's breathable inside the force field?"

"If by breathable, you mean Earth $CO_2$ levels, then no, not yet. But the atmosphere's been bearable for twenty years. It simply takes a little getting used to. The need for breathers is a myth perpetuated by business associates of mine looking to keep their profits up."

"Thanks, but I think I'll keep it on."

A French bulldog hopped up onto the sofa next to Alex. "Here that, Deimos? Girl wants to spark, but she's afraid of a little $CO_2$." She scratched behind the dog's ears. "So, how did you plan to pay?"

"Um, euros?"

"Euros, huh? You wouldn't be with the UN, now, would you?" Alex's symmetrical face stiffened. "The organization preventing me from purchasing the technology I need to speak with associates elsewhere in the solar system?"

Brooke swallowed.

Alex's tight frown upturned and she erupted with laughter. "There was a time where I would've enjoyed breaking in a prude like you." She leered at her guest. "But I no longer have the patience." One hand reached beneath the sofa cushions and pulled out a small case. With a flick of the wrist, Alex flung it at her visitor like a sports disc.

Hunching over, Brooke caught the spinning case before it floated down past her knees. On Earth, the heavy box would've smacked the floor halfway to her. "Where do you want me to upload the payment?"

"They're on me. You can thank a mutual friend of ours."

*Mutual friend? But Vik would never . . .*

"Not that little troll," Alex said as if reading her mind. "Do you really think I'd do a favor for a low-level distributor?" She stood. "You'll figure it out. You're a smart girl, and from what I hear, my little gift should make you a whole lot smarter." The old woman glided past her and descended the steps. "Good luck, Lieutenant."

♦

The heavy weight on Brooke's chest plagued her only until the next morning, when the sparks changed everything. Hypergeometry made sense. When she studied the shapes, she felt like she could perceive them in four spatial dimensions rather than by three-dimensional analogy. The answers to the exam questions came to her so readily that she intentionally got problems wrong for fear of showing perfection. The no-win attack sims still gave her trouble, but no more than anyone else. And like old times, no one could touch her in conventional combat. As long as she sparked often enough, the withdrawal symptoms didn't return.

By the end of the following week, she had climbed into second place. Only Colonel Richthofen, the Earth fighter wing commander, stood in her way.

Best of all, her elation returned with her dream within reach.

With her fellow candidates, she sat in a flight simulation chair in the training room. A new kind of helmet with enhanced neurotronic padding rested atop her head.

"Every sim I've put you through up to this point has been to school you on the phase shuttle, the craft one of you will operate by the end of the year." Lee's voice echoed from her helmet speakers. "Now, I want you to be my guinea pigs as we explore the hypothetical combat of the future."

The neurotronics activated with a mild static shock, hijacking her eyesight. Stars replaced the bare walls of the training room, situating her in a cockpit unlike any she had seen. Two fighters, each belonging to one of her classmates, held position beyond the canopy. They resembled sleeker versions of Starthroats but with translucent fuselages, like ghosts of planes.

Bright white exhaust flared out in front of her. Enhanced mental displays identified it as Lee's fighter.

"We've still got a number of issues to work out before the first phase fighter prototype is built," he said. "Drive charge times need to be reduced, the gravity wakes need to be eliminated, and so on. However, I think you guys have earned a sneak peak at what's coming years down the road." He cut his engines, leaving his phase fighter drifting in space. "Svenka, I want you to attack me."

Igniting her afterburners, Svenka closed in on him but held her fire. "Aren't you going to fight back?"

"No. C'mon, Svenka, waste me."

"Okay, if you insist." She unloaded her particle cannons.

His fighter vanished. The beams sailed through empty space.

Brooke guessed what would come next. Lee's craft reemerged in normal space above Svenka's fighter and blew her to simulated smithereens.

Shudders of awe rushed through Brooke's limbs when she contemplated the possibilities. The true reasons for all the math and physics crystallized in her mind. They would prove critical in such maneuvers.

"Now," Lee said after Svenka's craft reappeared. "That stunt I pulled may've looked easy, but in real life it won't be. There are precise AI-assisted calculations involved in the position shifts, and you have to wait for your drive to charge before you can shift again." He cleared his throat. "The phase shuttle's drive charge time will start out at fifteen minutes, making such maneuvers impractical in live combat. However, we hope to reduce that time to two minutes for the prototype phase fighter. For now, I'll set your charge times to ten seconds. That should interject a little strategy and allow you to have some fun. On the count of three, may the best pilot win. One . . ."

Brooke noted the positions of the other fighters.

"Two . . ."

Anticipation welled up inside of her. She plotted her first move.

"Three!"

The stars disappeared, replaced by the bland gray walls of the training room.

"Hey, what happened?" she yelled.

Her fellow candidates echoed the sentiment.

"At ease, everyone. I have unpleasant news."

Brooke whipped off her helmet to find the four-star general standing at the front of the training room.

After the last pilot removed his helmet, the general said, "It is with great regret that I announce the UN's decision to suspend this candidacy program indefinitely."

Murmurs propagated throughout the room.

Brooke expected to wilt and die, but shock numbed her to everything.

"Why?" Svenka asked.

This may be hard to believe," the general said, "but a more pressing matter has come up, one that requires every able pilot to return to active duty."

"What could possibly take precedence?" Brooke muttered.

"It's a classified matter for now, but expect new orders within the hour. Dismissed."

## Thirteen—Titanomachy
## Saturnian System, July 2247 AD

Captain Brooke Davis bounded into the mission briefing room aboard the *Ariane*. With each long stride, she sailed across one of the viewports in the aisles. Stars scrolled past beneath her feet as the carrier rotated. *Always makes me feel like I'm inside a kaleidoscope.*

Other pilots filed into the briefing room, which resembled a lecture hall crammed into a cross section of a big metal pipe.

During her time on Earth and Mars, she had grown accustomed to higher gravity. Now, only a quarter-gee tugged her toward the carrier's hull. Her first day aboard the *Ariane*, she drilled her head into the ceiling with an effortless skip.

She settled into a seat two rows back from the front podium and threw on her specs. An image of Maya wearing a party hat and blowing out five candles popped up on one lens. *Happy birthday, squirt.* She smiled. *I'm glad to be back, but I still wish I was there with you.*

Her shoulders sagged whenever she thought about the abrupt cancellation of the candidacy program. Being back in space, on duty, had buoyed her mood somewhat, but nothing could compensate for the loss of her dream. *I started sparking again for nothing, and now I can't stop.*

The UN hadn't uttered one word to the media about whether the overall project would continue without a pilot, and if her superiors knew, they weren't saying. She only knew that whatever crisis had ended the program had required the *Ariane* to depart Mars for the outer solar system within five hours of her receiving orders to board it.

A young pilot floated down into the seat next to her. The junior-grade lieutenant had recently earned his wings, evident by the officer candidate patches on his uniform.

He rocked back and forth in his chair, twitching.

"You feeling okay, newbie?" she asked.

He hesitated a moment before nodding. "Yes . . . yes, ma'am."

"First-mission jitters?"

"Yes, ma'am. Just graduated from the Defense Academy near Red Rock City." He inhaled and let his breath out over the course of several seconds. "Do you know where we're headed, ma'am?"

She raised an eyebrow. "Isn't it obvious?"

He shrugged.

"C'mon, newbie. We've been en route for two and a half weeks."

"The Jovian system?"

"Nope." She closed her eyes. "Feel that?"

"Feel what?"

"The deck vibrating."

"I don't feel anything."

"The engine room's pushing all six reactors to max output, and we've been cruising at top speed since the acceleration lockdown. Mars and Jupiter are on the same side of the sun, so we passed beyond Jovian orbit a week ago."

"Then we must be headed to Saturn."

"Right, but where exactly?"

"Well, the only human settlement near Saturn is the Huygens colony on Titan."

"Exactly. Except for the Neptune expedition the UN lost, nobody's set foot any further out than Titan. So, the sixth moon is our most likely destination."

"Huh." The newbie clasped his hands in his lap. "I've never understood why we haven't ventured further. Why not settle the moons of Uranus or Neptune? Or any of the Kuiper belt dwarf planets?"

"It's simple economics." Brooke regurgitated what she had learned on SolNet. "Each planet is farther from the sun than the previous one, so the travel time and required fuel increase exponentially. Not many people want to spend months in transit, and few companies see profit in it." She crinkled her nose. "The phase drive might've changed all that, but now—"

"Attention!" A colonel's voice echoed off the bulkheads.

Brooke stood at attention along with the other pilots in the briefing room.

The *Ariane*'s captain strode up to the podium. "We're now four hours from arrival." He stood rigid as a statue, his frown perpetual. "I'm sure most of you have figured out by now our destination is Titan. Three weeks ago, unknown forces attacked the Huygens colony, and we've been unable to establish communications with the settlement since the attack. Fortunately, a satellite got a look at the assailants prior to being blown out of orbit." He directed a nod at the colonel.

A screen congealed on the wall behind the captain, displaying the curvature of Titan's thick orange horizon. The blackness of space hung above the moon.

Nothing happened for a minute except the rotation of the moon. Then two gray dots, SF-515 Cormorants, rose up from the orange haze. A white blur shot past the camera from left to right, reducing the Cormorants to brief flashbulb explosions.

Whispers broke out among the pilots.

The colonel replayed the vid. He paused it when the blur appeared.

Brooke's back stiffened when she recognized the tri-fighter.

The captain's serious tone cut through the side discussions. "That's all we know. The obvious speculation is that the UFO is of extrasolar origin. I find it hard to believe, but that's why we're here—to find out what happened and who we're up against." He turned to the officer standing to his right. "The colonel will brief you on the flight plan."

♦

"Do you think we'll end up duking it out with aliens?" The newbie pilot posed the question from his cockpit over the comm net.

"The proper term is 'exobeings,'" a second pilot said. "'Aliens' sounds so fictional."

A third sniggered. "Maybe it's little green men operating those tri-fighters."

Brooke studied Saturn's rings through the canopy of her Starthroat. The outermost layer of powdery haze, known as the G ring, loomed to her left. The next inner section, the F ring, formed a horizontal wall stretching as far as she could see. It looked like someone had etched a white line across an antique chalkboard and smudged it.

Her mind struggled to reconcile the briefing with what happened near Jupiter and Europa. *The official reports claimed separatists attacked* Terminus *and the water plant but made no mention of the unidentified craft.* She bit her lower lip. *Was the intruder I saw in the plant's reactor room an exobeing? But if that's the case, what was he doing with two UN pilots?* Her orders required her to keep her mouth shut. She couldn't set the record straight or warn any of her comrades about the tri-fighters' tactical superiority.

"Stow the chatter, kids," she told her squadron. "And stay focused. I've watched more than one playmate eat it because they lost focus."

"Roger, Angel." Fifteen different voices sounded off in acknowledgement.

The fighter group that had launched from the *Ariane* consisted of three squadrons: Alpha, Beta, and Delta. Sixteen Starthroats made up each squadron. Brooke's fighter rocketed along at the fore of Beta Squad, the unit under her command. The colonel who had issued their flight instructions led Alpha Squad and commanded the overall group. Her recent promotion to captain designated her as second-in-command.

The fighter group resembled three triangular flocks of hummingbirds. Alpha Squad held position above, in front, and to her right with respect to her orientation. Their running lights and blazing blue backwash set them apart from the blackness of space. Delta Squad followed behind, silhouettes pockmarking Saturn's dull-banded atmosphere.

*<Five minutes, seventeen seconds to Titan orbit, ma'am,>* a familiar voice mind-spoke.

*Thanks, Bob. I've missed you.*

*<I'm not capable of human longing, ma'am. However, I do tend to function best when interfacing with your specific brainwave patterns.>*

*I'll take that as an "I missed you, too."* She patted the redundant dashboard readouts, happy she had downloaded Bob's program from Callisto. That had proven the easy part. Convincing the *Ariane's* flight crew she couldn't fly without it had presented the greater challenge. "Why do you need that specific AI?" the techs had asked, but she'd gotten her way in the end.

Brooke watched the tiny orange speck hanging in front of her fighter's nose expand. *I've always wanted to see Titan.*

Her mental readouts beeped and flashed.

*<Three spacecraft of triangular configuration detected ascending from the moon's surface, ma'am. One hundred thousand kilometers dead ahead.>*

*We've got a sixteen-to-one advantage, and they're not sneaking up on us this time. Let's hope that's enough.*

“Look sharp, people,” the colonel said. “Slow to rendezvous velocity. I’m transmitting a standard greeting on all frequencies. We’ll hold out for some kind of peaceful gesture as long as possible, but be prepared to engage.”

“Roger,” Brooke and the Delta Squad leader replied.

She reviewed Bob’s scans while watching three tiny white dots glimmer in front of the orange sphere. The isosceles triangles looked like their makers had carved them out of ice. Each tri-fighter possessed a volume and mass comparable to a Starthroat.

“Nothing so far,” the colonel said. “Wait a second. I think I’m receiving a response.”

He relayed the message over the comm net. A sound like a seal imitating an ancient fax transmission broke the static.

The newbie pilot cursed in awe.

Brooke’s brow dipped. *That doesn’t make any sense.*

*<Thirty thousand kilometers and closing, ma’am. The approaching spacecraft are holding their intercept course.>*

*They’re moving awful slow for an attack.*

“What the—?” The colonel yelled. “My flight instruments just went dead.”

“My matrix isn’t responding, either,” another pilot said.

Brooke listened to two-thirds of the fighter group report the same issues. *It’s the same quantum jamming virus. Bob, execute the defense we used before.*

*<I’m sorry, ma’am, but I’m unfamiliar with the countermeasure of which you speak.>*

*What?*

The tri-fighters accelerated at the immobilized Starthroats. White lightning reduced the front five UN fighters to atoms, including the colonel’s craft.

Particle beams, spiraling missile contrails, and flashbulb bursts cluttered local space.

Brooke didn’t know what chilled her more, the colonel’s death or the fact that his demise placed her in charge. “All units, firewall all data ports and reboot all subsystems to counteract the virus.” She instructed Bob to do as much. “Squad Alpha, scatter and evade but stick with your wingmen. Delta, break formation and provide cover. Beta, we’re going on the offensive.” She let the throttle out. “Stick with me, Nightmare.”

“Roger.” The newbie’s response skipped and crackled like an ancient vinyl record.

While her heart thumped, her Starthroat rocketed toward the

orange haze of Saturn's largest moon.

A display indicated incoming weapons discharges from one o'clock high.

On instinct, Brooke rolled toward the weapons fire. Pure white particle beams seared through the spaces she vacated.

A blinding flash forced her to squint.

The newbie's screams gurgled over the comm net.

Pangs of regret scalded her chest.

She fired retrorockets and flipped sideways. White death tore through her previous flight path. G-forces bore down on her. The gravgel staved off unconsciousness.

She stabilized her orientation, targeted the attacking tri-fighter in her mental heads-up display, and fired particle cannons.

The triangle darted back and forth like a rapid pendulum. After avoiding her shots, it spun around and loosed two seekers.

Brooke widened the beam-widths of her fighter's particle cannons and sprayed a continuous burst.

Both projectiles exploded less than a hundred meters away. Debris and backwash struck the Starthroat's force field. Shudders undulated through the fuselage.

"*Ariane*, this is Captain Davis. Enemy jamming compromised our control systems initially, but we've managed to counteract it." She glanced at her displays. Only thirteen of the original forty-eight Starthroats remained. She swallowed the grief. "We're getting slaughtered out here. Request instructions, over."

Static crackled within her helmet.

"Flight control, please respond, over. Nightmare? Anyone, please respond!"

*<Both long and short range communications systems are being jammed, ma'am.>*

How did they determine our frequencies and break the encryption?

*<I cannot answer that question, ma'am—Incoming particle beam discharges from seven o'clock high. Recommend evasive—>*

Brooke fired retrorockets, jerking her fighter backwards. Searing white lines pierced empty space.

*I've had enough of playing the victim. Let's see if the same trick works a second time*. Her mental targeting system locked onto the tri-fighter behind her. She spun her Starthroat, fired its afterburners, and roared straight at the enemy.

It whipped left in an attempt to avoid the collision, but not quickly enough.

Electricity sizzled when her force field impacted the tri-fighter's shield. Per Newton's third law, the bandit spun away in one direction. Sucking in her stomach muscles, her fighter flew off in the other direction, but she knew to expect the ricochet this time.

While Bob corrected the Starthroat's attitude and trajectory, Brooke launched three seekers and fired particle cannons. The triangle weaved through the intense bombardment, avoiding her ordinance.

Brooke turned tail and rocketed toward Titan at max thrust.

The tri-fighter hung with her but held its fire.

*<I'm receiving a transmission from the pursuing bandit, ma'am. It's using a Defense comm net channel.>*

*The enemy's using our jammed comm system?* She considered her next move. *Isolate the signal so it can't interface with our systems. Then patch it through.*

*<Done, ma'am. Channel open.>*

Seconds passed. The channel hissed with thermal background noise.

"What do you want?" Brooke asked.

"You're quite the formidable adversary," an eloquent male voice said. "I find myself humbled once again."

She recognized the voice as the one belonging to the tall intruder from the water plant on Europa. "You're speaking to me in English—again."

"Would you prefer another language?"

"No, I mean, if we're able to talk, why did your forces transmit gibberish?"

He chuckled. "Is that not what you expect?"

"What we expect?"

Interference fizzled over the comm net.

"Who—and what—are you?" Brooke asked.

"We are that which will save you from yourself."

"You said that before, but it doesn't make any more sense now. Are you an exobeing?"

"Such details lack importance. You need only do as you would so we may lead you to your tomorrow."

"I heard you say that on Europa. What does it mean?"

"You shall discover that in due time."

Brooke grunted. "Great conversation."

"I've enjoyed it as well."

"Well, I didn't enjoy you trampling my dream."

"My apologies, but never fear. We've only delayed the inevitable." His tri-fighter lurched forward, accelerating toward her. The channel closed.

White lightning lashed out at her fighter.

She avoided the beams through a series of mosquito-like zigzags.

Her Starthroat dove at Titan's atmosphere, descending into the ballooning sphere of orange foam. She attempted to lose her pursuer in the cloud cover.

*It's so damn thick!*

*<Titan's atmosphere consists primarily of nitrogen, some methane, and other trace gases, ma'am. It's thicker than Earth's atmosphere with about half the pressure. The bandit has re-entered weapons range.>*

Brooke spun her fighter around. Orange soap-like suds washed across her canopy. She targeted a spot in the path of her assailant's trajectory, launched a seeker, and detonated it when it neared her enemy.

A flaming methane shockwave burst forth in all directions.

The tri-fighter skirted the wall of flame by meters.

A loud thunk propagated out from the explosion. The thick clouds muffled the burning puff of cotton candy. A second later, the atmosphere's plentiful supply of nitrogen and low temperature smothered the fireworks.

Brooke dropped below the mesosphere and emerged from the clouds.

*<Now descending over Xanadu, ma'am,>* Bob informed her brain. *<The Huygens colony is six hundred kilometers north-northeast.>*

At first glance, the surface bore a striking resemblance to Earth. However, Titan's lakes and rivers consisted of ethane and methane, not water, and the landscape had an orange-tan tint. Few craters pockmarked the surface. Dunes created ripples in the sand. Saturn's faded silhouette dominated the sky above a dipping horizon, and a yellow-orange haze shrouded everything.

*<Bandit approaching from two o'clock even, ma'am. Same one as before.>*

Brooke dove down into a valley surrounded by mountains of water-ice. A blue-black methane river flowed beneath her Starthroat as it roared along.

*<Incoming—>*

She jerked her fighter right.

A searing white bolt scorched the river beneath her.

She gasped as a fireball rose up to swallow her craft.

**Fourteen—Foundered**
**Titan, July, 2247 AD**

Brooke gritted her teeth, maxed out the fighter's afterburners, and rolled her craft. Extreme g-force compressed her brain, blurring her vision.

*<Reduce velocity, ma'am. The atmospheric pressure on the SF-522's fuselage has exceeded design tolerances.>*

Rear cameras panned upward, tracking the methane-infused fireball as it climbed up into the clouds.

She cut speed.

*<Methane gas is highly flammable, ma'am. I recommend maintaining an altitude of at least one hundred meters above the surface.>*

*Thanks for the belated advice, Bob.* She targeted the pursuing tri-fighter with her aft particle cannons and fired, but her adversary dove to avoid the attack.

She pummeled the river with a spread of seekers from the Starthroat's rear launch tubes. Blazing pillars lashed up at the sky from the impact points.

Her adversary weaved around the first two pillars but couldn't avoid the third. The searing geyser torched the pursuing spacecraft like a flame thrower. The tri-fighter disappeared, consumed by the firestorm.

It emerged a second later, trailing smoke, its force field disabled. It plunged toward the river, wobbling through the soupy air.

Meters before impact, the craft pulled up, avoiding a combustive splashdown. It rocketed up and away into the yellow clouds.

Brooke sank down into her seat and watched it retreat.

♦

A mountain-sized dome rose above the skyline as Brooke's Starthroat hurtled toward the Huygens colony. The dome housed the colony's hydrocarbon refinery, which stood on the shore of Lake Cassini, a body of liquid ethane-methane comparable in size to any of America's Great Lakes. *If only that were water.* A cold sweat soaked the skintight garment beneath her flight armor. *I wouldn't mind taking a swim about now.* Automated pumps within the refinery siphoned hydrocarbons from the lake and atmosphere. Hundreds of cylindrical tanks pockmarked the nearby landscape. Processed propane and petroleum filled the tanks, awaiting transport to the inner solar system.

Six habitat domes hid in the refinery's shadow, each measuring half the diameter of those on Callisto. A network of above-ground tunnels connected them.

The adjoining UN base lay in ruins. Wreckage from four hydrocarbon tankers, along with a dozen Cormorants, cluttered the colony's spaceport pad.

Brooke had no intention of suffering the same fate. She ordered four of the nine surviving Starthroats to remain airborne and patrol the perimeter. Her displays showed no sign of the two other tri-fighters, but for all she knew, they lurked nearby, poised to attack.

Her instruments showed the *Ariane* beginning its approach toward the moon.

She opened a channel to the spacecraft carrier. Its captain expressed his regrets regarding the colonel and heavy losses but congratulated her on staying alive. "Determine the situation inside the colony," he ordered.

Brooke settled her Starthroat onto the landing strip and drained the gravgel from her cockpit. The air possessed a hazy, yellow glow like during a foggy sunset on Earth. Methane rivers fed into dark lakes. Dunes zigzagged across the desert to the east. Hills of water-ice dominated the western horizon.

Exhaustion weighed on her now that the adrenaline rush had worn off. Her limbs trembled. She spent ten frustrating seconds fumbling with her seat harness before it disengaged.

After pulling off her helmet, Brooke reached beneath her seat and grabbed a spark injector. Jabbing it into the base of her neck jolted her body like a defibrillator.

Her mind cleared, and her unaided vision improved to better than twenty-ten. The surroundings moved in slow motion, taking on increased definition and shape.

Via the comm net, she ordered the other five pilots to rendezvous at the nearest habitat dome's airlock.

Brooke reconnected her helmet to her flight armor and primed the charge on her particle rifle. After popping the canopy, she hopped out.

She expected to rise up out of the cockpit and drop down to the ground. Instead, Titan's low gravity and thick atmosphere took her for a ride. The modest hop sent her flying through the air, off-balance with arms flailing. She had traversed over thirty meters by the time her feet touched the landing pad.

Two of the other pilots made the same mistake.

*I hope the enemy isn't nearby. Somebody drifting along in midair might make for easy target practice.*

A second long stride carried Brooke to the entrance to the closest habitat dome.

The five pilots met up with her there.

She split the combined group of six, including her, into three pairs. One of the lieutenants, call sign Ruby, would enter the outer hatch along with Brooke. The other two teams would circle around the dome and locate a side airlock.

*Loop everyone in, Bob. Anybody inside?*

*<I detect two heat signatures, ma'am. They're bipedal, but I have insufficient data with which to distinguish between terrestrial and extrasolar life.>*

*There's no guarantee they're friendly even if they're human.* Brooke released her particle rifle's safety lockout and turned to her teammate. "Ready?"

Ruby held position the other side of the hatch and nodded. "Ready, Angel."

*Okay, Bob. Interface with the airlock controls and open it.*

*<Interface established, ma'am. Initiating airlock compression cycle. One moment . . .>*

The outer hatch slide aside. After Brooke and Ruby stepped into the cramped chamber, the hatch shut behind them.

*<Ma'am, I've encountered an error while attempting to initiate the pressurization sequence. Multiple breaches exist in the dome. Methane and other lethal trace gases have contaminated the biosphere.>*

"Not so good for the colonists," Ruby said.

Brooke stifled a rising pang of dread. *Open the door already.*

The inner hatch twisted open.

Brooke stuck her rifle through the entryway. Her head followed a couple seconds later. Puffs of poison fog seeped inside from breaches in the overhead dome, spilling onto rows of igloo-shaped habitats. Frost-covered trees and grass had turned to putrid greens and rotting browns. Abandoned cars sat parked at awkward angles in the middle the streets, doors flung open. Everything showed signs of charring, as if the invaders had torched the place with flamethrowers.

*Did the enemy burn everything?*

*<Unlikely, ma'am,>* Bob explained. *<When the dome ruptured, the methane in the atmosphere combusted with the oxygen inside. Given the relative exterior and interior temperatures, and factoring in the available amount of oxygen, the process would've lasted no more than eight seconds.>*

Brooke tried not to picture flames proliferating through the air, burning people alive.

Swinging her rifle back and forth, she crept inside. She stayed close to buildings, senses at the height of awareness. Her visor's infrared failed to register any heat signatures.

Ruby followed Brooke from habitat to habitat, lawn to lawn. They took turns providing cover for one another. Brooke hid behind bushes and traipsed across flowerbeds. At one point, Ruby ducked behind a swing set.

Frozen corpses with singed purple skin littered roads and sidewalks. Fingernail marks gashed their necks. The residents had clawed at their throats, straining for their last few gasps.

*<They died from asphyxiation and atmospheric contamination, ma'am.>*

*After frying?*

*<Unfortunately, ma'am.>*

"Not how I want to go," Ruby said, shaking her head.

Particle beams had torn gaping holes in torsos. A beam had seared off and cauterized one man's head from the jaw up. It reminded Brooke of the damage to Jeff's suit on Europa.

Near each victim, she searched for net specs or other personal devices that might have recorded the incident, but the invaders had smashed the few items she found.

With Ruby close behind, she followed the stone walkway leading into the town square. Eight fountains encircled a round slab of concrete situated in the center of the courtyard. On top of the slab sat the first unmanned space probe to visit Titan, launched two hundred fifty years ago. An oversized satellite dish sprouted up from the top of the spacecraft, a design common to many olden-day probes.

Thin red beams of laser light lashed out at Brooke from behind the probe.

She dove behind the block-shaped base of the statue honoring the colony's founder. The lasers chipped away at the statue. Chunks of concrete rained down on her, falling like feathers in Titan's low-gravity.

Ruby ducked behind a ledge two meters from her superior. "Those aren't exos shooting at us."

"Pulsed laser rifles," Brooke said. "Non-military issue." *Which is fortunate for us.* The lasers would take minutes to bore through the statue, whereas her rifle could pulverize it with a single shot. "I think we're dealing with civvies," she said over the comm net.

"Aren't we lucky."

*Bob, patch me into the colony's emergency comm channel.* "Hold your fire! We're with UN Aerospace Defense, and we're here to help you."

Another round of laser fire severed the statue's head.

She repeated the request a second and third time. Each plea received the same rebuttal.

"Perhaps we need to respond in kind," Ruby said.

"We can't start shooting at civilians. Plus—" Brooke nudged her head out from behind the base of the statue. "—that old space probe might get caught in the crossfire."

"Yeah, the top brass wouldn't be too thrilled about that."

*That gives me an idea. Bob, can you fire up the probe?*

*<I'll attempt to establish a data uplink with the Cassini-Huygens spacecraft, ma'am.>*

The probe hummed to life after more than two centuries of disuse.

*<I downloaded the NASA command protocols from the Defense archives and transmitted them, ma'am. The spacecraft has enough propellant to initiate a one-second burn.>*

*Do it.*

*<Transmitting startup sequence now, ma'am.>*

Plumes of exhaust escaped the underside of the ancient unmanned spacecraft.

Two suited figures rushed out from behind the probe's concrete perch. Their boots broke the ice covering the fountains. Water splashed in slow motion. Every few steps, one of them twisted around and fired an awkward pulse.

Brooke peeked around the base of the statue, sighted her rifle, and squeezed the trigger. Her stream of blue bolts blasted the ground behind the runners, tossing brick and dirt into the air, knocking them off their feet.

Brooke and Ruby sprinted over to the pair and kicked their laser rifles away.

Both civilians lay on their backs. Through their face shields Brooke discerned a teenage boy and girl. Their skin possessed a putrid green paleness, and their irises wobbled, unable to focus on anything.

"Just a couple of scared kids," Ruby said, lowering her weapon.

Brooke did the same. "It's okay now," she said over the emergency channel. "You're safe. No one's going to hurt you."

The teens panted and shook.

"What happened here?" she asked.

The boy screamed, sprang to his feet, and stumbled away.

Brooke gave chase. Each lunge resembled a lackadaisical long jump.

The teen bounded along at half her speed, tripping over his feet. She caught him at the edge of the town square and tackled him to the ground.

She flipped him over and straddled him, pinning him down.

"Leave me alone!" he cried.

Brooke held him down. "What did they do to you?"

*<I doubt anyone caused his condition, ma'am. Your suit scans indicate he's suffering from a combination of malnutrition, oxygen deprivation, and hydrogen cyanide poisoning.>*

*He probably hasn't had a decent meal in weeks. She looked his suit. Are the tiny burn marks I see due to leaking oxygen?*

*<Affirmative, ma'am. His suit wasn't designed for long-term use.>*

♦

After rejoining the other pilots, Brooke checked in with the *Ariane*. The spacecraft carrier remained on approach toward the moon. Based on its trajectory and speed, it needed five deceleration orbits to establish a geosynchronous position above Huygens. In the meantime, the captain ordered her to stabilize the survivors and survey the colony.

She located an airtight habitat for use as a temporary base of operations. Its designers had certified the building as a shelter, intended for refuge if the dome depressurized. The habitat had kept a group of colonists alive until the invaders had torn through the front hatch and killed its occupants. She found similar scenes in most of the other structures.

Her team removed the bodies and borrowed a hatch from another habitat. With a bit of improvised repair work, they managed to minimize atmospheric leakage.

Ruby worked the teens out of their space suits with the help of another pilot. Afterwards, she laid the kids down on a pair of cots and fed them IV drips from the Starthroats' med kits.

Color returned to the girl's face. She appeared to have suffered fewer symptoms than the boy.

"What's your name?" Brooke asked her.

"Cassie."

"Cassie, I'm Captain Brooke Davis. Can you tell me what happened here?"

"They attacked the dome a few weeks ago. Everybody ran for the shelters, but they appeared out of nowhere and started shooting everyone."

"Who do you mean by 'they'?"

"Tall, skinny creatures in white space suits," Cassie said. "They fired these powerful beams that dissolved people. The adults got us into suits. They told us to hide and tried to fight, but none of them survived." She buried her face in her hands, sobbing. "I found my parents' bodies . . ."

"You're going to be okay." Brooke sat next to the girl on the bed and patted her on the back. "Are any of the other children still alive?"

The girl wiped away the tears, nodding between sniffles. "Yes. Tyler and I went out to find food for them. They're hiding in the refinery, where the, um, where it is."

"Where what is?"

"The dead exo," Tyler said from his cot.

Brooke whipped her gaze in his direction. "Dead exobeing?"

"There was a big shootout in the refinery's main control room. All that's left is a bunch of corpses, including one dead exo." Tyler put a finger to his chin. "At least, I think it's an exobeing. It's taller than anybody I've ever seen, but you can't see what it looks like in its suit."

The other pilots gathered around his cot.

"You didn't disrobe it?" Ruby asked with a grin.

Tyler recoiled. "I'm not going anywhere near it."

"Why'd you go into the refinery in the first place?" one of the other pilots asked.

"It still has breathable air," Cassie said, "and a lot of places to hide."

Brooke rose to her feet. "If you feel up to it, I'd like you to take us to the other kids."

The teens traded glances and nodded. Brooke ordered everyone to suit back up.

Cassie and Tyler led Brooke and her team through the corridor connecting the dome to the refinery. Tiny droplets of liquid methane drifted down from yellow clouds. The raindrops popped and clinked when they struck the clear walkway tube.

After the airlock shut behind her, Brooke used her suit's instruments to sample the atmosphere. Oxygen and contaminant levels registered as acceptable. She signaled the okay for her team to remove their helmets.

The refinery stretched for hundreds of meters in all directions. The curved underside of the dome shone a bright white. Cylindrical tanks stood on end or sprawled lengthwise across the floor, each polished to reflective silver. Multicolored tubes and hoses snaked across every surface, pumping hydrocarbons throughout the refinery. Automated pumps chugged and centrifuges spun. Vats boiled while vacuums inhaled.

The teens led Brooke through a maze. She ducked beneath drums, leapt over pipes, and sidestepped worker bots motoring through the aisles.

Five minutes later, she reached a dead end marked by a dozen vertical tanks the size of silos. Water dripped from a faucet protruding from one of the tanks. Freeze-dried food wrappers—the colony's emergency rations—littered the floor.

Twenty children sat in the middle of the mess. Their ages appeared to range between five and thirteen years. The kids' faces had paled, and their movements were lethargic, although none of them seemed as bad as Cassie or Tyler. Brooke figured the two teens hadn't allowed any of the youngsters to venture outside the refinery.

The children scurried over to greet the returning teens. Tyler rustled the hair of a couple of boys while Carrie embraced three girls.

One of the girls—a small, energetic one with short black hair—reminded Brooke of Maya. "You're all safe now," she said.

They bombarded her with complaints.

"I'm hungry."

"I don't feel good."

"I have to pee."

"Where's my mommy?"

Tyler shushed them and turned to Brooke. "What's going to happen to us now?"

"We'll leave Titan once we complete our investigation." She turned to one of her men. "Penguin, stay here and watch the kids. The rest of us will check on the, um, uninvited guest."

"Ma'am?" Penguin asked. "With all due respect, I'm no babysitter."

"Trust me, you'll learn quickly."

♦

Engineers had situated the refinery's command center below the apex of the dome. Hundreds of displays projected out from a curved wall encircling the center. Screens not holed by weapons fire flashed with flow rates, schematics, and system statuses. Interface terminals lined the wall beneath the displays.

The refinery's operations team, five colony policemen, and two UN soldiers lay dead on the crimson-coated floor.

A tall, thin body in a white space suit lay face down in the midst of the massacre. Particle beams had minced its torso. Dried, brown-yellow blood caked the edges of its wounds and stained the floor beneath it. Six gloved fingers sprouted out from its hands.

Brooke's team kept their rifles sighted on the body while she crept toward it. Weeks had passed since the exobeing had died, but the service had trained her not to assume anything.

She poked the body with her rifle. When it failed to shriek, she knelt down, set her helmet and weapon aside, and tapped the corpse with a gloved finger. Its suit was made of a smooth, thin material.

Brooke flipped the body over onto its back.

A black visor wrapped around the front of its white, bowl-shaped helmet. She couldn't see inside it.

She checked its neck for a switch to unlatch the helmet but found none. *How do you get the thing off?*

At this point, procedure required her to contact the *Ariane* for further instructions.

*To hell with it.* She produced a knife from the toolkit affixed to her left hip.

Pressing the blade to the neck of the suit, she applied gentle pressure, expecting the material to defy penetration. Instead, the serrated blade ripped right through, revealing smooth, grey skin.

Brooke cut all the way around and lifted away the helmet.

Gasps rang out.

Brooke glared back over her shoulder. Numerous small heads poked out from behind tanks and peeked over matrix terminals. "Penguin! What're the kids doing here?"

"Sorry." The pilot shrugged. "I couldn't hold them all back."

She sighed and turned back around.

Her angst dissipated at the sight. The being resembled the classic alien straight from ancient myth, replete with egg-shaped head, oval eyes, and slits for nostrils. Centuries ago, people had referred to them as the Greys, although this specimen seemed taller than the legends.

"Unreal . . ." Ruby whispered.

The refinery's whirring, humming, and bubbling faded into the background. No one said a word for minutes—not even a peep out of the youngest child.

Brooke sat back on her hind legs, staring at the exobeing. Her mind tried to reconcile it with the intruder from the Artemis reactor hold. *He looked human, not like this. I don't get it.*

The transmitter in the collar of her suit squawked. "Incoming unidentified object," the tactical officer reported from the bridge of the *Ariane*. "It's big. Distance: three hundred thousand kilometers and closing."

Brooke rejoined her team.

The *Ariane's* operations officer said, "It measures about a kilometer from stem to stern, roughly the same length as us but a lot wider. Mass: maybe four hundred million kilos. Shape: pyramidal."

The captain's voice remained calm. "Transmit friendly greeting but launch all remaining fighters. Why didn't we detect it sooner?"

"Not sure," the tactical officer said. "It might've been hiding on the far side of Rhea—"

Operations interrupted him. "Now at two hundred thousand kilometers."

The *Ariane's* flight controller confirmed the launch of all star fighters.

"The unidentified carrier has launched tri-fighters," tactical reported. "Neudar shows eight in total."

"We still outnumber them, but . . ." the captain mused.

"Fighter group now engaging the enemy," flight control said.

Grunts, screams, tactical updates, and calls for support bombarded the comm net.

"Fighter group has incurred heavy losses," flight control reported. "Enemy tri-fighters are approaching the *Ariane*."

"We're taking fire from all sides," tactical reported. "Major decompressions reported. Compartments are venting atmosphere all throughout the ship!"

"Slide emergency bulkheads into place," the captain barked. "Evacuate all affected areas. Get us the hell out of here!"

"Thrusters inoperative," navigation reported.

Operations' voice cracked. "Destabilization detected in antimatter reactor number five!"

"The ship's caught in Titan's gravity well," navigation reported. "Now descending into the atmosphere. Projected point of impact is Lake Cassini."

The captain's voice boomed. "Brace for re-entry and impact!"

Static.

Brooke sprinted toward the east side of the refinery. She wound her way around tanks, ducked robotic arms, and hurdled pipes.

She reached a set of panoramic windows overlooking Lake Cassini.

With her eyezoom, she searched the yellow cloud-covered sky. Methane rain floated down and pinged against the window. The repetitive popping sounded like an antique mechanical clock ticking down the seconds.

A flaming pillar pierced the clouds in the distance. Brooke watched, mouth agape, as the kilometer-long spacecraft carrier splashed down into the lake and exploded.

The shockwave thudded against the dome, bending the windows inward, throwing her off her feet.

## Fifteen—Waif
## Titan, July 2247 AD

After the interior hatch sealed behind her, Brooke removed her helmet, frowning.

Pilots and children crowded around her in the habitat with expectant looks. Some coughed due to the rising carbon dioxide levels within the cramped living area. Engineers hadn't designed the environmental system of the single family residence to support over thirty people.

"You were out there forever, Captain," Penguin said. "What did Command say?"

Cassie pressed her hands together in a prayer-like gesture. "Is a ship going to rescue us soon?"

Wide eyes fixated on Brooke, making it difficult for her to speak. "The enemy destroyed the comm sats in orbit and all the equipment on the UN base. None of our Starthroats have phase tunneling capability."

"Meaning it took hours to communicate via radio," Ruby said.

"Right. When I finally received a response, Command assured me that our safe recovery is a top priority. A ship should be here in less than two months."

"Two months?" Vishnu, a pilot who often complained, placed his hands on his hips. "At present alignment, it should take two and a half weeks—three, tops—for a carrier to get here from Mars. Why the delay?"

"Separatists bombed Earhart the day after we left."

Vishnu paled and stepped back.

"They targeted the training areas," Brooke said, "so there were no casualties."

"Thank goodness." Trillium placed her hand over her heart.

"For whatever reason, Command can't spare any carriers from Earth or Mars, so they're sending *Opportunity* from Callisto."

Tyler scratched his temple. "Jupiter's the next planet in from Saturn, so shouldn't a ship from Callisto get here sooner than one from Earth or Mars?"

"Jupiter's on the other side of the sun." Bumba folded his thick arms. "So right now, it's much farther away than Earth or Mars."

"Oh . . ." The way Tyler's chest deflated cast an air of gloom over the habitat.

Brooke didn't want to deal with this—with being stranded, with them, or any of it. She had died a little inside with the cancellation of the program. By the time she made it back, they might have started up again and picked someone. Or they might never resume because of the bombing. But when she studied the sagging postures of the children—and pictured Maya among them—she knew she had to set aside her selfishness and show nothing but strength.

Rubbing her palms together, she used her most upbeat tone. "All right, two months isn't so bad. There are thirty-two of us in a colony built to support ten thousand, so we shouldn't have any trouble surviving. We simply need to get organized." She marched over to a window and stared out. "First priority is food." She whirled back around. "Cassie, Tyler, how many rations do you have left?"

"Only a few days' worth for us kids, but if we include everyone else here—"

"No need for that. We've got enough rations in our planes to hold out for a month, but after divvying that up amongst everyone, we're going to run out soon. Ideas?"

Trillium stepped forward. "I saw a greenhouse when scouting around the easternmost habitat. The casing looked intact, and I saw maintenance bots watering plants inside. I like to garden in my spare time, so I'm happy to check the place out."

"I've got some experience with hypergrowth," Tango added. "I can try to get whatever's in there sprouting as fast as possible."

"Good thinking." Brooke nodded toward the hatch. "The two of you get going right away." While they suited up, she said, "The next issue is to locate better accommodations."

"There must be more habs that can be patched up without too much trouble," Vishnu said. He still looked shaky, but his voice was firm. "I volunteer to find them."

"Sounds good. Go with Trillium's team and start by surveying the east dome. Let's see if we can find refuge close to the food."

"Yes, ma'am."

Penguin spoke up. "My family's in the construction biz on Mars. I've been studying the damage to the domes, and all I've seen is a crack here or a puncture there. If I can get the repair bots working, they could have one of the roofs stitched up in a matter of days."

The ideas continued to pour out: ensuring that the piping running from the factory brought water to them, using the processed hydrocarbons for power, finding working lavatories, and allowing the older children to help out. Given that the enemy might still be nearby, Brooke decided two Starthroats would remain in the air at all times. Ruby and Sienna volunteered for the first four-hour watch.

After the majority of her team had departed with eight of the eldest youths, Brooke turned to Bumba. "You've got five kids at home, right?"

"I'm the proud father of three boys and two girls, yes."

"Great. I'm going to take a look around the colony and see if I can find out more about what happened. I want you to hang back and watch the children." She reached for her helmet on a nearby table.

One of the little girls—Isabelle, if she remembered correctly—latched onto her leg. "Don't leave us."

"Bumba here's got more experience with your kind." She gave her leg a light shake. "You're far better off with him."

Sweet-faced Amir tugged on her arm. "Stay and play with us."

Brooke suppressed a grumble.

Bumba placed a hand on her shoulder. "It seems they want you."

"Why?"

"They look up to you. You're the one in charge, the one they've seen take action to keep them safe." The stocky pilot stroked the stubble on his wide chin. "And you've got a certain motherly aura about you."

Brooke couldn't stop her nose from bunching up.

"Don't worry," he said. "I'll stick around and help you out."

She mouthed a drawn-out thank-you.

While Bumba held storytime with half the group, Brooke played with the rest. Somehow, a game of duck, duck, goose turned into a let's-all-jump-on-the-furniture free-for-all, which in Titan's low gravity meant heads bumping the ceiling and a multitude of boo-boos from uncontrolled landings. Hide-and-go-seek involved less hiding and more seeking—or more accurately, Brooke crawling under tables and chasing after gigglers with short attention spans. And then came the crying, screaming, and whining, which made her want to rip every last hair out her head.

Throughout it all, a boy named Jevon refused to participate in any activity. He sat on the end of a couch in one corner of the living area, staring down with hands on his knees.

Brooke sent the other children to join in Bumba's storytelling session and took a seat next to Jevon. "Are you okay?"

The boy shied away from her.

"Do you miss your folks?" When she touched his wrist, she felt him trembling.

She tried and tried, but he refused to acknowledge her. "Well, I won't bother you anymore. If you need anything, let me know." She leaned forward, about to get up.

Jevon grabbed her arm. The wavering of his big brown eyes melted her insides. "I need to find my dad," he whispered.

"I'm sorry, but he's gone away, and I don't think he's coming back." She averted her gaze.

"I know he's dead, but I still want to see him."

"I don't know if that's such a good idea."

"Please, it's important."

"Why?"

"Hey, they're back!" a girl shouted.

The children rushed the inner hatch while it opened.

Trillium bounded inside, followed by the squad mate and two teens who had gone with her. All four carried crates overflowing with fruits and vegetables.

"Who's hungry?" Trillium asked.

"Me, me, me!" shouted at least ten little voices.

Brooke hopped up off the couch and inspected the contents of the boxes. "Radishes, melons, lettuce, potatoes, apples . . . There was this much?"

Smiling, Trillium set the crate down on a table. "I didn't want to get anyone's hopes up at first, but . . ." She unfastened the helmet dangling from her hip and set it down. "As I suspected, the greenhouse was the top-level entrance to the underground hydroponics farm. Much of the food's starting to rot, so we'll need to get back and get things growing again, but there's enough down there to last for some time."

"Good work."

Her three companions placed their crates next to hers. The children stared at the heaping mounds of nourishment, drooling.

*I guess eating emergency rations and facing starvation is enough to make any kid eat their veggies.* "Go ahead and dig in," she told them.

The famished tykes reached out and swiped oranges, pears, and peppers like little purse-snatchers. Bumba and the other pilots handed out items to smaller children.

A girl bit into a tomato. Juice and seeds ran down her face.

Brooke grabbed a carrot, nibbled, and wrinkled her nose. *It's not Fruity Planets, but I guess it'll have to do.*

♦

Throughout the next month, Brooke helped everyone make the best of things. With the automated subterranean farm, no one wanted for food, although she developed a craving for steak thanks to the forced vegetarian diet. Power from the factory and her squad's willingness to pull maintenance shifts kept everything running. Other members of her team fixed up four habitats in the east dome, providing each person with a bit more personal space, and Penguin got the construction bots to seal the dome's roof, so she relocated everyone there.

The situation presented its share of trials and tribulations as well. No one relished moving the bodies of the dead colonists, and a malaise thicker than the atmosphere shrouded the colony after the burial ceremony. Refrigerating the exocorpse for Command had also proven tricky, if not a little unnerving. As for the children, they could be quite endearing when they weren't pouting, screaming, stomping, or bawling. A couple of troublemakers tried running away but soon realized the futility of eluding a Starthroat's thermal imaging system.

Now entering month two, Brooke sat on the rear porch of an unrepaired habitat. *Alone at last.* She stared at the birdfeeder in the middle of the backyard, ready to claw her eyes out at the latest incident.

"You're not my mom. You can't tell me what to do!" a particularly vile girl had spat at her.

And then there was the perpetually despondent Jevon. He refused to play with the other children or interact with any of the pilots, choosing instead to lie on his bed for most of each day. No matter what she tried, he refused to come out of his funk.

*Is that how I seem to people?* She had never realized how contagious gloom could be to those around her.

She reached into a crevice beneath the porch and pulled out her last spark injector. Holding the device at eye level, she read its graphic display and felt her limbs quiver. *Ugh, only five normal doses left.* Each injection lasted four or five days, so the remaining quantity might hold her over until *Opportunity* arrived. However, she needed to plan ahead or else spend the two-month trip back to the Jovian system convulsing in the medical bay.

With her thumb, she rolled the volumetric dial on the injector all the way down, reducing the dosage to the bare minimum. Pressing the device to her neck yielded a mild zap but lacked the charge of the full amount. Her extremities ceased their shaking, but pangs of anxiety still plagued her. *It's going to be a long three months . . . and if I'm forced to use less anyway, I might as well try to wean myself off them.*

Cassie poked her head around the corner of the habitat.

Brooke whipped the injector behind her back. "What is it?"

"It's going to start in fifteen minutes, Brooke. C'mon."

"I'll be there in a sec."

Once Cassie disappeared back around the bend, Brooke returned the device to its hiding place. Then she jogged after the teen and climbed a staircase that began at the edge of the dome. Halfway into her ascent, at the point where the dome wall curved downward and became more of a ceiling, the staircase gave way to a suspended tunnel. She tried not to look down through the transparent floor of the passageway but couldn't help staring at the cookie-cutter streets and habitats. *Why am I fine flying high above the clouds, yet standing a few stories up bothers me?*

The tunnel ended at the central observation platform, which hung from the apex of the dome. Most of her team had arrived ahead of her along with the children, who had plenty of room to run around. Bumba and Ruby supervised the game of tag that had broken out.

Brooke stepped over to the group. Most everyone stood or sat on benches near the railing, gazing out over the ink-black Lake Cassini. The breathtaking view, she had to admit, made the climb worthwhile. Light winds sent methane waves crashing against islands and ice-boulders. Rivers snaked away from the lake and stretched toward mountains of water-ice towering in the distance. Saturn and its rings hovered above the horizon in an orange haze, six times bigger than Luna in Earth's sky. Amber rays from a tiny sun glared around the edge of the gas giant. Any minute now, the star would slip behind the planet.

She took a seat on an unoccupied section of bench only to have three little ones snuggle up close to her.

"I was looking forward to watching this with my dad." Tyler leaned over the rail in front of her, shoulders sagging. "He says—he said—the eclipse period only happens once every twenty years. Then you get four over the course of two months and wait again." He held his hand up, shielding his eyes. "I never understood why it doesn't get dark every time Titan moves behind Saturn."

"Because of the angle of the moon's orbit," Brooke said, stroking Isabelle's hair. "Titan orbits far enough above or below Saturn's equator that the planet doesn't get in the way most of the time."

"Huh." He stepped over to a set of binoculars mounted on a post and peered through them.

"You sure know a lot." Cassie slid closer along the bench.

"Comes with the job, I guess."

"The view's simply amazing."

"It is, but it's nothing compared to what's out there."

Cassie rested her chin on her fist. "Out there? You mean, beyond our solar system?"

"Oh, yes. Gas giants orbiting so close to their suns you can see the stars sucking away the atmosphere. Planets of red dwarfs where the plant life is black, not green. And binary stars racing around each other so fast you get dizzy watching."

"I'd love to see all that stuff."

"Me too," Tyler said.

"Me too. Me too!" Isabelle chimed in.

Brooke managed a wan smile. "Me too," she whispered.

Darkness engulfed the colony, met by more than one high-pitched scream.

Additional illumination switched on within the dome. Lights from the mountainous factory reflected off the lake.

"How long until it gets light again?" Cassie asked.

Tyler said, "A little over three hour—"

"Jevon!"

Brooke turned to see a silhouette approach from the tunnel.

Penguin lunged past her. After checking out each person on the observation deck, he cursed. "He's not here."

Her stomach tightened. "What's going on, Lieutenant?"

"It's Jevon, Captain. He was in his room. I went to the head—took me a little longer to take care of business than usual—and when I came out, he was gone. I was hoping he came up here, but I don't see him."

She shot to her feet, pressing her hands to the dome to keep from knocking her head, and pulled her fighter's portable comm unit out of her pocket. "Bob, scan for human life signs not at my position."

A second elapsed before the AI matrix came out of standby mode.

*<Scanning now, ma'am. I show one suited heat signature moving away from the east habitat dome, heading toward the lake.>*

*No*— Brooke enabled her eyes' night vision mode, flew into the tunnel, and bounded down the steps to ground level. Gliding strides carried her to the main hatch leading outside. "Bob, take off immediately." The hatch spiraled open; she ran into the airlock, barely glancing back to make sure the hatch had sealed behind her. As she jammed a leg into her flight armor, she checked the alcoves of environmental gear. One of the youth suits was missing. "If he's looking to do what I think, block him."

*<Inadvisable, ma'am. My engines generate too much thrust. Given the atmospheric density and low gravity, I'm liable to knock the youth off his feet and inflict serious injury.>*

"Damn—but good catch." She latched her helmet onto her suit. A mild electric shock tickled her hair, and her neurotronics activated.

Not bothering with the decompression cycle, she banged the emergency release button, forcing the outer hatch open. Thick air pummeled her, almost knocking her off her feet.

*Where is he now, Bob?* She craned her neck. The running lights of her Starthroat brightened the dark sky.

*<Ten meters from the shore, ma'am.>*

A series of leaping sprints carried her toward the lake. She enabled her suit's infrared display, which showed a small orange-red smudge up ahead. *Can I catch him before he enters the water—I mean, the—*

*<Negative, ma'am. He'll reach the body of liquid methane-ethane seven-point-two seconds before you can close the distance.>*

Cursing, she coaxed every last shred of strength out of her muscles and armor.

After reaching the shore, she descended the rocky beach and rushed into the lake.

*<Ma'am, I wouldn't recommend—>*

She expected the liquid to restrict her movements or buoy her up somewhat, but she passed through it like a thick cloud. *I lost him. This stuff is so weird . . .*

*<To your right—south, ma'am. Hydrocarbons in their fluid state possess half the density of liquid water and are much colder.>*

The bottom dropped off, and her head submerged. Pitch blackness cloaked her surroundings. Infrared showed everything as a single shade of blue, but neudar traced the outlines of rocks and the lake bed. She kept expecting a gigantic sea monster to swim up and swallow her.

Chills crept into the joints of her armor. *Is my gear going to freeze,*

*Bob?*

*<No, ma'am, but you may experience some stiffness, resulting in decreased mobility. The commercial suit worn by the youth, however, may not fare as well.>*

*I do feel a little less flexible, but not too bad.* She jumped, rising all the way out of the liquid. After following a graceful arc, she broke the surface and descended to the bottom.

An island surrounded by boulders loomed just up ahead. After weaving her away around the tall rocks, she caught sight of an orange-red figure above her on the island.

She leapt out of the lake and landed near the figure. Turning on her suit lights revealed Jevon sprawled out over a suited body. The adult's face wasn't visible through the ice crystals covering the inside of his face bowl.

"Are you okay, Jevon?" she asked over the comm net.

Weak moans and the chattering of teeth reached her ears.

After rolling the body onto his back, she discovered ice forming on the inside of his helmet.

*Bob, we need to get him back inside, and fast.* She picked him up.

*<Acknowledged, ma'am.>* Bob brought the fighter out over the lake.

"No . . ." Jevon whimpered. "Daddy . . ."

Her knees almost buckled from thoughts of her father. "I'm so sorry, Jevon, but he's dead."

"No . . . he has . . ."

"He has what?"

The boy's chin dipped, and he didn't respond.

Her Starthroat hovered nearby. Bob nudged its nose toward her. She had to increase the power to her armor's musculoskeletal system to keep the rushing air from blowing her back.

She carried Jevon to the cockpit and set him inside. *Get him back to the dome. Hurry!*

*<What about you, ma'am?>*

*I can get back on my own. Go!*

The canopy retracted. After she stepped out of the way, the Starthroat turned and flew toward the east dome.

She bent down next to Jevon's father. A particle beam impact had scorched his chest and ripped open his suit. She considered letting him rest in peace, but the boy's last words nagged at her.

A pat-down turned up nothing of interest, although the corpse was frozen stiff.

The latching system connecting his helmet to his suit no longer functioned, so she raised a fist in the air. *Sorry.* The first hammering strike cracked the face bowl and a second blow shattered it. The nanoplastic disintegrated, reduced to the consistency of sand.

The man wore a pair of net specs.

♦

Unsure of what the specs might reveal, and considering her orders from General Douglas and conversation with the security president, Brooke kept her discovery a secret after returning to the dome. She checked in on Jevon—the boy seemed to have avoided serious injury—and then found an unrepaired habitat in a remote section of the dome.

Brooke put the specs on. She had to tap them four or five times before they booted.

The last recorded vidsim showed footage of the factory from a first-person perspective. *Jevon's father must've been one of the factory controllers.* The man crouched behind a tangle of pipes. Beyond them, two tall, white-suited intruders like the one she had seen on Europa placed the exocorpse amongst the dead. *I knew it.*

The intruders flinched and swung their rifles at the boy's father, who turned and ran. Already suited up, he exited the factory through a side airlock and made it all the way to the shore before bright light knocked him off his feet. He crawled on his hands and knees into the flowing black abyss. Beams of light rained down all around him, at which point the footage ended.

She yanked off the specs. *Obviously, they want us to cart the corpse home. Once the media finds out, the whole solar system will think we're fighting exobeings. But if the invaders are working with the UN, it would mean . . .* The specs dangled from one limp arm.

"So this is where you like to hide out."

Her head spun to find Penguin standing behind her.

"Don't worry, Captain." He held his hands up, grinning. "We all need a break from each other every now and then. Your secret's safe with me."

Both her knees locked. "Thanks for understanding."

He shuffled over to her and stood far too close for her liking. "Hey, a pair of specs. I lost mine when the *Ariane* went down. There's this killer game I'm dying from not being able to play. I wonder if these have it." He swiped the specs out of her hand.

"Hey!"

Startled, Penguin recoiled, stumbled, and dropped them. With an exaggerated stomp, he brought the heel of his boot down on top of the eyewear.

The crunch of plastic echoed throughout the empty dwelling.

"I'm so sorry, Captain. I'm such a klutz."

Brooke swiped the specs up off the ground. She whacked them, shook them, and swore at them, but they refused to work.

Her subordinate backpedaled toward the hatch. "I feel horrible. As soon as we get back, I'll buy you a new pair. I promise."

He locked stares with her. His eyes twinkled without a hint of guilt.

"Again, so sorry." He exited the habitat.

She stood rooted in place, unable to speak.

## Sixteen—Deliberate
## UN Headquarters, New York City, September 2247 AD

Edward Collins rose from an armchair as the room's transparent doors whooshed open. UN Secretary-General Danuwa Ajunwa strode into her office on the 605th floor of the cloud-piercing stratoscraper.

The office's sterile white upholstery, stainless steel coffee tables, and square light fixtures struck Collins as too ultra-modern. The building possessed none of the old-world charm of London's 10 Downing Street, but he couldn't help but admire the view beyond the windows. The megalopolis of New York City sprawled for as far as he could see in every direction. The gleaming zeniths of skyscrapers looked like a bed of nails hundreds of stories below. Cars raced along the multi-tiered highways hanging above the ground-level streets of Manhattan.

The windows tinted opaque. Upper body shots of top-level UN executives materialized on each pane along with the leaders of other nations and solar colonies.

Ajunwa strode across the UN emblem dominating the center of the marble floor, stepped behind her desk, and settled into her seat. "Thank you all for meeting on such short notice." Her deep, formal voice resounded throughout the room. "How is everyone?"

The execs offered the standard positive responses.

"Couldn't be better," Collins said cheerily. "Leeds is at the top of the league."

"Indeed. My great-grandson plays for the Nigerian Super Eagles, who took the 2245 African Cup of Nations."

"Life wouldn't be the same without footy, now, would it?"

Ajunwa leaned back and mimicked swinging a racquet. "Tennis will always be my first love. After seventy years, I'm still working on my backhand." She cleared her throat. "Now, on to business. It's imperative we discuss what happened on Titan before the General Assembly convenes." Her pitch-black eyes targeted the only other person physically present. "Mr. Collins, please begin."

"Certainly, Madam Secretary." Collins faced the images of the other execs. He tapped the control in his hand, dimming the lights. "What I'm about to show you is a simulation of the battle near Titan. The sim was extrapolated from footage shot by the *Ariane* and its fighters."

Stars blinked into existence, filling the dark office. Orange pixels congealed into a sphere the size of a weather balloon, forming Titan. A gray cylinder, the *Ariane*, approached the moon from a few meters away.

"Impressive," said Olivia Fisher, the prime minister of Australia.

"That it is," Collins said. "Correct me if I'm wrong, Madam Secretary, but this holographic facility is the first and only of its kind—and cost a euro or two, might I add."

Ajunwa nodded, more to tell him to get on with it than to agree.

Collins magnified the volume of space near the *Ariane*. Titan expanded, pushing its way out the room. Forty-eight points of light grew into the shapes of Starthroats, each outlined by blue to distinguish them from the blackness. Three tiny white triangles approached them.

He stepped into the sim. "Observe as our forces engage this unknown enemy."

The sim zoomed in further, focusing on the formation of Starthroats. Straight white lines lashed out from the tri-fighters. The five leading UN fighters exploded. Pixelated flame and shrapnel lit up the office, passing through Collins's body without harm. The remaining star fighters scattered into disarray.

"Typical military spectacle," said the president of the Court of Justice, Nubia Sebutinde. She folded both arms across a thickset torso. "Shoot first and ask questions later. The report says you transmitted the standard friendly greeting messages. Obviously, you didn't try hard enough to avert the confrontation."

Collins frowned. "We made every attempt to establish a dialogue."

"You should've pulled your forces back until you could establish peaceful contact."

"That wasn't possible. The enemy fried our fighters' neurotronics and pounced before my pilots could react."

White and blue lightning crisscrossed like a laser light show throughout the room. Spherical flashes burst in and out of existence. Starthroats exploded one after the next.

Sebutinde furrowed her brow. "Why did we launch a group of armed fighters toward Titan in the first place? The reason these invaders are now our 'enemy' is because we treated them as such from the start. " She snorted. "If I showed up to a meeting waving a gun, I might not make many friends, either."

Collins kept his tone even. "These unknown assailants attacked the Huygens colony first, without provocation. Based on their initial show of hostility, I wasn't about to send in an unarmed team."

"Well, caution was clearly lacking—"

Ajunwa's voice cut through the rumbling of fusion reactor detonations. "Pause."

Digital explosions froze in random starburst shapes. Particle beams remained lit, reminding Collins of an antique laser security system. The holographic beams pierced him through his chest and legs.

He turned to Ajunwa.

"Jump back fifteen seconds," she said.

Collins rewound the sim. Debris assembled back into the shapes of spacecraft. Bolts of light retraced their paths back to fighters, which spun and flew in reverse.

The sim reverted to the fifteen-second mark and moved forward again.

Collins followed Ajunwa's gaze, which tracked the progress of one particular Starthroat. It wove through the fireworks with mind-bending precision and held its own against the pursuing triangle.

"Who is the pilot of that craft?" she asked.

He flicked a finger over his control. The battle space faded away.

Three translucent human figures appeared above the UN emblem, each a different view of the same young woman. Lavender streaked the flight-suited figure's raven hair, which she had tied back in a ponytail. Her face featured narrow violet eyes, a small pug nose, and a frown.

"Captain Brooke Davis," Collins read from his slip. "Age twenty-four. Mixed American and Japanese heritage. Her neurotronic response rates are off the charts. Over a thousand career kills, better than triple any other pilot in the last six years."

Ajunwa sat back and clasped her hands atop her desk. "If I had flown against such talent in the African Unification War, I doubt I'd be sitting here now."

"Davis might well be the best in the Defense Force. The lass managed to incapacitate a tri-fighter while most of her teammates fled and died. The *Ariane* sent forty-eight Starthroats up against three enemy spacecraft. Only ten of the carrier's fighters survived and made it to the colony."

"Only ten?" the American Colonies president, James Pierce, asked.

"Correct, Mr. President. The tri-fighters possess technological superiority over our Starthroats, but rest assured our engineers and strategists are working to improve these numbers."

"I hope so."

"Please continue your briefing, Mr. Collins," Ajunwa said.

Collins played the available footage of Davis neutralizing the lead tri-fighter, investigating the situation inside the colony, and finding the children. He paused after she removed the exocorpse's helmet. Virtual blood stained the office floor. A tall, thin body in a white space suit lay motionless in front of Ajunwa's desk. Bulbous black eyes protruded from its grey head.

The faces of each exec contorted in contemplation.

Pierce ran a hand through silver hair. "Not the most aesthetically pleasing creature I've ever seen."

"They're not so different from us," said Serena Reinhart, the president of the Economic and Social Council. "Bipedal with hands, feet, eyes, and a mouth."

"The discovery of this corpse," Collins said, "confirms we're dealing with genuine extrasolar beings, the first intelligent life we've encountered. In fact, they appear to resemble the Greys of ancient mythology."

"And they're here to destroy us," Pierce said.

"We don't know that." Sebutinde shook her head. "For all we know, Titan was a misunderstanding."

"I would hardly call the massacre of ten thousand colonists a misunderstand—"

"Where's the body now?" Ajunwa asked.

"It's on its way here," Collins said.

"Inform me the moment it arrives."

"Of course, Madam Secretary."

As Collins worked his control, the office jumped above the refinery. The Huygens colony and Lake Cassini plummeted away. The moon's surface disappeared below an orange horizon, which curved across the room's floor.

Collins waded in Titan's atmosphere.

The *Ariane* hung in front of him. Starthroats rocketed out of its launch bays.

A white ship fatter than a UN spacecraft carrier encroached on the office. The spacecraft possessed the shape of two pyramids stuck together at their bases.

The execs shifted in their seats.

*I shouldn't take pleasure in watching them squirm*, Collins thought. A twinge of guilt helped him suppress a grin.

Triangular specks shot forth from the pyramidal carrier. Sparks and streamers erupted between the two ships. The fireworks waned, and bright light leapt from the pyramid.

The *Ariane* shuddered, flared, and fell toward Titan.

Sweat slicked more than one exec's forehead. Francisco Muñoz, the General Assembly president, loosened his collar.

"After the *Ariane* went down," Collins said, "Captain Davis kept twenty-two children and the other nine surviving pilots alive for two months."

Yellow haze filled the office as he summarized Davis's work. Finally the sim showed Davis and her team leading the children across Titan's surface toward a descending shuttle.

Collins walked alongside them. "The shuttle ferried everyone up to the *Opportunity*. After rendezvousing with *Spirit* to transfer the corpse and children, *Opportunity* should arrive back at Callisto by early December."

The sim dissolved into nothingness, and the room brightened. Collins squinted, waiting for his pupils to adjust. He made a mental note to get ocular implants.

"Well, our next step seems clear," Pierce said. "We need to put all military installations on alert and tighten our defenses."

Collins ran a hand over his smooth-shaven scalp. "I've repositioned our forces, but there are other considerations. We can only spread our assets so thin without leaving ourselves vulnerable to separatist threats. The hit-and-run attacks continue on and around Earth, Mars, the asteroid belt, and the Jovian system. The latest projections indicate these skirmishes will erupt into full-scale wars in a matter of months."

"Before long, private entities won't be exempt from the fighting," said Reinhart, "which will collapse the intrasolar economy and throw the solar system into anarchy."

The prime minister of the United Kingdom, Anne Wellington, crinkled her brow. "And God help us when one of these separatists manages to stabilize an antimatter device."

Ajunwa exhaled. "We're all too close to destroying ourselves. We don't need anyone else to do it for us."

Collins knew his cue. "Do we inform the public about the existence of the Greys?"

. Ajunwa turned to Reinhart. "How do you think the general public would respond?"

"It's hard to say for certain, Madam Secretary. Centuries ago, an announcement would've caused mass suicides and panic. But today, we're a spacefaring civilization. Talk of other intelligent life, like talk of the phase drive, might be taken in stride."

Pierce slapped his desk. "There's no way we reveal this yet. Not until we know more."

"People deserve to know," Sebutinde declared.

"From a military standpoint," Collins said, "we stand to gain a tactical advantage by disclosing the truth. If we give the separatists something else to worry about, they may cease their attacks." He brushed the lint off his lapels. "Think about it. How significant is any conflict amongst humans in the face of an external, common threat?"

Wellington sat up straight. "Territories and political groups will not only stop succeeding but start begging for the UN's protection."

"This is what we've been waiting for, Madam Secretary," Pierce said, "the excuse we need to bring the strays back into the fold."

"Perhaps." Ajunwa inclined her head. "It's an intriguing prospect, but until we learn more about these exobeings, it's all speculation." She leaned forward in her chair. "There's one more item we need to address, and that's the project. The phase shuttle test flight is scheduled for December, but we cancelled the candidacy program in light of the exothreat, meaning we still don't have a pilot. Should we postpone or cancel the flight?"

"Absolutely not, Madam Secretary," Collins said. "If exobeings have traveled here from another star system, they must have faster-than-light capability. We need the phase drive to gain equal footing. The drive also offers a way to smite the separatist movement. Assuming the shuttle flight goes according to plan, we'll begin tier four. Designs are already on the drawing board for a prototype phase fighter. If anything, we should accelerate the timetable."

"What about the location? Is it wise to launch the flight from the Jovian system with the Greys lurking out there?"

"No. We're providing a fleet for maximum protection, and we also need the particle collectors to produce enough antimatter for a manned FTL spacecraft. Sommerfield and his team have already relocated to Callisto to oversee assembly of the drive and shuttle in Base HOPE's aerospace facility."

Sebutinde snorted. "You know, it's quite a coincidence. Exobeings show up right as we're about to develop a way to come to them."

"I've never believed in coincidences," Ajunwa said. "Very well, Mr. Collins, the shuttle test flight will proceed at your discretion."

Warm shudders coursed through Collins's limbs.

Ajunwa placed both palms flat on her desk. "So, you've got your location, your fuel, and your ship, but no pilot. Do we need to reinitiate the candidacy program?"

He shook his head. "No need, Madam Secretary. The committee's made its selection."

## Seventeen—Sojourn
## Base HOPE, Callisto, December 2247 AD

"Home at last." Brooke directed a tired smile at the door to her quarters, which beckoned to her with the promise of sugary cereal and sweet solitude. She couldn't believe nine months had passed since she had last set foot inside.

After spending two months stranded with a bunch of kids, she had welcomed the uneventful trip home. No further separatist attacks had occurred since the bombing of Earhart. The disgruntled political entities had recoiled in response to the secretary-general's announcement of the existence of extrasolar invaders. Images of the dead exobeing had left everyone stunned. The e-media networks had asked whether this creature belonged to the same race responsible for the alleged abductions hundreds of years ago. Talk shows had questioned the sanity of conflicts among humans given the existence of other intelligent life. Protesters had clamored for governments both official and otherwise to stop the fighting. Brooke hadn't been able to find a feed streaming anything else, not even Project Luminosity. The UN had offered no comment on the cancellation of the candidacy program or when the phase shuttle might fly.

A hot flash undulated through her body. She clutched her wrist to keep her arm from twitching.

Her last rationed spark had begun to wear off. *I'll run inside quick, drop off my bag, and then head to Vik's.* She pressed her thumb to the bioscan pad, and the door swished open.

"Surprise!"

Brooke blinked and dropped her bag.

Marie aimed her eyecam at her. "The triumphant heroine returns." She grinned. "Tell me, Captain Davis, how are your illegitimate children? Your uterus must've been working overtime to pump out twenty-two on such short notice."

Maya ran over and clamped onto her leg. "Auntie!"

Brooke stepped into the room, and the door sealed behind her. "Shut that damn thing off." She held a hand up in front of her face while jiggling Maya off her leg.

Marie tapped the cam, switching off the red light. "Still no sense of humor." She pulled the device off her head. "I thought you might be happy to see us."

"I am." Brooke locked her stare on the ceiling. "But I wasn't expecting you. You should've called."

"I did, but you didn't answer."

"Look what I can do, Auntie." Maya pulled away from her aunt's leg, dashed toward the bunk bed, and bounded into the air. "Quadruple super fusion burst!" She rose all the way to the ceiling in Callisto's low gravity. When her hands touched the metal paneling, she pushed off. One foot touched down on the top bunk and then the other. The silly monkey faces on each shoe flailed their tongues. "Wasn't that amazing?"

"Way to go, squirt." Brooke's focus remained on her sister. "How'd you get in here? The base is off-limits to civilians."

Marie held up the ID badge dangling around her neck and made it dance. "Somebody's moved up in the solar system." The ISN logo zoomed in and out.

"ISN—as in IntraSolar News?"

"That's right. You're looking at a full-fledged field reporter." Marie set her cam on the desk, kicked off her heels, and plopped down on the bottom bunk. "After seeing my *Tribune* feeds, ISN's executive producer called and offered me a job. Maya and I relocated to a posh New York flat two months ago."

"Congratulations, I guess."

"Thanks for your heartwarming support."

"That still doesn't explain how you got on base or into my room."

"Yes it does. With this badge, I can go pretty much wherever I want." Marie tapped her lower lip. "Granted, an officer or two needed a little extra convincing, but the point is, ISN struck an exclusive deal with the UN to cover the phase shuttle test flight, so—"

"What?" Brooke grabbed fistfuls of her hair. "The project's back on—and launching from here?"

"Sure hope so," Marie said. "Otherwise, I'm in the wrong place."

Seething, Brooke unbuttoned her blazer, tossed it aside, and unzipped the skintight jumper. Shivers undulated through her every appendage.

"Are you okay?" Marie dipped her brow. "You've looked better, even by your standards. I guess Titan really took its toll."

Brooke heaved in slow breaths, which did little to subdue her welling dread. "Who's the pilot?"

Her sister stretched out and yawned. "Some guy named Richthofen."

"Colonel Richthofen." *He was in first place—one spot ahead of me—when they cut the program.* Brooke's shoulders slumped.

"Sorry."

After pulling out a chair, Brooke slumped down and buried her face in her hands.

The ventilation system whirred. Maya lay on the upper mattress, pounding her heels against it.

"Well, look at the positives," Marie said. "We're staying at the New Gallilei Grand Hotel, so we'll be around to—Maya, what are you doing?"

Brooke took one look above the top bunk and shot to her feet. The chair tipped over and drifted to the floor.

Marie hopped up and spun around. "Maya!"

The ventilation shaft grating dangled from the ceiling above the top bunk. Brooke could only assume Maya had crawled up inside the shaft.

"How did she get it open?" Marie asked.

After leaping up onto the top bunk, Brooke crawled to the vent. "The grating snaps in and out of place. She could've pulled it off with ease."

"I guess I shouldn't expect a military base to be childproofed."

"This is why you shouldn't be here." Brooke rose up on her knees and stuck her head into the shaft. "Maya!" Her voice echoed down the narrow tunnel. "Maya, are you in there?" She waited a few seconds and then hoisted her body up inside, fitting with only centimeters to spare.

"Do you see her?"

The shaft disappeared into the darkness five meters ahead. Brooke enabled her implants' night vision mode but saw no movement. "No."

"Well, what are we going to—?"

The door to her quarters whooshed open below.

"Ta-da!"

Brooke scooted back and plopped down onto the top bunk.

Maya stood inside, bouncing up and down. "I found a secret passageway, Mommy."

Marie rushed over to her, went down on one knee, and embraced her daughter. "What were you thinking? A big fan could've chopped you to pieces. Don't ever do that again."

The little girl frowned. "Sorry."

Brooke drifted down to the floor and rushed out into the corridor. She rounded two corners before discovering a grating lying on the floor in front of an open vent in the wall.

Despite her welling angst, she cracked a slight smile.

After snapping the grating back into place, she returned to the room. Marie sat on the bottom bunk, engaged in a tickling fight with Maya. The girl squirmed in delight.

The giggling grated on her nerves, bringing her to the brink of convulsion.

♦

After shooing her sister and niece off to their hotel, Brooke rode the lift down to the subway station below the base. There she hopped on a hovertram that took her into New Galilei.

The passengers gave her long looks when she plopped down into her seat. *Why is everyone staring at me?* She wiped the sweat from her brow.

A woman sitting next to her said, "Hey, you're the pilot who rescued those children from Titan, right? You're all over the news feeds. I just wanted to tell you how wonderful—"

"Gagarin Street Junction now approaching," the tram's AI announced. "Next junction is Armstrong Central Station."

Brooke sprang up and darted for the nearest exit. Recent events had thrust her into the public eye more than she realized. *I better not end up a celebrity!* Her rapid breaths bordered on hyperventilation. The cramped cabin seemed to shrink.

The tram slid to a smooth stop and the doors parted.

She leapt out into New Galilei's subterranean downtown and sucked in a gust of frigid air. It stung her lungs but liberated her senses.

Every December, city engineers set the climate control system to winter mode. She never understood why anyone went to the trouble of creating an authentic holiday environment when it resulted in half a million people freezing their asses off for a month. The temperature stayed a constant one degree below freezing. Flurries wafted down like feathers, created from purified water-ice found in Callisto's crust. Holographic clouds obscured the imitation night sky. She caught glimpses of the dome through small, flickering breaches in need of repair.

She zipped up her jacket and buried her hands in the pockets.

The tallest building stood twenty stories above the city streets. Shops, restaurants, and far too many smiling people lined her route while she hurried along. She shivered at all the wreaths, giant candy canes, and Christmas trees. A group of off-key carolers assaulted her eardrums.

A boy holding his mother's hand pointed at Brooke. "Look, it's her, Mommy!"

Brooke quickened her pace.

A trash collection bot strayed into her path. Someone had tied a festive bow around its oblong body. She sent it on its way with a heartfelt kick.

Tromping through the snow brought her from Gagarin Street to Shepard Road, past Liwei Boulevard, and down Jemison Street.

She veered left at Aldrin Way and hung a right two blocks later. Low-income rental habitats and other crumbling buildings lined the street. Other points of disinterest included a pawn shop, an adult e-media store, and one of those E-Z Credit places that preyed on the financially inept.

Fifty meters later, she arrived at her destination, a hole-in-the-wall known as Vik's Virtual Gaming.

Shelves stocked with high-tech equipment surrounded her when she walked in the door. Screens flickered and flashed, providing the only source of light in the dim shop. Virtual goggles, zettabyte hard drives, AI matrix boards, and overclocked quantum processors represented just a few of the items in this gamer's paradise. A heat wave washed over her, banishing the chill outside.

Brooke marched toward the checkout counter at the back of the shop.

Two teenage boys stood near a far shelf, ogling her. Both wore shiny black jackets with animated flames leaping across their chests, and spiked hair jutted from their heads. The taller boy had colored his hair red, the other blue.

The boys' mouths hung open, almost foaming.

"That's her," Red whispered to Blue.

She flared her eyes at them without breaking stride.

"Oh my God, she looked at me." Blue drooled. "We gotta go home so I can get with her."

Red bobbed his head. "It's my game." He grinned, stretching his pimpled face. "I go first."

The teens scampered out the exit.

*What the hell were they babbling about?* Brooke reached the counter.

A short Indian man with spiked orange hair reclined in a chair behind the counter, his attention absorbed by the flashing within his virtual goggles. He worked the joysticks affixed his seat's armrests. Sweat beaded down honey skin. "Oh, yeah. That's right, baby. Keep doing what you're doing. Victory never felt so good."

"Vik," Brooke said. When he failed to respond, she yelled, "Vik!"

"Huh?" Vik pushed up his goggles and blinked. Then he lowered them, took them off again, and furrowed his brow. "Well, well." A crooked grin stretched across his thin face. "What a coincidence. You and I were just—how should I put this—having an adventure together."

Brooke hurdled the counter, pried Vik's goggles off, and put them on. The battle in Titan orbit consumed her. She sat within an inaccurate rendition of a Starthroat's cockpit. A lingerie-clad Captain Brooke Davis straddled her lap. The facsimile's breasts ballooned to five times her actual bust size, and her body gyrated.

"Hey, babe, it's the latest and greatest from HoloSoft. What went down on Titan has made you a superstar."

She growled. "Not this."

Vik stood, stretched, yawned, and shrugged. "I might've hacked it a little. Sells even better now."

Brooke tossed the goggles to the floor and grabbed a fistful of his t-shirt. "You wipe this program right now or—"

"Better let go of me if you want to spark again."

She shoved him away.

"Lucky for you I like it rough."

Brooke balled a fist.

"Now, now." He wagged a finger. "This is an employees-only area."

She stomped around to the front of the counter. "Hurry up so I can get the hell out of here."

Vik disappeared into the back storeroom, cackling all the way. When he emerged, the smirk still contorted his face. "Here they are." He tossed the case onto the counter, popped open the top, pulled out a spark injector, and waved it in front of her face. "That'll be five hundred million euros."

"You can't be serious. That's twice what you charged me last time."

"Hey, babe, sparks are getting harder to come by. They're not cheap to begin with. The product has to be smuggled all the way from Earth, and the UN keeps tightening security and customs checks. Plus, with everybody all worked up about the Greys, there are fewer transit liners running. Five hundred's doing you a favor."

"No way am I spending two months' pay. Three hundred."

"Four-fifty. That's my final offer."

Panic knotted her stomach. "Three-fifty."

"I said four-fifty was final." He stroked the stubble on his chin, eyeing her up and down. "Then again, if you'd be willing to turn my virtual experience into a real one—"

"I'll hand over my life savings before that, you pervert." Brooke whipped her net specs on. "Fine. Four-fifty." She enabled her personal credit app and wired the payment into his account.

Vik popped on his specs, nodded, and pushed the case toward her.

"And to think I was going to thank you for sending me to Alex," she said, swiping her purchase off the counter.

"Who's Alex?"

"You know, your distributor on Mars?"

He lowered his chin, staring at her over his specs. "You mean the Alex Rhodes who owns the biotech company that supposedly makes the sparks?" He folded his arms and shook his head. "Girl, if I knew a quadrillionaire, do you think I'd still be in this hole?"

"But we messaged a few months ago, and you told me she—"

"Wasn't me. You must know another Vik. And here I thought I was one of a kind."

She stood rooted in place, staring at the case. *She did say someone else arranged the favor.* A chill surged through her chest. *She couldn't have meant . . .*

"Alex Rhodes, beautiful, rich, and domineering," Vik mused, "'congratulates' the shy, innocent heroine of Titan. That oughta be how the game ends—"

Brooke slapped the counter, making Vik flinch. Her body juddered.

"Damn, girl, go on and get your fix, already."

"I'm . . . I'm fine. You'd better wipe that sick game, or else . . ."

"Don't worry. The kids will be onto something new by tomorrow."

Growling, Brooke rushed outside, found the nearest alley, and ducked into it. Her body convulsed.

*I'm a lowlife drug addict!* She slid down the side of a building, choking on sobs. Images of sex-starved gamers violating her body flooded her mind. Bile pooled in her throat.

Her butt hit the cold, snow-covered concrete.

When she ran out of tears, she pulled an injector out of the case and stabbed the back of her neck.

**Eighteen—Simulty**
**Base HOPE, Callisto, December 2247 AD**

"Thanks so much," Marie said over her shoulder as she stepped inside Brooke's quarters.

The soldier out in the hall nodded. "My pleasure, ma'am."

As the door slid shut behind her, Marie approached the desk. "Ah, there you are." She grabbed her cam and dropped it in her purse. *Okay, time to pick up Maya from preschool. I bet she's exhausted after bounding all over the playground.*

She glanced at the bunk and fought the urge to take a nap. All the walking and tech talk during her tour of the base's aerospace factory had fatigued her muscles and brain. Without her cam, she hadn't been able to record any footage—not that ISN could air anything until the day of the test flight. The UN refused to disclose the details of the flight until the launch ceremony because of the separatists and these new invaders. Lawyers had insisted she sign a stack of nondisclosure e-slips requiring her to keep her mouth shut or face charges of treason. She grumbled at the degree of control the UN maintained over the media. Citizens only enjoyed freedom of speech and the press provided individual rights didn't inconvenience the state.

*Brooke's sourness must be rubbing off on me.* She slapped her cheeks. *Think happy thoughts. You've got a beautiful daughter, your dream job, and a great life. Heck, you're about to cover the first crewed FTL spaceflight.*

She grinned. So far, her sister didn't suspect a thing.

Marie rubbed her arms. Her skirt and blouse failed to trap body heat. Brooke's quarters felt like a meat locker, both in temperature and décor. The base's designers had constructed everything out of metal, and the room's surfaces remained barren except for a desk matrix, at least twenty boxes of cereal, and an e-slip pinned to the wall near the bunk.

When she tapped the slip, it lit up with one of Maya's animated creations. Three waving stick figures—Brooke and Marie with Maya in the middle—stood holding hands atop a burning sun. A dialogue balloon hovered above Brooke's head with her saying, "Owie! Feet hot!"

*Admit it, Kishi. You've got a big heart, so stop pretending otherwise.*

Marie brought a finger to her lip, wondering what other objects of sentimentality her sister might have hidden away.

Plopping down in a chair, she opened one of the desk drawers. *I shouldn't snoop, but . . .*

Buried at the bottom of the drawer, she found an autographed slip of Brooke and her posing with Kid Fusion, a Martian boy band they had idolized in late elementary school. One of the band members held his arm around Brooke's waist. A glaze shrouded her distant eyes, and her face flushed.

Marie covered her mouth, stifling her laughter. Her side ached while she sifted through the other drawers.

In the bottom dresser drawer, she stumbled upon a small plastic case. She held it up to her ear and shook it like a Christmas present. A collection of heavy items rattled around inside.

When she opened the case, she found several cylinders resembling medical autosyringes.

Her body shuddered in dread.

She fished her specs out of her purse and snapped a picture of the cylinders. An image-matching app interfaced with SolNet and identified the injectors.

♦

"Captain Brooke Davis, please report to the main conference room."

Brooke jerked up from her seat, spoon protruding from her mouth. The base matrix repeated its message over the integrated audio system in the mess hall. She tossed her cereal bowl into the recyclers and made her way to the conference room.

The brass had given her three days leave upon returning, an unheard-of gesture since Defense had placed every member on active duty. The bombing on Mars almost half a year ago still marked the most recent separatist attack, but that didn't mean the movement had ended. Despite her protests, General Douglas insisted she take time off after her ordeal on Titan. She hadn't resumed duty, a fact she had yet to share with Marie.

A chill rippled through her. *Do they know about the sparks? One anonymous message from Alex or Vik could end my career. Maybe I should've kept my temper in check last night.* She halted. *What am I saying? How can I even consider apologizing to that pervert?* She shook her arms out and marched down the corridor.

She flinched when the conference room doors parted. Some of the most important people in the solar system sat at the table with General Douglas. Security president Collins, one of her least favorite people, occupied the seat next to him. Professor Kevin Sommerfield sat to Collins's right and directed a warm smile in Brooke's direction. Danuwa Ajunwa, leader of the greater part of the human race, loomed at the head of the table.

Brooke straightened her uniform, stepped over to the table, and saluted. "Captain Davis reporting as ordered, sir."

"At ease, Captain," Douglas said. "You're on leave, remember?"

"Yes, sir." Her stance stiffened.

Ajunwa clasped her hands together. "Captain Davis, please accept my sincere gratitude for your exceptional conduct on Titan." She adjusted her head scarf and leaned back in her seat. "I trust you and your family are in good health?"

Both of Brooke's eyes bulged, and she couldn't breathe. *Does she know?* "Everything's fine, I guess."

Kevin gave a subtle nod and mouthed Ajunwa's title.

"I mean, everyone's doing well, Madam Secretary," Brooke said.

The secretary-general smiled. "Please relax, Captain. This is an informal gathering." She stood and rounded the table. "I'd also like to express my awe at your prowess in the cockpit. I was a pilot in the African Union, so I appreciate your abilities." She held out her right hand.

Brooke stared at Ajunwa, as if in a trance. It took a few moments for her to work up the nerve to shake the woman's hand. "I . . . I don't know what to say, ma'am."

"You could say thank you."

"Right. Thank you, Madam Secretary."

Collins's gaze shifted toward the general.

"We're promoting you to major." General Douglas's deep baritone rumbled. "You're now the Jovian Fighter Wing Commander."

"Lead pilot?" Brooke blinked in disbelief.

"We want the best leading our fighters into battle," Collins said.

General Douglas nodded. "Congratulations, Major Davis. You'll assume your new position after completing Thursday's test flight."

Brooke cocked her head, studying the faces in the room. Everyone seemed to be suppressing smiles. "Sir?"

Douglas peered at Collins, who looked at Ajunwa.

The secretary-general turned to Kevin Sommerfield. "It's your ship, professor. You tell her."

Kevin stood and ran a hand through his hair. "The attack on Titan provided the UN with an official reason to shut down the candidacy program, but to be honest, Major Davis, it wasn't getting us anywhere. We completed the training portion and then terminated things after realizing a conventional competition wouldn't distinguish one pilot above the rest. For weeks, we tried to define what qualifications truly mattered." His face lit up brighter than the plasma strips illuminating the ceiling. "Then we saw what you did on Titan, which left an impression on the entire solar system. The committee was wary of reducing the selection process to a popularity contest, but we couldn't ignore the feelings of the general public." He paused and glanced at the others sitting around the table. "In the end, we felt that your actions best represented what we're looking for. Therefore, I'm pleased to offer you the opportunity to pilot the phase shuttle."

Brooke's mouth hung open. "Wasn't Colonel Richthofen selected as the pilot?"

Ajunwa, Collins, and Douglas furrowed their brows. "Richthofen was on the narrowed list of candidates," Collins said. "However, we've made no announcement, official or otherwise, until this moment."

"Rumors have been running rampant," Kevin said, "and the media's been speculating. I wouldn't be surprised if some 'misinformed reporter' made a brash assumption."

Brooke threw her head back in realization. *Marie!*

"This is strictly a volunteer assignment," General Douglas said. "You're not being ordered to accept."

"I'll do it, sir," she whispered. "It's a dream come true." She resisted the urge to drop to her knees.

"Great," Kevin said. "I know I'll feel a lot safer with you at the helm."

"You'll feel safer?"

"The phase shuttle seats four, which means three passengers will accompany you, including me."

"I see." For some reason, Brooke had pictured the phase shuttle as a tiny capsule. A black and white feed of a daredevil blasting out of a cannon ran through her mind.

"The full plan, of course, is for you to perform a solo shakedown flight before the official maiden voyage, which ISN will broadcast live. President Collins will join us for the latter—" Kevin gave a subtle wink. "—along with the reporter from ISN."

*A reporter I need to find and have a little chat with*, Brooke mused.

♦

The first officer she passed in the corridor gawked at her like she was one of the Greys. Then the technician who serviced her fighter did a double take.

No matter how hard she tried, Brooke couldn't straighten her smile. She had risen to the top pilot spot, and soon she'd make history as the first human being to travel faster than light. Her body tingled with elation, a sensation as foreign to her as clinical depression was to Marie.

With a bounce in her step, she danced around an automated delivery bot, head bowed in thought. Memories of gazing up at the Colorado night sky, watching her father point out the constellations, brought tears to her eyes. *I'm actually going to do it, Dad.*

She rounded a corner and ricocheted off a flight-armored chest. The impact jarred the pilot's helmet out of his arm and sent it clanging against the floor.

On instinct, she dropped into a fighting stance.

Jeff Braxton contorted his freckled, country-boy mug. "Well, if it ain't the girl everybody's talking about." He bent down and scooped up his helmet.

She stared at him, unsure of what to say.

A stomach-churning thought popped into her head. She felt happy to see him. She had craved a return to normalcy since her ordeal, and for better or worse, he represented normalcy. Despite his backwater chauvinism, he kept his priorities straight.

He shifted his gaze to the new rank insignia on her right arm. "Major?" His brow lifted when he noticed the winged star on her collar. "They made you lead pilot?" He stood at attention and saluted, expression souring at the apparent taste of swallowed pride.

The old Brooke—the one from before she had left for Earth and Titan—would've scowled and blown past him. "As you were,

Lieutenant." She clasped her hands behind her back and strolled past him.

With eyebrows raised, Jeff stared at her.

She stopped and turned. "Hey, um . . ." She tapped her nose. "Sorry about your, well, you know."

He opened his mouth but no words came out.

She spun and continued down the corridor.

"Angel, wait up a sec."

Brooke halted and peered back.

"I've been transferred to Earth, so . . ." After catching up to her, he shrugged. "Try not to kill your next wingman, all right?"

The smile returned to her face. "No promises."

♦

Marie's abdomen knotted when the door swooshed open. She hadn't risen from the bottom bunk since her discovery. Both eyes remained locked on the metal bars supporting the top mattress. Her stomach hadn't done this many somersaults since she'd first learned of her pregnancy.

Out of the corner of one eye, Marie watched her twin march up to the bed.

"What're you doing back?" Brooke unbuttoned her blazer, grinning. "Where's Maya? I've got incredible news, which you already know, of course."

Marie continued to avert her gaze. *I haven't seen her this happy since before Dad died. I don't want to do this to her, but I can't allow her to go on killing herself.*

Brooke bent down and slapped Marie on the bare leg. It stung like hell, but she knew it wouldn't compare to the impending emotional pain.

"Don't try to deny it," Brooke said. "The professor told you they selected me as the pilot, so you decided to have a little fun." She stood up straight and placed her hands on her hips. "Well, congratulations. You got me." She laughed.

Marie's frown deepened. She couldn't remember the last time she heard her sister laugh.

"Hey, what's the matter?" Brooke dipped her brow. "Aren't you going to take credit?" She held her hands out to the side. "C'mon, rub it in good. Let me have it already."

Marie swallowed hard.

"Well, say something already."

Not knowing quite how to broach the subject, Marie lifted the spark injector up from behind her hip and studied it.

The glow in Brooke's eyes caught fire.

Marie glared back.

Brooke stabbed a finger at her twin. "You went through my stuff?"

"I'm sorry," Marie said. "I was curious about what childhood artifacts you had hidden away. I had no right." She hardened her stare. "But what's done is done." She held the injector out. "How long have you been sparking?"

Brooke threw her hands up. "It's none of your damn business."

"Like hell it isn't." Marie sat up and scooted to the edge of the bed. "I'm your sister, and anything you do affects me to some extent."

"That weak logic justifies violating my privacy? You're concerned over nothing."

"If it's nothing, why are you acting like I caught you in the act of murder?" Marie recoiled at her sister's dramatic physical changes. Brooke's face flushed, and her body shook. "It all makes sense now. When you came to Chicago, I thought six more years of bottling your emotions—vacuum sealed—had caused your pent-up anxiety. Or maybe there was some truth to your condition. But now, I see how wrong I was, how horribly wrong."

Flicking her wrist, Brooke said, "You don't know what you're talking about."

"No? Why don't you stop shaking, then—if you can?"

"That's only because I'm furious at you right now."

"Is that all?" Marie sprung to her feet, threw on her specs, and read out loud. "'Illegal nanorobotic stimulants, more commonly known as sparks due to their dramatic "sparking" of the nervous system, yield temporary increases in motor reflex control and heightened sensory perception. Microscopic nanites, each between one-to-two nanometers in length, attach themselves to neurons and synapses. The nanites act as signal amplifiers, enhancing reflexes for weeks. But as the nanites break down, they impede neurological functions. Studies have shown them to damage neurons during the decomposition process. Short-term side effects include the shakes, dizziness, nausea, and irritability.' Sound familiar? 'Long-term effects include shortened life spans, paralysis, and even death.'"

"Whatever. That's how they try to scare you."

"Did you listen to a word of what I read?" Marie waved the injector in the air. "This thing shoots tiny machines into your spine that eat away at it. Kishi, they're killing you."

Brooke faced away. "I . . . I'm fine, really." She gripped her quivering left hand.

"Who are you trying to convince, me or yourself?"

Brooke leaned over the desk. “I’m not an addict.” She rocked back and forth, and whined in fright. “I’m . . . I’m not . . . not a . . .” She held up her hands, trying to hold them still. She couldn’t.

With a fist, she hammered the desk. The clang of metal echoed off the walls.

Marie risked placing a hand on her back.

Her sister pushed her away. “I don’t want your pity.”

“Fine, but you’re getting my help whether you like it or not. We’ll work on getting you off these things. Together.”

Brooke whipped her head up. “I can’t stop taking them. There’s no way I can fly without them. Not anymore.”

“Well, you’re going to have to learn.”

“You don’t understand, Marie. The sparks help me react ten times faster.”

“You were a good pilot before the sparks, and you’ll be a good pilot after them.”

“But not a great one.” Brooke’s face looked as pale as Marie had ever seen it. “It’s too late. I’m too far gone.”

“No, you’re not. You—we—aren’t even twenty-five yet. You’re still young and—”

“It doesn’t matter, anyway. Enemy fire, the vacuum of space . . . Do you know the average life expectancy of a pilot? I’m not going to live long enough for the sparks to kill me.”

“Don’t talk stupid. Someday, you and I are going to be two old hens. We’ll bob up and down in floating rocking chairs and laugh about this whole thing.”

“Nice fantasy. Wish I could join you in it.”

Marie drilled a heel into the floor. She shook now as well. “Promise me you’ll quit and get some help.”

Her sister curled her lips into a weak smile. “Sorry.”

“Okay, then.” Marie stepped toward the door.

“Where are you going?”

“Wouldn’t you like to know?”

“Seriously . . .” Brooke grabbed her arm.

Marie tried to shrug her off, but Brooke clamped down. “Let go. You’re hurting me.”

“You wouldn’t dare tell my superiors about this . . .”

“You leave me little choice.”

“No!” Brooke cried. “You can’t. My career will be over. I’ll never fly again.”

“But you’ll live.”

“And the test flight. If you screw that up for me, I’ll never forgive you."

Marie spun to face her twin. Those desperate purple eyes chilled her, but she had to stand her ground. "Are you going to quit?"

"You won't do this to me." Brooke relaxed her hold. "You're bluffing, hoping I cave."

"You think so?" Marie reached for the control pad next to the door. "I refuse to ride in any ship flown by someone under the influence of—"

Brooke dug her fingernails into Marie's arm and yanked her back. "You're not leaving!"

Marie stumbled backwards. "Let go of me!"

"Shut up!"

With a balled fist, Marie whirled and swung. The blow connected with Brooke's left eye socket, jerking her head back and dropping her to the floor.

Hissing through clenched teeth, Marie clutched her throbbing hand. *Guess all those self-defense classes came in handy.*

Brooke curled up into the fetal position and sobbed. Both hands covered her eye.

"Sorry," Marie said.

Seeing her sister this way flashed Marie back to Brooke's suicide attempt. Two days after their mother overdosed on sleep medites, Marie stumbled upon her hysterical twin in her room, poised to slice her wrists with a laser shaver. It took Marie the entire night to talk Brooke into putting it down.

Marie knelt down beside her sister and stroked her hair.

"What's wrong with me?" Brooke pleaded.

"You're not well, Kishi."

Brooke wrapped her shaking arms around her torso and sobbed. "It's all my fault, Miko. I killed Dad, and Mom took her life because of it."

Blowing out a heavy sigh, Marie thought, *It always comes back them.* "Their deaths weren't your fault."

"Yes, they were, especially Dad's."

"You were ten years old."

"He let me fly his plane—taught me everything—and what did I do?" Brooke's tone shrank to a hoarse squeak. "I killed him, so I deserve to die."

Marie cupped her sister's face with both hands. "Listen to me carefully, Kishi. If Dad were alive, do you think he'd agree?" Her sister tried to pull away, but Marie held her head in place. "Answer the question."

After squirming in vain, Brooke lowered her eyes and shook her head.

"Of course he wouldn't. Nor would he want you to sacrifice your health or push away your family."

"I'm so sorry, Miko. You must hate me."

"I love you, Kishi, more than you'll ever know." Marie pulled Brooke into her embrace, and together, they wept.

## Nineteen—Shakedown
## Base HOPE, Callisto, December, 2247 AD

Brooke wiped the sweat from her forehead with the back of one hand. Her body ached from withdrawal. She reached into the pocket of her flight suit, grabbed a pill, popped it into her mouth, and slumped down into the pilot's seat. The anti-anxiety meds lessened the chills enough to allow her to focus on the phase shuttle's control readouts.

The scaffolding folded away from the forward viewport, giving her a clear view of the fighter assembly bays at the other end of the arena-sized factory. Robotic arms twisted. Android workers scurried about. Sparks flew in the vicinity of a half-completed Starthroat, one of the new SF-522A models. This latest fighter featured higher power, heavier armaments, improved neurotronics, greater maneuverability, anti-jamming, and double the top speed, making it a better match for the tri-fighters.

A shudder rippled through her body. She didn't know how much longer she could keep her word. Only the impending thrill of piloting the shuttle allowed her to endure the pain.

"Promise me you'll quit," Marie had insisted after their spat ended.

Brooke had pulled herself up off the floor. "Okay."

"Thank you. In return, I'll keep quiet as long as you stay off them and get help."

Technicians came and went beneath the shuttle's fuselage, prepping it for transfer to *Terminus* for the afternoon shakedown flight. The ringing echoes of clanging, drilling, and microwelding pierced her forehead.

Brooke's facial muscles twitched, and she manifested a smile despite the acoustic assault. *Today's the day. I'm finally going to fly faster than light—assuming I can keep from passing out.*

"Let's see. The shakes, dizziness, upset stomach, headache . . ." Brooke had rattled off a list of at least fifty ailments while sitting on an exam table in the base infirmary.

"What do you suppose might be causing these symptoms?" Doc Gordon had asked.

Dread had wrenched her stomach. "Unprescribed medication."

"Which would be what?"

After swallowing hard, Brooke had divulged the truth.

The white-haired physician had asked only one question after she'd finished. "Have you stopped sparking?" He'd run the soft blue light of a medscanner over her body.

She'd given a reluctant nod. "I didn't have a choice. My sister made sure of it."

"If only more patients had family like her." He'd poked his finger into the screen at the foot of the table. "I've transmitted a prescription for a nano-anxiolytic to the base pharmacy. One pill three times a day should help ease your symptoms. Time should allow your body to heal, but there's no cure, so you won't ever fully recover."

"I understand."

"Come back and see me in a week." Gordon had stepped toward the exam room door. His white coat had flowed like a cape in the low gravity.

"Doc," she'd said.

He'd stopped and turned back around.

Staring up at the lights on the ceiling, she'd asked, "Do you plan to inform, um . . ."

"Patient-doctor confidentiality." He'd shrugged. "Good luck to you, Major. I'll be watching next week with the rest of the solar system."

"How's your cold?" asked a jubilant voice.

Brooke jumped out of the pilot's seat.

Professor Kevin Sommerfield stepped through the shuttle's side hatch and handed her a steaming cup.

With a grunt, Brooke accepted the drink and sat back down. She didn't like coffee, but right now she'd try anything to subdue her anxiety.

The professor settled into the copilot's seat and ran a hand through his thick hair, gawking at the cockpit as if seeing it for the first time. He glanced over his shoulder at the empty third and fourth seats. Then his gaze moved to the rear cargo hold hatch and swept past her before returning to the forward viewport. He beamed.

Brooke shared his enthusiasm, although the stabbing at her temples subdued any outward expression of it.

Facing forward, Kevin logged into his console. Schematics and equations related to the shuttle's phase drive lit up his screen. Unlike a Starthroat, the decades-old cargo carrier featured no neural interface. The engineers had installed holographic display monitors, but the crew had to input instructions via old-fashioned touchscreens. "She's programmed and set. Ready to go down in history?"

"Today, yes, but can we skip the broadcast flight next week?"

Kevin nodded. "I know how you feel. Celebrity has its perks, but I preferred my anonymity."

Brooke nodded and took a swig of coffee.

While reviewing the shuttle's fusion reactor status, she caught Kevin glancing at her out of the corner of her eye. She had noticed earlier too, but didn't know what to think about it.

"I have to say I'm impressed," he said.

"By what?"

He waved a hand in the air, indicating the cockpit. "By the dramatic improvement you've shown since the start of the candidacy program."

"Oh." Her chest felt heavy.

"You seemed lost at first, but by the end, I almost swore you invented the drive."

"I simply did what I needed to do." *That's the truth, at least.*

"Well, I'm thrilled you were selected to fly my baby. I feel pretty lucky, and, um"— He turned away from her. —"I've enjoyed working with you the last few days."

Brooke hid behind another sip and contemplated his words. *Is he trying to indicate romantic interest?* She couldn't believe the inventor of the phase drive could feel that way about her—or that anyone might have feelings for her. *I've enjoyed the time I've spent with him, though.* Kevin had showed patience whenever tutoring her. Never once had he talked down to her like a high-and-mighty intellectual. *Could he really like me? No, he's only being nice.* "Yeah, me too, I guess." In her peripheral vision, she studied his expression.

He smiled and opened his mouth to say something.

The lead engineer popped his head inside the hatch. "We're ready to seal her up and ship her out."

"Okay," Kevin responded. "Excited?" he asked Brooke.

"If you're fond of understatements," she said.

♦

After initiating the startup sequence, Brooke gripped the control stick, fired the shuttle's thrusters, and maneuvered out of the hangar bay. *Terminus* receded in her rear camera views until it became one of the stars.

Her console beeped, indicating she had put enough distance between the carrier and shuttle to execute a dimensional shift. A hovering readout showed that the fifteen-minute drive charge time had elapsed.

"Everything looks good on this end," Kevin said from aboard the carrier. "Just remember your training and let the AI do the work. We're ready whenever you are."

"Good luck, Major," said Captain Hasluck, *Terminus's* skipper.

"Thanks." Her heart thumped against her ribcage, and she almost fainted from euphoria. "Okay, here we go. Upshifting to hyperspace." She slid her finger over the execution icon.

The whirring of the drive intensified. The deck, her seat, and everything around her vibrated with increasing frequency. The cabin pressure increased, and her ears popped. A pinpoint of light blinked into existence in front of the shuttle.

"Whoa—"An unidentified force pried the breath from her lungs.

Beyond the forward viewport, the light brightened and grew into a spinning vortex, warping and twisting the stars in the background. Its outer edge churned like the event horizon of a black hole. Space ahead of the shuttle collapsed like a dent punched into reality.

The shuttle stretched toward the light. The cabin's interior elongated and distorted like a reflection in a funhouse mirror. Her console and legs appeared meters out in front of her. The strange forces distorting her perspective squeezed in on her mind.

Like a rubber band, the cabin snapped forward, shrinking lengthwise and collapsing. Brooke flinched as the bow of the craft rushed toward her. She tried to throw her arms up for protection, but they wouldn't move. She wanted to cry out but her tongue had vanished.

She clamped her eyes shut.

When she opened them, calm had settled over the cabin, and a color she didn't recognize tinted everything. She knew the color didn't exist in the visible spectrum, but she didn't know how she knew. Her surroundings appeared to have flooded with a type of liquid, yet she could still breathe, and the air didn't feel wet. Perhaps the interior had filled with a substance that didn't exist in her reality. Maybe the substance was this reality.

Outside the shuttle's transparent walls—inside of which she could discern internal wiring, circuits, and insulation—stars waded in the same liquid-color. She seemed to exist both outside and inside the physical universe. It surrounded her, and she surrounded it.

She reached for her seat's armrest, feeling the need to grip something, anything to ground herself in this hyperspace. Multiple time-delayed images of her arm flailed about. Past, present, and future limb positions coexisted like overlapping apparitions. *Which one is my real arm? Or are they all real?* Her many hands passed through the armrest as if it were a hologram.

When she peered down, her vision dove beneath skin and muscle. A pulsating heart thumped her chest. Blood coursed through arteries and veins. White blood cells chased pesky bacteria.

Her perception plunged deeper. Double helices of adenine, thymine, guanine, and cytosine rotated around nucleobases. Coiled proteins resolved into polypeptide chains of amino acids. Molecules expanded to reveal atoms held together by covalent chemical bonds. Vast expanses of nothingness separated orbiting electrons from protons and neutrons. Quarks spun like tops. Strings vibrated in an infinite number of quantum melodies. Deeper still, she saw . . .

Brooke forced her many sets of lungs to draw deep, even breaths.

Confusion gave way to an omnipresent viewpoint. If she was still sitting in her seat—and she swore she hadn't moved—how could she see herself from above, below, and the side at the same time? She examined everything in the cabin from alternate angles without physical relocation.

When she thought of someone, her all-encompassing perspective showed her that person, no matter their location. Kevin stood behind the flight controller on the bridge of *Terminus*, asking for constant updates. Marie lay on the bed in her hotel in a white robe, flipping through channels with Maya curled up next to her, asleep. The sound of the girl's soft breathing reached Brooke's ears.

Brooke wondered about her own appearance, and her compound perspective turned to examine her expression. One narrow, violet eye wavered. The black strands in her ponytail drifted in microgravity. Her teeth chattered, and her skin had paled.

Beneath her skull, electrical current coursed through her brain.

She hyperventilated. Her many arms thrashed about, hands seeking the armrests, and she squeezed her eyelids shut.

Her awareness heightened, giving her a vague sense of an aura surrounding her body. Was there more to her than she knew existed, more than simple flesh and bone?

"Exit point in ten seconds," the AI announced. "Three, two, one, zero. Commencing downshift to normal space."

A whirlpool formed within the strange liquid-color beyond the forward viewport. Instead of bright light, blackness comprised the churning whirlpool. The cabin and shuttle elongated, allowing the vortex to suck her forward.

The next time she blinked, everything had returned to normal.

Normal lighting gave objects definition and shape. Two and only two hands gripped solid armrests. A bead of sweat trickled down her cheek, and perspiration soaked the garments beneath her flight suit. Every viewport showed a familiar starry backdrop.

Letting her body go limp, she exhaled in relief and then whooped with glee. She stomped her heels and slapped the armrests, laughing her throat hoarse.

♦

Brooke kept pace with Kevin, trying to articulate her experience without much success. They walked beside the shuttle while it rolled back into the aerospace factory for post-flight checkout.

"Four-dimensionality was like everyone predicted, yet nothing like it."

"You just said two opposite and contradictory things," Kevin said, smiling.

"I know, I know, but words can't describe it. I mean, I saw Marie sitting in her hotel room when I thought about her. I never expected that."

"Well, you literally existed across multiple planes of normal space-time at once. Who knows what you could have seen? Did you see anyone on Mars? Earth?"

"I didn't try."

"We'll definitely have to study that effect. I can't wait until I get my chance—oh, you've got to check this out." Kevin bounded away from the shuttle and toward the main spacecraft assembly area. "There she is." He sounded like he'd seen the most beautiful woman in the solar system. "I can't believe they've already completed the frame." He stopped, looked up, and stood in reverence.

Brooke caught up to him and followed his gaze. The skeleton of a star fighter sat on a wheeled platform, waiting its turn in line at a robotic welding station. Compared to a Starthroat, the craft's frame was bulkier aft and sleeker fore. "No, it couldn't be. Already?"

"Oh, yes." A boyish grin contorted his five o'clock shadow. "It's the prototype for the first phase fighter. Tier four is only a few months away."

A pang of elation shot through her aching sides. "Do you think it's possible to experience too much joy in one day?"

Chuckling, he said, "The UN began the structural designs the day I told them about the phase drive. An FTL fighter gives them a huge tactical advantage against the separatists, which explains their haste." He frowned. "I wasn't happy about it at first. I'm excited about the ship itself, not its ability to kill people. But now that we'll be using it against hostile exobeings, I don't feel so bad. Because of them, the UN has accelerated the timetable further still."

"Huh." Brooke folded her arms across her flight suit. "You're able to construct a drive small enough? The shuttle's ten times the size of the fighter."

"I'm still finalizing how that's going to work. I've been refining the equations in my off-hours."

The comment jolted Brooke's memory. She pulled her specs out and checked the time. "I have to go. Marie and Maya insisted on celebrating by dragging me to some lame restaurant with a nineteenth-century theme." She palmed a fist. "If a waiter so much as thinks about putting a cowboy hat on my head, I might start an old-fashioned bar brawl."

"Not much of a social butterfly, huh?"

"I prefer the cocoon."

Kevin smirked. "Yet you love to fly."

Brooke turned to leave. "You got me there."

Three steps later, Kevin called after her. "Hey, um, Brooke."

She stopped and turned around.

Wiping his pale forehead, he said, "There's something I, um, want to ask you."

Hyperspace had banished her withdrawal symptoms, but now twinges coursed through her body like jolts of electricity. "Okay . . ."

"I know you're not a big fan of social situations. Neither am I, but I was thinking maybe, after the broadcast flight, we could grab dinner someplace quiet. Just the two of us."

*He's asking me out on a date?* She wanted to say yes. *But what about when he learns about the sparks? No one wants to date an addict.*

*And besides—* "I thought . . . you know . . . you and my sister . . ."

"Marie's a great person, but she's, well . . ." He averted his gaze.

"To be honest, I like you better."

Her jaw practically smacked the floor. *He likes me better than Marie? The prettier, smarter, and more popular version of me?* She cocked her head. "Why?"

"Why not? You're intelligent, talented, good-looking—"

"Me?"

"Well, yeah."

"But you're . . ."

He swung his head from side to side. "Despite my accomplishments, I'm still a desk jockey, but you risk your life every day. I think that's amazing."

Brooke stood, gawking at him. *Why won't I let myself believe him?* Despite what she wanted to answer, she hesitated. "I . . . I don't know."

"Hey . . ." He held up a hand. "You don't have to answer now." The tension in his muscles relaxed. "I don't want to make things weird between us, so if you end up not wanting to, it's no big deal. Just think about it whenever you get a chance. Okay?"

She blinked, feeling stupid.

"Have fun with Marie and Maya tonight." He pivoted and hurried away to inspect the phase fighter. "Or don't. That's fine, too."

Brooke slumped as she watched him bound off.

## **Twenty—Spectacle**
## **Jovian System, December 2247 AD**

Eyecams recorded Marie's every twitch. Her cheeks ached from constant smiling. Hundreds of fellow reporters from Earth, Mars, Ganymede, and Callisto stood at the foot of the stage, cams transmitting the pre-flight ceremony to thirty-five billion people. The phase shuttle, now christened *Viking,* rested behind her on the flight deck within *Terminus*'s hanger bay.

Beyond the throng of reporters stretched the interior of the spacecraft carrier, which resembled the inside of a giant metal pipe. Its rate of rotation induced a quarter gee, gently pinning everything to the curvature of its surface. Two hundred meters above her head—on what looked like the ceiling relative to her position—upside-down flight crews prepared inverted Starthroats for launch. In the distance, she watched rovers drive up the sloping deck. When she had first stepped inside the bay, she had gone cross-eyed. *I've never had great depth perception.*

Her skin tingled despite the sensory overload. She would soon crew the first official FTL flight and broadcast it to the solar system in near-real time. *Brooke's not the only one with a dream. Thank the stars she stopped sparking. If she hadn't kept her promise, I would've had to turn down this assignment. I couldn't have done that to her.*

A reporter inquired how she planned to cover the flight. It felt a little odd to be on the other end of news coverage, not that she minded.

Brooke stood on the opposite end of the stage, surrounded by media hounds. The reporters insisted she strike various poses in her shiny uniform. They shot her in the act of saluting, from the side, and with sexy, pouty lips. Brooke scrunched her nose and grunted in protest after each request before relenting. The scene reminded Marie of a swimsuit calendar shoot showcasing the most disgruntled of models.

*I know she's enjoying this deep down. She'd never admit it—not even to herself—but a sister can tell these things. I mean, those sexy, pouty lips don't arise out of depression.* Marie caught her twin smoothing her hair when the reporters took a quick break.

Since the shakedown flight, Brooke's sour demeanor had sweetened. She had called—actually called—Marie in a blissful daze and rambled on about the experience of existing in a higher dimension.

Kevin stood a few meters away with Dr. Christine Yeager and the rest of his research team answering questions. He fielded each query without stammering, although the sweat on his brow suggested he still didn't revel in the spotlight.

His gaze wandered over in Brooke's direction. Their eyes connected, and they exchanged a smile.

*Brooke and Kevin seem to have struck an efficient working relationship.* Marie tapped her lower lip. *It makes sense in retrospect. He never made a move on me during those interviews at CERN.* She shrugged. *Well, if Brooke's found someone who makes her happy, I'm happy for her.*

With a couple of hops across the stage, Marie bounded to her sister's side. The press pounced like a pack of vultures, bombarding them with questions.

"Care to explain how two sisters were chosen for this historic flight? That can't be a coincidence."

"You both look an awful lot alike. Plan on switching places and letting the other one fly the ship for a while?"

"Do you two wear matching outfits? That would be so cute . . ."

"Let's get on with it already." Brooke huffed the words under her breath.

Chuckling, Marie said, "Whatever. You love it."

With her thin eyebrows raised, Brooke glared in her sister's direction, purple eyes radiating contention.

Marie patted her twin on the back.

The president of the UN Security Council stepped up to the

podium at center stage.

The hanger bay fell silent as reporters focused their eyecams on Collins. Marie, Brooke, and Kevin marched over and stood in line to his right. Captain Hasluck, General Douglas, Callisto's governor, New Galilei's mayor, and a couple of top UN execs occupied the stage's left wing.

Collins scanned the crowd from left to right, drawing out the suspense. "Ladies and gents, today we stand on the precipice of the future." He paused to adjust his tie, giving his voice time to echo throughout the bay. "In a few short hours, we will embark on a historic voyage. To recap a tad of history, the Vikings discovered the American continents—the New World, so to speak—around 1000 AD. Then, in the twentieth century, the *Viking* probe revealed the wonders of a new world named Mars. The upcoming flight marks the first step in humankind's journey to new worlds beyond our solar system. Therefore, naming the shuttle *Viking* seemed appropriate." He scanned the crowd. "In order to reach those worlds, *Viking* is about to travel faster than light, a feat once viewed as impossible."

"Still is, technically," Kevin muttered.

Marie weighed her opinion of Collins. His bellowing voice projected the power of his position, while his shaved scalp bestowed a degree of rugged handsomeness upon him. *He's definitely an alpha male—not my type, but one that attracts plenty of women.* He stood a mere half-head taller than Marie, although his air of authority gave him an imposing demeanor.

"Closer to home," Collins said, "the scientific community has discussed establishing gateways called phase tunnels, which will cut transit times of days, weeks, or months to hours or minutes. These tunnels may eliminate the need for spacecraft between colonies, which will make the solar system a much smaller place." Again, he paused for effect. "This technology will bring all nations and peoples closer together. We've been fighting each other for too long. Let us end it once and for all. The first steps have been taken. We have laid down arms because of a common enemy. Now, let's band together against those who would challenge our resolve."

Reporters, civilians, crewmen, pilots, and officers near the stage whooped and hooted. The two rows of hovering screens on either side of the crowd displayed reactions in major cities. People in Times Square in New York clapped and hugged one another. A woman stood arm-in-arm with a man in Red Rock City on Mars, cupping a breathing mask over her mouth. Pavonis Mons towered in the background. People wept in Beijing, Moscow, and São Paulo. Residents in London,

Mumbai, Sydney, and New Galilei demonstrated similar ebullience.

Collins drew in a deep breath and nodded. "I don't know about you, but I'm thrilled to be alive during such a time and proud to be a part of it." He turned to Marie, Brooke, and Kevin. "And speaking of being a part of it, it's about time you met the rest of *Viking's* crew."

Kevin stepped forward first, as rehearsed.

"Professor Kevin Sommerfield," Collins said, "the modern-day Einstein, who invented the phase drive, will monitor the drive during the flight."

Kevin held a hand up, forced a smile, and retreated to fervent clapping.

Collins held out his hand toward Brooke, who came forward next. "Major Brooke Davis, heroine of Titan, is the ace pilot who will operate *Viking*."

With hands clasped behind her back, Brooke nodded and then resumed her place in line.

"And finally," Collins said, "Marie Davis, the up-and-coming journalistic prodigy. You know her from IntraSolar News."

Marie stepped forward. In a euphoric daze, she waved like the queen of a parade.

Applause reverberated throughout the hangar.

Kevin, Brooke, and Marie strode to the other side of the stage.

A display screen materialized, filling the area they had vacated. The screen showed a star field with Jupiter and a much smaller Callisto in the bottom-left corner.

"This is our intended flight plan," Collins said.

The screen zoomed in on Callisto. Four animated spacecraft carriers drifted away from the moon. A simulated phase shuttle launched from the lead carrier and darted away.

"Presently," he said, "this ship and three other escorts are en route to deep space. Once we've cleared Jupiter's gravity well, we'll launch aboard *Viking* and upshift to hyperspace. Our destination . . ."

The shuttle blinked, disappeared, and reappeared near the top-right corner of the screen.

Leaning forward, the crowd adjusted their eyecams, hanging on Collins's timely pause.

". . . is the planet Neptune—specifically its largest moon, Triton."

A big blue planet and tiny, reddish-gray moon appeared in the screen's upper-right corner near the shuttle.

"Is the objective to recover the wreckage of the crashed expedition?" a reporter asked.

"Excellent guess." Collins inclined his head. "For viewers

unfamiliar with the incident, the UN lost contact with the crew we sent to Triton a decade ago. We launched an unmanned probe to discover what happened. When it surveyed the moon, it found pieces of the spacecraft strewn about the surface. Orbital scans failed to reveal what caused the mission to fail."

"Why didn't the UN attempt a manned rescue mission?" a young e-media rep asked.

"Unfortunately, the political climate soured before we could send anyone to investigate. The conflicts within and between nations sapped the UN of the necessary resources. In the last few years, no new colonies have been established. Nor have any new exploratory initiatives been launched. Huygens remains the only settlement near Saturn, and no one has ventured further out. Until now . . ."

Neptune slid out of the picture, and the reddish-gray Triton ballooned. The shuttle orbited the moon and disgorged a mini-star fighter.

"*Viking's* maiden voyage will double as a salvage operation." Collins gripped the podium with both hands. "The shuttle will carry one of the Defense Force's upgraded Starthroats in its cargo hold. Major Davis will descend to the moon's surface in the fighter and recover the flight recorder."

Marie glanced at Brooke, who nodded.

"What about the Greys?" A third reporter asked. "They attacked Titan. What if they're lurking around near Neptune and detect the shuttle?"

With a confident shake of his head, Collins said, "The UN's deep space sensor network hasn't detected any activity in the Neptunian system."

The phase shuttle christening ceremony followed Collins's speech. Marie stood near Brooke and Kevin, watching as he uncorked a bottle of champagne. The cork shot through the air and exploded into thousands of pieces of blinking candy-confetti, which drifted down to the deck. Marie caught a piece on her tongue. *Mmm, cherry!*

Kevin raised the fizzing bottle in tribute. After dousing *Viking's* bow with champagne, he took a swig and passed the bottle around.

♦

The tension in Brooke's muscles eased when she plopped down into the pilot's seat. *I'm glad that's over*. She had found a surprising amount of enjoyment in the ceremony, but Collins's talk of "a brighter tomorrow" struck her as shameless posturing. Now, at least, she could steal a few moments to herself while the others tended to last-minute business prior to launch.

She input a command into her touch console, bringing *Viking's* systems online. While studying her displays, she reached into her pocket and grabbed an anxiety pill.

"Someone seems eager to make history."

Brooke flinched. She jammed the pill down her throat and jumped up. "Oh, sir, I—"

Collins raised a palm. "As you were, Major. Don't let me interrupt."

"Yes . . . yes sir." She plopped down into her seat and focused on her displays, heart thumping her chest. She had hoped Kevin would enter the cabin first, or at the very least Marie.

Her mind flashed back to her confrontation with Collins on Earth. She had seen him a couple of times from afar in the aerospace factory but hadn't interacted with him. The hairs on her neck stood on end at the prospect of spending time in a cramped cabin with the man, even with others present.

He eased into the chair behind her and leaned forward. "Is everything in the green? All systems go for launch?"

"Um . . . yes. Yes, sir. No problems."

She heard him recline in his seat.

"Let me be direct with you, Major," he said. "Things seem a tad awkward between us."

"What do you mean, sir?" Loosening the collar of her uniform, she thought, *I swear someone messed with the shuttle's environmental controls and jacked the temperature way up.*

"Let's drop the ranks for a moment. I want to apologize for my choice of words when we spoke back at Dryden."

She threw herself into running a navigational subsystem diagnostic. "Okay . . ."

"The thing is, Brooke—may I call you Brooke? Or do you prefer Kishiko? Or Kishi?"

Brooke clenched her jaw.

"You see, Brooke, a few of us have been working on an important project, one to ensure a new era of peace. When you saw what you saw, well, let's say the reactors of certain colleagues of mine overheated. But I said, 'No, this can work to our advantage. Her abilities could be an asset.' You see, we believe strongly in our project, but most of us don't trust that everyone would understand. Is any of this making sense to you?"

She didn't respond at first, but he let emptiness hang in the air, waiting.

"I . . . I don't know, sir."

"You must have questions."

"I just follow orders, sir."

"You can drop the model soldier act. I know you're curious."

She twisted her body enough to spy him in her peripheral vision.

"Well, go on." He sat back and propped a leg up on his knee. "Now's your chance."

Her mouth opened, closed, and opened again. Collins sat with hands clasped in his lap, stare boring into her head.

*I know I shouldn't play this game with him, but . . .* "Well, I guess the biggest thing I've wondered is why none of what's happening now seems to make any sense."

"Go on."

"In the Artemis reactor hold, I met a supposed exobeing who looked more or less human. He—I think it was a he—spoke to me in English. He was with two Defense pilots who I served with before they transferred out of Base HOPE, and when I confronted them, they tried to kill me." She sucked in a breath and faced him. The questions poured out. "Sir, how can our people be working with the same extrasolar invaders who are attacking us? And why did the UN blow up the water plant and frame the separatists for the deaths of fifty thousand people?"

Collins stroked his chin. "Those are very interesting questions." He took his time brushing the lint off his suit. "I'm starting to feel that I can trust you, which is why I've applied a gentle nudge here and there to help you achieve your dream"— He glanced around the cabin and spoke in a hushed tone. —"despite, shall we say, your less than ideal health."

A chill began at her toes and shot up her spine. *How could he know?* She whipped back to face her console.

"I always wondered how you could be so much better than everyone else," he said. "Honestly, if your methods didn't only work for you, I might have every pilot do the same—not that it's necessary." He let out a long sigh. "I like you, Brooke, I really do, but I can't help you any more at this time." He stood. "We'll speak again when we get back, assuming we're both able."

Brooke froze stiff.

Long after Collins had exited the cabin, she sat staring off into the distance, grappling with questions and worry that no pill could cure.

## Twenty-one—Occident
## Jovian System, December 2247 AD

"This is Marie Davis, reporting live for ISN aboard *Viking*, the first manned faster-than-light vessel." She hovered behind the cabin's four seats, directing her eyecam straight ahead. Brooke sat in the pilot's seat, speaking to Control via her headset and implementing course adjustments. Kevin occupied the copilot's seat to her right, attention fixed on the equations and data scrolling across his screens. Collins reclined in his chair behind Brooke. A field of stars surrounded the shuttle outside the forward viewport.

Marie swung the cam in a slow arc, giving the viewers at home their first look at the interior of *Viking*. The cabin boasted a plethora of animated readouts. Screens flashed schematics of the shuttle. One diagram showed the hundreds of thrusters in the reaction control system. Another reported fuel cell, fusion, and antimatter power consumption. Other displays offered external camera views from multiple angles. Icons covered every touch panel.

IntraSolar News had spared no expense in purchasing the latest eyecam for her. In her mind's eye, a dozen screens hovered off to either side of her perspective. Marie could swing any of them into view with simple desire, and occasionally, she desired to arrange them in the shape of a smiley face. *Ha ha.*

The screen she focused on at the moment displayed her broadcast as the end viewer saw it. Her name appeared at the bottom with a news ticker below it and the ISN logo off to the right. Thanks to phase tunneling, the transmission delay lasted only two or three seconds. The cam linked with the shuttle's transmitter, which routed the signal via microscopic wormholes to other locations within the solar system.

Marie drifted up to the ceiling toward the back of the cabin. Rear viewports offered a view of the stars beyond the dorsal cargo bay doors.

Pointing her eyecam at the rear window, she said, "That shrinking brown and white ball in the distance is Jupiter." She increased magnification and angled the cam to the right. "And those silver slivers falling behind us are UN spacecraft carriers."

After descending to the deck, she pressed her thumb against a wall panel and opened the rear hatch. Overhead plasma strips switched on as she drifted into the cargo hold. "This is *Viking's* cargo bay, which is just big enough to hold one of the UN's upgraded fighter craft." The Starthroat resting in the bay looked meaner and bulkier than those she had seen in the past. "Major Davis plans to launch in this fighter through the overhead bay doors and descend to Triton's surface.

"The shuttle's phase drive and conventional engines are situated aft of the cargo bay, but there's no way to get back there. It's a shame, since I've heard gazing into the light given off by the drive's antimatter collider is a real trip. But no matter. We're minutes away from experiencing what the new drive can do."

She soared back into the main cabin.

"*Viking* has cleared Jupiter's gravity well," said the navigations officer aboard *Terminus*. His tinny voice squawked from a ceiling speaker above her head.

Brooke nodded. "Verifying . . ."

"Verified," Kevin said. "Local gravitational field confirmed as negligible." He tapped his console. "Now initiating the drive's charging sequence. T-minus fifteen minutes until we can execute a dimensional shift."

"Marie," Brooke said, looking back over her shoulder, "I want you back in your seat before then."

"Will do." Marie caught Brooke's frown. *What's the matter with her all of a sudden? She was ecstatic at the end of the ceremony.*

Kevin twisted around to face the cam. "Hello, everyone. I'm making final preparations for our first phase shift."

"Care to answer a question posed by one of our viewers, Professor?"

"Sure."

"Nikki from Toronto asks, 'How does the transdimensional phase drive work?'"

Kevin scratched his mop of brown hair. "Well, Nikki, the shuttle's antimatter drive focuses a large quantity of energy at a tiny point in space. This energy creates a tear in the fabric of space-time called a wormhole."

"I'm guessing it's a good idea to poke the hole far away from things," Marie said, "which is why we had to get clear of Jupiter."

"Right, a gravitational field makes it difficult to open a stable wormhole and skews all subsequent calculations. Shifting in the presence of significant gravity could tear the shuttle apart, and if it survived, space-time fluctuations at the mouth of the wormhole would shift the re-entry point. In that case, the shuttle might end up who knows where."

Motioning for Marie to swing the cam his way, Collins said, "A phase shift also creates a hazardous aftereffect. The event horizon of the wormhole distorts surrounding space, and gravity waves propagate out from the epicenter for hundreds of kilometers. This phase wake, as the professor calls it, could do a lot of damage to a nearby ship, space station, or moon."

"Sounds like it could be used as a weapon," Marie said.

Collins readjusted in his seat but said nothing.

"We're still working on minimizing the wake," Kevin said. "Anyway, after opening a wormhole, the drive reverses the angular momentum of every quark in every atom of the shuttle, giving it—and its passengers—negative mass. This repulsive, negative-gravity effect widens and holds open the wormhole long enough for us to pass through without being crushed." One corner of his mouth upturned. "Now, here's where the mind-bending starts. Once we pass through the wormhole, we enter a realm of existence 'above' our four-dimensional universe."

"Four dimensions?" Marie asked.

"Length, width, height, and time. Einstein showed that time isn't constant over three centuries ago. It slows down in the presence of extreme gravity or speed."

"Time dilation, right?"

"Exactly. So, the shuttle enters a higher dimension in which the universe functions according to higher-order spatial dynamics. Much of this 'hyperspace' is beyond human comprehension."

"Think about it this way," Brooke said. "If a two-dimensional being—one who only knew about length and width—stumbled into a world with height, basic concepts like up and down would make no sense to him."

Kevin nodded. "But even though the human mind might have difficulty grasping its surroundings, the drive's matrix won't. It'll interpret our surroundings in terms of mathematical equations and follow a shorter route through hyperspace than the one we would've traveled through normal space-time."

"Once we've traversed that route," Collins said as Marie refocused on him, "we create another wormhole and downshift back into reality."

"Thus, we'll have moved from point A to point B faster than light could've covered the equivalent straight-line distance through space-time." Kevin turned back to his console.

"Fascinating," Marie said. "Our viewership appreciates the explanation."

"And I'd appreciate it if you took your seat," Brooke said.

Marie drifted down into her chair and strapped into it. Her heartbeat quickened in anticipation.

"Thirty seconds and counting," Kevin said.

"Okay," Marie said to the billions tuned into the broadcast, "the moment we've been waiting for is almost here. Entry into hyperspace will cut off my signal, but I'll re-establish it once we emerge in about . . ." She tapped the professor on the shoulder.

"The drive shifts objects at a practical velocity equivalent to one-point-seven times the speed of light, meaning we'll 'disappear' for two and a half hours. The trip won't last anywhere near as long for us, though." He cracked his knuckles. "Five seconds . . . three, two, one, zero . . ."

♦

*Viking* emerged from hyperspace outside the orbit of Neso, Neptune's thirteenth moon. A distance of fifty million kilometers placed the shuttle beyond the range of significant gravity. Neptune hung in space as a blue half-crescent. Brooke blotted it out with her thumb.

Once again, the trip through hyperspace had quelled the shaking and anxiety that had plagued her since she quit the sparks, although Doc Gordon insisted her symptoms would return. *Temporary relief is better than nothing.*

The second go-round, the ethereal experience overwhelmed her to a lesser degree—not that a person ever acclimatized to a higher dimension. The euphoria that had overwhelmed her during the shakedown flight exhilarated every bit as much during flight two.

Such thrills allowed her mind to ignore the way Collins had wound her up before they launched. Because of it, she had avoided contact with him. *I can do this job even without the sparks. I can.*

A hand clasped the top of her arm.

She spun and yanked her arm away.

"That was simply . . ." Kevin's head swayed back and forth. "There are no words for it." His eyes glazed over.

Brooke relaxed. "Yeah, it was pretty okay."

"Pretty okay?" Marie scooted forward. "Stop pretending to be Miss Cool-as-Ice all the time. Hyperspace makes a zero-gee rollercoaster ride on acid seem about as exciting as watching grass grow."

Twisting partway around, Brooke said, "That camera better be off right now."

"What are you going to do if it isn't?"

"It far surpassed my expectations," Collins said, ending the squabble.

In her peripheral vision, Brooke saw something akin to reverence on his face.

Discussion centered on the hyperspace experience throughout the next thirteen hours. Marie, Kevin, and Collins rehashed every aspect over freeze-dried rations. Brooke listened as the others compared notes, trying to figure out what certain things meant and why other things happened.

The most awkward moment came when Collins insisted on relieving her. Having once served as a Defense pilot, he knew how to operate a spacecraft and had also trained on the phase drive's systems. She initially insisted on remaining in control, but he ordered her to take a break. After the briefest of salutes, she sprang to her feet, grabbed her flight bag, and headed for the cargo bay, citing the need to double-check the Starthroat's systems. She took a moment to admire the sleek lines of the SF-522A before climbing in and settling into the pilot's seat. It felt strange to sit there without her armor on. She pulled the helmet over her head.

*Bob, are you there?*

*<Yes, ma'am.>*

*Good. Talk me through the new systems. I want to know everything they changed.*

As Bob began his overview, Brooke reached into her flight bag and pulled out her last spark injector. Marie had cleared out the drawer in her quarters, but she hadn't found this one. Brooke stared at it for a moment, longing to press it to her neck. *There are only two charges left. I'd better save it for an emergency.* She reluctantly slipped it under the seat and then sat back, Bob's calm narration droning in her ears. Despite her best intentions, she eventually dozed off.

Brooke returned to the cabin and relieved Collins a few hours later. Not long after she settled back into the pilot's seat, her instruments indicated the gas giant's seventh moon had come into visual range. Her nose crinkled in response to the curious readings.

"What do you see, Major?" Collins asked from his seat behind her.

"I'm not sure, sir. Kevin, what's the composition of Triton's atmosphere?"

He shrugged. "It barely has an atmosphere. Very thin nitrogen content with trace amounts of carbon monoxide and methane."

After checking and rechecking the data, she asked, "Then why do my readings show a mix of sixty-six percent nitrogen and thirty-three percent oxygen with a pressure of about seventy kilopascals?"

"What?" He leaned in closer to her, peering at her displays. "I don't believe this. If these readings are accurate, it means—"

"I know."

He skimmed the full sensor report. "Traces of methane, nitrogen dioxide, and particulate matter?" His hand flew to his mouth. "Almost sounds like—"

"Earth's life-supporting yet polluted atmosphere."

Collins stood and leaned over her shoulder, much too close.

Kevin tapped several commands into her console. "We should be seeing frozen nitrogen and carbon dioxide on the surface along with water-ice. The moon's temperature ought to be minus two hundred degrees Celsius."

Brooke swiped a finger over her console. The cabin's main screen materialized above the forward dash, displaying a high-resolution image of Triton. The reddish-gray moon possessed modest oceans beneath thin, swirling white clouds.

"It looks like the moon's been terraformed, folks," Marie said, having reestablished her feed signal.

"How can this be?" Kevin ran a hand through shaggy, blue-brown hair. "We've applied planetary engineering on Mars for a century and a half, but it's still not this far along."

"I'm more concerned with how this was done without Defense knowing," Collins said. "Moons don't sprout biospheres overnight, so this must've begun decades ago, perhaps centuries. When we scanned for signs of the lost expedition, Triton looked nothing like this."

Brooke worked her console, which beeped and flashed as the shuttle's AI crunched more of the data. The results prompted her to increase magnification on one spot near Triton's equator. "Look at this." The main screen displayed a bright object over one hundred kilometers in diameter. It looked like a mini-sun. "Now we know part of how the terraforming was accomplished."

"It's a big mirror," Marie said, "like the orbital reflectors that focus the sun's heat on the surface of Mars."

"I show hundreds of them scattered all around Triton."

Kevin sucked in a sharp breath. His attention remained on Brooke's readouts. "That's not all. Somehow, they've harnessed Neptune's tidal force. They're using it to warm up the moon even more."

"Tidal force?" Marie asked.

"It's how the Moon causes Earth's tides, or what makes Io's volcanos erupt. In an elliptical orbit, Triton comes closer to Neptune at times and drifts farther away at others. When the moon gets closer, the planet's gravity pulls on it harder, and vice versa. This squeezing and uncompressing cause friction within the moon, heating it up. Tidal force often results in geological instability, but I'm not seeing that here."

"Could members of the lost expedition have survived and done this?" Marie shifted her eyecam between Kevin and the screen.

Collins shook his head firmly. "They only had the resources to carry out their survey mission. There's no way they did this in a decade."

"Then who? The Greys?"

"No doubt about it." Brooke put another image up on the screen, this time zooming in on a different location above Triton. A space station half the size of NISS hung in synchronous orbit over the northern hemisphere. When she increased magnification further, the screen showed triangular spacecraft leaving from and returning to the station. "Whoa." An asteroid twenty kilometers in diameter rose up over Triton's horizon. Brooke focused the shuttle's cameras on the giant rock and magnified it. Scaffolding affixed to the face of the asteroid enshrouded a pyramidal spacecraft carrier under construction. Hundreds of spider-like robots crawled throughout the pyramid, weaving the mammoth craft into existence. "It's similar to how we build carriers in the asteroid belt and the Trojans."

"I don't see how our telescopes and satellites missed all this," Kevin said. "And how have we failed to intercept one stray communications signal?"

Crimson lights flashed, casting shadows across the stubble on his face. Emergency klaxons buzzed.

Brooke gasped. "We'll have to ponder that later. Neudar shows three tri-fighters on an intercept course."

**Twenty-two—Fey**
**Neptunian System, December 2247 AD**

Adrenaline coursed through Brooke's veins. Her training and combat experience took over. "Back in your seats!" The moment the others strapped in, she fired thrusters, spun *Viking* around, and headed out of the Neptunian system. "Start charging the drive, Professor."

"It'll take another thirteen hours to clear Neptune's gravity well before we can shift."

"Can you find a way to make it work sooner? We can't outrun those bandits, not through conventional means, anyway."

"How long do we have, Major?" Collins asked.

"Based on distance and relative speed . . . about forty-five minutes, sir." Brooke turned to the professor. "Didn't you tell me gravity was just another variable in the equation?"

"Yeah, but . . ." A bead of sweat trickled down the creasing lines on Kevin's forehead. "It's theoretically possible to account for a local gravity field. I'm confident I'll figure it out eventually, but right now, the calculations get too convoluted, and it's a lot harder to predict what will happen."

"What's to stop us from trying? We can shift. We only risk destroying ourselves or ending up on the other side of the solar system."

He gave a slow nod. "The drive's matrix does have the algorithms I was working on to solve the issue. They're very preliminary, though."

She turned to Collins but avoided eye contact. "It's your call, sir."

The Security Council president tugged his collar in thought. Marie focused her eyecam on him. Thirty-five billion people hung on his decision. "One concern remains paramount," Collins said. "We cannot let these beings capture us or this ship." He looked at each of the others before speaking again. "That leaves one course of action. We make the attempt. If the shuttle brings us back, we keep it out of enemy hands. If it destroys us, we accomplish the same aim."

Brooke gave Kevin a nod and refaced her console.

"I started the power accumulation sequence when you first asked," he said. "Somehow, I knew what we would decide. T-minus five minutes."

The next five minutes felt more like hours to Brooke. Her carotid artery throbbed. The fusion reactor rumbled at max output, drowning out her heavy breathing. The vibrations shook the cramped, stuffy cabin like a baby's smart rattle.

"Well, ladies and gentlemen, this is it," Marie said to the solar system. "Seconds remain until we shift home, get blown to pieces, or end up who knows where."

Brooke kept her focus on her displays. The three tri-fighters accelerated toward *Viking*, closing the gap. The shuttle's phase drive might be the most advanced piece of technology humans had ever created, but the conventional engines were decades out of date.

"Five seconds," Kevin said. "Four, three, two, one . . . zero."

"Initiating upshift." Brooke tapped the command sequence. She heard the power buildup reach its highest pitch, felt the vibrations reach their uppermost frequency.

The whirring and shaking sputtered, waned, and ceased. Stars and space remained outside the viewports.

Glancing at Kevin, Brooke said, "It didn't work. What happened?"

"I don't know." Sweat soaked his hair, which he brushed away from his forehead. His breathing rate increased. "I'm working on it."

Anxious minutes passed.

Marie explained the situation to her viewers. Brooke imagined them sitting on the edges of their couch cushions.

She stared at the proximity timer. *Twenty-five minutes until they reach us.* She wondered whether the enemy wanted to capture the shuttle intact. It seemed likely since they hadn't fired anything long-range.

The timer read 20:16 when Kevin's hand slammed down on his console. "I can't believe this!"

"What?" Brooke asked.

"Key algorithms have been erased, thousands of lines of code deleted."

"How can that be? It worked before."

"The drive's matrix found a time-released virus set to activate after we got here."

She swallowed. "Sabotage."

"It looks that way."

"How could anyone get a virus into the shuttle's systems?" Collins's heightened tone startled Brooke. "Who has that kind of access?"

"Major Davis, my staff, the engineering team, me, and anyone with senior-level UN security clearance," Kevin said.

"Can you fix it?" Brooke asked.

He pulled at his hair. "I think so."

"Great. Then all we have to do is—"

"Unfortunately, the only way is to refresh the drive's operating system to a previous state. Rebooting from the last restore point should put it back to normal, at least in theory."

"How long will that take?"

"That's the unfortunate part. At least fifteen minutes, not counting the additional fifteen minutes needed for the drive to charge again."

"Half an hour . . ." Brooke eyed the proximity timer. Only half the time they needed remained. "We need to buy fifteen more minutes somehow." She thought of ways to delay the tri-fighters, but she couldn't coax any more speed out of the engines. The shuttle technicians hadn't installed any weapons. Only one act might give them—or at least the others—a chance.

Her stomach knotted. She didn't want to die, but she had to do it.

After pushing up out of her seat, Brooke gripped the backrest and spun around.

Kevin sat with his attention locked on his screen, busy with the OS refresh, unaware. The eyebrow not hidden by Marie's eyecam dipped in response to her sister's forlorn smile.

Brooke hadn't thought her abdomen could wrench any further, but when she caught Collins's lack of emotion, she almost heaved and fainted. *Anyone with senior-level security clearance.* Mental puzzle pieces interlocked at the periphery of her conscious mind. *I was never going down to Triton's surface. He knew this was going to happen, knew the choice I'd be forced to make.* She thought back to Europa, recalling the pair of Defense pilots who had worked with the intruder to blow up the water planet. *Somehow, the UN or part of the UN must be working with the enemy.* The notion sapped what little faith she held, like a loss of childhood innocence. *If that's the case, Collins must already know about the sabotage and wants the enemy to get hold of the shuttle. But what good would that do them if they have FTL—or do they?*

She ripped her gaze away from him, sweltering from head to toe. The fact remained that her suspicions didn't change anything. Only one thing mattered. Minutes separated the shuttle and approaching tri-fighters.

Brooke refaced Collins. "Sir, please relieve me."

He nodded. "It's the only way, isn't it?" He unfastened his harness.

"Wait, what?" Marie's eyecam darted between the two of them. "Would you mind telling the rest of the human race what's going on?"

"No time," Brooke said. "Sir, I've locked in a course for Nereid."

Collins cocked his head as he floated past her. "The eighth moon?" He settled into the pilot's seat.

"That's right." She drifted past Marie and descended the ramp to the cargo bay. "I preprogrammed the route earlier in case something like this happened. We're nearly there. If I can delay the enemy by a few minutes, you should be able to reach the moon. Use it for cover until the drive charges."

His face betrayed nothing. "Good thinking, Major. The best of luck to you."

Brooke slapped the control panel on the rear wall, opening the hatch. After stealing one last glance at a confused Marie and a concerned Kevin, she soared through the open hatch.

♦

After slipping into her flight suit, Brooke jammed a leg into her flight armor. A cursory glance showed Marie floating through the open hatch. Her twin had left her eyecam back in the cabin.

"What are you doing?" Marie asked.

"What does it look like?"

Marie stomped her foot in anger, but instead of pounding the deck, her foot and leg flailed backwards. She lurched forward, grabbing Brooke's shoulders to steady herself in the microgravity environment.

Brooke pushed back with one hand, stabilizing them both. "Damn it."

"Sorry." Marie leaned against the nose of the Starthroat and braced herself. "This is stupid. You don't have to do it."

"There's no other way, and you know it."

Her twin's eyes reddened. "Do you even stand a chance against three of those advanced ships?" Marie leaned closer and locked stares with her. "Don't you dare lie to me."

Brooke tore her gaze away. She pulled the suit up over one shoulder and slipped both arms through flexi-plated sleeves. "Probably not." The words came out almost as a whisper, carrying a finality not even she had expected. She choked up, hating herself for it.

"Then what's the point? Stop this nonsense. Come back to the cabin. We'll figure something else out."

For a fleeting moment, Brooke considered taking her sister's advice. She didn't want to throw her life away if she could help it, but deep down, she knew she couldn't stay, not if she had the slightest chance of buying her sister time to escape.

The thought froze Brooke. For over a year, she had dreamed of being accepted to the candidacy program and flying faster than light. The elation of having accomplished that had exceeded her wildest expectations, and yet, the sight of her sister's pale, tense face made her realize that some things were more important.

She pressed a button on her suit-arm's wrist, and the back auto-zipped. Ultra-strong carbon nanotubes hugged the contours of her body. "I can't because . . ." Brooke stopped short of revealing her suspicions about Collins. The knowledge might place her sister in danger. "There's no time." She slipped on her gloves, which melded to their respective sleeves on contact, creating airtight seals. "We've got less than five minutes."

"No, Kishi."

Brooke wilted at the sight of Marie's upper lip trembling.

The gravity of emotion pulled them into an embrace.

"I know." Brooke tried and failed to suppress a sob. "But my mind's made up. I have to do this. It's far more important you live than me."

Marie squeezed her tight. "No, it's not."

"Yes, it is." Brooke thought she might pop right out of her suit.

"Why would you say such a thing?"

Brooke indulged in the moment for a few seconds and then pushed her sister away. Little time remained.

Grabbing one of the handholds on the side of the Starthroat, she swung her body up into the open cockpit in one fluid motion.

After wiping the tears from her face, she reached down and collected her helmet. Grief-stricken purple eyes stared back at her from her reflection in its smooth black exterior. "Because Maya needs her mother."

Marie stared up at her. Her lips parted but no words came out.

"Now go!" Brooke yelled. "Get out so I can decompress the bay and launch."

Marie hesitated before pushing off toward the cabin.

Once the hatch slid shut, Brooke reached a hand beneath the fighter's front seat. "Sorry, Miko." She retrieved the spark injector and pricked the back of her neck.

♦

Extreme g-force hurtled Brooke's Starthroat toward Neptune. Gravgel absorbed most of the force, but a fractional amount still slammed her back into her seat. Stars vibrated outside the canopy, distorted by the gel. In one of her mental displays, she watched *Viking* plummet out of sight. Her augmented reality identified three digital triangles.

She couldn't help wondering which one of them would put her out of her misery.

*<Weapons range in twenty-three seconds, ma'am. Three bandits dead ahead. My programming requires me to recommend against engagement, given there is less than a zero-point-zero-zero—>*

*Thanks, Bob, but I prefer not to know the odds. We're doing this, regardless.* Her velocity climbed, stretching the circles under her eyes down to her cheeks. The twisting blue bands of the fist-sized gas giant expanded. The enhanced Starthroat achieved half its top speed.

*<Very well, ma'am. I did in fact calculate a ninety-nine-point-seven percent chance you would proceed in spite of my counsel.>*

She laughed out loud, releasing her pent-up terror. *Oh, Bob. Unlike me, you seem to have developed a sense of humor.*

*<Humor isn't in my programming, ma'am. Five seconds to weapons range.>*

*Ready with those targeting calculations?*

*<Affirmative, ma'am.>*

*Okay. We stick to the plan. Hold course no matter what. If this doesn't work, well, there's nothing left to say.*

*<Entering enemy weapons range, ma'am.>*

Pinpoint flashes erupted fore of her craft, and her instruments registered thirty-four warheads racing toward her. While Bob calculated their trajectories, Brooke fired her particle cannons in wide bursts. The SF-522A's enhanced targeting system increased her accuracy, allowing her to blow over half the warheads out of space.

She zigzagged her fighter in every direction, avoiding all but two of the projectiles. The survivors detonated against her force field along the underside of the Starthroat.

Blue haze fizzled outside the canopy. Energy from the blasts transferred through the field, denting the reinforced armor plating.

The force jostled her in the cockpit. Every muscle in her body tightened. Her shoulders strained against the seat harness while her brain rattled around in her skull. The gravgel distorted, blurring her surroundings.

Had she suffered the same damage in a standard model Starthroat, the explosions would have torn her fighter apart.

Bob assumed thruster control, calculated force vectors, and fired countering bursts to keep them on course.

Having weathered the initial onslaught, her Starthroat plunged toward the three tri-fighters, which scattered as she had hoped. A fraction of a second before she passed between them, Bob fired a hundred seekers in all directions.

The bandits fired countermeasures while parrying her attack with particle beams and warheads. Her shielding lit up like a fireworks display. Blinding light pierced the canopy. Brooke clung to the auxiliary control grips with all her strength and waited to be torn apart.

**Twenty-three—Bulwark**
**Neptunian System, December 2247 AD**

Marie held her breath and pressed two fingers to her neck. Her pulse throbbed.

Her nose hovered a centimeter away from one of the cabin's rear viewports. She hadn't pried her gaze from it since her sister's launch had rocked the shuttle.

By default, Marie's eyecam recorded the scene behind *Viking*, but she had shoved any thought of her journalistic responsibilities to the recesses of her mind. *Some things matter a lot more.* Red text scrolled across the bottom of her vision. Her producer demanded she say something.

Her stomach dropped at the sight of multiple explosions. Bright light propagated out from the center of a kaleidoscope pattern. Fireballs blinked in and out of existence along its edge.

She fell back, muffling a sob.

"Yes!" Kevin's voice echoed throughout the cabin.

Marie spun.

Kevin put the rear camera view up on the main screen and programmed it to follow the action. Tiny blue flames—the exhaust from Brooke's Starthroat—shot away from the epicenter of the carnage.

Marie pushed off from the rear wall and glided up behind him. "What happened?"

He looked like he might pump his fist in the air. "Brooke flew right between them, fired a bunch of missiles, and blew away one of the tri-fighters." He turned to face her. "Only two left to deal with."

"Definitely the most impressive—and desperate—maneuver I've ever seen." Collins's accent remained cool. "But celebration's a tad premature." From the pilot's seat he pointed a finger up at the main screen. One of the two surviving triangles tangled with Brooke. The other rocketed toward the shuttle. "How soon until we can shift, Professor?"

"The reboot's complete. Ten minutes until the drive charges."

Collins concentrated on his displays. "One of those bandits will intercept us in six minutes, although the major delayed it long enough to allow us to find cover. I suggest you take your seat and buckle up, Miss Davis."

While securing her safety harness, Marie directed her attention ahead. A gray dot grew bigger by the second in front of the shuttle. Navigational graphics built into the forward viewport identified the ballooning object as Nereid, Neptune's eighth moon. Length, mass, and other characteristics accompanied the red target bracketing the oblong rock.

The shuttle's cameras auto-zoomed and repositioned, keeping her sister's duel against one of the two tri-fighters centered on the main screen. A pure white beam stretched out from the bandit, missed the Starthroat by what looked like less than a millimeter, and continued off the edge of the screen.

Space combatants maneuvered nothing like planes in an aerial dogfight, Marie observed. Movements occurred abruptly rather than gradually. With no atmospheric drag, neither spacecraft banked. Instead of turning in a gradual circle, Brooke's Starthroat darted in any of three dimensions at any given instant.

Brooke's fighter launched a seeker, which zipped across the screen faster than any previous missile she had fired. The seeker struck the tri-fighter before it could react and overloaded its force field.

The Starthroat rocketed back toward the shuttle.

Having recovered, the tri-fighter fired a spread of missiles. Fireballs consumed Brooke's fighter.

Marie shrieked.

Kevin gasped.

"Now approaching Nereid," Collins said.

The shuttle rocketed along above the moon's cratered surface. The explosions surrounding Brooke's Starthroat disappeared below the horizon on the screen, replaced by rushing shades of gray. Collins dropped the shuttle to within meters of the jutting rocks.

Marie summoned her resolve and directed her eyecam forward. "The security president is searching for a place to hide until the phase drive charges," she told the viewers at home. "One tri-fighter is closing in on us with another on the way." She forced her next words out. "Major Davis is presumed dead."

"The closest bandit will reach us in ninety-six seconds." Collins reduced the shuttle's speed and darted right.

"Five and a half minutes to full charge," Kevin said.

*Viking* turned left near a small mountain. A few kilometers later it zipped right. Tense seconds passed.

A ridge rushed toward them. Collins pulled back on the control stick, directing them over the top of it.

The moment they cleared the ridge, displays flashed red and sirens blared.

"Incoming bandit," Collins yelled.

A white blur streaked past overhead.

Marie yelped.

Collins shook his head, tight-lipped, while studying his displays. "It would've been simple to destroy us, but it didn't."

"They want *Viking*," Kevin said.

"Or human prisoners." Collins dipped the shuttle down into a ravine that stretched off into the distance.

White lightning struck the canyon wall ahead of them. Rock and dust sprayed out from the impact point. Debris pummeled the shuttle's thin force field, causing the view outside to shimmer blue.

The tri-fighter hovered above *Viking* on the main screen.

"I'm receiving a transmission." Collins worked his console.

The cabin's speakers emitted screeching and hissing.

Cringing, Marie recognized the incomprehensible speech. ISN had replayed the messages from the attack on Titan numerous times. "Has the UN deciphered their language yet?"

"No," Collins replied, "but I know a demand for surrender when I hear it." He turned to the professor. "How long?"

Kevin's shoulders slumped. "Less than a minute."

Collins cut their speed and collapsed back in his seat. "We came so close . . ."

"Wait, that's it?" Marie stared at the back of his scalp. "We're giving up?"

"There's no point in running. They've got us bracketed in their sights."

"Yeah, but they've shown they're not going to kill us."

A second searing white line whizzed past the forward viewport.

Collins turned and glowered at her. "That was a lot closer. I've been in my share of combat situations, and I know what that last warning meant. 'Give up now or the next one's going through your hull.'"

Her body wilted.

"Professor," Collins asked, "the phase drive has a self-destruct mechanism, correct?"

Kevin gave a start. "It does." His console beeped. "And now that the drive's charged, we can blow ourselves to kingdom come any time."

"If we're going to die anyway," Marie asked, "why not try to escape?"

Collins stuck his chin out at the tri-fighter. "It's right on top of us at point blank range. We could never get far enough away from Nereid to upshift."

"He's right, Marie," Kevin said, "There's no way we can shift so close to Nereid. The drive can open a wormhole in near-vacuum conditions, but not when surrounded by solid rock. If we tried to shift right now, we'd rip this moon and ourselves apart in the process."

"I plan to take the enemy with us when we go." Collins almost sounded heroic. "Professor . . ." He paused, as if to consider his decision one last time. "Overload the drive."

Locking gazes with Marie, Kevin conveyed an unspoken apology.

She gave a tight-lipped nod.

He reached for his console.

"Well," Marie said to her audience, "*Viking's* maiden—and only—voyage is about to go down in history for very different reasons than we expected. Hopefully, the information we gathered will better prepare humanity to combat these invaders." She breathed in deep. "Finally, I want to say good-bye to my daughter . . ." A soft whimper escaped her mouth. "I'm going to miss watching you grow up, Maya, but I know Obaa-chan will take good care of you. I love you so very, very much."

The tri-fighter descended to within meters of the shuttle.

Kevin's fingers tapped his console, entering the destruct sequence.

The whir of the drive intensified. A whoosh-whoosh-whoosh thudded against metal. The sound rumbled through the walls from the rear of the shuttle. Marie imagined an evil robot attempting to bash its way free from its confinement.

The disgruntled drive ceased its racket, and its hum returned to normal.

"Again?" Kevin grunted.

"What is it, Professor?" Collins asked.

"Apparently, I didn't restore the operating system to a point far enough in the past. Another virus has overridden the self-destruct sequence." The lines on his forehead scrunched as he studied his readouts. "No, it couldn't be." He jerked back from his console. When he turned to Collins and Marie, his face had paled. "It's not a virus at all. Nor was the program that kept us from shifting earlier." Kevin whacked his control console with a fist. She had never seen the skinny intellectual lose his temper. "These aren't viruses. They're subroutines built into the drive system—intentionally."

"What does that mean?" Marie asked.

"It means the sabotage runs much deeper than we thought." The eerie, monotone way in which Collins said it revealed he had suspected all along.

Kevin vented his frustration with a closed-lipped growl. "Any number of people who worked on the project could've loaded a virus, but these algorithms exist within the drive's core source code. Only a member of my team could've implemented them."

"Someone wanted to strand us out here," Marie informed her viewers, "but whom and why?"

"Questions I plan to answer," Collins said, "although we have more pressing concerns at the moment." He shot the professor a glance. "Can you circumvent these algorithms somehow?"

Kevin tapped a finger on his console. "I think so. With the matrix's help, I should be able to rewrite or reroute around the rogue code."

"How long?"

Kevin blew out a long breath. "Longer than we have."

"Get started anyway."

Marie interfaced her eyecam with the main screen, allowing her viewership to see what she saw. A cylindrical docking apparatus extended from the approaching tri-fighter with a spinning drill bit protruding from the end.

"The tri-fighter must be planning to cut through the shuttle's hull." She cleared her throat, dismissing the fear from her tone. "Any minute now, we should see the Greys up close." She sent a neurofeed request to her crew at ISN Studios on New Galilei. The slimy grey body found on Titan appeared in a picture-in-picture window for the audience's benefit. "What do they have in store for us? Will they kill us? Hold us for ransom? Dissect us?" *Maybe they'll plant their eggs inside of us, and once the eggs hatch, they'll burst out of our chests like in ancient sci-fi feeds.*

She suppressed a gag. "All we can do now is wait."

The tri-fighter approaching the shuttle exploded.

Flame and shrapnel pummeled *Viking*'s force field. Blue electricity crackled, and the shuttle shook. Marie hissed as harness straps dug into her shoulders, locking her in place.

A bright blue trail of exhaust rocketed out ahead of the shuttle beyond the forward viewport. Less than a second later, a white blur darted after it.

Brooke's voice squawked from the shuttle's audio system. "Get out of there!"

Marie swallowed a squeal of delight. "It appears Major Davis survived after all."

Kevin's head swung toward Collins, who ran a hand over his bare scalp.

"Don't just sit there!" Brooke said. "Head for open space! Move!"

The security president's hands flew to the control stick. He fired *Viking's* fusion rockets, lifting them out of the ravine. Display text integrated into the forward viewport listed 3.2 gees of acceleration. The force pinned Marie back in her seat.

♦

*Two down, one to go,* Brooke thought. *As long as the last one's after me, it'll leave the shuttle—*

*<Incoming particle beam—>* Bob warned.

Brooke rolled her Starthroat. White lightning crackled past the canopy and shattered the tip of a mountain.

She kept her fighter low to the moon, leveraging its topography as cover whenever possible. White beams seared rock and ice all around her. Corkscrewing warheads pummeled the terrain. Bob fed her mind the information needed to avoid each attack and auto-targeted the Starthroat's rear batteries.

Retreating behind another mountain, she burned thrusters and spun to face her attacker. Momentum kept her fighter streaking forward along its previous course.

The tri-fighter emerged from behind the mountain.

Brooke fired the last of the upgraded Starthroat's trio of relativistic seekers. She had used the first to stun the bandit blocking her path to Nereid and the second to dispatch the craft attempting to capture the shuttle.

The r-seeker accelerated away at thousands of gees, approaching light speed. Milliseconds after she issued the launch command, the missile struck the tri-fighter, disabling its force field.

She launched her remaining conventional seekers at the top of the jagged mountain. The explosions flung shards of rock and ice up into the tri-fighter's path.

The bandit navigated the debris field.

With her particle cannons, she blew larger fragments into smaller pieces. Shards of rock and ice sliced into the unshielded tri-fighter. It weaved out of control and crashed into the moon's surface.

Brooke sunk into her seat and exhaled.

Standing her fighter on end, she rocketed up and away from Nereid. *Viking* resembled a wandering star on course out of the Neptunian system.

"Is everyone okay?" she asked over the comm net.

"We thought they got you when we first reached the moon," Marie said.

"I burned my retrorockets, and the seekers collided in front of me. You must've lost me behind the fireball."

"Glad to hear your voice." Kevin sounded confident. "I think I've got the drive working. T-minus one minute until it reaches full charge."

"Great. Let's get out of here." She accelerated hard. "I should reach you in time. Open the hanger bay doors in thirty seconds."

"Fearless superwoman dispatches three bad guys and saves the most historic day in human history," Marie said. "Now, that's a scoop."

"This A-model Starthroat was the difference—" Brooke gasped.

*<Enemy carrier emerging from the far side of Nereid, ma'am.>*

"Oh my . . ." Kevin said.

The carrier rose up over the moon's horizon like a pyramidal sun. It measured about the same length as a UN spacecraft carrier but possessed far greater girth.

*<The enemy carrier is launching tri-fighters toward Viking, ma'am. Twenty in total.>*

*Twenty? How long until the shuttle comes into range of their weapons?*

*<Forty-two seconds, ma'am.>*

"Max charge," Kevin said. "We can shift any time."

*I'll reach the shuttle before the bandits, but there's no way I can maneuver into the bay in time.* Brooke's chest deflated. "Sir, upshift now. Don't wait for me."

"Are you sure, Major?" Collins said. "You'll be stranded here."

"I can head back on my own, sir. Jupiter's only three or four months away."

"Your fighter might have enough fuel for the trip," Kevin said, "but how much emergency food and water do you have onboard? A week's worth? And your muscles and bones will atrophy in microgravity, if you don't go crazy first. You'd never survive, Brooke."

"Seriously," Marie said, "we're not leaving without you." Momentary silence consumed the comm net. "We're not leaving her, right?" Static. "You both can't be serious."

"Even if you plot a course toward me now"— Her mental displays showed *Viking* moving in her direction —"which it looks like you've done, we'll only gain a few seconds. That's not enough time for me to slow down, align my fighter with the bay, and land. That would leave us too exposed. A single shot could take us both out."

"Can't you eject and let us pick you up?"

"Retrieving me would take longer than docking."

"How about crash-landing into the bay? So what if it's not a perfect landing?"

"No, the timing required to place my moving fighter into the moving shuttle's cargo bay is beyond my abilities. I'd damage the shuttle. Then none of us would get out of here."

"Fine. How about—"

"Marie, please stop it. There's no other—"

"No, you stop it." Marie's heightened tone wavered. "I thought you were dead I don't how many times. Don't put me through this again."

"Marie, I . . . I don't know what to say except . . . I'm sorry, and I—"

*<Pardon the interruption, ma'am, but I can do it.>*

Brooke blinked away the tears blurring her vision. "Do it? Do what?"

*<I can determine the exact velocity and trajectory required to bring us into Viking's cargo hold as well as execute the hyperspace shift within the given time restraint, ma'am.>*

*"Really?"*

*<Affirmative, ma'am. A complex set of calculations would be involved, including continual course and thrust adjustments. I would, however, require complete control of both the SF-522A and Viking's flight systems.>*

She knocked the idea around in her head. If the consequences of failure would only affect her, she would attempt it without hesitation. "I don't know. I guess it's up to everyone else."

"You have to try it." The words leapt out of Marie's mouth.

"I'm with Marie," Kevin said. "If there's a way we can all get home together, we have to make the attempt."

Collins took his time responding. "I don't know how comfortable I am with your matrix assuming control, but I seem to be outnumbered. All right, Major. I'm transmitting the shuttle's command codes."

Brooke had half-expected him to cite an excuse why the maneuver was too dangerous, perhaps something about how risking both their lives and the phase shuttle wasn't worth saving her. She might've agreed with him if he had said it. *Either Collins is putting on one hell of a performance, ad-libbing when things haven't gone his way, or I've misjudged him.* The pang in her gut argued the former.

Precious few seconds remained in which to act, so she buried the feeling deep down.

She relinquished control of the Starthroat to her AI matrix. "Okay, Bob. You've never let me down before. I trust you."

*<Thank you, ma'am. I shall endeavor to perform this task to the best of my ability.>*

Bob accelerated the Starthroat at max thrust, slamming Brooke back into her seat. She watched the shuttle grow larger. Bob altered its orientation so the ventral bay doors faced her fighter.

*We're coming in too fast.*

*<The SF-522A's velocity and acceleration are within calculated tolerances, ma'am.>*

*I know, I know, but I get squeamish when I'm not in control.*

*<An understandable human reaction, ma'am. Thirteen seconds to dock—>*

Lateral force whipped Brooke to the side. *Viking* spun out of view as a beam of white light lit up the canopy. Bile filled her mouth.

Brooke thought she heard Marie cry her name.

"What . . . ?" she asked in a daze.

*<The lead bandit has entered weapons range, ma'am.>*

"If . . . if they're threatening the shuttle, we . . . we need to abort."

"It's firing again," Collins yelled.

Brooke's mind reached out for neurotronic control.

*<Five seconds to docking, ma'am. The equations now include extra variables, but I'm still able to execute this maneuver. Please trust me.>*

Dizziness twisted conscious thought, forcing her will to recede. "Okay, Bob." Her vision blurred.

*<Docking now, ma'am.>*

Jarring force threw her forward.

## Twenty-four—Promulgation
## New York City, January 2248 AD

The passersby scuttled along the multi-tiered streets of Times Square, breathing masks held tight against their faces. Men with polychromatic hair, women in smart suits, and people of all ethnicities and social classes brushed elbows, shoving their way past one another.

A brusque pedestrian bumped into a teenage boy, dislodging the neurophones wrapped around the teen's triple-spiked hairdo. Searing riffs and synthesized distortions ceased direct bombardment of his brain's pleasure centers. The neurophones fell to the sidewalk as the inconsiderate stranger disappeared amongst the mass of people. Rapid footsteps trampled and snapped the thin device into pieces.

The teen spat a curse over his shoulder, but he failed to identify the person who had collided with him.

A grunt and a stomp later, he resumed stride, forced to pay attention to the useless blather of the world outside his head. The establishment's standard propaganda emanated from the hundreds of billboard-sized screens tuned to ISN.

"Welcome to this edition of IntraSolar News for Tuesday, January fourth, 2248. I'm Marie Davis, reporting live from ISN Studios in New Galilei." The newswoman's transparent projection hovered above café tables, displayed on e-slips, and filled floating screens. Her smile brightened an otherwise drab day in the sprawling metropolis.

The teen scowled.

Below her, the local weather report for New York City appeared. An animated gray cloud rumbled next to a timer ticking down to the exact second the sky would start raining. The forecast included a temperature of fifty-two degrees Fahrenheit and a current Air Quality Index of Unhealthy.

The anchorwoman straightened the stack of e-slips on the desk in front of her. "Today's top story is the return of *Viking* from its almost-tragic maiden voyage to Neptune."

Footage of the shuttle puncturing space-time replaced her image. Space churned around a small, widening aperture. A streak of light leapt from it and contracted to the shape of the shuttle. Then the aperture shrank and disappeared. Black waves propagated outward through space. The ripples looked like the aftermath of a stone tossed into a pool of oil.

The news lady's round face returned to the screens. "This footage, recorded by a UN Defense satellite, shows *Viking* emerging from hyperspace. The shuttle reappeared between the orbits of Jupiter and Saturn, three hundred million kilometers distant from its intended return coordinates. It took *Terminus* six days round-trip to return us to Callisto." She picked the stack of e-slips up off the countertop and flipped through the pile for effect. "This was the scene three days ago when we disembarked."

The opening of the shuttle's hatch played across screens adorning high rises and vending machines. Professor Kevin Sommerfield emerged first, followed by Marie Davis, who helped Major Brooke Davis down the steps to the deck. A medical team lifted her onto a stretcher.

"Major Davis has been hospitalized for injuries relating to her astounding rendezvous maneuver with *Viking*. Based on data from the shuttle's systems provided courtesy of the UN, as well as testimony by the crew, ISN analysts have reconstructed what happened in those tense final moments near Neptune."

The teen watched the displays in Times Square project a reenactment. In the center of each screen hung a small reflective cylinder—*Viking*—in the blackness of space. Its bay doors opened, peeling away from the center of the shuttle. Then a speck of light—Major Davis's Starthroat—entered the screen from the top-right, following a curved path toward the shuttle. A second speck—a tri-fighter—emerged from the left side of the screen. White beams of light leapt from the extrasolar craft toward the Starthroat, which fluttered about like a mosquito, avoided the weapons fire, and disappeared into the bay.

*Viking* grew brighter, flashed, and disappeared. Ripples propagated through space. The tri-fighters on the left edge of the screen exploded when the waves reached them.

Marie returned to the screens. "*Viking* shifted in the presence of significant gravity, which damaged its phase drive beyond repair. Words cannot convey how ecstatic I am that it held out long enough to—"

The teen descended the stairs into the hypersonic subway station.

♦

A businessman sat on a park bench in Sydney, Australia, waving to a vending machine.

The machine's simple AI caught on to his desire to make a purchase after about ten seconds. It zoomed over to him like an eager puppy, bumping into a water fountain in the process. The mechanical whirring of its motor grew to a whine, almost sounding frustrated. Three changes of direction later, the dilapidated machine worked its way around the impediment. A crack in the sidewalk nearly toppled it before it reached him.

<How can I help you, sir?> its upbeat, synthesized tone asked. <Would you care to try the new Schweppes Anti-Aging Cream Soda? Only nine hundred ninety-nine dollars.>

The man shook his head. "Just today's edition."

<IntraSolar News for Thursday, January sixth, 2248. Do I have permission to charge your account, sir?>

He lowered his net specs down over his eyes and approved the purchase. "Yes."

One of the ads playing on the machine's rectangular body flipped to a display, which indicated the details of the transaction. <Your purchase is complete, sir.> A slip of nanoplastic one-tenth of a millimeter thick jutted out from a slot in its midsection.

The man lifted his specs and furrowed his brow. "No direct download?"

<I'm sorry, sir, but this basic unit lacks a SolNet uplink.>

He sighed and grabbed the e-slip. An ad for a sports car played across its smooth surface. He grumbled. He would have to wait for the ad to finish before he could watch any of the articles.

"Can I interest you in anything else today, sir? Martian Mint Gum? A Callisto Crunch Bar? Buy any two items, get a third of equal or lesser value free."

"No, thank you."

"Okay, sir. If you change your mind, I'll be nearby." The machine spun and wheeled off after an unsuspecting couple. Laser-grafted graffiti, replete with artful profanity, covered the back of its faded body.

The man leaned back against the bench. The ad finished, allowing him to flick through the e-slip's feeds.

He stopped at a stream entitled *Point/Counterpoint*. Two news correspondents stood in a studio on opposite sides of a high table. A holographic scale model of Red Rock City on Mars covered the wall behind them. Their stern voices grated into one another as the debate raged.

"It doesn't make any sense, Holly," the first correspondent said. "How could the Greys have settled Triton without us realizing?"

The other correspondent leaned forward and smirked. "You forget how big space is, Dan. Neptune is four and a half billion kilometers away from Earth and three-point-seven billion from Jupiter. It's way out there."

"But how could every UN Defense satellite and scientific probe fail to identify a terraformed moon?" Dan smoothed his tie, which sported a bouncing ISN logo, and perused an e-slip. "Latest expert analysis states the terraforming effort began about a century ago. Are you kidding me? We can locate microbial life on exoplanets a thousand light years away, but in the last hundred years, we've failed to notice a habitable moon in our own solar system?"

"That's the overriding question, isn't it?" Holly faced the camera and straightened the sleeves of her blazer. Its plaid patterns shifted and zigzagged like an ancient screensaver. "We've got an expert on the line who we hope can shed some light on this subject." The vid toggled to a split-screen with Holly on the left and a woman in uniform on the right. "Lieutenant Maria Mitchell is a tactical astronomer for UN Aerospace Defense. Thank you for joining us, Lieutenant."

"It's a pleasure to be here, Holly," Mitchell said.

"So tell us . . ." The left split-screen showed Dan, who placed both palms on the table. "How did we miss the settlement of Triton?"

"Defense has a number of theories. We think the Greys might have the ability to block or alter our instrument readings. High resolution telescopes directed at Triton continue to show the lifeless ball of rock you'd expect. The Greys could also be using holotech on an immense scale. Or perhaps they're employing light-refraction or cloaking technology, although if that were the case, they'd probably cloak their ships. Another possibility is altering local space-time to induce a time distortion effect, causing us to see back to a point in the past before they terraformed the moon. We're not certain what they're doing or how they're able to do it. The only thing we do know is *Viking* was finally able to see the truth up close."

"So," Holly said, "we can't see them, but shouldn't we have intercepted a stray communications signal in the last hundred years?"

Mitchell shook her short brown hair. "No, actually. We believe they communicate via a technology similar to phase tunneling. We've just begun implementing PT, so we haven't possessed the ability to intercept this type of advanced signal until recently. Phase communications don't travel through normal space. They pass through wormholes in and out of hyperspace. The possible entry and exit points are infinite, which makes the signals much harder to intercept."

Dan jabbed a finger into the table. "Perhaps there's a simpler explanation. Conspiracy theorists think the UN is staging this whole thing. They claim there are no exobeings. What do you say to that, Lieutenant?"

"That's beyond absurdity," Mitchell replied. "Think about what you're implying. Settling the Moon, Mars, and Jupiter has required the combined effort of humanity over the course of multiple centuries. How could you hide the misappropriation of resources on such a large scale? The settlement of Triton began back when humans had taken the first steps on the moons of Jupiter. Such a conspiracy wouldn't have been feasible even if the nations of the world had worked together behind the general public's back."

The man on the park bench swiped his finger across the e-slip, jumping ahead to a later point in the debate.

"—and UN investigators continue to hunt for the shuttle saboteurs," Dan said. "But according to a reliable source, they're not optimistic given how many private companies and individuals were involved in the project."

"Let's back up for a moment, Dan," Holly said. "The shuttle was sabotaged." She over-enunciated her last word while staring down the camera. "Let that sink in for a moment. Some person—some human being—may have wanted the Greys to get their hands on *Viking*."

"Not necessarily." Dan waved a finger at her. "Whoever planted that virus in the shuttle's systems wanted its maiden voyage to fail, but they couldn't have known what *Viking* would encounter at Triton. Perhaps the saboteurs did it for no other reason than to prove they could. No, the fact that sabotage almost allowed the Greys to commandeer the shuttle is pure coincidence."

"I don't know if I buy that, Dan. A saboteur would've programmed the virus to prevent the first flight. However, the virus didn't activate until the crew attempted to shift back home."

"Maybe the goal was to strand them out there?"

"Okay, but if not for the Greys, then why? What was the point?"

"Who knows? But consider the full extent of what you're saying, Holly. If someone planted the virus to help the Greys nab the shuttle, it means humans are in league with them. It means humans knew these extrasolar beings were out there, and it means, quite probably, these humans are conspiring in the genocide of their own race."

Holly jerked back from the counter. "Now hold on a minute. Let's not rocket to conclusions. Genocide? Do we really think the Greys intend to wipe out the human race?"

"So what's your theory, then?" Dan asked. "Why're they here?"

"The fact is we still don't know. If they intended genocide, you'd think they'd attack more often and in greater force. All they've done is destroy the Huygens colony." She waved an arm in the air. "That's one attack in the last hundred years, not counting the shuttle incident, which we might've provoked. In my book, what we've seen so far hardly qualifies as intent to exterminate."

Dan folded his arms. "If they're intelligent life—which, as a spacefaring culture, we have to assume they are—then they're not stupid. They must be biding their time, studying us, gauging our weaknesses, searching for the easiest way to wipe us out."

"I think you've seen too many bad science fiction feeds, Dan. Why would intelligent exobeings expend the resources to travel trillions of kilometers to kill us?"

"I don't know, but who can understand an inhuman mind? We still haven't been able to talk to them, to decipher their language. We know nothing of their culture. We refer to them as 'the Greys' because we still don't know what they call themselves. And the only reason we know what they look like is because of the corpse recovered at Huygens—which, for all you skeptics out there, was found to be one hundred percent authentic. The thing's got a DNA structure unlike anything on Earth."

Footage of the grey exocorpse appeared in a picture-in-picture window to Dan's right. The body lay on an operating table, its chest and lower body covered by a white sheet. The caption below the image stated the body resided at the UN MedCenter in New York.

"These beings might not function according to reasoning we can understand," he said. "Destroying other life might be instinctual for them."

Holly blew out an exasperated sigh. "The Greys tried to capture the shuttle intact. They could've destroyed it, but they didn't. I think that rules out instinctual carnage. I submit they want to learn about us and our technology. They may simply be curious. This whole mess might be one big misunderstanding."

"They probably wanted to capture *Viking*'s crew so they could study them. The better they learn our physiology and psychology, the better equipped they'll be to take us out. I doubt they have any interest in the shuttle or its technology because theirs is superior. If they're here, they must already have FTL capability."

"The Greys don't have to possess FTL," Holly said. "They could've traveled here over the course of thousands of years. Generational ships. Cryogenic freezing. Embryonic transference. There are plenty of slower, less ideal methods of traversing interstellar space. Spending multiple lifetimes getting here might make them awful eager to get their hands on the phase drive."

"They traversed untold distances over far-stretching time periods and arrived, coincidentally, only a hundred years before we developed FTL? I find that hard to—"

"Nobody knows what's going on." The man on the park bench rose to his feet. On his stroll back to the office, he pressed the e-slip's recycle icon and tossed the device aside. The slip crumbled to biodegradable dust the moment it struck the ground.

♦

An eleven-year-old girl sat next to her mother in a restaurant in Tokyo, Japan. The girl kept her specs in her lap below the table top, surfing SolNet in stealth.

Major Brooke Davis's voice squawked from the specs in censored English. "Marie, get that"—Bleep—"cam out of my face."

Her mom's gaze descended upon the girl's lap. Parental nostrils flared.

The girl read her mother's irises as clearly as the text on the slip. *Motoko, put that thing away.* The stern voice echoed throughout her head as if her mother possessed telepathic powers.

Motoko stared down at her specs.

"C'mon, Major." Marie Davis's response emanated from the device on low volume. "Your fans want to get to know you."

With a defeated sigh, Brooke sank down into the hospital bed, picked a slip up off the covers, and stared at it.

She flung the slip toward the cam. "Who cares what my favorite color is?"

Motoko's mom leaned toward her and whispered, "That woman is hardly a good role model. Now, put that thing away."

*Not a good role model?* The girl swiped a finger across the slip, selecting a different vid feed. *Here she is getting the most important award ever for bringing* Viking *back home!*

Brooke stood beside the president of the UN Security Council on stage. With two hands, Edward Collins pinned the Medal of Honor on her dress uniform. Applause erupted.

Motoko's mother pried the specs out of her grasp.

The girl's torso slumped. Disappointment burned in her chest, and she glared at the table. *I don't care what you say. Someday, I'm going to be a pilot like Major Davis.*

With a mischievous smile, she grabbed a set of chopsticks, held one stick in each hand, and aimed at the lion-dog statue near the wall. Then she made spitting noises and shook the sticks, pretending to shoot the statue with particle beam turrets.

♦

Marie stood inside the UN General Assembly Hall, fighting for a decent angle against the hundreds of reporters crammed toward the back of the room.

After settling into a semi-comfortable stance, she enabled her eyecam and began shooting. The date appeared in the bottom-right corner of her mind's eye: January 24th, 2248.

ISN had sent her straight to UN Headquarters the moment she returned to Earth from Callisto, and with good reason. An event more historic than the phase shuttle flight loomed imminent.

Five thousand dignitaries filled the rows of seats lining the circular hall. Those present included the elected officials of each terrestrial nation and space colony as well as the leaders of every separatist political group. The lines on the faces of bureaucrats struggled to hide the tension and unease. Marie wondered how many of them had managed to sneak concealed microweapons past security. *An untimely glower might be enough to cause a massacre.*

People had never filled this place to capacity as far as she knew.

She zoomed in toward the front of the hall. A holographic UN emblem the size of a parade balloon hovered in front of a gold backdrop. Three-story-tall screens adorned the curved walls to either side. Below the emblem stood the iconic marble podium from which the UN secretary-general would make her speech.

The president of the General Assembly, Francisco Muñoz, stepped up to the podium and cleared his throat. The billboard-sized screens magnified the graying man's face. After the many voices quieted, he spoke. "Thank you all for convening on such short notice. I'd like to offer special thanks to those of you who have set aside your differing viewpoints in order to attend."

A low snort escaped Marie's nose. *Differing viewpoints, huh?*

"Ladies and gentlemen, we all know why we're here, so let's get to business. Please welcome the UN secretary-general, Danuwa Ajunwa."

Everyone in the hall stood, watching without applause while Ajunwa ascended to the stage. The aged leader took her time, stepping with grace and dignity. After reaching the podium, she gazed out at the audience before speaking.

Marie focused her eyecam on Ajunwa's face as the woman glanced from one side of the room to the other, nodding. Lines creased her forehead, and black braids with streaks of gray fell from her patterned headscarf like the leaves of a mighty tree. Marie felt her presence all the way at the back of the hall.

"It's good to see this place full," Ajunwa said, smiling. "I hope this day finds you and your families in good health." Her loud, booming tone enveloped the hall. Goose bumps popped up on Marie's arms. "One month ago, the faster-than-light spacecraft *Viking* discovered the extrasolar settlement of Triton. The Greys terraformed the moon, meaning they've been there observing us for at least a century. This is beyond unsettling." Her face grew stern, tense. "Especially since the attack on the Huygens colony—the one where we learned of the exobeings' existence—wasn't the first attack after all. It turns out the separatist group who claimed responsibility for the attack on the Artemis water treatment plant was lying and did so only to draw attention."

Ajunwa looked up at one of the floating screens. Each display showed a grainy image of a tri-fighter above the surface of Europa. "Our most sophisticated matrices have reconstructed these images from fragments of jammed satellite surveillance feeds. They reveal how the Greys caused the destruction of Artemis and the death of fifty thousand people months before Huygens." Her head swung back to face her audience. "Which begs the question, just how long have these exobeings been meddling in our affairs?"

Nervous whispers echoed throughout the assembly hall.

"Aerospace Defense is in the process of investigating this question," Ajunwa said, "but right now, the length of time the Greys have been here or how they've managed to hide themselves isn't important." She stepped away from the podium and paced the right wing of the stage. "A few months ago, we laid down arms. For the first time in years, human beings stopped fighting one another, and that peace has held steady thus far." She halted, whirled, and raised her hands. “My fellow leaders, the time has come to bring an official end to our petty conflicts.”

As she strode back toward the podium, she said, “The Greys’ objectives remain a mystery, although their attacks imply less than beneficial intentions. We cannot continue to allow them to destroy colonies and take lives, but we cannot stand divided against them. If they should choose to threaten our survival as a species, we must show a united front. We must put our differences aside and focus on the one thing we all have in common, our humanity. Only by combining resources can we ensure victory.”

Ajunwa picked an e-slip off the podium and waved it in the air. “And so, my brothers and sisters, I implore you to sign the armistice I have drafted, which will guarantee the salvation of every man, woman, and child. Let us come together for the greater good of all mankind.”

The UN secretary-general marched down the steps and out of the hall.

Thousands of conversations erupted.

♦

A woman stood in front of the kitchen sink in her home in New Galilei, washing dishes. She could have stuffed her dinnerware into the dish recycler, but she preferred the manual task. It helped her think, and she rather enjoyed the feel of the sudsy water on her skin.

She gazed out the window above the sink. Her eight-year-old granddaughter bounded about the yard, spinning a holo-hoop around her waist. She kept it churning with minimal effort, focusing her attention on one of the games projected from the top of the hoop.

Today’s imitation sky possessed a deep blue tint. Puffy white clouds floated along, flickering. Sometimes, the woman almost forgot she resided on a moon hundreds of millions of kilometers from Earth.

A plate slipped from her grasp and drifted downward. On Earth, the good china would have plummeted to the floor and shattered to pieces. Here on Callisto, she had time to bend down, hold her hand out, and catch the plate like a sinking balloon.

She set the plate in the dish rack and pressed her finger to the window. The integrated display screen came to life, showing a transparent anchorwoman in the pane.

The woman dipped her hands back into the soapy water, which swished in slow motion. She felt around for the next dish and scrubbed while listening.

“Welcome back to this edition of IntraSolar News for Thursday, January twenty-seventh, 2248. I’m Marie Davis. For the past three days, the UN General Assembly has convened in special session to discuss the secretary-general's proposed armistice. Separatist parties from South America, the Middle East, and Russia were the last to sign the peace agreement less than an hour ago. All 4,967 nations, colonies, and groups have agreed to the terms of the armistice, which includes immediate military consolidation and eventual government centralization. The fighting has officially ended."

Scenes of people celebrating in the streets of cities around the solar system played across the window pane.

The news lady's image returned. "This is the greatest level of unification the human race has achieved in its history. Many experts see this as the first step toward a true united solar government and—hold on a second."

The woman stopped drying the bowl in her hands. She devoted her full attention to the newscast.

Marie Davis put one finger to her ear and listened. A frown formed on her young face. "IntraSolar News has just received a disturbing report." Her symmetrical features tensed. "UN Defense's deep space sensor grid has detected a fleet of spacecraft en route to the Jovian system. At this time it is unknown whether—"

The bowl slipped from the woman's inattentive hands. She didn't bother to halt its glide to the floor.

## Twenty-five—Decrescent
## Jovian System, February 2248 AD

The sun's rays reflected off Jupiter's engulfing presence. The gas giant illuminated local space like a spotlight the size of a thousand Earths. Brooke's canopy tinted, dimming the light. The gravgel refracted glare out of her field of vision. Twinkling streamers dangled in her peripheral vision.

She squeezed the auxiliary control grips, but the act did little to calm her apprehension about the coming skirmish.

Her gaze magnified the 960 multinational fighters holding position in front of her: Chinese Dragonflies, Russian Foxbats, South American Condors, UN Starthroats, patchwork separatist craft, and more. Twenty UN spacecraft carriers waded among the fighters like whales swimming in a school of fish. The bright reds and blues and yellows of plasma exhausts hung in space like Christmas tree lights. Jupiter's peanut-shaped ninth moon, Themisto, dominated the scene beyond them.

For the first time in years, humankind's once-disparate forces refrained from firing at each other. Instead, they had banded together to fight against a common enemy.

Now, she would lead them into battle as the Jovian Fighter Wing Commander.

Despite humanity's newfound cooperation, projections by UN statisticians gave them, at best, a fifty-fifty chance of fending off the Greys. The approaching enemy fleet consisted of three pyramid carriers. Each packed the firepower of ten UN carriers and could launch at least twenty tri-fighters. Strategists theorized the Greys wanted to steal humankind's FTL technology. The invaders' projected destination, Callisto, seemed to support this assumption, although Brooke didn't know what to think.

While contemplating how to turn the odds in humanity's favor, she had dreamed up a brilliant addition to the top brass's defense strategy. Given her suspicions regarding members of the UN working with the Greys, she refrained from bringing the idea to General Douglas's attention. If she informed him, Collins might learn of it and inform his colleagues.

She didn't understand why the Greys didn't obliterate the human race with the commander-in-chief of its armed forces on their side. There had to be more to things, a hidden agenda she couldn't yet discern. The UN officers who tried to kill her on Europa, her confrontations with the tall pilot, General Douglas's order of silence, the sabotage of the shuttle, and Collins's attempt to orchestrate her death convinced her of that much.

Instead, she raised the idea with Captain Hasluck, *Terminus*'s skipper. After initial reluctance, he agreed to implement it without informing their superiors. The plan increased the chances of success to eighty-twenty, his tacticians said, although it demanded a sacrifice with possible repercussions. If it worked, people would forgive the cost. If it didn't, no one would remain alive to object.

"Hostile fleet now passing inside the Hill sphere," *Terminus*'s flight controller reported over the comm net. "Enemy carrier count confirmed at three," the controller said. "They're decelerating from—wow—speeds over one percent light speed. Entering visual range now."

Brooke focused on the trio of white specks drifting against the stars in the background. Their double-pyramid shapes grew more pronounced by the minute.

*How long, Bob?*

*<Fifty-four minutes remain until enemy forces reach our defense perimeter, ma'am.>*

She opened a channel. "Group leaders, report."

The lead pilots of the groups within the Jovian Fighter Wing confirmed their combat readiness. Multinational accents bombarded her ears.

Her breathing grew heavy as her proximity timer counted down. Shivers coursed through her body even though she had sparked before launch.

She reviewed the official defense strategy again. UN tacticians had identified Themisto as the location where humanity should make its stand. The timing of the ninth moon's orbital period would bring it to within tens of kilometers of the enemy's approach vector. The invaders would have to navigate around the eight-kilometer-wide rock, which would provide cover for UN forces and serve as a launch point for surface-to-space missiles.

General Douglas had deployed the fleet in two waves. Defense Wave One consisted of two hundred and forty-five fighters and five carriers positioned beyond Themisto. They would welcome the Greys with an initial barrage, turn tail, and lure them back. When the enemy neared the moon, surface elements would bombard them. Then Defense Wave Two—the nine hundred sixty fighters and twenty carriers hiding behind Themisto, including her—would move in and finish the job.

A pang of guilt pressed into Brooke's gut. Her plan would increase the casualties suffered by the first wave and test the second wave's ability to follow orders.

When the time came, Captain Hasluck would issue commands altering the general's defense strategy. Such insubordination might mean a court-martial for both her and the captain, but it seemed a small price to pay for saving Callisto, if not the entire Jovian system.

The flight controller's voice interrupted her thoughts. "Hostile fleet has approached to within three hundred thousand kilometers of Themisto. The enemy will enter weapons range of the first wave in ten seconds."

The captain's voice boomed. "Defense Wave One, engage."

A smattering of pixels converged within her mind's eye.

Flashes of light outside her canopy forced her to squint. Space beyond Themisto erupted.

"I can't stand sitting here while all the action's over there, Angel," a pilot said.

"Stay focused, Lieutenant," Brooke said. "Your chance will come soon enough."

She studied the digital representation of the clash. *Status, Bob.*

*<The three enemy carriers have incurred minimal damage. They deployed thirty tri-fighters against the first wave. Data collected near Neptune suggests this is half of the attacking force's overall fighter complement. Four of the five first-wave carriers have sustained hull*

*breaches. Fewer than one hundred friendly fighters remain.*>

*We're losing the initial encounter as expected. Any time now, the captain should—*

"Defense Wave One, initiate withdrawal," Hasluck said.

Friendly fighters blinked out of existence as the first wave retreated

"Defense Wave One now approaching Themisto," the flight controller said. "Enemy forces in pursuit. Themisto ground elements initiating counterstrike."

Brooke's instruments registered thousands of missiles launching from the far side of the ninth moon. The complement of projectiles ranged from conventional seekers all the way to one-gram antimatter warheads.

A bright flash consumed space beyond Themisto. Brooke threw a suited arm up in front of her face until her face shield and canopy compensated.

The flight controller remained cool. "Multiple detonations detected." Her voice quivered. "One enemy carrier has suffered moderate damage but none were destroyed." She paused. "Captain, the enemy's deployed a wide-angle energy beam. It neutralized most of our missiles."

Brooke felt the fleet's collective tension rise.

"Defense Wave One has fallen into disarray, sir," the flight controller said. "Hostile fleet is targeting their weapons on Themisto. Remaining surface defenses are being wiped out. Captain, Defense Wave Two is standing by to engage on your order."

*And now, the moment of truth . . .*

"Tell them to stand by," Hasluck said.

*Terminus's* second-in-command protested in the background. "We should move in, sir. This is the best tactical advantage we're going to get. We can surround them, pin them between Themisto and our fleet. These are the general's—"

"I'm aware of the general's orders," Hasluck said. "Defense Wave Two shall hold its position until I say otherwise."

"But sir—"

"Tell Wave One to remain engaged. Keep hitting them hard."

An uncomfortable silence consumed the comm net. Brooke imagined every member of humanity's armed forces questioning Hasluck's sanity.

"Defense Wave One has been wiped out." The comm net crackled in response to the flight controller's sharp inhalation. "Hostile fleet launching additional fighters, sir. Fifty-eight total tri-fighters with two destroyed. Enemy now passing inside Themisto orbit."

Brooke's cameras zoomed in, showing the enemy carriers emerging from behind Themisto. Three white, pyramidal mountains seemed to grow out of the cratered landscape. Bright specks surrounded their mother ships like flakes in a snow globe.

"Sir," the second-in-command shouted. "We have to engage now."

The captain's tone exhibited a steadfast calm. "Hold positions." He cleared his throat. "Major, it's time."

"Roger," Brooke replied. *Here we go. Bob, detonate the charges.*

*<Transmitting destruct sequence now, ma'am.>*

Light burst forth from Themisto's canyons and craters. Crevices formed in the moon's surface, which shook and flew apart.

The pyramids and triangles darted away but failed to react in time. Lunar chunks hundreds of meters wide hurtled toward the enemy, directed by embedded thrusters. Two of the three pyramids collided with large chunks, buckled, and exploded. The third pyramid, the apparent flagship, suffered serious blows from smaller fragments. Shards of rock pelted the tri-fighters like pellets from an antique shotgun, destroying most of them.

Celebratory curse words reverberated over the comm net.

"Defense Group Two, engage," Hasluck ordered.

"Beta, Gamma, Epsilon, and Omega Groups, attack your assigned targets," Brooke said. "Alpha, Delta, Zeta, and Omicron Groups, provide support."

Fusion rockets flared. Plasma plumes of every conceivable color flung allied fighters and carriers toward the reeling enemy.

She let them go and followed behind.

*<Ma'am—>*

The fighters ahead of her scattered. *I see it, Bob*. She swung her Starthroat out of the path of a boulder-sized fragment.

Ahead, squadrons surrounded tri-fighters fleeing the debris field. Particle beams crisscrossed like a techno light show. Flash bulb explosions expanded and dissipated faster than she could blink. Force fields crackled as weapons fire and shards of rock struck home. Out beyond the chaos, she dodged a high-velocity pebble every few seconds.

Brooke directed the fighters within Defense Wave Two, deploying them to concentrate on the weakest elements of the enemy fleet and to achieve an advantage in numbers wherever possible. The upgraded Starthroats fared best against the tri-fighters, achieving one-to-one kill-ratios. The standard-model Starthroats and the rest of the less advanced spacecraft perished more often than not, so she instructed them to work in groups.

Only once did she tangle with a tri-fighter that escaped the combat zone. She dispatched the damaged bandit with an r-seeker and minimal maneuvering.

Smoking tri-fighters retreated here and there, outnumbered ten-to-one or more. The flaming hulks of the two incapacitated pyramids floated adrift in what would expand to become a new ring system. A definitive victory seemed assured.

The remaining tri-fighters self-destructed. Brooke guessed the enemy would rather commit suicide than allow their technology or pilots to fall into human hands. The notion heightened her anxiety level. *What would we find if we did capture one intact?*

Only the apparent flagship continued to offer resistance. It cleared the debris field, following a return trajectory toward Neptune.

General Douglas had said nothing about the unauthorized destruction of Themisto up to this point. Now, with the battle winding down, his voice came over a restricted command channel. "Captain, I'll require an explanation for your actions when you return." The general's calm baritone unsettled her far more than if he had shouted.

"Yes sir," Hasluck said.

"And Captain, Major . . . good work."

"Thank you, sir." The words leapt from both their mouths.

Brooke let her limbs float in the gravgel. It sounded like the general might commend their initiative rather than reprimand them. *Perhaps I overestimated the extent of this conspiracy.*

"Should we pursue the enemy flagship, sir?" Hasluck asked.

"No, let it go," the general said. "We've lost too many lives today. Have the fleet regroup and return to base."

"Yes, sir."

The general closed the channel.

The tall intruder, the self-termination of the tri-fighters, and the decision to not pursue the fleeing flagship weighed on Brooke's mind. *Bob, establish a private channel to Captain Hasluck.*

*<Channel open, ma'am.>*

"What is it, Major?" Hasluck asked.

"Captain, we have to go after that ship."

"I think General Douglas was clear on that point, Major, and I agree with him. There's been enough bloodshed. Destroying one last retreating enemy carrier won't make any difference in the long run."

"We shouldn't destroy it, sir. We need to board it."

"Major, we might yet avoid the stockade. Let's not press our luck."

"Sir, we kept my idea secret because human beings might be in league with the Greys." She laced her tone with as much emphatic determination as she could muster. "The proof we need is on that ship."

"Major, I'm still not convinced. I only implemented your plan because it increased our chances of success."

"Then why didn't you bring it to the general's attention?" She didn't wait for him to respond. "We know next to nothing about this enemy, so why wouldn't Command want us to board that ship? Is someone worried about what we might find if we do? Not going after that ship is a tactical error." She took a deep breath.

"Major, I share your concerns, but you ask too much. The brass might forgive us for blowing up Themisto. It was a lie of omission rather than direct disobedience, and it saved the day. Sending the fleet after that ship, however, would qualify as insubordination. I won't do that based on your unsubstantiated theory. I'm sorry."

Brooke smacked her armrest with a fist. The gesture lacked punch within the gravgel. Hasluck had a point, as much as she didn't want to admit it.

*I've got to find out if these invaders are exobeings. The answers are on that ship.*

She set course for the limping flagship and fired her Starhroat's afterburners.

"Major, don't do anything stupid," Hasluck said.

"Sorry, sir." She terminated the channel.

*<Ma'am, I'm receiving a remote command sequence from* Terminus. *An attempt is being made to take control of the SF-522A's systems.>*

*Block it, Bob. Close the port and change the encryption codes.*

*<Done, ma'am, with zero-point-two-eight milliseconds to spare. The remote access attempt has failed. However, I must recommend against this course of action. The probability of surviving an encounter with an enemy carrier is less than—>*

*This is something I have to do, Bob. I need answers.* Her heart pummeled her chest. *Since when did I start caring about more than flying?* Sweat soaked her skin, and she couldn't stop her limbs from shaking. *Damn withdrawal. I'm not a drug addict!*

Brooke matched the pyramid's course. It had entered open space minutes ago, velocity climbing at a stunning pace. She didn't understand how such a large ship—one carrying hundreds or perhaps thousands of people—could accelerate so rapidly.

*I feel like a mosquito trying to attack a mountain.* From a distance, the ship looked like two smooth white pyramids stuck together at their bases. Up close, the hull possessed countless protrusions, ridges, and grooves. Blocks and cylinders tens of meters tall jutted up from the sloping exterior. Particle beam and missile impacts charred sections of paneling. Crystalizing smoke vented from breaches not sealed by force fields.

*<Incoming—>*

She spun her fighter out of the way. A beam with the diameter of a house pierced the space she vacated.

Brooke fired a spread of seekers at a skyscraper-sized exhaust port. Particle beam turrets destroyed half of the warheads before they reached the pure white blaze. Her remaining seekers detonated against magnetic shielding. Electricity crackled across the impact point.

Enemy beams and missiles countered, forcing Brooke to cut her speed and fall back. It took all her concentration to avoid the attack. Explosions detonated all around her.

*<The enemy carrier's velocity continues to increase, ma'am.>*

Another salvo almost finished her.

She growled in frustration. *Bob, open a communications channel. Set it to the same frequency used by previous enemy transmissions.*

*<Done, ma'am.>*

"I know you can understand me," she screamed. "I know you're humans, and I won't let you get away with this!"

Seconds passed.

Seconds added up to minutes.

The pyramid continued to accelerate. Her Starthroat rocketed forward, requiring more and more thrust to keep pace. No further attacks threatened her.

*Why have they stopped shooting at me? Did they hear my message? Are they trying to rub my helplessness in my face?*

*<I cannot answer your questions, ma'am, but the enemy carrier has achieved a velocity greater than our maximum speed. We cannot maintain pursuit.>*

*Damn it!* She snarled and tried to coax more thrust out of the engines without success. *If we disable the speed limiter, can we keep up, Bob?*

*<Ma'am, I don't recommend—>*

*Answer the question, damn it!*

*<Without the limiter, our theoretical maximum velocity would exceed the carrier's projected velocity for eighty-two seconds unless it keeps accelerating, ma'am. However, the fusion drive will likely lose containment before then.>*

*I don't care. Do it.*

*<Very well, ma'am. I have disengaged the safeties that limit the fusion reaction rate.>*

Her mental speedometer climbed higher than she had ever seen, and her fighter shook. The gravgel blurred, no longer compensating for the increased forces, which drilled her back into her seat.

The distance to the pyramid decreased.

She fired her remaining seekers and blasted away with her particle cannons. What the ship's weapons failed to repel deflected off its force field. "Come back here!" she gasped.

*<Ma'am, the fusion drive is—>*

Her mental displays flickered and dropped offline.

She switched to manual control systems.

"Bob?"

Her matrix didn't respond.

The pulsations of an internal explosion propagated from the engines, through the frame of her fighter, and to the cockpit.

All around her, the gravgel boiled.

## Twenty-six—Consanguine
## Somewhere in Space, February 2248 AD

Disjointed images of Themisto bursting apart, interweaving beams of light, and a pyramidal landscape scintillated through Brooke's mind. *The Little Angel* receded into fiery oblivion behind the Rocky Mountains, and the explosion expanded to encompass her.

Brooke roused like a ship breaking free of atmosphere. She fluttered her eyelids and squinted. Brightness obscured her surroundings, and pain stabbed her temples. She blinked, bringing an array of glowing plasma strips into focus.

When she tried to move, she couldn't turn her head or lift her arms and legs. She could only blink and shift her eyes, or tense and relax her facial muscles.

*Am I paralyzed?* A chill surged through her body like waves rippling through liquid nitrogen. *No, no, no! I can't be paralyzed!*

She shivered at the thought of living the rest of her life in such a decrepit state. She also shivered because she felt a draft. Her skin tingled—no, not tingling, but more of a burning, crawling sensation. It didn't feel right, but at least she felt something.

Each digit twitched when she tried wiggling her toes and fingers.

She blew out a prolonged breath, feeling like a deflating aerostat.

*I'm restrained, but I don't feel any straps. Is it a force field?*

The human race didn't possess that level of technology—almost, but not quite. At present, engineers and scientists could manipulate force fields into simple shapes around objects possessing an internal power source. Encompassing star fighters and spacecraft carriers proved a simple matter, but a field tracing the contours of the human body, such as the one holding her, required far greater precision than they had achieved.

She thought of the intruder's personal force field back on Europa. *I must be aboard the enemy flagship.* Hot and cold flashes boiled her blood and chilled her bones.

With all her strength, she pushed and resisted, but she achieved little except exhaustion and an increased sense of helplessness.

"You'll hurt yourself if you persist in that endeavor, Major Brooke Davis."

She recognized the calm, well-mannered voice. It belonged to the tall pilot who had almost killed her twice.

"You know my name?" Her vocal cords rasped as if she had emphysema. "Let me go."

"I'm afraid releasing you at this juncture wouldn't be advisable."

"Let me out now!" A sweltering prickle radiated from head to toe. *Are they dissecting me? Turning me into one of them?* She gulped. "What are you doing to me?"

"Healing your wounds," he said. "You incurred severe injuries in your brave but imprudent assault against us. By struggling, you impede your treatment."

"Oh." She relaxed, but only marginally. "Who—and what—are you?"

The table beneath her tilted forward, slanting to a forty-five-degree angle so that she could see around the room. Floating cubes displayed animated simulations of her internal organs. Mechanical servo arms, counters, sinks, instrument trays, and displays furnished her surroundings.

The sterile white room looked more advanced than its equivalent back at Base HOPE, but she recognized a medical bay when she saw one.

A figure entered her peripheral vision. She shifted her gaze toward it.

The man standing next to her stood over three meters tall, taller than the tallest person she had ever seen. His forehead, nose, chin, and body appeared elongated, as if someone had stretched him like putty. His pale skin and blonde hair shared a grey, almost anemic tint, like a holoscreen lacking contrast. Other than these superficial differences, he seemed human enough.

"As you can see," he answered her question, "I'm not much different than you."

"You're not an exobeing?"

He shook his head. "If by use of the term 'exobeing' you mean extrasolar in ancestry, then no, I'm not."

While gawking at the man, Brooke sifted through the many questions vying for position in her head. She noted his white uniform coat and his black pants. The outfit resembled a military tuxedo sans buttons, pockets, or medals. The center seam had intermittent fasteners. A blue band similar to a priest's collar adorned his neck, the only decoration or hint of rank.

She opened her mouth, intending to put forth the first of many queries, but shrieked when she saw a cube display her arm.

Searing heat had ripped away most of the skin and muscle, exposing her radius and ulna bones. Necrotic black tissue charred what little dermis remained. *I must have suffered third- and fourth-degree burns when my fighter's reactor overloaded.*

The tingling sensation, she realized, didn't stem from her injuries. Her circulatory system, muscle fiber, and skin tissue regrew in slow motion. Her mutilation reversed like a time-delayed feed played backwards.

The tall man's oblong expression remained tranquil, but his occasional raising of an eyebrow betrayed a hint of concern.

"I . . . I want to see what I look like," she said.

He drew his wide lips to a thin line. "In a matter of hours, the mediquantites will have healed you. You'll appear as if the incident never took place. I see no reason for you to endure the negative psychological impact."

"I don't care. I have to see."

Her adversary hesitated before nodding to someone behind her.

A full-length mirror materialized in front of her.

She wished she had taken his advice.

The butterflies in her stomach drowned in gurgling bile. She whined in high pitch and sucked back a sob. It took all her energy to keep from fainting.

A burnt, bloodied, purple-eyed zombie stared back at her. Her body looked like a butcher had skinned her down to raw meat, hacking out the occasional chunk.

She exhaled when she saw the redness receding like a slow ocean tide, filled in by amalgamating dermal layers.

The mirror dissolved into nothingness.

Brooke clamped her eyelids shut and sucked in a succession of deep breaths.

"You may choose to consider yourself lucky," the man said. "Had your people recovered you, you wouldn't have survived."

"Why do this?" She opened her lids. "Why bring me aboard and fix me up?"

He paced in front of her. "When I heard your voice transmission and realized it was you, I convinced my superiors to hold their fire. Only after your accident transpired did we make the decision to retrieve you."

"Why do you care about me?"

He stopped pacing. "I have my reasons." His gaze remained fixed on the floor.

"If you think I'll betray the Earth," she spat, "you might as well shove me out an airlock right now."

The tall man lifted an eyebrow. "Betraying the Earth is the furthest item from our agenda." His steel-blue irises shimmered. "We intend quite the opposite, in fact."

"You've got a strange way of showing—ohhhh . . ." The room spun out of control. Her mind lost its grip on consciousness.

♦

Brooke's eyes popped open. She lay on her back, staring up at the same blue-white illumination.

The voice of a woman echoed from somewhere behind her. "Yes, master. I won't tamper with the neurofeed to the patient's implants." A beep indicated the closing of a comm channel.

*Neurofeed?* Brooke's mind strained to regain focus. "What . . . what happened?" Her vocal cords no longer rasped.

Another beep. "She's awake, Armin," the woman said.

The comm distorted the tall man's response. "I shall return at once." A final beep.

Brooke's bed tilted forward again.

The woman, presumably a physician, leaned over her. She wore a longer white coat than the tall man. With one hand she held a scanning device above her patient's head and ran it down the length of her body. "The only damage I failed to rectify was that to your nervous system," the physician said, "which occurred prior to your accident. Other than that, you've mended with greater haste than my estimates projected. You're quite the resilient little thing."

Brooke frowned at the remark, although she understood her perspective. While shorter than the tall man, the woman still dwarfed her patient.

After retrieving another device from a tray floating next to her, the physician said, "You know, he hasn't been able to stop scrutinizing his encounters with you."

"What do you mean?"

"Armin is our most accomplished pilot. He has no equal among our kind. You bested him in a one-on-one duel when he held the advantage—twice."

Pursing her lips, Brooke said, "Guess I got lucky a couple of times."

"Your expression betrays your false modesty. Triumphing against him required great skill, not luck."

"Maybe luck is one of my skills."

The physician stepped back, gray-green eyes intrigued. "Is this what is referred to as humor?"

Her patient had to think about it. "I guess so."

"You Innards are truly perplexing." The doctor resumed her scans.

"Innards?"

"Vernacular for humans occupying the inner solar system." Armin encroached into Brooke's field of vision.

"That makes you, what, an Outie?"

Armin inclined his egg-shaped head. "No less accurate than our term."

"What do you call yourselves?"

His brow dipped. "What do you call yourself? We're humans, same as you."

"I mean, your nation or group or whatever must have a name, right?"

"We have no such designation."

Brooke tried to shrug without success. "Can I move now?"

"Epidermal tissue regrowth is complete," the physician said. "She needn't remain in the infirmary any longer."

Armin drew in a deep breath. His chest ballooned. The air pressure in the room seemed to drop.

He disappeared behind her. A moment later, she found she could lean forward and sit up. The force field still pressed against her but to a lesser extent. Moving her upper body required greater than normal effort, like swimming in a viscous fluid. From the waist down she remained locked in place. *Smart*, she thought. *I can't run off, and any attack I try will pack the punch of a love tap.* Her mind replayed scenes from ancient feeds she had watched as a kid. When the bad guys captured the good guys, the heroes found ways to stage miraculous escapes. Somehow, she doubted that would work in this case.

"Thanks." She set aside her getaway plans and examined herself. Although still pink and tender in places, the skin on her arms had regrown. Someone had also fitted her into an oversized surgical gown. Her captors' inability to find clothing in her size came as no surprise given their proportions.

Brooke swung her head around, testing the regrown muscles in her neck. Predictably, they ached. She sat in an examination room, one of several along the side of a thirty-meter-wide hospital facility. Through transparent walls she saw medical personnel scurrying between rows of long beds, tending to the injured. Distant conversations—in English—jumbled together. Overhead lights flickered. Tubes and paneling dangled from the ceiling, reminding her she had almost destroyed this damaged carrier. "I guess I'm not the only one who was hurt." She suppressed a twinge of guilt.

"Speaking of which, they have need of me elsewhere." The physician exited the room.

Armin returned to Brooke's side, although he kept his distance. "This is the result of our unsuccessful assault against you." He shook his head. "We failed to foresee you would destroy a small moon."

"Why are you attacking us?" Questions overwhelmed her. "Where did you come from? How did you create a civilization on Triton without anyone knowing? How have you kept it hidden from us? Where did the infrastructure necessary to build everything come from? How can you possess more advanced technology than the rest of humanity when we have so many more resources at our disposal? Why—"

He held up a hand to silence her. His index finger measured half the width of her wrist. "Some of these questions I intend to answer. Others I cannot. For now, I'll begin by showing you." He ambled over to a cube hovering behind her and dipped his fingers into it.

The force binding her lower body dissipated to the level restraining her upper half.

She heaved her legs over the side of the bed. They dangled half a meter above the deck.

After dropping to the floor, she noticed a pair of slippers twice her size. She stuck her feet into them, and they shrank, gripping her skin.

The top of her head rose to Armin's stomach. *I feel like a kid all over again.*

Armin led her out of the room, through the medical bay, and into a hallway with five-meter-high ceilings. Square-meter sections of white composite alloy covered every surface. Blue display cubes projected from the walls every few meters.

"This way," he said.

Brooke plodded along beside the gangly pilot, the invisible magnetic field impeding her motions. She expended considerable energy keeping pace with her host. He took fluid strides that indicated minimal gravity within the ship, perhaps a tenth of a gee or less. She hadn't realized it before with the force field holding her down. Low gravity made sense, since Triton possessed about eight percent of Earth's pull. Without significant force to weigh on these people, they would've sprouted up after a few generations. The same thing had begun to happen to inner system humanity, although not as yet to this extreme. *How does the ship generate gravity without spinning, though?*

The individuals she passed towered to heights near three meters. Most directed quizzical glances her way. Others scowled in disapproval. All wore the same white and black uniforms with different-colored collars. Without exception, each person nodded at Armin in a show of respect.

After following Armin around a corner, she entered a wider corridor. Sunlight gleamed through an archway at the end.

She passed through the archway and stepped out onto a balcony. "Oh my . . ."

Hills, lakes, rivers, trees, and buildings stretched in every direction up the bowl-shaped terrestrial landscape. The sloping terrain rotated clockwise, its scenery matted to the inside of a giant rotating sphere. A haze of clouds, thicker in some areas than others, obscured her view. A central ball of light—a mini-sun—illuminated the interior. She felt like she stood inside a planet which some unimaginable force had flipped inside-out.

Not all appeared well with this artificial paradise. Forests burned. Collisions with lunar fragments had dented mountains into the countryside. Stars twinkled through hull breaches. Force fields prevented the air inside from blowing everything out into the vacuum of space.

"It's similar to NISS or New Galilei," she said, "but I've never seen such realism on this large of a scale." The biodomes on Callisto featured Earth-imitation environments with holographic skies, but they resembled mere greenhouses compared to her present surroundings.

"This is what's referred to as a Dyson Sphere," Armin said. "We've implemented it on a much smaller scale than the idea's originator envisioned and without a real star in the center."

"I think I've heard the term somewhere—wait, you said 'sphere,' yet this ship's exterior has the shape of two pyramids stuck together at their bases."

"You're familiar with ball bearings, yes?"

Brooke nodded slowly. "This sphere must rotate inside the double pyramid. That's what generates the gravity."

He dipped his chin.

"I'll bet the sphere spins within some sort of gravgel, which cushions the biosphere during high-g acceleration."

"Precisely correct." He stepped over to the railing and pointed up.

She leaned forward and zoomed in on the sky. A trio of thick metal pillars stretched away from the mini-sun and intersected with the landscape. "There's a triple axis, which must provide structural integrity and help drive the rotation."

He turned to her. "Your powers of deduction equal your prowess in combat."

The comment flattered her, but she dismissed the feeling. He still qualified as the enemy, and she remained a prisoner aboard his ship, one that had attacked the Jovian system. *I have to keep my guard up.* "A full biosphere seems like overkill for a warship."

"Who says this is a vessel of destruction? Our intentions for creating such an environment have nothing to do with military conquest." He gripped the railing. "No, these ships were built for conquest of a different sort." He stared out beyond the landscape. "The conquest of the stars."

She jerked her chin forward. "It looks like you've got everything you need for your journey except a proper means of propulsion."

"Indeed."

"I don't get it." Brooke indicated their surroundings by sweeping her arm. "You've shown me technology beyond what we 'Innards' have accomplished, yet you haven't developed FTL capability?"

Armin shook his head. "That advancement has thus far eluded us. You said it yourself. Inner system humanity has greater resources and many more minds to devote to the problem."

*Minds like Kevin's*, she mused.

"We're proficient at working with what we're given, but ingenuity is not our strong suit."

She pushed back from the railing. "What you're given?" Mental gears spun. "You mean, from the inner system humans working with you?"

"Yes."

"Who are they?"

"Those responsible for all of this? They are who created us, gave us purpose."

"Created you? You mean they cloned your race?"

"Yes."

"And these same creators secretly terraformed Triton and birthed your civilization a hundred years ago?"

"Yes, although their plan predates us by many years."

"Really?"

"In a way, they're our gods."

"Gods, huh?" She snorted. "So what do these 'gods' call themselves?"

"The Vril."

"The Vril?"

"Yes." Armin kept his focus on the rolling landscape. "We're their society's vision, a vision of a better humanity."

The implications twisted into her gut. "This secret society wants you to exterminate the rest of us? That way, their new, improved human race can take over."

"No, no, no." He swung his head from side to side. "We hardly intend genocide."

"I don't get it. Why attack us? Why kill tens of thousands of people?"

"I shall answer your question by posing another." He faced her. "What would the end result have been had the separatist movement continued?"

She lifted a heavy finger to her chin. "Territories would've kept seceding, and the fighting would've spread. The American Colonies and European Union might've eventually split, bringing about the collapse of the UN Sooner or later, somebody would've stolen or developed an antimatter device and detonated it. The outlook was grim."

"And what's the current state of the Earth?"

"Well, global warming and pollution are at all-time highs. Saving the planet has taken a backseat to holding the fragile solar economy together. The experts think Earth's deserts may become uninhabitable within a century or two, and—" The point to Armin's line of questioning hit her like the wrench she'd taken to Jeff's nose. It seemed like a lifetime ago. "No . . ."

"I see the truth has dawned on you at last."

Brooke staggered backwards. "Keeping your existence a secret. All the attacks. Posing as exobeings. Everything has been orchestrated to stop the fighting." She pressed her hands to her mouth and tried to control her breathing.

"We wish only to bring humanity together in peace."

"Peace by mass deception." The plots of old science fiction feeds filled her head, movies where the human race rallied together to defeat evil alien invaders hell-bent on eradication.

"We view it as saving you from yourselves. It's the main reason for our existence."

"But it's a lie."

"Lies have shaped human history. How many butchers have been lauded as heroes? How many religions have promised the illusion of salvation? How many secrets have been withheld by governments in the best interest of its populace? Sometimes a lie that ensures one's survival is preferable to a fatal truth."

"What 'truth'? You think we'll destroy ourselves if left to our own designs?"

Armin shrugged. "Basic human nature might argue so. Human beings thrive on conflict. In prehistoric times, you expended great effort to survive. If you hadn't evolved to accept and even welcome the struggle, you wouldn't have developed the resolve necessary to perpetuate yourselves this far."

"I happen to agree, but such theories don't justify what you're doing."

"Our leaders wrestled with the same ethical dilemma. After weighing the consequences of many possibilities, they chose this course of action. Therefore, we must proceed with the belief that our actions will benefit humanity in the long run despite the short-term loss of life." He clasped his hands behind his back. "For tomorrow."

Brooke clenched a fist. "Will your actions really lead to a better tomorrow?" A surge of conviction made her flush. "Nothing you could ever say would make lying and killing right."

Her host stepped away from the railing, studying her with eyes the color of a gray terrestrial sky. "I've failed to make you understand." He hung his head and sighed.

She lifted an eyebrow. "Why do you care what I think?"

"You asked me why I brought you aboard and spared your life."

The artificial sunlight had dimmed since their conversation began. Early dusk tinted the landscape to shades of amber.

"I know you developed a kind of respect for me since you've never lost before," she said.

"I would characterize my feelings as curious admiration. I couldn't let pass the opportunity to meet you face to face."

"You have a surprising sense of honor. At first, I didn't understand why two enemies would bother to talk if they still planned on fighting.

but I get it now." She risked a step toward him and tilted her head all the way back to see his expression. "That same sense of honor is forcing you to question your actions. I think you wanted to get the other side of the story."

"You continue to astonish me." Armin smiled a knowing smile. "Yes, you may be right. Perhaps I wanted to test my convictions against you in the same way I test my skills in battle. If I can convince you, my greatest enemy, of the righteousness of my cause, I can convince myself."

"But you've failed to convince me, just as you failed to beat me. How deep are those convictions now? Not so certain, I'll bet."

His smile burgeoned into a grin. "On the contrary. Your fresh perspective has renewed my resolve. My purpose henceforth will be to prove to you our cause is necessary and just. With heightened vigor, I shall ensure humankind sheds conflict once and for all. Neither guilt nor regret shall weigh on my conscience when such things become reality."

Brooke held his gaze for a few seconds before turning away. A manufactured breeze whipped her newly-grown hair into her face.

Armin's steadfast dedication forced her to second-guess her position. *Maybe he has a point. Maybe ethics can bend to excuse death and deception if they usher in an unparalleled golden age. Would I rather live in a utopia based on a lie or a true yet imperfect world? How can I possibly answer such a question?*

"Okay," she said. "For the moment, let's say you accomplish your goal. We stop fighting ourselves, band together, and live happily ever after. What then? In order to maintain paradise, the truth has to stay hidden. If humans triumph over exobeings, people can't know there were no exos. They can't ever find out about you. So, how'll you hide what's on Triton, your ships, your technology—all your people?"

"Our leaders have spent decades preparing for the aftermath of our final act. A plan exists to erase all revealing evidence from our colonies."

"Final act? And colonies, as in plural?"

Her adversary stiffened his posture. "I fear I've said too much."

"What does that mean?" Every muscle in her abdomen clenched.

"I've enjoyed my time with you, and I hope you share the sentiment. When next we meet, only one of us shall emerge from the encounter. I look forward to that time."

The force field shimmered, sending a jolt of electricity coursing through her. Brooke felt her body go limp as darkness shrouded her mind.

## Twenty-seven—Indictment
## Jovian System, February 2248 AD

Brooke sprang to a sitting position and whipped her head back and forth. She sat on a bed in Base HOPE's medical bay, wearing a hospital gown. Displays flashed, and life support systems beeped. Wounded patients occupied most of the other beds in the room.

With a sigh, she leaned back.

"Ah, you're awake." Doc Gordon, the head base physician, sauntered over to her and poked his fingers into the screen at the foot of her bed. An approving grunt escaped from beneath a white mustache. "All vital signs appear normal. How do you feel?"

"My sinuses are throbbing." She pinched the bridge of her nose with her thumb and forefinger. "I'm also a little dizzy."

"That's understandable given what you've been through."

"What I've been through?" A thick haze clouded her mind.

"What's the last thing you remember?"

She thought back. Her brain refused to focus. It took a minute to coax her most recent memories out of obscurity. "I went after the enemy carrier, my reactor overloaded, and . . ." The encounter with Armin gushed back into her head. Suppressing a gasp, she decided against revealing what had happened. ". . . and then I don't know."

"The *Asimov* picked up your fighter's transponder signal," Gordon explained. "It took the carrier almost a week to retrieve you. The crew pried you from your torched spacecraft and melted flight armor. They said the seat in your cockpit looked like a charbroiled steak. What the *Asimov*'s head physician couldn't understand was how you escaped without injury."

"The gravgel?"

"The gravgel should've cooked you alive." The doctor retrieved an electrohammer from the cabinet next to her bed and zapped a spot beneath her left knee. Her leg kicked without her consent. "You need to take better care of yourself." He shocked her right knee. "The next near-death encounter might exclude the 'near' part."

She gave a slow nod.

The hammer jolted her left arm into the air.

"Have you been taking the meds I prescribed?" Gordon spoke in a hushed tone. "Are you back on the sparks?"

She averted her stare. "No . . ."

Gordon raised his brow. The lines on his forehead creased in doubt.

She grumbled. "I stopped for a while, but I had to choose between a sober death and staying alive."

The doctor returned his attention to the screen. "Well, you're as healthy as I've ever seen you." He glowered at her. "And the patient has been informed of what she needs to do to stay that way."

Brooke shifted uncomfortably.

He strolled around the bed and stood beside her. "The good news is that you're cleared for duty. The bad news . . ." Doc pointed a thumb in the direction of two Intrasolar Military Police officers. They stood on either side of the medical bay's entrance, staring her down.

"IMPs." Her stomach cramped. "Let me guess." She recalled her direct defiance of Captain Hasluck's orders. "They're my chaperons."

"They're here to escort you to General Douglas."

Brooke leaned back, recoiling. "I don't feel so well. Not fit for duty."

Gordon placed a hand on her shoulder. "Sorry."

She sulked for a minute before scooting off the edge of the bed. When her bare feet contacted cold tile, the room spun. It took a moment for her to regain her balance.

After shaking it off, she approached the two IMPs with frayed nerves.

"You're to report to General Douglas," the woman on the left said. Her chiseled jawline appeared locked in place, incapable of smiling. "Immediately."

Peering down at her hospital gown, she asked, “Like this?”

“We’ll escort you to your quarters so you can change first,” the equally humorless man on the right said.

The first IMP led the way out of the medical bay. The second brought up the rear, following her through Base HOPE’s corridors. Every fourth or fifth plasma strip flickered, and she passed at least three scorched control panels. “What happened here?”

“Guess you wouldn’t know, would you, Major?” the second IMP said.

The first IMP didn’t break stride or look back. “Word is this is all your fault.”

Brooke’s eyelids fluttered. “My fault?”

The IMPs guided her into a lift, and its door slid shut. The brief, momentary lurch of the compartment shooting upward disoriented her.

Two sets of fingers dug into her arms. The IMPs supported her weight, holding her up.

The elevator doors opened.

She shrugged the IMPs aside and stepped out into the hall.

When she reached her room, her escorts took position on either side of the door.

“Let’s not keep the general waiting,” the woman said.

Brooke hurried inside.

Her hands pulled at her hair the instant the door slid shut behind her. *They’re going to court-martial me for disobeying orders. I’ll never fly again!* She wrapped her arms around her torso. A tear ran down one cheek. *Oh, Marie, Maya, Kevin. I’ve kept you at arm’s length, and now, I’m all alone.*

She dragged her feet into the bathroom and slipped off her gown. After pressing both palms to the counter, she hung her head. The weight of her broken life buckled her shoulders.

When she lifted her chin, she caught her reflection in the mirror. The image of a charred zombie glared back at her.

She wailed so loudly, the scream grated her throat.

Clamping her eyelids shut, she stumbled backwards until her back smacked against the tile wall.

When she opened her eyes, the mirror showed her normal reflection. *It’s all in my head.* Brooke trudged out of the bathroom and fell to her knees, gasping for breath. Drowned in perspiration, her naked body trembled.

She knew what she needed. Only one thing could make it all go away.

After crawling to her dresser, she yanked open the bottom drawer and grabbed the new safe. Then she pressed her fumbling thumb to the fingerprint reader until lid popped open. She snatched the first spark injector her shaking hand found and jabbed it into the base of her neck.

A concussive shock pulsed through her body and mind.

The weight lifted. Her head cleared.

She shot to her feet and threw on her uniform, all the while glowering at the door. The IMPs stood outside, waiting to usher her to the end of her career—if not further. *Collins must be a member of the Vril. First he set me up to pilot the phase shuttle, but then he tried to eliminate me. I don't get it, but if he knows about my visit with Armin, he'll probably be more motivated to get rid of me. My insubordination will give him the excuse he needs.* Her chest tightened. *What do I do? Think, think, think!* She paced, gripping her head. *Kevin, Marie, Maya, I may never—Maya!*

Her eyezoom locked onto the vent above the top bunk.

♦

Kevin stood on the floor of the aerospace factory, arms hugging an e-slip flickering with schematics. A yawn displaced his grin. He hadn't slept for more than four hours each night in the past few weeks, although the sacrifice seemed well worth it now.

The most advanced star fighter ever built sat on the deck in front of him. Neurotronic wires interlaced the frame like a circulatory system. Without its exterior molding, the plane resembled a medical diagram of a three-dimensional creature with exposed internal organs.

A crane lowered the scaled-down version of the phase drive into the fighter's aft section. The drive's casing possessed the shape of an antique jet turbine, but this engine hid a raging antimatter cascade held in check by precision force fields.

Kevin ran a hand through his hair and turned to Christine. "Great work. Let's start interconnecting the power systems."

"Right." Christine nodded at the lead engineer, who pressed a command on his control slip. Mechanical arms extended from the surrounding scaffolding toward the drive section. Sparks flew.

The progress of the integration displayed on Kevin's slip. "Connectivity in nodes one through twenty-seven appears stable. Let's—"

"Kevin!"

He turned to find Brooke sprinting around the nose of the phase fighter and smiled. "Hey." He hadn't seen her in weeks.

She stopped less than an arm's length away from him, panting. Fear had drained her face of color.

"Hey, you got your hair cut," he said, "and no more highlights."

She blinked. One hand flew to her head. She rubbed the jet-black strands between her fingers as if she had realized the difference only now.

“Something the matter?” he asked.

“We need to talk.” Brooke looked pointedly at Christine and the lead engineer. “In private.”

“Sure, but can it wait a few minutes? We’re in the middle of connecting the phase fighter’s power systems.”

“Oh.” She turned and peered up. “This is it?”

“That’s right.” He couldn’t keep his chest from puffing out. “You’re looking at the YPF-1 Quasar. This prototype packs more maneuverability and firepower than the SF-522A, plus the FTL capability of the phase shuttle. She’ll be ready for shakedown one week from today.” He winked. “I don’t suppose you know of anyone who might want to fly it?”

Brooke’s mouth drooped as if someone had shut off her robotic dog. “I don’t think that’s going to happen.”

She stepped closer to him. *Some sort of strawberry shampoo?* Her hair smelled good.

“Please, we need to talk now,” she whispered. “I’m in big trouble.”

Kevin drew his lips to a thin line and nodded. “Of course.” To Christine, he said, “Take over. I’ll be back as soon as I can.”

“No problem,” she said.

Kevin led Brooke toward the offices adjacent to the aerospace factory.

She increased her pace, overtaking him. Every few steps, she peered back over her shoulder.

He followed her into his office. Its transparent doors slid shut behind him.

“So what’s up?” he asked.

Brooke shook her head, staring up at the ceiling. “I don’t know where to begin.”

“Let’s start with what you said before.” He sat on the edge of his desk in the midst of a floating screen. Blueprints and equations danced across his chest. “Why wouldn’t you be able to fly the phase fighter?”

“I’m facing a court-martial.”

“Why?”

She told him about her idea to destroy Themisto and how it had won the battle.

“That’s how all the damage happened,” he said.

“Damage?”

“Lunar fragments hit the colonies here on Callisto. One of the New

Galilei biodomes bore the full brunt of a twenty-meter rock. It slammed into the dome and decompressed it, killing thirty thousand people. Then the tremors caused as much destruction as the initial impact."

Brooke cupped a hand over her mouth. "The IMPs were right. It was my fault."

"It's horrible." Kevin dug his hands into the pockets of his lab coat and studied the floor. "But based on what you said, there might have been more casualties had you not done what you did. They should be giving you another medal, not court-martialing you."

"They might've done that, except . . ." She told him about her unauthorized pursuit of the enemy carrier and the overload of her fighter's reactor.

"Surely they can overlook one act of disobedience given all you've accomplished and endured. I bet they let you off with a reprimand."

Swinging her head back and forth, she said, "If only that were the real issue." She approached the desk and did that cute thing where she crinkled her nose. Kevin's skin tingled. "You're going to think I'm crazy, but I died when my reactor exploded." She grabbed a lock of her hair and held it up. "It's shorter with no highlights, but not because it was cut or styled. It burnt away and regrew in less than a day along with all my skin."

"How?"

"The enemy brought me aboard their ship. They revived and regenerated me."

"You mean the Greys?"

"They're not Greys. They're humans like us."

Kevin jerked back. "Humans? How can that be?"

She recapped everything she learned aboard Armin's ship.

"A secret society that created a genetically superior race of human beings, provided them with advanced technology, and settled them at the edge of the solar system, all without the rest of us knowing?" His brow lifted up past his forehead. "Do you have any idea how implausible that sounds?" He sprung up off the desk and launched into lecture mode. "The expenditure of the resources necessary to terraform Triton couldn't have gone unnoticed. I can't begin to fathom where they would've found the raw materials or how they could've processed them. Satellites, probes, and telescopes would've detected activity out there. And then there's—"

"I said you'd think I was crazy, but it's the truth."

"Don't you think it's more likely you had an elaborate dream? Your reactor exploded, leaving you hanging in the vacuum of space. A new hairstyle isn't conclusive proof."

"If that'd been the only incident, I might agree, but my time aboard the enemy ship confirmed my suspicions about everything else."

"Everything else?"

She revealed how UN pilots, in cooperation with Armin, had blown up Artemis, how she'd faced Armin on Europa and Titan, and how Collins seemed to be in the middle of all of it.

Reason argued otherwise, but everything she told him fit together too well for casual dismissal. The attacks made little sense if enacted by extrasolar beings intent on exterminating the human race, but the timely assaults on well-chosen targets had instilled the perfect amount of fear and camaraderie in the human race to bring it together.

"The Vril are staging this invasion," Brooke concluded, "although I still can't explain Collins's role in it. Why hasn't he given the designs for the phase drive to the Vril or hauled you out to Triton to build it for them? It doesn't make sense."

The knotting of his intestines became a wrestling match. "It makes perfect sense."

"It does?"

Kevin waved his arm in the direction of the fighter construction bays. "The automated robotic assemblers are programmed via encrypted algorithms. Thousands of countries, companies, and people are involved in this project. Only the manufacturer of a given part can activate its assembly algorithm." He strolled behind his desk, plopped down in his chair, and pointed at his screen. "This component is one of tens of thousands that make up the drive. Each part's design is encrypted like the fabrication algorithms. To work on any one piece, I have to submit a request to the owning entity. Only they can unlock it. Same with the umpteen software applications required to operate the drive's systems." He leaned back. "It's a decentralized security system that makes stealing the overall design next to impossible."

"So, if a thief couldn't get his hands on the blueprints, the next best thing would be to seize the drive and reverse engineer it."

"It'd take detailed analyses and a lot of time, but yes, that'd be the next best option." Kevin studied Brooke. She stood, slouching and staring out the walls, arms dangling at her sides. Her body trembled. He wanted to pull her into his embrace and comfort her.

His mind grappled with everything she had told him. *The Greys don't exist after all? Instead, there's an organization with the ability to create a clandestine civilization for the purpose of implementing a noble conspiracy to unite humanity under false pretenses?* His brain grappled with the ethical implications. *But most of all, I'm worried about Brooke. This organization knows she knows everything, which means they'll try to remove her as a threat.* "There's only one thing to do. We need proof."

"You believe me?"

"Yes."

Her posture relaxed. "Thank you." Her eyes shone like amethysts.

Giddiness gave him goose bumps. "Okay, where do we get our evidence?" He stroked the stubble on his chin. "Doesn't your fighter's matrix keep a log of everything that happens?"

"It does, but to interface with Bob, I'd need to be in my fighter with my helmet on."

<Actually, that assertion no longer holds, ma'am.>

Brooke jumped. "What the—? Bob, is that you?"

Kevin chuckled.

<Correct, ma'am.> The speakers embedded within the office walls emitted her matrix's synthesized male voice.

She gawked at Kevin.

"After your matrix—sorry, after Bob—performed the calculations necessary to bring your fighter back to the phase shuttle," he said, "I had the techs copy and install him on the base mainframe. Bob's one of the smartest AIs I've ever encountered. If it weren't for him, I wouldn't have been able to complete the scaled-down version of the drive."

"I see."

<The professor has applied my faculties to a number of challenging tasks, ma'am, and also provided me with full access to SolNet. I've accumulated yottabytes of data. I never realized so much existed.>

"That's great, Bob. So . . . about that log."

<Using the base network, I've determined software engineers were unable to retrieve the copy of me that accompanied you during your defense of Callisto. The SF-522A's neurotronic systems were damaged beyond recovery thresholds. I'm sorry, ma'am, but there's no record of your most recent flight.>

Brooke's body teetered to one side. "Why am I not surprised?"

"Okay, fine," Kevin said. "What else? There must be a record of something that happened to you." He paced again. "How about Europa?"

With a nod, she said, "Bob, did you get a look at the pilots you shot when we escaped from the water plant?"

<I'm unfamiliar with the aforementioned individuals, ma'am. However, I do show a memory purge event logged after returning from

that engagement. If that data existed, it was deleted.>

Kevin stared at Brooke. Her claims seemed more plausible than ever.

"What about my conversation with Armin near Titan?"

<A transmission was received during that incident, ma'am, but I was unable to save the content or trace the source.>

"Damn it!" She drove a booted heel into the deck.

Kevin grumbled. "I guess you don't keep a civilization secret for over a century without knowing how to cover your tracks." He approached her. "What else?"

"I . . . I don't know."

He risked placing a hand on her shoulder. "There must be. Think."

A tear escaped the corner of her eye. "I . . . I can't think straight anymore." She rested her head against his arm.

"Well, keep thinking." He did his best to suppress his elation. *This is no time to think about romance.* "Don't give up."

They stood in silence. Kevin allowed himself to enjoy the moment despite the circumstances.

"Hey, um . . ." She pried her gaze away and stared out the window walls. "About what you asked me before, I—" She sucked in a sharp breath.

Two military police officers stood talking to Christine, who pointed in the direction of his office.

Kevin's heart practically struck the floor.

The IMPs jogged toward them.

Stepping closer to the office door, Brooke said, "You can't let them get their hands on the phase drive, but don't do anything to put yourself at risk."

"Brooke—"

The IMPs darted through the sliding doors. The first officer carried a pair of magnetic restraints. She raced up behind Brooke, pulled her wrists behind her back, and cuffed her.

"Major Brooke Davis," the IMP said, "you're under arrest for evasion of military law enforcement." She yanked her backwards with the help of the second officer.

Brooke yelled while backpedaling. "The answer is yes."

Kevin could only stare, helplessly, as they dragged her away.

## Twenty-eight—Animus
## Yokohama, Earth, February 2248 AD

A temperate breeze caressed Marie's skin as she strolled through Sankeien Garden. The wind rustled cherry blossoms and nudged a wooden boat down a stream lined by blue irises.

With sunlight warming her face, she drew in a steady breath. Fresh air invigorated her. *No respirator. This is the life.* Eighteen-hour days, which had included running around the planet covering the latest breaking news, had left her a bit high-strung. Her producer at ISN had noticed and insisted she take a week off.

Maya skipped along next to her, holding her hand. Marie's grandmother walked beside them, bobbing and weaving to the noise booming from her specs. A man and woman who passed them flashed scowls at the beeping and crackling and thumping.

"Grandma, do you think you could take those off for two seconds and appreciate where we are?" Marie asked.

The old woman ignored her.

"Obaa-chan!" Marie yanked the specs off her grandmother's head.

The outburst scattered a flock of birds. Nearby tourists stared at them.

The old woman grabbed her specs back and shoved them on. "Mariko, you could've killed me."

Holding her breath, Marie said, “I didn’t think . . . is your heart acting up again?”

“No, but some kid in Argentina almost blasted me.”

Marie rolled her eyes.

“Obaa’s playing Stellar Combat Five,” Maya said.

Trying her best not to sound sarcastic, her mother said, “Thank you, dear.”

“Can I play, too?”

“Grab a pair of specs and join in the bloodshed, little one.” Obaa-chan said cheerfully.

“Absolutely not,” Marie said. “First of all, Maya’s not playing anything with graphic violence, and secondly, she’s here to appreciate nature, unlike—”

A twenty-first-century hip hop song blared from the pocket in her skirt. Further vehement glowers found her.

“Still infatuated with antique sound bytes?” Grandma’s shoulders swayed, dodging virtual weapons fire. “And I thought I was the old lady.”

Grumbling, Marie fumbled for her net specs. “Darn it.” She swore she’d turned them off before entering the garden. *Oh, right. I forgot to switch them off again after I looked up that flower.*

Maya tugged at her mother’s skirt. “Who, Mommy? Is it Auntie Brooke? Is she going to take us for a ride in her ship?”

“Quiet, please.” Marie found the specs and put them on. *This better not be work calling. I don’t care if Mars just exploded. Somebody else can cover the story.*

The text blinking on the lenses indicated an incoming call from Kevin Sommerfield.

She led her daughter and grandmother over to a park bench. “Sit here with Obaa-chan, Maya, and stay put. I’ll be right back.” Her feet shuffled through carpet-like grass to the edge of a stream, out of earshot but still in view of her family.

With a wink, she connected the call. “Hi, Professor.”

“Marie,” Kevin said. He looked disheveled and upset. “I’m glad I finally got a hold of you.”

“Sorry about being incommunicado, but I’m in Japan on vacation.”

He ran his fingers through his hair. “Brooke, well, I don’t know if she’d be happy with me contacting you, but I thought you needed to know.”

“It figures she wouldn’t call me. What doesn’t she want me to know?”

“She’s in trouble, Marie. It’s pretty bad.”

"What sort of trouble?"

The rate and intensity of his speech increased. "I don't know what's going to happen to her, but military police officers dragged her away right in front of me."

"Why?"

"She almost killed herself because she disobeyed orders, but that's not the half of it."

A biting cold coursed down Marie's spine. "What do you mean?"

"Look, I'm not sure if it's a good idea to tell you over the comm. Someone might be eavesdropping."

"Kevin, you're starting to scare me." She gazed across the stream at a traditional tea house, feeling her stomach constrict. "You wouldn't have called unless you intended to tell me, so drop the pretense."

The professor spent the next ten minutes rambling off an unbelievable story.

When he finished, Marie could only say, "You can't be serious."

"I wish I were making it up," Kevin said. "I wouldn't have contacted you if I didn't believe it."

She tapped her shoe against a rock. "Do you have any idea how big a story this is?"

"Marie, you can't report this—"

"Of course I can't report it. Not yet, anyway. Not without proof."

"Which we don't have, and have no way to obtain."

"If the Vril are responsible for everything you claim, there has to be evidence somewhere."

"Marie, I only told you because I know you care about your sister."

"No, you told me because I'm an investigative reporter, and this situation clearly calls for investigative reporting."

"Seriously, don't do anything stupid."

"I'm not one to sit back and pray. People deserve to know the truth, and the only thing that can absolve my sister is proof, right? The question is how to get it."

♦

Marie led Maya into the cramped dining room of their elder's unkempt home, settled her daughter into a seat at the table, and sat down next to her.

Grandma shuffled in after them, carrying a stack of three small dinner trays. The one hundred and three-year-old woman slid two of the dinners across the table at them.

"Seriously?" With a pair of chopsticks, Marie nabbed a rubbery chunk of raw tuna and held it up. "I came to Japan for fresh sushi. I can get imitation fish made in a lab anywhere." She sighed and swallowed. “Why didn’t we go out to eat again?”

“Grandma’s on a budget.” The old woman deftly plucked one roll after another off her tray.

“I could’ve paid.” Marie shoved the pile of matrix hardware to the end of the table. “I like circuit boards as much as the next girl, but you might try spending more on groceries and less on gadgets.”

Maya sniffed the food on her plate and stuck out her tongue. “Can I have Fruity Planets instead, Mommy?”

“For once, I think we both might have cereal.”

Gripping a chopstick, Maya batted a crab roll off her plate. The roll soared between two desktop speakers and onto the floor. “Score!” She held both arms straight up.

“Touchdown!” Grandma held her hand up. “High-five.”

Her daughter and grandmother slapped palms, eliciting a headshake from Marie.

After cleaning up the mess, Marie returned to the unpalatable meal. “It must be time for the evening news.” She forced another bite down her throat. “Screen on.”

A display materialized on the wall.

“ISN network,” she said.

Picture-in-picture screens, scrolling headlines, and the 3D ISN logo surrounded a thin-faced anchorwoman.

“Looks like McKenzie nabbed the lead anchor spot,” Marie muttered.

“—and in other news, the UN secretary-general has issued an official thank-you to the nations and political groups who signed the armistice.”

A vid of Danuwa Ajunwa appeared on the screen next to quoted text. “Only through mutual cooperation were we able to safeguard the lives of each and every person in the Jovian system,” the UN secretary-general said. “I extend my whole-hearted gratitude to each and every man, woman, and child. Let this be but the first step toward a unified One Humanity, one where petty squabbles amongst human beings go the way of the dinosaurs.”

Footage of the battle near Callisto replaced the vid of Ajunwa. The only topic the major networks had discussed in the last couple of days was the successful defense of Callisto against the Greys. The UN credited General Frederick Douglas with the brilliant strategy to sacrifice Themisto. Vids showed the military spacecraft of cooperating nations dealing crippling blows to extrasolar ships.

McKenzie’s suited figure returned to the screen. “The UN still lacks the slightest insight into their culture or why they’re here.”

A frame showed the exocorpse lying on its bed within the UN MedCenter. "This specimen remains the only evidence mankind has regarding the Greys' appearance. Medical experts from around the solar system have authenticated it as a genuine exobeing."

Marie paused mid-chew. *Or have they?*

In light of what Kevin had told her, she wondered. How might a group that had infiltrated the UN go about fooling everyone into believing the corpse was real? Had the doctors not examined it, or were the examining physicians in on the conspiracy? ISN showed interviews with the experts, and all of them vouched for the authenticity of the corpse.

Her body tingled with anticipation and dread.

She told the screen to switch off and stared at her tray, tapping her lower lip. A plan formed in her head.

♦

Bending over, Marie kissed her daughter's forehead. "You behave for Obaa-chan now."

Maya whipped her hair from side to side. "I don't wanna stay with Obaa. I wanna go with you, Mommy."

The autocab honked from the street in front of the house.

Marie held up her index finger. "One minute!" She squatted in front of Maya, meeting her gaze. "Mommy has to do something that might be dangerous. It's best if you stay here with Obaa." She gave her a big squeeze. "Don't worry. I'll be back before you know it."

Her daughter sniffled and squeezed back until Marie pulled away.

Grandma rested her hands on her great-granddaughter's shoulders.

Maya rubbed her eyes.

"I'll back as soon as I can. Please feed Maya something decent, and no graphic violence."

The old woman nodded. "Be careful, Mariko." For once, she almost sounded like a grandmother.

"I will."

"And tell Kishiko to contact me, preferably before I die. She may be a pilot, but I can still waste her in any flight sim of her choosing."

Marie smiled. "I'll relay the message."

♦

Two IMPs marched Brooke through the door of Base HOPE's main conference room. She lurched forward, tripping but not falling. They hadn't restrained her legs, but magnetic cuffs chafed her wrists behind her back.

She regained her balance and glanced around the room. President Collins, General Douglas, a colonel, and a judge advocate general sat on the far side conference table. A second JAG officer, a lieutenant general, rose from a seat on the near side.

*Prosecution and defense counsel.* Her stomach sank.

The IMPs escorted her to the table. Along the way, she caught the horrific view outside the panoramic window.

A towering, jagged rock—a fragment of Themisto—jutted up from a smashed New Galilei dome. Drilling machines and mining vehicles worked atop the shard. A small section of the fragment broke away from one side. Under thruster control, the detached section maneuvered away from the city and descended to the surface.

She had seen the damage in the corridors, and Kevin had told her about the casualties, but his explanation had failed to prepare her for the sight of the stake she had driven through the heart of Callisto's largest population center.

The IMPs saluted and stepped back. Brooke couldn't salute with her hands bound.

General Douglas's deep baritone was frosty. "Four months, three weeks, and five days. That's how long it's going to take to clear that monstrosity away."

She closed her eyes, struggling to control the wave of guilt that washed through her.

Her legal advisor took his place at her side.

"Major Brooke Davis," the judge advocate recorder said. "We've summoned you, the respondent, before this administrative discharge board to review your alleged misconduct."

*Discharge?* Her breathing quickened.

The recorder interlocked her fingers. "We've taken statements from President Collins and General Douglas, which have led to four formal charges. The first is whether the respondent, an officer of the United Nations Aerospace Defense Force, acted in an insubordinate manner. Major Davis allegedly conspired with Captain Hasluck to hide her intent to destroy Themisto. Per General Douglas, alterations to any defense strategy should be approved through the proper chain of command."

"Yes sir, but I—"

The legal advisor leaned toward her and whispered, "Remain silent until prosecution has presented their case."

She grumbled.

"Furthermore," the recorder said, "the respondent allegedly disobeyed a direct order issued by Captain Hasluck, an offense which violated Article Ninety-Two of the Intrasolar Code of Military Jurisdiction. Instead of returning to base, the major pursued an enemy carrier in a suicidal maneuver, thereby destroying government property and almost killing herself. Based on these actions, this board questions whether the major suffers from psychological impairment resulting from a genetic disorder, which limits her capacity to pilot a spacecraft."

Brooke opened her mouth.

"I provided counsel for Captain Hasluck," her advisor said, maintaining his hushed tone. "Your best chance of avoiding discharge is to forgo accusations about implausible conspiracies and keep your mouth shut."

Her expression soured.

The recorder cleared her throat. "If I may continue? Charge number two is a violation of Article One-Nineteen, manslaughter."

Brooke's knees almost buckled.

"As a direct result of the unauthorized act of destroying a small moon, almost thirty thousand people lost their lives. The verbiage of the ICMJ Article states, 'Any unlawful act performed by an officer outside of military purview, such as illegal action taken in direct violation of an order, makes that officer subject to criminal prosecution.' This board seeks to determine whether the respondent is culpable for those deaths."

The advisor stared at Brooke. The recorder paused. Brooke kept her jaw clamped.

"Charge three corresponds to Article Ninety-Five, resistance, flight, breach of arrest, or escape from military law enforcement. After the head base physician cleared the respondent for active duty, General Douglas ordered her to report to him immediately. Instead, the major allegedly fled from the two military police officers assigned as escort.

"Now, this board plans to take the major's impressive seven-year service record into account." The middle-aged woman read from an e-slip. "The rescue of twenty-two children from Titan. Operation of the first manned FTL spacecraft. Bringing *Viking* back home safely, for which the officer received the Medal of Honor. Based on the respondent's accomplishments, rank, and time in service, we felt it appropriate to convene in-person for board processing." She slapped the slip down on the table, addressing Brooke for the first time. "But these deeds cannot excuse your actions. You may be an icon in the eyes of the general populace—" she jabbed the table with her index finger —"but your celebrity status has not placed you above the Defense command structure."

Brooke couldn't hold it in any longer. "I took these actions because I believe this 'command structure' has been compromised by—"

"Defense wishes to exercise the right to withhold testimony, which could be construed as to incriminate the defendant," her legal advisor said.

The recorder inclined her head. "That is her right under—"

Something snapped inside Brooke. "No." She whirled on her advisor. "Are you on my side or just another lackey?" *Collins must've arranged this façade to get rid of me. They couldn't care less about hearing my side of the story, but they're going to get it, anyway.* She faced the prosecution. "I got on board the enemy flagship. There were no exobeings, only humans."

"Major, please cease—" her advisor pleaded.

Brooke whipped her head back over her shoulder toward the window. "They've settled more than Triton. Multiple Kuiper belt dwarf worlds. I don't know how many. The Europa, Titan, Triton, and Themisto incidents were instigated by a secret society known as the Vril." Her stare narrowed at Collins. "A society of which that traitor is a member."

The IMPs grabbed her arms.

Collins wore a tired frown, like a schoolteacher disappointed in a prized pupil. His face betrayed no signs of anger or guilt, nothing to give him away.

Brooke scowled in disgust.

"These are serious charges," the recorder said. "Are you prepared to present evidence to support these allegations?"

Brooke's body went limp.

The IMPs held her up.

"Well, then." The recorder raised an eyebrow. "What seems more plausible"— she picked up her slip —"is that the respondent is suffering from delusions brought on by alleged drug use."

Brooke stopped breathing.

Collins's expression didn't change, but she swore she caught a brief twinkle in his eye.

Her nostrils flared.

"The fourth and final charge," the recorder read aloud, "is violation of Article One-Twelve Alpha, wrongful use or possession of controlled substances. According to a medical report filed by Base HOPE's chief flight surgeon, the respondent has been injecting nanorobotic stimulants, or 'sparks' as they are more commonly known, for years." She set the slip down and leaned back in her chair. "Unlawful substance abuse is grounds for immediate discharge Under Other Than Honorable Conditions."

*So that's it.* Brooke swallowed a panicked gag. *My career just imploded, and nothing I can say or do will make any difference.* She felt hot and cold all over. *No one will ever believe the word of an addict.*

"I won't let you get away with this," she hissed at Collins.

He patronized her with a pitying glower.

"Does defense wish to add anything else to the record?" the recorder asked.

The legal advisor wearily shook his head.

"Very well." The recorder exchanged glances with Collins and Douglas. "We are adjourned. This board shall convene in closed deliberation to consider whether the respondent, Major Brooke Davis, shall be discharged from the Defense Force."

"Take her to the brig," General Douglas said.

**Twenty-nine—Muckrake**
**New York City, February 2248 AD**

The automated taxicab veered onto United Nations Plaza. Marie worked her specs while the cab slowed to a halt. An electronic ding announced the draining of funds from her account.

<Payment accepted, Ms. Davis,> the front dash said. <Yellow Cab wishes you a pleasant night in Manhattan. Current Air Quality Index is moderately unhealthy. Please remember to wear your respirator. If you don't have a mask, one can be purchased for only—>

"I've got one, thanks." She slipped her breather up over her mouth, stepped out of the taxi, and craned her neck upward. New York possessed a daunting scale rivaled by few other cities. Multi-level streets wound around skyscrapers like concrete vines. The Doppler-shifted whooshing of cars and trucks raced along above her. Moonlight peaked through sporadic patches in the overhead infrastructure. Streetlights and floating advertisements lit up the area.

The windowed exterior of the UN Headquarters stratoscraper directed shimmering light on the fountains, flowerbeds, and statues in the grassy courtyard. The massive tower jutted up through the tangle of streets and disappeared above the clouds.

To her left, the UN MedCenter stretched for half a kilometer. The building looked like a skyscraper fallen on its side.

ISN Studios loomed only a few miles away. So did the apartment she had settled into after taking the job with ISN, although she hadn't found the time to stop at home. She had rushed straight from JFK Intrasolar Spaceport to make it here on time.

Marie strode through the courtyard, heels clacking against the concrete pathway. Two minutes later, she reached an occupied park bench.

The man sitting on it removed his breather. "Marie Davis." He sprung to his feet.

She stopped at arm's length and pulled down her mask. "Zach Mitchell." She smirked. "I bet you didn't think you'd see me again so soon."

"You got me there." The green streaks in Zach's light-brown hair glowed in the moonlight. "To be honest, I was surprised you remembered me at the five-year reunion."

"What are you talking about? Of course I remembered you."

"It's not like we hung out in high school." He peered down at his shoes. "I was a big nobody. You were one of the prettiest, most popular girls in school."

"You weren't a nobody." Marie shook her head. "And while I thought of myself as a likeable person, it's not like I was prom queen or captain of the cheerleading squad."

"Maybe so, but you never got picked on or embarrassed."

The image of two seniors yanking down a scrawny freshman's pants flashed through her mind. She could still picture the dancing comic book characters on Zach's underwear. "Oh, come on." She stifled a guilt-ridden snicker. "That was freshman year."

"Junior year, actually."

"Oh." Her finger tapped her lip. "Right." *No wonder I remember it as well as I do.*

They stood in awkward silence until a huckster vending machine insisted she buy an authentic New York hot dog.

Zach shooed it away.

"Hey," Marie said, "I remembered what you do. IT help desk at the UN MedCenter."

"And you're a big celebrity reporter now, one who wants an illicit look at the exocorpse and needs me to sneak her in." He folded his arms. "But as I said when you called, I've got serious reservations. If we get caught, they'll fire me, maybe worse."

"I know. I wouldn't ask you to do it if it wasn't important."

"That's what you kept saying." Zach shoved his hands into his jacket pockets. "Damn this stupid little crush I've had on you since high school. It won't let me say no."

Her brow furrowed. "Crush? I never knew—"

"Why's it so important you see the body? The UN let a bunch of reporters see the thing months ago."

Marie's mind still clung to his previous statement, but she let it go for the time being. "I have reason to believe it's a fake."

His eyebrows lifted. "A fake? Marie, the best and brightest have examined the thing backwards and forwards. What do you think you can do?"

"I don't know." That, at least, was the truth. She hadn't a clue what she would do once she reached the body. Still, she had to try. Visions of shadowy men tossing Brooke in a dark, rat-infested dungeon to rot for all eternity spurred her onward. "I'll figure something out."

He glared at her, unconvinced.

Marie's eyes adjusted to the darkness, and she noticed the green of his irises. The man standing before her no longer resembled the skinny, frightened teen from high school.

"This is insane." He sighed. "But you do know how to pique my interest. I live for conspiracy theories." He turned toward the MedCenter. "If nothing else, this gives me an excuse to see the body, too."

She followed Zach through the MedCenter's front entrance. Its transparent doors peeled out of her way like curtains.

Two security guards sat behind a black marble desk inside the lobby.

"What's up, Dante, Mack?" Zach directed a chin-nod at them as he passed.

First-name basis didn't stop them from scrutinizing her. The first guard—Dante, she presumed—seemed to recognize her, probably from ISN. The other guard, Mack, leaned forward, about to stand up.

Her intestines knotted.

Marie flinched when Zach wrapped his arm around her waist. In her peripheral vision, she saw him direct a sly grin toward the guards and wink.

Knowing smiles wiped all suspicion off the guards' faces. Mack's beefy figure collapsed back into his chair. He leaned back, bit his lower lip, and nodded.

"Nice," Dante mouthed with a not-so-subtle thumbs-up.

She didn't appreciate them ogling her like a piece of meat, but it was nice to know she could still pull in looks despite being fresh off a plane.

Zach led her through one sterile white hallway after another. Only two MedCenter personnel passed her within a span of ten minutes.

"We're in the research and administrative wing," he said. "The hospital's on the opposite side. Most everyone works nine-to-five, so we should have the place more or less to ourselves."

The majority of the office and lab doors she passed remained shut, windows tinted opaque. "I hope nobody's around near the corpse," she whispered. "Where is it?"

"Up on the fifty-first floor." Zach guided her into an elevator room. A lift door opened when he neared it.

"Hello, Zach Mitchell," said the MedCenter AI "Security clearance verified."

"Provide visitor clearance for my friend on my authorization." He turned to Marie. "Put on your specs."

She hesitated.

"Don't worry. You need them for initial verification, but I'll erase the security logs later."

After zipping open her purse, she retrieved her specs, put them on, and enabled her identity app.

"Visitor pass granted. Welcome, Marie Davis. Your temporary clearance will expire in twenty-four hours."

*We'd better be gone long before then.* She put away her specs and trailed Zach into the elevator.

"The fifty-first floor is restricted," he said as the doors closed. "Only the medical director and top-ranking UN officials have clearance. I couldn't figure out any way to give myself access without tripping the alarm."

"If we can't get up there, why did we bother—"

"However, being the help desk guru I am, I figured out a way around it. I granted myself clearance to the fiftieth floor. We'll get off there and take the stairs up. I spent all last night figuring how to override the security lock on the stairwell door."

She cocked her head to the side. "You'd think they would've thought of that."

"They did, but the type of lock on the stairwell door is easier to override. The elevator uses newer technology and is better integrated into the hospital network." He cleared his throat and spoke into the panel on the wall. "Fiftieth floor."

"Help desk authorization confirmed," the MedCenter AI said.

The compartment climbed upward.

Zach stuck his fingers down the collar of his shirt, loosening it. "Look, um, Marie," he stuttered. "This is probably horrible timing, but in case I never get another chance, there's something I have to tell you."

"What's that?"

"Remember our social studies class together senior year?"

"Of course. It wasn't that long ago."

"Every day, you plopped down into the seat in front of me with a big, bright smile." He flushed. "I was crazy about you back then, and my feelings haven't changed."

Marie blinked. Heat washed through her body.

"Anyway, I didn't have the courage to say anything back then. I was scared you'd reject me. But now . . . well, even if you don't feel the same way, I had to at least tell you."

"Hold elevator," Marie said.

"Suspending ascent," the AI said. The display above the door read twenty-sixth floor.

"Why'd you stop it?" Zach asked.

Marie turned away from Zach and thought back to social studies.

"Look, I didn't mean to make things awkward," he said. "I don't expect you to share my feelings, so just say the word, and I won't mention it again."

She whirled back around. "Do you know why I always had smile on my face when I got to class?"

"Well, you did tend to smile a lot."

"True, but I always smiled extra big in anticipation of your corny jokes." She tapped her lower lip. "I remember one about exos and measurements or something . . ."

Zach grinned. "Oh, you mean, 'What's the first thing exobeings would say to us after learning the metric system?'"

"I don't know, what?"

"'Take me to your liter.'"

Marie held Zach's gaze with a straight face for as long as possible. He had grown into a handsome man, one with the willingness to risk his career for her.

They both burst out laughing.

Once the aching in Marie's abdomen subsided, she stood beside him, staring at the compartment wall. Her skin tingled.

"So," Zach said, "does that mean you felt the same way?"

"Maybe a little—but that was high school. In this day and age, a mature woman requires more sophisticated humor."

He nodded. "Well, here's a funny idea." He took a deep breath. "Kiss me."

"Here? Now?" Despite her misgivings, the notion of forbidden romance during a perilous quest—one to uncover the greatest conspiracy in mankind's history, no less—presented a certain appeal. "I mean, I'm not opposed to the idea, but we should probably get moving."

"You stopped the elevator." He folded his arms. "You start it."

Marie tapped a toe against the floor. "Okay, fine. Let's do it quick."

"Wow, you're a true romantic."

"You know what I mean."

He eyed the ceiling. "Anything less than, say, sixty seconds would leave me feeling used. I'm not a piece of meat."

She placed her hands on her hips. "Unsophisticated jokes merit ten seconds, tops."

His face lit up. "Forty-five."

"Seriously?" Her head jerked back. "We're haggling over a make-out session?" She cracked a smirk. "Twenty."

"Thirty."

"Done." She extended her palm to the side, intending to shake on the deal.

Zach grabbed her hand and yanked her into his embrace.

♦

Kevin slouched in his chair while tapping his fingers on his desk. With heavy eyelids, he studied the snow globe sitting atop a stack of e-slips, below his screen. Another explosion erupted inside the globe, reenacting the Big Bang for the umpteenth time.

Not long ago, the culmination of his life's work had buoyed his spirits to new heights. The phase shuttle test flights had succeeded, and his team had completed construction of the phase fighter. Designs for interstellar ships now sat on the proverbial drawing board. Soon, humanity would take flight from the solar system to discover wonders untold.

*What does any of it matter when it's all shrouded by lies? The fighting ended but under false pretenses. We're still struggling against ourselves, only we don't even know it. Should an unscrupulous race of beings such as ourselves be allowed to spread throughout the galaxy?*

He ran his fingers through his hair, recalling the moment two military police officers had dragged Brooke away. After a bit of digital digging, Bob discovered her locked away in the brig. The AI matrix also detected signals emanating from her implants as if she sat in her fighter wearing her helmet. So far, Bob couldn't explain it.

*I guess I should at least take comfort in knowing Brooke's alive and well.*

He couldn't stop his chest from burning, though, not in light of the unthinkable act of betrayal Bob had discovered.

During the phase shuttle flight, Kevin had realized that someone created the malicious shutdown algorithm as part of the OS during its development. Through a comparison of programming styles, and by cross-referencing software audit trails with building entry and exit logs, security camera footage, and other records, Bob had identified the saboteur.

Dr. Christine Yeager.

Kevin slapped both palms against his desk. *My friend from college and closest confidante. A member of my original research team. The person who helped me muster the strength to make the initial phase drive announcement!*

He didn't know what to do about it. While Bob's findings implicated Christine beyond any reasonable doubt, the evidence remained circumstantial. *If she sabotaged the shuttle for the Vril and I expose her, who knows what steps they might take to cover it up? I can't tell the authorities.*

Someone knocked on the transparent walls of the office.

He flinched in his seat. When he saw the visitor, he relaxed and grumbled. "Come in."

Colonel Richthofen pushed his way into the office. "Professor."

"What can I do for you, Colonel?"

Richthofen stood stiff as sheet metal in front of Kevin's desk, clasping his hands behind his back. "It's oh nine hundred hours, sir. We scheduled a meeting to go over the phase fighter's systems." His dark, inset eyes appeared far too small for his square head.

"Oh. Right." Kevin had forgotten about the appointment.

His brain had blocked it out on purpose, probably. He had designed the phase fighter with another pilot in mind, and he still intended for her to fly it.

He focused his gaze beyond Richthofen's bulky chest and arms out the window-walls. The floor of the aerospace factory seemed far too empty now that the engineering team had transferred the Quasar to a hangar bay to await its shakedown flight.

Vindictive thoughts compelled him. He dug an e-slip out from under a pile on his desk and handed the slip to Richthofen. "I know you were trained on the phase fighter's systems during the candidacy program, so I think it's time to take things to the next level. Read this thoroughly. Then come back with questions."

"Yes, sir . . ."

Kevin watched the pilot's face contort as he perused the slip. It contained the professor's original published paper, replete with theoretical proofs, complex mathematical equations, technical terminology, and simulations. He could count the number of people who understood the content on one hand.

With slow steps, Richthofen filed out of the office.

*That should keep him busy for the next ten lifetimes*. Guilt pressed into his gut, which he shook off. He had come to a decision the moment the pilot stepped into his office. “Bob.”

<Yes, Professor?>

Kevin’s fingers wiggled atop a holographic keyboard. “Transmit the following command sequence to all entities collaborating on the phase fighter project.”

<Professor, the authorization codes you’ve entered are incorrect. Transmitting invalid codes will cause each intelligence matrix to block further communications. Reapplying with all entities—>

“Will take weeks, if not months, of cutting through red tape, delaying the construction of anything beyond the prototype. Yes, I know.” He held his breath. “Do it anyway.”

<Codes transmitting, Professor.>

Kevin felt light-headed, but he ignored it. “Also, encrypt the phase fighter’s control systems. Grant access to one and only one person’s brainwave patterns, excluding me.”

## Thirty—Corpus Delicti
## New York City, February 2248 AD

The elevator doors swished aside, revealing the fiftieth floor of the UN MedCenter.

Marie fanned her neck as she stepped out. Zach emerged behind her, adjusting his shirt.

She checked her specs. Ten minutes had passed since the innocent handshake. *So much for thirty seconds.* "Well, Mr. Tour Guide," she said, fixing her hair, "lead the way."

Marie speed-walked down the corridor behind him. Every fourth plasma strip on the ceiling remained lit during off-hours. The occasional light flickered, adding to the hall's eerie ambiance.

Zach reached a fork in the hall and rounded a corner.

He yelped.

The woman he collided with shrieked. E-slips scattered everywhere.

"Oh, crap," Zach said. "I'm so sorry, Dr. Blackwell." He bent down and scooped up the slips.

Marie helped him.

The middle-aged physician waved a hand in front of her lab coat, fanning herself. "Zach." She inhaled quick, successive breaths. "I didn't expect to run into anyone so late."

Standing, he handed her the slips he had collected so far. "I decided to give my friend a tour at the last minute."

"Of the fiftieth floor?" Her head darted between Marie and Zach. "What about you? Why're you still here?"

E-slips slid out of the doctor's grasp. "I'm working late." She adjusted to catch them. "On the floor where I belong."

"I drew the graveyard shift tonight, which means I have to cover every floor. There's a matrix in need of troubleshooting down the hall."

"I see." Blackwell shrugged. "Well, as long as you're up here, could you take a look at my matrix? It keeps fuzzing every time I swipe my finger through it."

"I'm not sure now's the best—"

Jumping in front of Zach, Marie handed the slips she'd retrieved to the physician.

"You look familiar," Dr. Blackwell said. "Aren't you . . .?" Her jaw extended. "You're Marie Davis, the ISN news anchor."

"Guilty as charged," Marie said.

Blackwell wedged her stack of slips under one arm. "Dr. Elizabeth Blackwell." She shook Marie's hand. "I loved your coverage of *Viking*'s flight. Tell me, what was it like to travel faster than light?"

"Truly indescribable."

"I'm sure."

"You're an exopathologist, correct?" Marie thrust her chin toward the slips. "I couldn't help but notice the jargon about Martian diseases."

The physician's eyebrows rose. "Yes, I'm studying the effects of Martian terraforming bacteria on Earth immigrants." Her face lit up. "Why, are you familiar with my work?"

"No, but it dawned on me you might be able to help us."

"Help you?"

"Help us?" Zach said. "Marie, I don't think we should involve—"

"Involve me in what?" Blackwell asked.

*Things have a way of working out.* Marie flipped to serious reporter mode. "Dr. Blackwell, I'll be honest with you. We're not up here taking a tour or fixing broken matrices. We're on our way to the floor above us."

Blackwell gave a slow nod. "You're interested in the exocorpse."

"Diagnosis one hundred percent accurate."

"The fifty-first floor is off-limits, though."

Zach winked. "Only to the technically-inept."

Blackwell scrutinized them both. "Why do you want to see it?"

"I believe the body is a fake," Marie said.

"That's impossible. The UN commissioned its top physicians to examine the corpse. A close colleague of mine was one of them. He swore the specimen was the most amazing creature he had ever studied."

"I won't accuse your colleague of lying, but according to a reliable source, he may not have understood what he saw." Marie took a step closer to her. "I'd like your help verifying it."

"Me?" The physician blinked. "No, no. If anyone found out, I'd lose my grant. My career would be over."

Marie held Blackwell's gaze. "Doctor, there are things going on behind the back of the everyday citizen. Either the UN is lying to us, or they're being manipulated. Either way, the fate of the human race is on our shoulders." She slipped in a white lie. "ISN has irrefutable proof."

"What proof might that be?"

"I'm not at liberty to disclose that at the moment. All I can say is we need further evidence of the exobeing's true origins to expose the conspiracy." *I should've pursued a career in acting,* Marie thought. "Only you can help me do it."

Blackwell hugged her slips. "I'm . . ." She stared down the tile flooring. "I'm not sure . . ."

"I know you're scared, believe me. My heart's trying to bash its way out of my chest." Marie placed a hand on her shoulder. "But I'm facing my fears for the greater good."

The physician fixed a questioning eye on Zach.

"Don't worry," he said. "There won't be any record of us going up there. I've made sure of it."

♦

Gaining access to the fifty-first floor proved simpler than Marie had imagined. She had pictured Zach hotwiring the stairwell door panel like in an old heist feed, but when he reached the door, the red light next to it flashed green, followed by the click of metal unlatching.

"What did I tell you?" Zach said, opening the door for Dr. Blackwell. "No worries."

Marie followed them through low-lit hallways with white walls and black floor tiling. Every door she passed featured state-of-the-art security panels and no labeling of any kind. She wondered what secrets the UN had hidden behind them.

Minutes later, they reached a four-meter-tall door, which reminded her of the entrance to a meat locker. Two robotic sentries stood on either side of it, possessing vague humanoid form. Their thin metal torsos sat atop twin belts of triangular tire treads. Antennas and cameras protruded from their heads, and particle cannons hung from either side of their bodies.

Dr. Blackwell gulped at the sight of them.

"Don't worry," Zach said. "I put them in sleep mode. They won't give us any trouble."

Marie waved a hand in front of one of the sentry's camera-eyes. Nothing happened.

When Zach approached the door, a wide-angle beam bathed him in violet light.

The door rumbled open.

"Looks like a morgue," Marie said as she stepped into the room.

Zach and the doctor followed.

The door slid shut, sealing them inside with an echoing clang.

Two rows of metal drawers, each a square meter in area, lined the far wall. Tens of displays and interface terminals occupied the wall to the left. Mechanical arms equipped with lasers and other scanning apparatuses hung from the ceiling above the drawers.

"Cryogenic stasis units," Blackwell said. "The corpse is in one of them."

"Unit 3B," Zach said. "Third from the left, bottom row." He strolled over to unit 3B and pressed a button on the drawer. Cold air billowed out from its edges with the hiss of decompression.

Centimeter by centimeter, the drawer extended open.

Marie stood next to it, waiting. Her heart fluttered in anticipation.

Two feet jutted up beneath a white sheet. A tall, skinny body lay underneath it.

A narrow chin emerged, followed by a tiny slit for a mouth and two more for nostrils. The being's grey head increased in size closer to its top, much like a balloon. Two solid black, oval eyes stared up at the ceiling.

*How many old feeds have I seen you in?* Marie studied Blackwell. The physician stood next to Zach on the other side of the drawer, her face pale, mesmerized.

Zach stuffed his hands into his jacket pockets and stared.

"Okay," Marie said, breaking the awestruck silence, "it looks like the real thing to me, so it's up to us show otherwise. Doctor?"

The physician lifted her gaze.

"How long will it take to examine the body?" Marie asked.

"The autopsy should only take a few minutes."

"Please get started. The sooner you finish, the sooner we can get out of here."

Blackwell strode over to a screen and ran her index finger through it. The apparatuses on the ceiling came to life. Motors whirred and lights flashed. Arms extended down to the body.

"In the meantime," Zach said to Marie, "you can review the corpse's charts." He led her to the interface terminals, rolled out a swivel chair, and plopped down. His fingers dipped into the nearest screen, signing in and working menus. An image of the corpse with accompanying data materialized. "This is the patient's medical record."

Marie squinted at the screen. "No allergies."

"I don't think pollen and dander bother the deceased, human or otherwise."

"Hmm . . ." She leaned over his shoulder, poked the screen, and flipped through the menus. "Looks like every doctor who examined the thing made chart entries." She tugged on Zach's shirt, urging him out of the chair so she could sit. "This should make for interesting reading."

Marie perused the records. Medical scanners hummed in the background.

Five minutes later, the hum dissipated.

"The autopsy's complete." Dr. Blackwell approached the terminals. "I've routed the results over here."

After prying her nose away from her screen, Marie leaned back. Data and images washed over six hovering displays. One screen showed internal organs. A second showed skeletal structure. Nervous and circulatory systems occupied a third, while a three-dimensional quadruple helix rotated on the fourth.

The final two screens listed height, weight, mass, molecular composition, and other data. A particle beam discharge to the upper torso was the assumed cause of death. The AI couldn't determine the rate of necrotic tissue breakdown or carbon-14 decay due to insufficient physiological data, so it couldn't estimate the corpse's date of death or age.

"I'm afraid I must echo my colleague's sentiments," Blackwell said. "This being is the most intriguing medical specimen I've ever examined." She buried her hands in the pockets of her lab coat. "Its DNA is more complex than a human's. Not even our most advanced genetic engineering techniques could produce it."

"Like all the news feeds claimed," Zach said.

"I'm sorry, Ms. Davis, but I don't need to look any further. This creature didn't evolve here on Earth. Nor could it have been created or faked by human science."

Marie wilted. Is Brooke delusional after all? Did the sparks drive her mad? And Kevin didn't tell me anything I can't explain away as coincidence.

*No, I believe in her. I'm missing something.*

Discrepancies in the exobeing's EMR had also failed to turn up during Marie's reading. No surprise there. An actual physician would've caught the obvious, yet something in what she had read struck her as odd. She didn't know what, specifically. Somehow, she knew she glossed over the answer that could vindicate her sister, something hidden in plain sight no one would think twice about it. She could feel it churning her journalist's gut. "A good reporter knows the right questions to ask," she muttered.

"The right questions?" Zach said.

"That's what my editor back in Chicago used to say." Marie sprung to her feet and paced around the room. "I need to ask the right questions." Her wandering brought her back to the corpse, and she considered the contraptions hanging from the ceiling over it.

She whirled to face the physician. "Doctor, how did you perform the autopsy?"

Blackwell approached the body. "The machines do all the work, really."

"What exactly do they do?"

"Well, emitters bombard the subject with lasers, x-rays, neutrinos, radio waves, magnetic fields, and more. We use multiple scanning techniques at once to map internal structure and composition."

Marie thought back to what she had read. "It's called a passive autopsy, right?"

"That's correct."

"In other words, you don't cut into the body."

Blackwell lifted an eyebrow. "Of course not. Surgical incisions haven't been performed in autopsies for over a century. There's no need with modern scanning techniques. We can create sims of internal organs as lifelike as the real thing."

"I see."

"Surgery in the traditional sense is becoming a thing of the past. Lasers and scalpels are used in rare cases. Nowadays, we inject medites into a patient to diagnose, heal cuts, repair broken bones, rebuild organs, and decompose foreign objects."

"A teammate hit my collar bone with a bat in a softball game." Zach pulled down the front of his shirt. "He broke the bone clean through, so the doctor shot me full of medites. A week later, I was good as new."

Marie placed an index finger to her lower lip. "According to the chart entries, none of the examining physicians injected medites into the body."

"The MedCenter director imposed a medite ban," Blackwell said. "He didn't want to pollute the only specimen we have with foreign contaminants. Medites break down in a living human's bloodstream, but not in a corpse, and not in a dead exobeing's physiology."

"Every doctor performed a passive autopsy." Marie's pulse quickened. "No one did a physical inspection of the body." *Am I on the verge of something?* "And if I recall, every physician examined the body here at the MedCenter. In this room."

"Obviously, they came here to see it," Zach said. "The UN's not about to ship the body all over the solar system. Something could happen to it. Think about the security measures they'd have to put in place to safeguard the thing."

"Yes, yes, it all makes sense—far too much sense, if you ask me." Marie waved a hand at the screens. "What do you think, Mr. IT Guru? Could someone program the scanners to show false readings?"

"Maybe." His brow scrunched. "If a bunch of hardcore programmers put their minds to something, they'll accomplish it."

"They might be able to fake certain results," Dr. Blackwell said, "but not the DNA. I have a hard time believing even our most sophisticated matrices could conceive of such a complex structure."

"The doc's right. That would be one hell of a feat."

"Difficult," Marie said, "but not impossible, right?"

Both Zach and Dr. Blackwell looked at each other.

Marie rubbed her hands together. "There's only one way to find out." She turned to Blackwell.

The physician stepped back, alarmed. "No, I won't cross that line."

"I'm with her, Marie," Zach said. "I can erase the evidence of everything we've done so far, but I can't cover up physical alterations done to the corpse."

"I agree we shouldn't slice into the thing," Marie said, "but can't we inject a few medites? Surely no one would notice a handful?"

"Yes, they would." Blackwell jabbed a finger at the screens. "The scans we took would catch one lone medite. It would stand out like the sun in the sky."

"No, it wouldn't."

The physician blinked at the reporter in disbelief.

"I'm willing to bet," Marie said, "we could chop the corpse into tiny little pieces, and the scan results wouldn't change."

Zach nodded. "I know what you're thinking. If the scanners aren't scanning the body, they won't find the medite."

"Precisely."

"It might not be that simple, though. Anyone capable of this kind of technical feat probably didn't rig it to return static results. I'd bet only a few of our results are skewed, but the majority are accurate."

"Like I said, only one way to find out."

Marie and Zach fixed pleading stares on Dr. Blackwell.

The doctor sighed. "If we get caught—"

"I forced you into it at gunpoint." Marie looked around. "Now all I need is a gun."

Zach escorted the doctor out of the room so she could retrieve the medites.

Standing alone in the dark morgue, Marie gazed into the lifeless black eyes of the exocorpse. It took her a minute to work up the courage to run a finger across its smooth head. Her body shivered at the cold grooves and pores in its skin. *If you're a fake, you're one hell of a fake.* The more she studied the being, the larger the pit in her stomach grew, partly because of her eerie solitude and partly because her gut gurgled with mixed signals. She second-guessed her original assumption about the corpse's authenticity, yet she still believed something wasn't right.

The entrance whooshed open. Marie held her breath until the door closed behind Zach and the doctor.

Blackwell carried a small cylinder and an auto-syringe over to the body. "These are molecular imaging medites." She loaded the cylinder into the syringe like a handgun clip. "I've prepared a solution with ten thousand parts per milliliter. Once injected into the subject, the medites will spread and start transmitting data."

Carrying a shoebox-sized AI tower, Zach made his way over to the terminals. "I brought my personal matrix, and Dr. Blackwell gave me the wireless frequencies used by the medites. We'll route the signals through my matrix to make sure nothing tampers with them." He set the tower down on a table, picked up an e-slip, and ran his fingers over it. "All right, it's all set up. The results will appear left of the existing screens."

Dr. Blackwell pulled the white sheet back to the reveal the body's grey, nippleless chest. Drawing in a deep breath, she held the autosyringe above it. "Last chance to back out."

"Do it," Marie said.

The doctor drove the syringe into the corpse's torso and pushed a button. The syringe emitted a faint buzz. "It's done."

The first images and data appeared within seconds. Eight new screens popped up, filling with information similar to the earlier scans.

Marie worked her fingers through the various screens, understanding very little. She gave up after a couple minutes. The data proved far too technical.

"So far, we've got the same results in more detail," Dr. Blackwell said. "The medites resolved the DNA's quadruple helix structure down to the molecular bonds."

Marie frowned. "So, it's definitely a genuine exobeing."

"You couldn't prove it any more conclusively."

"Okay, then. Keep looking for anything different from the initial scans." Marie slumped down into a chair next to Zach and observed the doctor.

Blackwell shuffled from screen to screen, striking one thoughtful pose after another.

During her second pass of the fifth screen, she did a double take. "Well, I'll be damned." She wiggled furious fingers within the screen, writing out an equation.

Marie rushed up behind her. "What is it?"

"Give me one moment." She scribbled two lines of mathematical formulas, which the screen rendered into three-dimensional font. "There." She spun around, face lit up. "The medites have deciphered the subject's physiology in enough detail to estimate the subject's age and date of death. The matrix is crunching the numbers now."

Marie stared at the screen. Digits scrolled down it.

Two large numerical figures usurped the screen, flanked by number ranges associated with probabilities.

"It appears our friend here is very old," Blackwell said. "More than five thousand years."

Zach whistled.

"As for the time of death . . ." The doctor cocked her head. "No, this can't be right." She dipped her fingers into the screen again. "I must've screwed up the equations somewhere. They found the body on Titan last July, right? We should be getting about seven months or so."

Marie blinked at the screen. It indicated the exobeing had died three hundred years ago.

The door to the room thundered open.

Twirling around, Marie found the lobby security guards, Dante and Mack, standing with laser pistols aimed at her. The two robotic sentries flanked the human guards, particle cannons raised, camera-eyes glowing red.

**Thirty-one—Entreaty**
**Base HOPE, Callisto, March 2248 AD**

Edward Collins sat alone in General Douglas's office, tapping one finger against the desktop. Outside the window, a dismantled chunk of Themisto broke away from the main rock, flew above New Galilei's biodomes toward the base, and disappeared overhead.

Pangs of despair washed over him when he considered the destruction and loss of life, but he accepted their necessity. *Everything up to this point was necessary, and everything has gone according to plan—amazingly so, in fact. And why shouldn't it have? Millennia of tireless planning by my mother, grandfather, and ancient ancestors have ensured success.* A jolt of pride coursed through his body. *Soon, their dreams will come to fruition, ushering in an unprecedented era in human history.*

Before that day came to pass, he had to deal with a handful of minor inconveniences.

The door to the office chimed.

"Enter."

Professor Kevin Sommerfield lurched through the doors as they parted. Two IMPs followed, shoving him inside.

"I'm going," Sommerfield said, tripping over his feet. "You don't have to push."

The IMPs escorted him over to the desk.

"Wait outside," Collins told them.

After the IMPs exited, he extended a palm toward a chair. "Have a seat, Professor."

The scientist folded his arms across his chest and narrowed his eyes.

"Come now, Professor. Let's discuss this like two civil adults."

Ten seconds of pouting followed before Sommerfield took a seat.

"Let me come straight to the point." Collins clasped his hands together and leaned forward. "Sabotaging the phase fighter production system and encrypting the prototype's interface could be considered acts of treason."

Sommerfield averted his gaze. "I've apologized for the accidental transmission of the wrong authorization codes. As for the prototype, it's not ready yet. The drive software has a few bugs. It's not safe to operate until I've resolved them."

"Why didn't you submit the proper notices? We didn't know until the fighter denied Colonel Richthofen access at the start of the shakedown. You've thrown off the entire schedule."

"It slipped my mind. Sorry."

Collins smiled. "Let's drop the pretense, shall we?" He jabbed a finger into the screen floating above the desk.

An audio stream filled the room.

"So you believe me?" Brooke's recorded voice said.

"Yes," Sommerfield said.

Collins let their conversation play for another few seconds before switching it off.

The professor ran a shaking hand through his hair.

"I know everything you spoke to Major Davis about," Collins said. "I understand why you did what you did, but Davis is a troubled individual. She's addicted to nanorobotic narcotics—to sparks."

The professor's face drooped.

"Didn't you know? How else could anyone pilot a star fighter with such skill? She did it with illegal drugs, trading her health for improved cognition and reflexes. But now, the sparks have wreaked havoc on her body and mind, causing her to hallucinate. They're the source of the absurd accusations she's made about conspiracies and the exothreat being staged, accusations about my involvement. She's delusional, Professor, and I want to make sure she gets help."

Collins studied Sommerfield's face, trying to read his reaction. The lines on the man's forehead scrunched while he grappled with the dilemma.

The tension in Sommerfield's face relaxed, and he snorted. "Discrediting one woman must be a trivial matter for an organization that's stayed hidden for over a century."

"Professor, listen to what you're saying. Right now, we're at war with beings that might bloody well intend our extermination. We need the phase fighter to combat them, and you're putting the human race at risk. I'll ask you again. Please release control of the prototype and transmit the proper authorization codes to the appropriate entities."

"Sorry, I won't do it."

"Very well. The UN is funding the phase fighter's construction, which makes it government property. Therefore, I'm giving you a direct order as commander-in-chief of UN Aerospace Defense. Unlock the control systems and transmit the codes."

Sommerfield lifted his chin. The timid little man had come a long way since stuttering on stage back at Dryden. "I'm not one of your soldiers. I don't take orders from you. The UN may be funding the fighter's physical manufacture, but the private sector maintains intellectual property rights to many of the designs. They're not mine to hand out."

Collins clenched a fist. He lifted it above the desk but stopped short of slamming it.

He poked a finger into his screen. "Dr. Yeager, please report to my office."

The professor's body tensed at the mention of her name.

A minute later, the office door swished open. Christine Yeager strode into the room and approached Collins.

Sommerfield drilled a vehement stare into her head, which she ignored.

Collins considered Sommerfield's reaction. *How does he know the identity of the saboteur? Not that it matters . . .*

While glaring at the professor, Collins said, "Dr. Yeager, you're now in charge of Project Quasar, effective immediately."

"Thank you, sir. It's a great honor."

Sommerfield scowled. His face burned redder than Martian soil.

"How long will it take to decrypt the prototype's control system?" Collins asked.

Yeager stuck her hands into the pockets of her lab coat, keeping her back to her former colleague. "It'll be quicker to wipe each operating system, reinstall, and reintegrate them. A week. Maybe two."

"What about getting the production lines up and running?"

"I've begun contacting all entities about the professor's 'mishap' and started reapplying for authorization. It could take a month to get things going again."

"I'm not sure we have that much time."

"I'll do what I can to speed up the process."

Collins dipped his chin. "See that you do."

The doctor turned and headed for the door.

"I know it was you," Sommerfield hissed when she passed him.

She hesitated for a moment before exiting the office.

"Last chance to have a change of heart," Collins said to him. "As you can see, you've caused only a minor setback. I'd prefer to get things going straight away, but if you want to be difficult, we can make do without you."

The professor took his time folding his arms across his chest.

"Have it your way." Collins considered tossing the professor in the stockade but decided against it. Justification existed for throwing Davis in solitary. The soldier disobeyed orders. But if Collins imprisoned the civilian scientist who invented faster-than-light-travel, he'd have a lot more explaining to do. It might even cause an intrasolar incident.

He poked his screen.

The two IMPs reentered the room.

"Orders, sir?" the first IMP asked.

"Escort Professor Sommerfield to his quarters and keep him there. Post a guard outside at all times—for his protection, of course."

Sommerfield growled under his breath. "You have no right to do this."

Collins opened his mouth, but the desk matrix chimed before he could voice his rebuttal. The screen indicated an urgent message required his attention.

The IMPs grabbed the professor under the armpits and forced him to his feet. He squirmed but gave up struggling after a couple seconds. His strength paled in comparison to the two trained military men.

After the IMPs dragged the man away, Collins spat his authorization code at the screen. A loyal subordinate's image took shape within it.

"We've apprehended the reporter, sir."

The previous encounter faded from Collins's mind. "Did she learn the truth?"

"She wouldn't talk, but medites were injected into the body."

"Indeed. Have you collected our insurance policy?"

"Yes, sir."

The tension in his muscles dissipated. "Then patch me through."

♦

Darkness had shrouded Marie since she awoke in a daze. Her discovery in the MedCenter felt like hours or even days ago, although she had no way to know for sure.

The lack of external stimuli had, at least, given her the chance to mull over Dr. Blackwell's results. In that time, she reached the epiphany of all epiphanies.

Marie tugged at the restraints binding her wrists behind the backrest of the metal chair. Her struggles caused the seat to wobble and tip sideways. She toppled over in slow motion, gasping. The backrest pinned her left arm against the concrete floor.

Her head smacked the floor next. She yelped. The impact jarred her but didn't inflict overwhelming pain. The crash might have cracked her skull in Earth-standard gravity.

*I'm no longer on Earth. Where am I?* She felt lighter than usual, but not as light as on Callisto. *Fairly low gravity. Concrete floor. Can't be a ship or space station. Luna?*

A door swished open behind her, but the darkness didn't fade. *Is the whole place unlit, or is something wrong with my sight?* A chill rippled through her body.

Footsteps scuffled along the concrete. Two pairs of hands grasped her along with the chair, hoisting her upright.

An object pressed to her temple, shooting stabbing pain through her forehead. Her eyes burned and watered, and she hissed through clenched teeth.

The door whooshed shut behind her.

Light encroached on her vision as she blinked away the moisture. A gray blur replaced the darkness. With each blink, her surroundings took on definition and shape. She sat in a room the size of a walk-in closet. Three plasma strips cast dim illumination on gray walls. A metal table outfitted with a screen emitter loomed in front of her.

"Hello?" Her voice echoed.

The emitter beeped and flashed. Pixels formed a narrow face with a shaved scalp.

Marie glared at him. "Oh, it's you."

Collins shook his head. "Marie, Marie, Marie. You've put me in a difficult position."

She knew she'd broken more than one law with the stunt she pulled, but that didn't stop her from shuddering in fury. "Where am I? Why was I drugged and dragged away like a kidnapping victim?" She fought against her restraints.

The chair swayed, so she ceased her struggles. She didn't want to end up on the floor again.

"Marie, you're guilty of breaking and entering, as well as destruction of government property. Do you have any idea what the penalty is for—"

"Where are Zach and Dr. Blackwell? And what've you done with Brooke?"

Collins clasped his hands together. "I'd be more concerned about myself if I was you."

Fear wrenched her abdomen. "What's . . . what's going to happen to me?" She stifled her trembling and feigned a hard outer shell.

"That depends."

"On what?"

"On your willingness to cooperate."

"Cooperate how?"

He shrugged.

Marie took a guess. "You want me to keep quiet about what I've figured out?"

"Oh, and what do you think you've figured out?"

"Everything."

Collins smiled. "Please do elaborate."

"I had to dig deep into my knowledge of ancient history. Most of this stuff isn't common knowledge today." She circled her gaze around the featureless room. "Let's start with the secret society that's staging the attack by the Greys. The Vril were a covert organization that supposedly helped Nazi Germany develop technology far outclassing the Allies during World War II. Conspiracy theorists claimed the Vril gained advanced knowledge through contact with extrasolar beings."

"How interesting."

Marie tilted her head. "And then there's Roswell."

He sat back and tugged his lapel, no longer smiling.

"Dr. Blackwell determined the exobeing in the MedCenter died three hundred years ago," she said. "She assumed she made a mistake, but it got me thinking. What happened three centuries ago that might explain her findings?

"Then it hit me. The year was 1947, I believe, when a UFO allegedly crashed near Roswell, New Mexico. The government of the American Colonies denied it, of course. They insisted the craft was a weather balloon and released a number of reports debunking the existence of 'aliens,' but that didn't stop the event from spawning a mythology about the Greys, one which lasted for a century and a half."

"That's quite an intriguing theory."

"It's more than theory." Marie snorted. "It's shocking irony. Only now, centuries after people accepted aliens and UFOs as myth, do we discover extrasolar beings did, in fact, visit us in the past. The Greys are real, but they're not the ones attacking us right now."

"Well," he said after a minute, "allow me to extend my congratulations. You, Marie Davis, are the first person to uncover the truth."

"So, I'm right. Brooke's not crazy after all."

"It no longer serves me to deny it."

"You can't believe you'll get away with duping the entire human race into uniting."

"We already have. The separatists have relented because of us. All nations and colonies have joined the UN"

"Maybe so, but the truth will come out sooner or later. Somebody will figure out the exocorpse's true origins or realize there're humans aboard 'extrasolar' ships."

Collins inclined his head. "Which is where you come in."

"Me?"

"That's right. I want you to tell the solar system all about it."

Marie leaned back in the chair, brow dipping. "You want me to go on the air and tell everyone the truth?"

"Yes—well . . ." He held up a palm. "I need you to phrase the truth in a specific manner."

She rolled her eyes. "In what 'manner' are we talking?"

"You'll announce that the UN has captured a tri-fighter."

"But the exo fighters self-destruct."

"Most of the time, yes, but through extreme diligence, the UN got its mitts on one at last. When we opened it up, it contained a human being."

"You want to reveal that humans are the actual pilots? That'd blow your cover."

Collins intertwined his fingers and leaned forward. "We believe in flipping disadvantages to advantages, which is why UN experts will determine that the Greys are using human abductees as pilots. This has been going on for three hundred years."

"Why would . . .?" The answer hit her. *Greys using us as pilots will explain away any human bodies found amongst wrecked tri-fighters. The story will also support ancient abduction theories, and who'll think twice if no one finds another exocorpse?*

"Forget it." She whipped her hair from side to side. "I'm not your messenger girl. 'Phrase the truth in a specific manner.' You're asking me to lie to thirty-five billion people to further your agenda. I won't have any part of it."

"Well, that's gratitude for you."

"What do you mean?"

"I thought you'd be more grateful given my efforts to advance your career."

Marie tilted her head and dug deep. When she found the answer, she almost fainted. "You changed my editor's mind about sending me to Dryden? But how could you have known?"

"Consider my offer, Marie. We're bringing the human race together, which means no more war. As a single government—one with us pulling the strings in the background—the UN will wield the influence necessary to eliminate crime, poverty, and hunger."

She shook off the shock. "Maybe so, but it's a lie. Plus, you're killing thousands of people in the process."

Collins jabbed a finger in her direction, but he did it to interact with his screen, she realized.

A ten-digit integer appeared on the display.

"Take one guess what this number represents, Marie."

"I'm not in the mood."

"It's the projected death toll for one year from now given continued territorial secession."

She took a deep breath, feeling her heart pound.

"That's right," he said. "A billion people dead, along with our modern way of life. Now, do you know how many people have died since Europa because of the Vril's actions?"

Marie glowered at him.

"About one hundred thousand," he said. "Bloody hell. If we'd intervened sooner, we could've saved millions more lives."

"No moral or ethical considerations, huh? It all comes down to the numbers."

"When you're the commander in chief of humanity's armed forces, you maintain a higher-level perspective than the everyday citizen. Morals and ethics are foremost on my mind, I assure you. But sometimes, yes, it does come down to numbers."

Marie considered his words. She hated to admit it, but he had a point. The death of a hundred thousand people seemed better than a billion. If the Vril succeeded in their attempt to unify everyone—and if they eliminated crime, poverty, and hunger—would such an act not prove worth it? She might even prefer to live in such a world.

*Still* . . . "It's not right. We should have the chance to get there on our own. If we destroy ourselves beforehand, maybe we don't deserve the Promised Land."

"Funny," he said. "Your sister uttered similar words. The two of you are more alike than either of you would care to admit."

Marie raised an eyebrow.

"I implore you again," he said. "Join with me to usher in a better tomorrow."

She held his penetrating stare. "Absolutely not. Kill me if you must." Her heart stopped beating for a nanosecond. *Did I just say that?*

"I have no desire to kill you, Marie. Our organization's intent is to eliminate such acts in the long term. Killing in the short term is an unfortunate necessity." He blew out a long sigh. "I hoped you'd see the bigger picture, but if you won't help us, there're ways to ensure your cooperation."

An empty cabin inside a spacecraft replaced Collins's image.

The view panned downward. A little girl sat in one corner of the room, hugging her legs. Tears slicked her cheeks.

"Maya!" Marie cried. "Maya, can you hear me?"

Her daughter lifted her head. "Mommy?"

Collins's deplorable face returned, eschewing Maya's image.

"You evil prick," Marie said. "Is there nothing you won't—" She gasped. "Obaa-chan . . . you better not have hurt my grandmother."

"No, my men sedated her when they took the girl. She's fine."

"Thank the stars." Her body released a miniscule amount of tension. "If you harm a single cell in my daughter's body, so help me . . ."

"Marie, I'm not a monster. I spared the children on Titan, didn't I?" He sat back. "I'm holding her for insurance. That's all. I promise a blissful mother-daughter reunion once you've fulfilled my request. You have my word." His face stiffened. "As long as you do as you're told."

Marie hung her head, no longer able to suppress her sobs.

## Thirty-two—Parley
## Base HOPE, Callisto, April 2248 AD

Dried tears crusted the corners of Brooke's eyes. She lay atop her bunk, staring up at the ceiling of her detention cell. A repair crew had applied smart sealant to a corner because of the damage she caused to New Galilei. The cracks in the metal receded at a barely perceptible rate. *I wish I could apply something similar to fix my flaws . . .*

Another spasm shook her body. She'd reached the point where she never stopped trembling. Thousands of tiny, invisible creatures gnawed at her head—or so it felt. Sweat beaded off her skin, chilling her to the core, and every molecule in her body reeled. She'd never gone this long without sparking or anti-anxiety meds.

The meal schedule provided her only sense of time. A guard delivered breakfast, lunch, and dinner each day. *How many have passed? Fifty? A hundred? I've lost count.*

She'd long since grown numb to the pain and monotony. *My career—my life—is probably over. Never mind flying faster than light. I may never fly again at all.*

Moaning, she broke into a fit of rage. She didn't have any tears left to cry, but that didn't stop her from wailing. With clenched fists, she pounded the mattress until she couldn't pound it any longer. The feeling of wanting to end it all hadn't consumed her since her mother's suicide.

The door swished open, flooding the cell with light. Brooke squinted and propped herself up on her forearms. *Feeding time already?*

Two guards rushed in and grabbed her. She twisted and flailed, but they pinned her face and stomach against the bed. One guard sat on top of her while the other cuffed her legs and wrists.

The guard hopped off of her, and both exited the room.

Brooke rolled onto her back, finding Collins in the doorway. She sprang to a sitting position and snarled.

"How're we holding up?" he asked.

The door closed behind him, dismissing the bright light.

Collins sat on the bunk opposite her and placed a screen emitter on the mattress beside him. "I thought you might want to see this." To the emitter, he said, "Enable ISN network."

A display materialized above his bunk. Flickering text read, "Phase tunneling in progress." Then it stated, "SolNet link established."

A commercial for a clinic offering cybernetic arm and leg replacements appeared. At the end of the ad, the saleswoman said, "Go out on an artificial limb with us."

Collins cleared his throat to mask a snigger. "I always liked that one."

Brooke's stomach constricted.

A familiar face appeared on the screen.

"Welcome back to IntraSolar News for Monday, April tenth, 2248. I'm Marie Davis."

*April?* Brooke groaned.

"As ISN first reported two days ago, UN Aerospace Defense has recovered the wreckage of an extrasolar spacecraft. The tri-fighter was found adrift in Jupiter's new outer ring system, which was created as a result of the destruction of its ninth moon, Themisto. Apparently, the craft's self-destruct system malfunctioned, leaving it intact."

Footage of the wrecked tri-fighter floating in space replaced Marie's image. The craft somersaulted past asteroids big and small. The occasional pebble-sized chunk of debris pummeled it.

The footage skipped ahead to the triangle sitting inside a spacecraft carrier hangar bay. Soldiers and members of an engineering crew stood near it, watching a crane lift away the upper section of the fighter's smooth, white hull.

"When technicians opened up the craft," Marie said, "they found a deceased pilot. However—" the camera altered its angle and zoomed in, showing the interior of the cockpit "—the pilot turned out be human."

The pilot wore a white helmet with black visor. A technician lifted the headgear away, revealing a tall woman with gray skin and an elongated face.

The weight lifted from Brooke for the first time in weeks. "She's one of them." Hope buoyed her spirits. "The truth's finally coming out."

"So it would seem," Collins said.

Marie returned to the screen. "When physicians aboard *Terminus* examined the woman's body, they reached a startling conclusion." She stared down the camera and paused for effect. "The woman was a human abductee, stolen from Earth by the Greys."

The notion sapped every last shred of Brooke's short-lived elation. "What the hell? That's not true at all."

"So far, analysts have been unable to extract any data from the craft. Furthermore, questions about the pilot's altered physiology remain unanswered, although experts theorize the woman isn't a first-generation abductee. The fact the settlement of Triton occurred at least a century ago seems to support—"

Collins told the emitter to switch off. "As you can see, Major, you were partially right all along."

"Partially?" she said. "You've twisted the truth to better serve your ploy." An anxious pang rippled through her arm. She gripped her wrist and breathed. *Then again, I wonder how much truth there is to this story. Perhaps the Vril abducted people in their early efforts to create Armin's ancestors.*

"That's not what your sister thinks about what we're doing."

"You're admitting it?" Brooke shuddered with relief and abhorrence. "But what's Marie got to do with . . .?" In her mind, she replayed her sister's telecast. Something in her voice and demeanor hadn't seemed right, something only a twin sibling could discern. "She knows?"

"Following a candid conversation, Marie dedicated herself to our cause. She appreciates the better life it'll bring about for everyone."

"No. She wouldn't."

He leaned back against the wall. "She has a different perspective than you. She wants her daughter to grow up in a world without suffering."

Brooke bowed her head. She'd never felt so alone.

Bending forward, Collins rested an arm on his upper leg. "Which brings me to why I'm here. I came to offer you one final opportunity to improve your situation."

Her chin lifted.

"That's right, Brooke. You can fly again. Spark all you want, and perhaps our advanced medicine can eliminate the harmful side effects. You can be a part of the future we're creating. Come pilot the phase fighter, Brooke."

Hope welled up inside of her, straightening her spine. "What . . . what do I have to do?"

"That a lass." Collins nodded. "We'd planned on sending a fleet of phase fighters to deal a crippling blow to the colony on Triton, an operation you would've commanded."

"A crippling blow?" Her head swayed. "You mean you're setting up your patsy race to lose?" It made perfect sense. The act of defeating them would unify the human race. The Vril had intended it all along. "What about all those people?"

"That's their purpose, Brooke. It's why we created them. And not all of them will die. We have important plans for some of them."

"I see . . . you said you 'had planned' on attacking Triton. It's not happening anymore?"

"Yes, the professor's actions forced us to alter our strategy."

"What did he do?"

"The bloody twit sabotaged mass production of the phase fighter and rigged the prototype so only you can operate it."

She tossed her head back and cackled.

Collins grimaced. "Care to include me in the joke?"

When she whipped around to face him, she saw his Adam's apple gulp. "No wonder I'm still alive. You need me. Otherwise, the Vril can't get their hands on the phase drive."

"Don't flatter yourself." He bounded to his feet. "It's more convenient for us if you operate the fighter, but we don't need you."

"I don't think so. You didn't plan on Kevin uncovering your plot, did you? I'm sure you thought you had everything under control, but he screwed you good, didn't he?"

The security president took a deep breath and forced a weak smile. "He's presented us with an unforeseen obstacle, but it's nothing we can't hurdle. We'll get the phase drive, and we've devised an alternate stratagem, one that's an improvement over the original plan. As a matter of fact . . ." His eyes shifted, reading a message in his new smart vision. "They should've revealed themselves by now." He stepped over to the opposite bunk. "Screen on."

"—breaking news," Marie said as the display congealed. "UN Aerospace Defense has detected an enemy fleet passing inside Martian orbit. Its projected course is Earth."

Five specks of light much too big and bright to mistake for stars replaced Marie's image. The specks were pyramidal spacecraft carriers.

"You could be out there, piloting the phase fighter," Collins said. "You'd be almost invincible."

Brooke wanted to accept his offer. She yearned to sit in a cockpit again, to be free. *So what if the Vril deceive thirty-five billion people if it gives them a utopia? I'm not sure why I have such a problem with it . . . but I do.* "I'd rather rot in here."

"You're condemning yourself. Why fight the future?"

"What you're doing robs people of their humanity." She refused to cry. "Maybe I've lived with pain for too long, but because of it, I've learned why people need it. We need things not to be perfect so we can recognize the truth, even if we're not always conscious of it."

"You and I may never understand each other." Collins gave a pitying shake of his head. "So be it." He reached into the pocket of his suit coat, pulled out a black pill, and held it up to the dim light. "I offer you one final choice. You're going to help us whether you want to or not. If you remain alive, you'll go through a court-martial proceeding. We'll use it to reinforce the things that aid our cause and to discredit anything that reveals too much of the truth. Or"—he held the pill out to her—"you can take this. It's quick and painless, I assure you. Either way, your life is over, but if you end it now, you'll die as a heroine rather than a traitor."

The cell door opened. Two guards rushed in, demagnetized her cuffs, and held her arms.

Collins clamped a hand around her wrist, yanked her arm out, and dropped the pill into her palm. "It's up to you." He swiped the emitter off the opposite bunk, straightened his blazer, and exited the room.

After freeing her legs, the guards followed him out. The doors whooshed shut, sealing with a click of finality.

She held the pill between her thumb and middle finger, regarding it. Her teeth chattered with each choking sob. *Marie's sided with them. My sister. My best friend. I'm all alone.*

Brooke had never felt like she belonged anywhere. She knew she'd never fit into the society the Vril intended to create. Maybe Kevin still cared for her, but she could never have a life with him. She could never live any life, for that matter, not with what they planned to do with her.

After collapsing back onto her cot, she stared at the pill for what felt like hours. When she couldn't stand it anymore, she closed her eyes, opened her mouth, and touched the pill to her tongue.

## **Thirty-three—Skyjack**
## **Base HOPE, Callisto, April 2248 AD**

The door to Brooke’s cell swished open.

She withdrew the pill from her mouth, sat upright on the bunk, and stared at the empty doorway.

More than a minute later, the door remained ajar without anyone entering.

The pill rolled out of her hand and onto the mattress.

When she slid her legs off the bunk and stood, her stance wobbled. She hadn’t left the bed in days. Weekly gravite injections helped to maintain her strength, but her muscles and bones still strained.

Brooke poked her head out the doorway. The guard at the far end of the hallway had disappeared, and someone had deactivated the shimmering blue force field separating the stockade from the rest of the base.

*Is this a setup? Does Collins want me to try to escape so he can kill me in the act? But if that’s the case, why bother with the pill?*

She crept her way down the corridor.

A familiar voice emanated from the wall speakers. <Ma’am, turn left when you reach the upcoming intersection.>

“Bob!” Her outburst echoed throughout the metallic passageway. “I didn’t think I’d ever hear your voice again,” she whispered and rushed over to a control panel on the wall. “What’s going on?”

<I’ve been observing you throughout your detention, ma’am, executing a program created by Professor Sommerfield. I wasn’t supposed to initiate the extrication sequence for another two hours and sixteen minutes, but when I detected your imminent ingestion of a lethal chemical substance, I decided to take initiative.>

“Initiative?”

<Please keep moving, ma’am. I calculate an eighty-four-point-six percent chance you’ll avoid discovery if you follow my instructions. Each passing second decreases that percentage.>

She quickened her pace.

Her peripheral vision caught the empty chair behind the desk. “What happened to the officer on duty?” Regulations required a guard to man the post at all times.

<I’ve executed diversionary tactics with the intent of eliminating encounters with base personnel, ma’am. Concerning the guard in question, Second Lieutenant Scott Wilson, I cross-referenced his profile with the records of his spouse. The information I accumulated about her predicted gestation timeline allowed me to preoccupy the lieutenant via a message to his personal communication device.>

“Predicted gestation?” Feeling her energy return, she broke into a jog, laughing. “You mean you told him his wife was in labor.”

<Correct, ma’am. Thus far, I’ve removed eleven potential obstacles in similar fashion.>

“I’m impressed. So, where are you leading me?”

<Level B1, section twenty-three, ma’am. The test launch hangar.>

Her skin tingled in anticipation. Adrenaline propelled her forward.

Several corridors later, a lift elevated her to level B1. When she reached the door to her destination, Bob released the lock, and the doors parted.

She ran into the test hangar locker room.

Ceiling speakers projected Bob’s voice. <The delivery bot, ma’am.>

The bot sat next to the bench between the lockers, holding a cargo container.

Plopping down on the bench, she tapped the top of the container. Its upper surface peeled back. “Bob, how did you . . .?” Elation surged through her veins at the sight of her helmet and flight armor.

<Your personal belongings were confiscated following your incarceration, ma’am. I altered the Intrasolar Military Police inventory manifest and requisitioned them here.>

Her hand quavered when she reached for the helmet. “I want to,

Bob, but I don't know if I can."

<Look in the container, ma'am.>

She dumped the box. Her personal effects, including her flight suit, specs, and the safe with her spark injectors, drifted to the floor. "How did you manage to get the safe? The IMPs wouldn't have kept it with my stuff."

<I checked the safe out of an evidence locker for presentation in a falsified trial, ma'am. I made sure the bot delivered it and your belongings here without human intervention.>

"Kevin was right. You might be the smartest AI ever." After opening the safe, she pulled out an injector and stared at it, rehashing the negative consequences the sparks had wrought upon her life. Regret wrenched her intestines, but her withdrawal symptoms—the shakes and shivers and hot flashes and dizziness and perspiration and dejection and anxiety and dependency—outweighed any and all higher sentimentalities.

Brooke jabbed the injector into the base of her neck.

With newfound vigor, she hopped to her feet and donned her flight suit and armor.

She wedged her helmet beneath her armpit and entered the hangar bay through the exit on the opposite side of the locker room.

"Oh, wow . . ." She almost fell to her knees.

At the center of the test hangar rested the YPF-1 Quasar, its wings retracted into its sleek body. Six afterburners and four retrorockets jutted out from the front and rear of the fighter. The prototype's fat midsection contained the phase drive. Engineers had affixed two stubby cylinders, the drive's graviton-focusing nacelles, to the top of the fighter and two below it. Anyone not familiar with their purpose might mistake them for oversized missiles.

The Quasar's hull reflected the interior of the bay like a mirror. At the same time, light passed through the fighter's translucent fuselage. The spacecraft looked like the ghost of a plane, as if it didn't quite exist.

"It's the most beautiful thing I've ever seen," Brooke murmured.

"Personally, I'd rank her number two."

Whirling, she found the professor standing to one side of the locker room entrance. "Kevin!" She wanted to throw herself into his arms, but a fear more potent than any force field seized her.

Instead, she said, "I'm glad to see you."

"Me, too."

"Bob said you arranged my escape."

"That's right."

She jabbed a thumb toward the Quasar. "I also heard you sabotaged this thing."

"Well, sabotage is a strong word."

"You shouldn't have done anything."

He held his hands out. "I had to do something. Like it or not, I'm involved. If I hadn't encrypted the prototype's systems and put a stop to more being created, the drive would be in the Vril's hands right now."

Brooke nodded.

"Besides," he said, "Collins made a few threats, but I doubt my life's in danger. My death would result in a thorough investigation I'm sure the Vril would prefer to avoid. All Collins did was confine me to quarters and try to cut off my network access." He wiggled his bushy eyebrows. "But I let Bob loose beforehand. He replaced the base's AI without anyone knowing and took control of everything."

<Correction, Professor,> Bob said from the Quasar's external speakers. <I've gained control of ninety-eight-point-one percent of all base networks and matrices. However, I still lack access to the most heavily-encrypted communications and data storage systems.>

Shuffling over to the phase fighter, Brooke said, "Which are probably the same systems used by the Vril."

"That wouldn't surprise me." Kevin followed her. "Bob's access level was more than enough to re-establish my network connection, divert the guard away from my room, and get me here. And that's not all."

She reached the fighter, stopped, and turned around. "Oh?"

He dug into his pocket and held up a data chip the size of his thumbnail. "Were you aware Collins has been watching and listening to everything you do and say?"

"What do you mean?"

He directed his attention toward the Quasar. "Bob, display the footage from the chip."

A floating screen projected from the side of the fighter's nose below the canopy. The display provided engineers with an external systems interface during maintenance, but now, it showed something all too familiar to Brooke.

"What . . . what do I have to do?" her recorded image said.

"That a lass." Collins nodded as she had seen him do in person. "We'd planned on sending a fleet of phase fighters to deal a crippling blow to the colony on Triton, an operation you would've commanded."

Kevin told Bob to dismiss the screen.

"That was my conversation with Collins," she said. "What did you do, Bob? Hack into the stockade surveillance system?"

<I attempted that at first, ma'am, but—>

"Collins scrambled all the vid feeds," Kevin said. "Obviously, he thought of that much."

Brooke's brow dipped. "Then, how?"

"Route the feed from her implants to the screen, Bob."

The Quasar's exterior display showed her image repeated to infinity.

She turned toward Kevin. The screen showed him.

"That's what I'm seeing."

"That's what I'm seeing," the display repeated in her voice.

"Enough, Bob," Kevin said.

The screen dematerialized.

Her free hand flew to her temple. "Collins tapped my implants and has been seeing everything I see." She thought back to the exam Doc Gordon had given her before she departed for Earth a year ago. "That's how he knew about Marie and me, the sparks . . ."

"Bob noticed a signal coming from your implants when I told him to keep an eye on you in your cell," Kevin said. "It took him weeks to break the encryption."

Brooke nodded. Then she gasped. "What am I showing Collins now?"

"For all he knows, you're still asleep in your cell."

"Nice work, Bob. We've finally got the proof we need."

Kevin stepped closer to her. "As much as I don't want you to go, you have to take the chip to the UN secretary-general." He handed it to her.

"Take it to Earth?" She stared at the all-important evidence resting in her gloved palm. "Why not post the footage on SolNet? Billions of people would see it in a matter of seconds."

He shook his head. "That was the first thing I tried, but the moment I uploaded it, a censor matrix purged all traces of it."

"Censor matrix?"

"You know the AIs that filter online content, bleep out bad words, and edit out sensitive information, right? Well, something much more advanced intercepted my upload and back-traced it here to Base HOPE. If I hadn't saved and isolated the footage on the chip beforehand, I would've lost everything. This leaves us with only one option."

"I guess so." She opened a slot in the arm of her flight armor and inserted the chip.

"Also, I've included the production authorization codes on the chip."

"Codes?"

"In order to build more phase fighters, the proper codes have to be transmitted to the designers and manufacturers. Only they can program the robotic assembly arrays and initiate construction." He grinned deviously. "Christine thought she could break Bob's encryption on the prototype and get production going in a matter of weeks. Boy, was Collins livid when it turned out she couldn't."

"I see." Brooke stared up at the Quasar's canopy, feeling the weight of the task ahead. *It's up to you, me, and Bob, huh?* She crept up to the fighter, reached out, and touched her fingers to its nose.

Kevin stood beside her and wrapped his arm around her waist.

Turning, she gazed up into his hazel eyes and stopped breathing for a moment.

She held his gaze for the longest period of time she had ever made eye contact with anyone. Her knees weakened.

He closed his eyes and crossed the distance between them.

Before their lips touched, she twisted her head to the side.

Kevin backpedaled. "Oh, I'm sorry." His cheeks flushed. "I didn't mean to—"

"No, you don't have anything to be sorry about." She forced back mounting tears. "It's just that I . . . I . . ." Her stomach cramped, but she forced herself to admit the embarrassing truth. "I've never kissed anyone before."

"Really?"

"Well, technically, I did once. A boy tried to kiss me back in high school. Our lips made contact for a second or two before his hands made too much contact." She crinkled her nose. "I think I knocked out at least three of his teeth."

Kevin gave a generous nod. "If you don't want to, I understand."

"No, I want to. I just . . ." She looked around helplessly. "It's stupid. I'm not anywhere near as scared about going into combat. It doesn't make much sense, does it?"

"I don't know. A lot of people have the same difficulty. Emotional pain hurts far worse than physical pain. Maybe that's because the latter doesn't require opening up."

"Maybe."

Brooke couldn't think of anything else to say. Kevin went mum as well. With each passing second, Brooke's heart dropped further and further.

It made sense. Her destiny didn't include love.

<Ma'am, my latest attempt at diversion almost failed. I predict one attempt within the next three will fail and reveal our ruse. I recommend launching immediately.>

"Okay, Bob." Brooke rounded the phase fighter to a set of rollaway stairs leading up to the cockpit. "Thanks for everything, Kevin." Grabbing the side rail, she placed her boot on the first step. "You're the most wonderful man I've ever known. I only wish—"

"Oh, I almost forgot." He hurried over to her. "I have one more thing for you." He reached inside his lab coat and pulled a small box out of the side pocket. "I know you love this stuff, and I figured you might be hungry, so . . ."

The label on the travel box read "Fruity Planets Cereal."

With a smile, she accepted the box, although it felt too light, even in Callisto's low gravity. She shook it. "Hey, it's empty."

"Sorry. I guess I ate a few of them."

"A few of them?" She shoved the box back into his hand. "You finished it off."

Kevin rattled it. "Not the entire thing." He tapped the top, and the box transformed into a bowl. A single Jupiter marshmallow lay at the bottom of the dish, blinking red. "I guess we'll have to share." He held it up between them and smiled.

Brooke inched her face closer to the piece. Kevin did the same.

Her chest thumped. When her mouth contacted the marshmallow, she closed her eyes.

She touched her lips to Kevin's. Every inhibition cried out for her to pull away, but she reached deep down and found the courage to break through them.

Goosebumps tickled her skin. Her muscles released years' worth of tension. A rising euphoria buoyed her very essence.

Kevin wrapped his arms around her, and she melted into them. Her flight armor prevented a closer embrace, but she didn't care.

It took all her willpower to break away. "So, what did you do with the milk?"

He shrugged. "A brilliant scientist never reveals his secrets."

"Not completely original, though."

"Maybe so, but it worked, didn't it?'"

She raised an eyebrow for as long as she could hold it. Then her frown morphed into the warmest smile to ever grace her face. "Yes. Yes, it did." She grabbed a fistful of his coat, yanked him close, and kissed him again. Hard.

A deep-seated sadness welled up inside her chest. She never wanted the moment to end.

Kevin looked into her eyes and cupped her face with one hand.

<Ma'am,> Bob said, making them both jump, <an officer has noticed your vacant cell.>

Klaxons sounded. Red lights affixed to the walls near the ceiling flashed.

He let go of her hands and stepped back. "Come back to me safely, Brooke."

"I will."

"You still owe me a date."

"We'll go on one when I get back. That's a promise." After one last look at him, she ascended the stairs and hopped into the Quasar's cockpit.

Brooke settled into the seat and wedged her head into her helmet. Her face shield emerged from the edges of her helmet and created an airtight seal.

As the seat harness locked her into place, she squeezed the auxiliary control grips and scanned the compartment. The light-gray shades of upholstery contrasted with her black armor and the darker interior of a Starthroat.

<Brainwave patterns recognized, ma'am. Disengaging control lockout. Initiating neurotronic interlinks.>

*<Neural connections established, ma'am.>*

Translucent screens crowded her field of vision. She whipped through them, bumping most into her peripheral vision. Directed desire manifested the pre-flight systems checks and launch sequence startup menus within her direct line of sight.

Brooke shooed the pre-flight screen away and cold-started the Quasar's systems.

Gravgel rushed in to submerge her while the engines rumbled to life. Their low hum erupted into a growl, shaking the cockpit. The phase drive began charging, the required time reduced to two minutes from *Viking's* fifteen-minute cycle.

*<All systems ready for launch, ma'am. However, Control has secured the bay doors. I cannot override the locking mechanisms.>*

*Bob, determine the minimum explosive yield necessary to remove our obstruction, and let me know when Kevin is out of harm's way.*

*<Calculations complete, ma'am. Professor Sommerfield has exited the hangar.>*

With a thought, she thumbed the trigger. A seeker tore away from the forward launch tubes and blasted a hole in the bay doors. Shrapnel glanced off the Quasar's shimmering force field. Rushing air blew the fireworks out into space.

She nudged the Quasar forward toward the opening. When her fighter reached the bay door, she raised the nose and engaged thrusters, lifting away with minimal acceleration. Base HOPE and New Galilei shrank within her rear camera views.

*<Gravgel immersion complete, ma'am.>*

The fusion afterburners bellowed plasma, hurtling the phase fighter away from Callisto. Jupiter's eighth moon plummeted out of view like a gray ball dropped into a black abyss. The sun crested Jupiter to starboard.

*<Ma'am, the phase drive has reached its full charge capacity.>*

*All right, Bob. Let's go expose this—*

<Terminus *has launched r-seekers, ma'am. Impact imminent.*>

*Shift now—*

Detonations and distortions tore local space apart.

**Thirty-four—Naumachia**
**New York City, April 2248 AD**

"This just in," McKenzie Pierce informed the solar system. "Extrasolar forces have breached the UN's defenses in lunar orbit."

Marie sat off-set, not far from the sound and vid crew. She stared sullenly at McKenzie while the anchorwoman delivered the latest breaking news.

It had taken Marie about a week to succumb to guilt. Unable to continue spreading Collins's propaganda, she had given up the lead anchor spot.

Her intestines tangled into knots. She gripped the bridge of her nose and squeezed, trying to ease the sinus pressure.

McKenzie leaned over her desk and put two fingers to her earpiece. "Hold on." She stared into the camera, unwavering. "ISN has just received an update. The Greys have engaged the unified fleet in high Earth orbit. What you're about to see is real-time battle footage streamed from the New International Space Station."

Fireworks erupted against the backdrop of space on the screen nearest to Marie. Another display showed what the viewers at home saw. Flashbulb explosions flickered and faded within a picture-in-picture window to McKenzie's right.

The anchorwoman shuffled the stack of e-slips on the desk. "The

UN secretary-general has issued a statement asking people to remain calm. The Security Council president is confident in the unified fleet's ability to defend the Earth."

Marie choked.

"Here you go," Denise said in a cheery tone. She handed Marie a can of Relief Cola, the latest product to include pain killers, antacids, cut healers, caffeine, and other medite remedies. "This should make you feel better." She tapped the top of the can, opening it. Holographic fizz billowed up like a fountain. Pixelated droplets of cola sprayed in all directions. "Mmm," said the can's child-like voice. Cartoon characters danced around the can's exterior, drinking from longneck bottles designed centuries earlier.

A prolonged sigh escaped Marie's lips.

"You haven't been your confident self lately," Denise said, "not since you got me this job. I can't thank you enough for it. The VidStreamer was such a dead end." When Marie failed to respond, Denise added, "You need to get well so you can reclaim the spotlight." She waved a slip in the air. "Your ratings were way higher than McKenzie's. People like you a lot better."

"In other news," McKenzie said, "the Vatican has issued a statement asking people to pray for the souls of the humans abducted by the Greys."

Denise waved a fist in the air. "Despicable exos. Using us to do their dirty work. I hope we pummel them back to wherever they came from."

*That's exactly how they want you to feel*, Marie mused.

McKenzie reported the extrasolar attack force consisted of five pyramid carriers and one hundred tri-fighters. While still on the air, Marie had referred to these figures as "daunting," given the enemy's technical superiority. Now, McKenzie revealed the complement of spacecraft within the unified fleet, which consisted of two hundred spacecraft carriers, almost ten thousand star fighters, and hundreds of orbital defense platforms and satellites. These figures included everything assembled in Earth orbit. The fleet from Mars had yet to arrive.

*All to put on the greatest charade in human history...*

"How's Maya doing?" Denise asked.

Marie sunk deeper into her chair and stifled a whimper.

Vibrations shook the entire building. She gripped the arms of her chair.

"What the—?" a man yelled from beyond the studio exit.

Marie leapt out of her chair, overtook a waddling Denise, and rushed out into the hallway. Half a dozen people had their faces plastered against the windows.

The eighty-ninth floor of the refurbished New York Times Building provided Marie with a bird's eye view of the city. Vehicles crowded the winding, multi-tiered concrete streets below. Horns blared. Not a single car or truck budged. Masses of panic-stricken people gathered at ground level.

More of Marie's coworkers filled the hall, crowding her.

"Look!" A woman pointed up into the sky.

A ball of flame thundered down from above, parting the clouds as it bore down on Manhattan.

Marie shrieked.

The fireball struck the Empire State Building blocks away, shaking the floor and tossing people off their feet. A cloud of debris ballooned out from the impact point near the top of the building.

The hallway windows warbled when the shock wave thudded against them. Bits of concrete and metal pelted and cracked the panes.

Standing as rigid as the once-mighty building, Marie watched the dust cloud dissipate. Her gaze refused to waver from the gouge.

Dazed journalists struggled to pick themselves up off the floor.

The wall screen behind Marie projected McKenzie's image and voice. "—State Building has been struck by wreckage from the battle in orbit. All of us here at ISN Studios in New York felt the impact. UN ground forces are attempting to confirm whether the object was part of a spacecraft carrier, star fighter, space station, or extrasolar ship. Again, Aerospace Defense is asking people to remain calm, as incidents such as these should occur infrequently."

"Define 'infrequently,'" Marie grumbled.

"Marie, a word, please."

She peered down the hall.

Her producer wove his way around a mass of disheveled employees. "Walk with me." He grabbed her by the arm and tugged her along. "I hope you've worked yourself out of your little funk. Your refusal to go on-air has cost this company significant ratings, not to mention trillions of dollars." The producer stopped once they reached an unoccupied section of the corridor. The ISN logo on the breast pocket of his jacket spun and flickered. "The secretary-general is holding a press conference at UN Headquarters in less than an hour. I want you there to cover it."

Marie blinked.

"Come on, Marie. Don't leave me hanging. If you value your job, you'll—"

Her skin tingled. A tiny seed of hope—and an idea—sprouted within her. "I'll do it."

♦

Captain Jeff Braxton engaged his Starthroat's thrusters, ducking a bolt of white lightning. Burning his forward retrorockets, he slipped behind the pursuing tri-fighter and fired a series of particle bursts. The bursts missed the target but directed it into his wingman's line of fire. Bolts from the second Starthroat connected with the tri-fighter's force field, inflicting enough damage to chase it away from the New International Space Station.

"Nice shooting," Jeff shouted over the comm net. His mental displays showed no other tri-fighters within his group's assigned sector.

He gazed out the canopy to port. NISS floated a few thousand kilometers away above a blue and white half-crescent. Command had assigned him the responsibility of protecting the station. So far, none of the enemy carriers or main tri-fighter groups had targeted it. The bulk of the fighting remained in higher orbit.

"Attention all units," the fleet flight controller announced from on board the *Enterprise*. "We've received word the YPF-1 Quasar, the phase fighter prototype, has been stolen from Base HOPE on Callisto."

Jeff stiffened his posture.

The controller added, "The Quasar's assumed destination is Earth. Ignore all transmissions from the fighter, as we believe the human hijacker is an enemy sympathizer. Do not, I repeat, do not allow the Quasar to enter Earth's atmosphere under any circumstances. All units are authorized to use deadly force. Be advised the fighter is more maneuverable and more heavily armed than the A-type Starthroats."

The comm net returned to its usual medley of chaos.

Jeff ordered his squad to stay alert.

He gazed up through the canopy at the pyrotechnics. Explosions fell along the curvature of the Earth and disappeared over the horizon. Every thirty seconds, a directed energy beam stretched out from one of the antimatter cannons in low orbit. The beams possessed a quarter-kilometer diameter and packed intense energy no force field could withstand. The cannons took time to aim and possessed limited accuracy, but when their destructive power struck a target, nothing remained of it.

Within the center of the combat zone, an explosion burst forth, large enough to indicate the demise of a carrier.

The sphere of light ballooned larger still. It blotted out a volume of space hundreds of kilometers wide, the biggest Jeff had seen yet.

Space rippled. Stars wavered and disappeared all around the fireball. Light churned around its epicenter, which shone with colors he didn't recognize. Secondary explosions erupted along the edges of the storm.

He focused on the area, magnified it, and held his breath. Something had ripped a hole in the very fabric of space.

♦

A firestorm trailed the Quasar as it exited the wormhole.

Brooke wailed. The Quasar shuddered.

The encompassing light receded behind her, granting the Quasar passage into open space. All around her fighter, explosions big and small swelled and waned. Particle beams of every color streaked the blackness. Pinpoints of light danced and weaved around one another.

*The battle's begun.* She armed all weapons. *Bob, you were supposed to downshift beyond Luna's orbit, not drop us in the middle of the combat zone.*

*<I warned you about the possible variance in our point of egress, ma'am,>* the intelligence matrix transmitted to her brain. *<Luna orbits within Earth's gravitational influence. Any attempt to execute a phase shift within a gravity field increases the unpredictability of—>*

*Yeah, okay. I remember my training.* Brooke's rear displays caught her attention. *Holy . . .*

The shimmering and convulsing surrounding the shrinking wormhole dissipated, returning space-time to normal. A half-kilometer section of a once-intact pyramid carrier drifted away from the mending tear. Smaller chunks of debris littered the area, creating a mini-metal asteroid field.

*The Quasar's re-entry must've ripped the carrier apart.*

*<Ma'am, incoming—>*

She yo-yoed the Quasar out of the way of a pair of seekers.

Her augmented reality identified her attacker as a Chinese Dragonfly. *What the hell?* She finagled into position behind the Dragonfly. *Why's it shooting at me?*

*<This is why, ma'am.>* Bob replayed a transmission he'd intercepted in which the *Enterprise's* flight controller issued orders to terminate her.

*Collins, you lying bastard.* Brooke opened the comm net tactical frequency. "This is Major Brooke Davis aboard the Quasar. Cease fire. I'm not your enemy—"

A Starthroat's particle cannon discharge came within a meter of puncturing her canopy.

*Fine. If that's how it's going to be, I'll take you all on.* She targeted the craft.

*<I recommend against engaging friendly forces, ma'am. Killing people will only strengthen the position against you.>*

Brooke let the bracket slide away from the Starthroat. *What else am I supposed to do?* She wanted to beat her fist against the dash but couldn't while immersed within the gravgel.

*<Ma'am, our objective is to deliver critical data to the UN secretary-general. Therefore, I suggest—>*

*We get to UN Headquarters as quickly as possible. Right.* She took a breath and ignited her afterburners. *I'm relying on your calculations to navigate this obstacle course.*

*<I shall devote my full processing capacity to determining the optimal route to our destination, ma'am.>*

The next few minutes proved the most perilous of Brooke's life. She dodged thousands of beams and missiles fired by both friend and foe. Millimeters separated her from oblivion on innumerable occasions.

Pain stabbed her brain due to intense concentration. Split-second decisions taxed the limits of her cognitive abilities, even with the sparks. She almost blew away two Russian Foxbats and mistook a pair of South American Condors for tri-fighters. In each instance, she held back at the last moment.

Very quickly, she learned the full extent to which the Quasar gave her the edge over every other spacecraft. Her thruster control software provided her with increased maneuvering precision. She used it to zig-zag out of aggressors' lines of fire, dance around them, and weave into their blind spots. The Quasar could also accelerate and decelerate much faster than an A-type Starthroat or tri-fighter. The maneuvers she pulled would've crushed the pilot of any other craft. And her antimatter reserves rendered power and fuel consumption negligible in all cases except when executing a phase shift.

The weapons systems provided her with the arsenal of an entire fighter wing. Her particle cannons auto-aimed with minimal conscious targeting. The onboard nanofabrication chambers assembled new seekers within seconds, giving her a near-unlimited supply of ordinance. The chambers couldn't fabricate r-seekers, though. She did her best to conserve her complement of twenty-five, but counteracting the Starthroats' r-seekers forced her to exhaust her supply.

She held back from employing the Quasar's phase shielding, Kevin's most astounding breakthrough. The shielding would suck her antimatter reserves dry in a matter of minutes.

Bob's calculations saved her time and again. Between her AI, the

Quasar, the sparks, and her natural ability, nothing touched her.

The phase fighter's retrorockets hurled her backward. After blasting a pursuing tri-fighter to atoms, she whipped her orientation forward. The combat zone dwindled behind her. Swirling clouds, oceans, and continents shrouded the canopy.

*We made it.*

*<Atmospheric entry in sixty seconds, ma'am.>*

Brooke flipped the Quasar so its underbelly faced the Earth. She sifted through her mental screens to the re-entry system, toggling her force field to thermal protection mode.

Something twinkled in her peripheral vision.

NISS emerged over the horizon. The two-kilometer-diameter habitat ring rotated around a central cylinder. In the time since she'd last visited it, construction had commenced on two smaller rings above and below the main one.

Explosions detonated near the civilian space station. Thirty-five thousand kilometers distant, in higher orbit, a pyramid carrier approached it.

*They wouldn't destroy the station, would they? If this war is an act, what's the point?* The more she thought about it, the more the pangs bit into her stomach. *But that's precisely the point, isn't it? Killing twenty thousand civilians will sell the believability of it all and provide humanity with yet another cause to rally around.*

*<Thirty seconds to contact with the mesosphere, ma'am.>*

Brooke focused on her mental displays. *It's not my problem.*

*<Twenty seconds, ma'am.>*

*Not my problem.* Her gaze crept its way back to the station. A flaming Russian spacecraft carrier fell away from NISS toward the Earth. A missile impacted one of the station's newer rings, tearing it apart.

*<Ten sec—>*

*Damn it!* She reoriented her afterburners to face the Earth. The Quasar rocketed up and away toward the space station.

*<Ma'am, should I assume your objective is to prevent the destruction of the New International Space Station?>*

*I have to do something, Bob. Tens of thousands of people have already died because of my actions—and inactions.*

*<I have little doubt a human would find your intentions admirable, ma'am. However, not even in this craft do we possess the ability to save the station.>*

*Maybe—*

She dodged a blue beam and weaved through a spread of seekers.

Two A-type Starthroats hurtled past her.

"Stop shooting at me," she yelled over the comm net. "I'm trying to help you!"

The tactical frequency crackled with the static of an incoming transmission. "Is that you, Angel?" came a thick southern drawl.

"Cobra! I'm glad to hear your voice."

"Hold your fire. Angel, did you hijack that fighter like they say?"

She cut her speed. "Well, yes, but I had to because—"

"They say the Greys are using you to make a surgical strike on UN Headquarters. My orders are to prevent that by any means necessary."

"Didn't you see me abort re-entry and change course toward NISS? Why would I do that if I planned to blow up headquarters?"

"I don't know. You might have some other agenda."

"That's ridiculous."

"Why, then?"

"This is going to sound crazy, but this invasion isn't what it seems. A secret organization is faking the whole thing. There are no exos. I'm on my way to deliver proof of it to the secretary-general."

He hesitated again. "You're right. That sounds crazy."

"I know, but you have to trust me."

"I don't know if I can risk it. They say the exos are controlling your mind. How do I know you aren't saying this to get me to drop my guard?"

Brooke watched the pyramid close the distance to the station. Her muscles tensed. "Jeff, please listen to me." She took a deep breath to keep from tensing. "I know I've been a bitch to you in the past, and I'm sorry, sorry for insulting you and for breaking your nose. I know one apology can't make up for everything, but twenty thousand lives are at stake. Please, I'm begging you . . ."

The comm net went dead.

"Well, I'll be a monkey's uncle," Jeff said. "I never thought I'd live to hear you say that. All right, Angel. If you can do something to save the station, go ahead. My team'll watch your back. But if I see the slightest hint of any funny business . . ."

"Thank you." Brooke directed the Quasar toward the space station. *Charge the phase drive, Bob.*

*<Ma'am, I determined your intentions one minute and twenty seconds ago. Forty seconds remain to full charge capacity.>*

*More of that initiative?*

*<Yes, although I must recommend against the maneuver you're about to perform. I cannot calculate the likelihood of our remaining undamaged with any degree of certainty. Although the relatively short*

*distance we plan to traverse will lessen the error in our exit coordinates, I cannot determine our precise point of egress.>*

*That's all right, Bob. We're doing it, regardless.*

The pyramid carrier expanded from the size of a child's toy to a white wall blocking out the stars. With the pyramid looming a couple thousand kilometers away from NISS, she could gauge its relative size. It possessed half the diameter of the station but filled out a much greater volume.

Scorch marks and breaches covered the carrier's hull.

*<Drive fully charged, ma'am.>*

*Upshifting to hyperspace . . .*

♦

Jeff's eyes bulged when the Quasar plunged toward the pyramid. A vortex formed in front of the pyramid carrier, swallowing the phase fighter and rippling space.

The vortex drilled through the center of the pyramid. Forces beyond his comprehension twisted it, wringing it out like a rag. The innermost sections of the pyramid collapsed to nowhere. Sparks and shrapnel flew. A series of solar flares lashed out from the epicenter.

Jeff maneuvered his Starthroat, gaining a better view of what remained of the pyramid. The Quasar rocketed out of another vortex—or perhaps the opposite end of the same one.

"Way to go, Angel," he whispered.

His displays alerted him to a bandit above his relative position. Before he could react, white-hot light disintegrated his fighter.

♦

"Cobra!" Brooke shouted. "Jeff . . ."

A tri-fighter holed his Starthroat through and through.

The triangle dispatched the other members of Jeff's fighter group with graceful ease.

Brooke shot off after it. *Bob, open a channel.* "I know it's you, Armin!" she called out. Her nostrils twitched. "You just killed someone who was important to me."

"Seeing as how you destroyed my home and slew my crewmates," Armin replied, "I can extend only minimal sympathy."

"That was your ship, the one I visited?"

"Yes." A wavering sigh filled the channel. "Once again, I fear I've underestimated you. My plan was to lure you here with a timely attack on that civilian space station. I knew your convictions wouldn't allow you turn your back on them. However, I failed to consider the awe-inspiring power you now wield."

"That's what you get for scheming and plotting. If you and the Vril would've left well enough alone, all of these deaths could've been avoided."

"Our lack of intervention might have brought about humanity's extinction."

"I'm not going to have this argument with you again." She altered course for Earth. "I've got places to be."

"I see, but before you take leave, perhaps you'd care to witness the ramifications of your actions."

"What're you talking—?"

*<Ma'am, the New International Space Station is losing altitude.>*

Brooke's attention whipped through mental screens, analyzing data collected by her remote sensing instruments. The gravitational eddies caused by her phase shift had knocked NISS out of its orbit. The station plummeted toward the Earth, picking up speed, atmospheric entry imminent.

"No . . ."

By trying to save twenty thousand civilians, she had condemned them.

"Your efforts were commendable," Armin said, "but you failed to take into account all potential consequences."

Her fighter rocketed after the station while she tried to think of a way to save it. NISS possessed an array of station-keeping thrusters but nothing powerful enough to reverse its descent. Its commercial-grade force field deflected low-mass space debris. The field might prevent portions of the station from burning up in the atmosphere, but it wouldn't spare its occupants from the lethal heat.

"And so," Armin said, maneuvering his tri-fighter behind her, "I shall use this turn of events to defeat you once and for all."

"Forget it. I've got to figure out how to save these people."

"Don't indulge in delusions. They're beyond help."

The underside and edges of the station radiated a violent orange.

"I'm afraid you have little choice in the matter, Major Brooke Davis. You and I shall duel until one of us can duel no more."

"Armin, there's no reason for us to fight. You don't have to do this." Molecules of oxygen and nitrogen scraped her force field, tinting the inside of the cockpit red.

"But I do, my dear nemesis. I have no other recourse. My people's final act is nearing its completion. My ship no longer exists. I have nowhere to go, no purpose other than to commit myself to your demise." Armin fired a salvo of white bursts.

Brooke avoided them but realized he hadn't intended to hit her.

His pulses struck the plummeting space station's force field, dissipating it. He bombarded the station again and again. Sections of the burning rings broke away.

The station ripped apart. Buildings, electrocars, and bodies tumbled out of breaches. Thousands of degrees of scorching heat set everything ablaze.

Flaming chunks of the station raced up at her. Bob calculated their predicted trajectories. She spun, shifted, flipped, and dodged, but drag impeded the Quasar's movements.

A section of paneling bigger than her fighter slammed into its force field. The air around the Quasar crackled blue and red. Her neurotronics flickered. Thrusters and fusion rockets stopped responding, followed by attitude control. The Quasar twirled and twisted like a gyroscope.

Brooke's mind cried out to Bob, but he didn't respond.

The cockpit temperature skyrocketed. Her vision blurred. She sprayed vomit all over her face shield.

Another station fragment bashed into the Quasar, knocking her out.

**Thirty-five—Catastasis**
**New York City, April 2248 AD**

"I ask that each and every citizen remains composed and level-headed," Danuwa Ajunwa said. "Return to your homes and jobs. Go back to your lives. There's no reason for panic."

Marie stood inside the UN Headquarters briefing room, at the foot of the stage in the front row. A mob of reporters surrounded her. She directed her eyecam at the secretary-general behind the podium and increased magnification.

Ajunwa smoothly brought her speech to a close. "I ask every man, woman, and child to put their trust in the UN We've narrowed the technological gap separating us from the Greys. The combined might and ingenuity of the human race can and will win this fight."

Every artery and vein in Marie's body pulsated. Guilt knotted her stomach. She wiped her forehead and fanned her torso. Sweat plastered her blouse to her skin.

She'd reached a decision while covering this glorified pep rally. Now, as she waited for the right moment, she wondered whether her plan would accomplish what she hoped or backfire and place her daughter in greater jeopardy. She didn't know, but she had to do something. She couldn't live with what she'd agreed to do any longer.

"Thank you." Ajunwa stepped away from the podium.

Arms and shouts flailed into the air.

"Madam Secretary," a reporter yelled, "you didn't provide any specifics about casualties or the remaining strength of either party. What's the current state of the battle?"

"When is the Martian fleet expected to arrive?"

"You say not to panic, but can you guarantee no more debris will strike our cities?"

Marie worked her way to the end of the first row, closest to the edge of the stage where the secretary-general would step down.

The press gravitated toward Marie, carrying her away from the stage like a river current. They shouted questions in vain.

Ajunwa descended from the stage. A line of security guards separated the aged woman from the mob. They cordoned off a path toward her point of egress.

Marie's heart thumped. Text scrolled across the bottom of her field of vision, transmitted via her eyecam's neural connection. Her producer wanted her to blurt out a question. *Sorry*, she mused, *but I'll be asking something different today.*

The crowd shepherded her along the secretary-general's path.

She approached one of the guards, a towering woman wearing a black suit and thick set of solid black wraparound goggles. The eye gear, a much more advanced version of Marie's device, no doubt gave her a direct interface to the building's security system.

*Almost time.*

When the secretary-general drew near, Marie stopped her cam from recording, cutting off the signal to billions of people. Angry red text from her producer scrolled across the bottom of her vision.

She disabled the cam's neural interface and sucked as much air into her lungs as she could muster. Then she pointed her finger behind the crowd and shrieked at high pitch.

Everyone's heads whipped around.

The guard standing closest to her turned.

*Oldest trick in the slip*, she mused.

Her diversionary outburst provided the fraction of a second she needed to slip past the guard and into Ajunwa's path.

The secretary-general stopped and stared at Marie.

Marie directed her cam at the leader of mankind, pretending to record. "Madam Secretary, would you care to comment on the allegation that the Greys aren't the ones attacking us? Rumor has it the reason we found a human pilot in a tri-fighter is because we're fighting humans, not extrasolar beings."

Ajunwa frowned at her.

A guard grabbed Marie's arm and yanked her back.

She wiggled out of her hold and scurried back to the secretary-general.

"Is it also not true," Marie said, "this sham of a war is, in fact, being orchestrated by a secret society, one which has infiltrated the UN at the highest levels?"

Ajunwa blinked.

A much bigger and stronger guard grabbed her around the waist. He scooped her up off the floor and stuffed her under one armpit.

Marie blanched at the horde of gaping reporters. Hundreds of eyecams recorded the guard carrying her away like a disobedient child.

Chills undulated through her body. *What did I just do?*

She could only pray the secretary-general had understood her intentions.

♦

The secretary-general resumed stride toward her personal exit.

Her chief bodyguard paced her. "Madam Secretary, I apologize for my guard's lapse in attention. I take full responsibility."

Ajunwa clasped her hands behind her back and bowed her head. Thoughts and questions rattled around in her mind. Misgivings rimmed the edge of her perception.

When she reached the exit, she turned and gazed back at the commotion in the briefing room. Half the press had their cameras pointed in her direction. The other half faced the back of the room, filming a group of guards in the act of cuffing the reporter.

The bodyguard shook her head. "Two seconds in the spotlight, and she's trashed her career. What a waste."

Ajunwa lifted her head. "No."

"Pardon, Madam Secretary?"

"Bring the reporter to my office. Immediately."

♦

Brooke's thoughts stumbled through delirium. Centripetal force squeezed her perception.

She gasped, awakening. Her lungs sucked in pure oxygen from inside her helmet while she gazed around the cockpit.

A fire raged outside the canopy. Her blood felt ready to boil beneath her sweat-soaked skin. The Starthroat shook, jarring every bone in her body.

*Bob?*

*<Ma'am, you've regained consciousness.>*

*How long was I out?*

*<Eight-point-seven seconds, ma'am.>*

*It's so hot.*

*<We're descending through Earth's atmosphere, ma'am. A collision resulted in an electrical overload, knocking the fusion and antimatter cores offline. The YPF-1 is running on battery reserves. I've restored life support and the neurotronic control systems. Thrusters will fire, but the main rockets are unavailable without primary power.>*

*Can you get things back online?*

*<Not without additional energy, ma'am. The battery reserves lack the necessary charge.>*

*In other words, we're headed for a sure splat.*

*<I concur the probability of our survival is negligible, ma'am. Also, the force field won't function without main power.>*

*If force field's offline, why haven't we burnt to ashes?*

*<I've relocated us, ma'am.>*

Brooke focused on the view outside.

Her jaw drooped when she realized how Bob had saved them.

The Quasar rested atop a section of metal paneling which had once belonged to NISS. The underside of the panel continued to absorb much of the heat of reentry. Walls of flame climbed past her fighter in all directions. It looked as if she sat within a box made of shooting fire. Chunks of flaming wreckage paced her fighter farther away.

*<We need to relocate, ma'am. Our improvised heat shield will disintegrate in twenty-three seconds. The YPF-1's fuselage should be able to withstand brief intervals of high-temperature exposure.>*

*Okay.* Her augmented reality showed Armin's tri-fighter descending above her several kilometers away. *Why hasn't he finished me off?*

*<I calculate a ninety-three percent chance he's unable to distinguish the YPF-1 from the rest of the debris, ma'am. Extreme temperatures and our lack of power have left him reliant on visual identification.>*

A mental timer ticked down the seconds to the panel's disintegration. Frantically, she searched for her next hiding place and contemplated ways to restore main power.

Another timer counted down the time until surface impact. Five minutes and thirty-two seconds separated the Quasar from a projected collision with the Himalayan Mountains.

She plotted a path toward a tumbling metal barrel.

*<Two seconds, ma'am.>*

Brooke fired a directed thruster burst and leapt the Quasar across a five hundred-meter-wide atmospheric gap.

Her world tinted to crimson, and the external temperature gauge soared. Flames engulfed her fighter.

The Quasar settled above the barrel. The temperature dropped.

*<Ma'am—>*

She leapt her fighter clear of the barrel as a white particle beam tore it apart.

"I knew you couldn't have perished," Armin said.

Gritting her teeth, she dashed for the nearest object.

The phase fighter spent three seconds above a semi-circular section of the habitat ring before Armin reduced it to shrapnel.

*<Ma'am, we need to remain in a low temperature location. The YPF-1's hull is experiencing structural degradation.>*

*I know, I know.* Brooke hopped her fighter-turned-fireball from fragment to fragment, heading for the largest plummeting section of NISS. She darted away from each place of refuge microseconds before Armin destroyed it.

The timer indicated three minutes to surface impact.

At last, she reached what had served as the space station's central axis. Habitat rings once rotated around the mostly-intact metal cylinder. With an even distribution of mass, the immense tube fell sideways, its length parallel to the surface of the Earth.

The Quasar zoomed across the curvature of the axis' cool upper half. Brooke ducked beneath the tube's blazing underside and dove into recesses to avoid Armin's particle bursts.

After a few seconds of the cat-and-mouse game, Armin ceased his attacks. "Why do you refrain from returning fire?"

"I told you, there's no reason for us to fight."

"No, that's not it. Your craft has sustained damage. Main power is offline. No wonder I lost you for a time."

She reached the end of the axis and spun the Quasar around. Armin's tri-fighter settled above the tube meters away, cornering her.

Her heart thumped her chest as she waited for him to finish her off.

"No." He powered down his particle weapons. "I don't want to kill you this way."

His helmet and visor appeared in one of her mental windows.

"Who's going to know?" she said. "Get it over with already."

"The object shielding us from the heat will strike the ground in less than two minutes. You and I shall die together, two kindred souls with no place in the future to come."

"Is that what the Vril tell you to believe?"

"I reason for myself."

"What do they do with people who 'reason' against your masters' wishes?"

Crackling and heavy breathing carried over the frequency.

"We believe in our cause, no matter the hardship," Armin said. "I believe it to be just."

"Of course you do. You can't believe any other way with how they've raised you."

His visor dipped ever so slightly.

Her timer indicated forty-seven seconds to impact.

The Quasar's rate of descent slowed, and the flames around the axis subsided. Mountains and glistening oceans surrounded her.

*Bob, if we dump every last remaining watt into the force field, can we activate it?*

*<Yes, ma'am, although it'll only last for two-point-three seconds—two-point-one since your planned maneuver will require a brief thruster burst.>*

"Back when I visited your ship, you told me you had misgivings," she said. "Are they still so strong after watching your people led to the slaughter?"

"I can only be who and what I am," Armin said. "I cannot deny the purpose for which I was created. I have no other choice." He looked to the side. "Not that it matters any longer."

"You do have a choice. We always have a choice, even though we might often feel otherwise. I decide whether to shy away from people or open up and start living my life, and I'm planning on the latter. You can choose any destiny you desire."

Twenty-two seconds to impact. She could feel the mountain range rising up to smite her.

He faced her. "Compelling words. Part of me wishes I had more time to contemplate them. Perhaps, in the next lifetime . . ."

Ten seconds.

"I'm sorry, Armin, but I plan to live out this one." *Now, Bob.*

*<Shunting all available power. Force field enabled, ma'am.>*

She burned the aft thrusters.

The Quasar lurched forward and collided with the tri-fighter. Force fields fizzled. Electromagnetism crackled, repelling. The spacecraft ricocheted off one another, hurtling in opposite directions.

Explosions erupted around Armin's fighter, which plunged over the edge of the axis.

Energy surged through the Quasar, which rebounded upward. Brooke's flight armor prevented the current coursing through the gravgel from electrocuting her.

Rushing air threw her fighter into an uncontrolled tumble.

Five seconds.

*<Fusion core reinitialized, ma'am. Stabilizing orientation . . .>*

With Bob's help, Brooke brought the Quasar under control and pointed its nose upward. The phase fighter's afterburners flared. Crushing acceleration drilled her back into her seat.

♦

A boy stood atop high rocky terrain outside the mountain village of Askole, focusing his net specs on the meteors raining down from above. He shouted back over his shoulder.

Members of the boy's family scurried up behind him. Oohs and aahs escaped each and every mouth.

Shooting stars pelted the Himalayas. Rocks, ice, and billows of soot erupted into the air.

The boy panned his specs higher into the overcast sky.

A horizontal column of flaming metal plummeted toward K2, the second-tallest mountain in the world.

He cringed when the column thudded against one side of the mountain, shaking the ridge beneath his feet. A deafening explosion mushroomed up from the impact point.

His ears popped. The wind knocked his little sister off her feet.

The boy dug his shoes into the rocks, held onto his specs, and zoomed in closer.

A contrail of superheated exhaust arced up and away from the swelling cloud of dirt.

## Thirty-six—Quietus
## New York City, April 2248 AD

The security guard demagnetized Marie's cuffs and removed them.

She rubbed her wrists and gazed around the secretary-general's office within the UN Headquarters stratoscraper. Five-meter-tall projection windows lined the room, displaying footage of the skirmish in orbit, battle statistics, and situation reports from cities and space stations around the globe.

The guard marched over to the secretary-general's desk, leaving Marie standing atop the planets within the central UN emblem. When the guard reached the desk, she twirled and froze into a statue. A second guard stood at attention on the other side of the secretary-general.

"That was quite the stunt you pulled down in the briefing room, Ms. Davis," Ajunwa said from behind the desk. With her deep mahogany eyes, she scrutinized the reporter.

"I needed to get your attention," Marie said. "I knew you'd understand."

"I appreciate the confidence you showed in me. I only wish a greater number of the voting populace shared it." Ajunwa interlocked her fingers and leaned forward. "Normally, I'd ask how you're doing, but in this case I think we should dispense with the pleasantries. Please elaborate on what you were trying to tell me."

Marie stepped closer but hesitated to speak when she noticed the two guards.

"Anything you have to say can be said in front of them," Ajunwa said. "They're sworn to secrecy. They have to be. I can't so much as use the ladies' room without one of them in the stall with me." She directed a palm toward the chair in front of her desk. "Please, take a seat."

The padded chair Marie settled into auto-adjusted for optimal comfort—a shame, since she didn't want to feel comfortable right now.

She scooted to the edge of her seat and divulged everything, including the true origins of the exocorpse, the Vril, their cloned patsy race, Collins's involvement, and the plot to dupe the human race into uniting.

The secretary-general absorbed the tale with the expressionless professionalism of a world leader. "Your story fits the facts, albeit in a coincidental manner. Do you have any proof?"

"I did when we examined the body," Marie grumbled. "But I doubt you'll find anything on the fifty-first floor of the MedCenter now."

"We moved the body to a more secure location after the terrorist break-in. No one's allowed near it any longer."

"See what I mean?"

Ajunwa reclined in her chair and crossed her arms. "Everything you've revealed strikes me as an elaborate story contrived to fit the events of the last year."

Marie slumped in her chair.

"However," said the secretary-general, "I've chosen to entertain your assertions because they fit with undisclosed intelligence reports I've received. These reports aren't much more than rumors, but . . ." She swiveled to face the windows. "They question the accidental deaths and strange behavior of high-ranking officials, funds misappropriation, and anomalous satellite sensor readings—things which could be construed as the actions of a covert entity."

Popping up in her seat, Marie said, "All that can't be coincidence."

"Perhaps."

A screen flickered to life above Ajunwa's desk, accompanied by incessant beeping.

She waved a hand in front of the screen. "Yes, what is it?"

"Madam Secretary," an aide's voice said in haste. "Are you tuned into the footage being shot by NISS?"

Ajunwa directed her attention toward a window cross-sectioned into sixteen subscreens. Explosions, particle beams, and spacecraft darted across fifteen of them. Static crackled across the sixteenth subscreen. "We've lost the signal from NISS."

"That's because the station's no longer in orbit."

"Where is it?"

Amateur vid of the Himalayan Mountains filled the window to the left of the cross-sectioned pane. A boy shouted in a language Marie didn't know. The mountains appeared to bounce up and down because he couldn't hold his specs still. Fireballs pummeled the mountains.

The boy panned the angle upward.

A horizontal pillar of fire dropped into the picture from above. The perspective zoomed out to encompass the full length of the pillar, following its descent toward K2.

The pillar exploded upon impact. A cloud mushroomed up, followed by avalanches.

"All those people . . ." Marie said.

A fighter arced up and away from the blast, heading east.

"Some kid made the post on SolNet only minutes ago," the aide said. "We're still confirming how it happened, but initial reports indicate—"

The desk screen beeped.

An aide reported, "Madam Secretary, a spacecraft has violated New York airspace. It appears to be the stolen phase fighter prototype. It's holding position a kilometer above us, and the pilot is demanding to speak with you."

Another window showed blue rocket exhaust flaring from the bottom of a translucent star fighter. Six Starthroats hovered around it.

Marie shot to her feet.

"Put the pilot through," Ajunwa said.

A sleek black helmet replaced the amateur vid. "Madam Secretary, I need to speak to you right away."

"Brooke." Marie rushed closer to her sister's image.

Her sister turned her helmet to face her. "Marie, is that you? What're you doing there?"

"I came to expose the conspiracy, of course." Marie grinned for the first time in weeks. "Why're you here?"

Behind her visor, Brooke blinked her purple eyes. "Same reason." Her head shifted toward Ajunwa. "Madam Secretary, I've come to inform you of the truth behind what's going on. I've got evidence, but every time I descend toward the roof landing pad, somebody gets in my way. Luckily, they stopped shooting at me when I reached New York."

"You shouldn't be operating that spacecraft, Major Davis," Ajunwa said. "Official word is you've stolen it and sided with the invaders."

"I know it looks bad, ma'am, but I had to steal the Quasar to bring you the proof. It was the only way. And I can't be controlled by exobeings that don't exist."

The aging woman drew her lips to a thin, contemplative line.

"She's telling the truth, Madam Secretary," Marie said. "If my sister were lying, I'd know."

Ajunwa nodded. "Very well, Major Davis. I'll order those fighters to stand down."

♦

Brooke settled her fighter atop the three-kilometer-high stratoscraper

*Okay, Bob. I hope it doesn't come to it, but feel free to take more of that initiative if something goes wrong.*

*<I understand, ma'am. Good luck.>*

After draining the cockpit of gravgel, she popped open the canopy.

A frigid wind whipped through her hair when she pulled off her helmet. After surviving thousands of degrees of searing heat, she welcomed the chill.

She jumped up and regretted it at once. Her knees wobbled as her muscles strained against the Earth's pull. Light-headed and dizzy, she almost toppled over.

The artificial muscle fibers within her flight armor powered up, compensating for her reduced strength.

Heaving in a breath, she shook off her disorientation and crawled down from the cockpit.

The Quasar's fuselage looked better than she would've guessed. The nanite repair systems slowly reversed the warping and scorching.

A guard wearing a black suit and goggles rushed up to her, brandishing a handheld security scanner.

"I'm unarmed," Brooke said.

"I'll be the judge of that." He ran the device up and down the length of her body. "You're clean. This way, please."

She jogged after him across the rooftop, through an open door, and down a flight of stairs. A short corridor later, she passed through a side entrance into the UN secretary-general's office.

Marie rushed over and wrapped her arms around her suited torso.

Brooke squeezed back.

Her sister pulled away and locked stares with her. Dark circles rimmed Marie's watering eyes. "He took her, Kishi," she whispered, lower lip trembling. “Collins kidnapped Maya so I’d report whatever he wanted. I don’t know where she is.”

Emotions washed over Brooke. Surprise at the news. Relief at knowing her sister hadn’t sided with the Vril. Anger at Collins for stooping to such a low. Fear when she imagined how Maya must feel right now. Guilt because she’d allowed her personal plight to consume her when others were suffering too.

Determination rippled through her. She placed both gloved hands on Marie’s shoulders. “I’ll get her back, Miko. I promise.”

Marie gave a slow nod.

“What’s this?” the secretary-general asked.

After releasing her sister, Brooke tapped the forearm of her suit, opening the tiny compartment. “The Security Council president has kidnapped my niece.” She pulled out the data chip and marched over to Ajunwa. “This,” she said, holding it at eye level, “proves Edward Collins’s collusion with a covert organization to create a civilization of subservient human beings, stage an invasion, and steal mankind’s phase technology. It also contains the authorization codes to enable mass production of that technology.”

Ajunwa stared at the chip. “This I must see.”

Brooke reached forward.

The matrix chimed. “Madam Secretary,” a voice said, “the Martian relief fleet has arrived and engaged the enemy.”

Every window displayed the battle in orbit from different angles. A hundred spacecraft carriers and thousands of fighter craft charged the combat zone. The frequency and intensity of explosions increased. The theater-sized displays gave Brooke the impression she was still out there.

She didn’t need to check the numbers to predict the end result. The Earth forces had outnumbered the attacking fleet from the beginning. Had the Martian forces not joined the effort, Earth would’ve won, anyway. But now, the invaders found themselves surrounded, outgunned from every angle. A hundred spacecraft carriers ganged up on each pyramid. Groups of Condors, Foxbats, Dragonflies, Starthroats, and patchwork craft swarmed single tri-fighters.

The invader’s lines collapsed. Only chaotic pockets of resistance remained.

One window flipped to ISN, showing the perfect symmetry of McKenzie Pierce’s face. “This just in. We’ve received word over ninety percent of the extrasolar forces have been destroyed, and those remaining appear to be in retreat.” The camera zoomed in to show her well-practiced conviction. “It’s over, everyone. We’ve won. Earth has won."

Scenes depicting Brazilians dancing in the streets, Arabs thrusting triumphant fists in the air, and Thai people crying replaced McKenzie's image.

The celebration of humanity's combined triumph had begun.

Brooke fought back the angst. "It's all a sham."

Marie stared past the windows, rooted in the same spot since releasing from their embrace.

Beeps and tones squawked from the desktop matrix.

"Madam Secretary, the networks are asking for statements."

"Madam Secretary, a crowd's forming outside headquarters."

"Madam Secretary. They're shouting your name all around the world."

"Madam Secretary—"

With a flick of her wrist, Ajunwa silenced her screen. "The chip, Major." She nodded toward a small data port integrated into the desk.

Inserting the chip into the port, Brooke said, "Access it in isolation mode. Disable your SolNet uplink and firewall the building's AI from your console. If one of the Vril's censors locates the content . . ."

"I'll take the necessary precautions, thank you."

Edward Collins usurped each and every window. The jail cell conversation played to its conclusion from Brooke's point of view through the speakers embedded in the walls.

When it had finished, Ajunwa said, "He asked you to kill yourself . . ."

Brooke averted her gaze, nodding. "I almost did, ma'am."

The secretary-general leaned back in her chair and blew out a protracted sigh.

"People will be appalled when they learn the truth," Marie said. "How will you make the announcement, Madam Secretary? A press conference?"

Standing, Ajunwa made her way over to one of the windows and waved her hand in front of it. The projected image faded, giving way to transparency. "No."

"How then?" Brooke frowned. "And when?"

Peering down at the city, Ajunwa said, "There will be no announcement. Not now. Perhaps not ever."

Marie's head turned.

"What?" Brooke bolted up behind her. "I don't understand."

Ajunwa spread her thumb and forefinger apart in front of the window. The square section of pane in front of her hand zoomed in on the streets below. "Do you see all those relieved and hopeful people below us?"

Brooke stepped closer. Six hundred stories below, a horde of people had amassed in the courtyard. "Don't tell me you don't want to disappoint anyone."

Ajunwa turned to her. "What do you think would happen if I told everyone this invasion was a lie? That it was staged like a play to manipulate them toward a scripted end?"

"Won't they be relieved to know the truth?"

"No, Major. You'll be relieved, but that's not how the general populace will react. People will feel violated, outraged. They won't believe a secret society was behind the deception. They'll blame the UN. There'll be protests. Riots. Countries and colonies will secede all over again. We'll lose the unity we've finally achieved, go back to war, and what chance do you think we'll have of reestablishing peace? No human institution will ever trust another again."

"Maybe, but what does it say about a race of beings that chooses to delude itself?" Brooke shook her head. "What about the human conscience?"

"I think having to face real consequences, such as the plunging of society back into the dark ages, weighs heavier than the knowledge of deceit held by a select few."

Brooke threw her arms up in the air. "Then why did I risk my life to come here?"

"Your efforts were far from in vain. Imagine the ensuing chaos if I didn't know about this. Now that I do, I can manage the situation."

"'Manage the situation'?" Brooke snapped. "I get what you're saying, but it's not right."

"But it is," Marie said.

Turning, Brooke found her sister standing beside her.

"It's not morally right," Marie said, "but withholding the truth is the correct decision."

"How can you say that?" Brooke gawked at her.

"I don't approve of the Vril's methods any more than you do, but there's no undoing the deed now that it's done. To try would cause far more damage than good."

"They've got your daughter."

"She's what this is all about, Kishi. It's about a better future for Maya, a better future for all children—for every child yet to be born. I won't take that away from them, away from Maya." She shrugged, smiling. "Being a parent means protecting your child no matter what, even if it means lying to them."

Ajunwa inclined her head at Marie.

Brooke glowered at the floor. Every cell in her body refused to accept it, yet deep down, she knew she must for her niece's sake.

The windows flickered.

"I'm pleased you've taken our cause to heart." The narrow cheekbones of Edward Collins, along with the rest of his face, appeared on every holographic pane.

With fists balled, Brooke opened her mouth, ready to rage.

The secretary-general beat her to it. "Your ploy may have succeeded, Mr. Collins, but your actions cannot be excused. I order you to return to Earth and submit to the authorities. And I want the names of each and every member of the Vril."

"I'm afraid I can't comply."

"No, Mr. Collins, I didn't imagine you would. But mark my words. If you don't, I shall spare no effort in hunting you down." She bared her teeth. "And since we're not publicizing the truth, there'll be no trial."

"Here's my counteroffer, Madam Secretary." His voice remained calm. "Give up any futile notion of opposing us—join us—and we'll let you live. You're a popular figurehead. We'd prefer to keep you around, but we'll do what must be done."

"You dare threaten me?" Ajunwa growled. "Where are you? I demand to know this instant."

Collins shrugged. "It might take you a while to reach me, and I'll be long gone by then."

"We'll see about that." She strode over to her desk and jabbed the screen. "Contact Aerospace Defense Command. I want the security president's exact location, and I want it now."

The screen fuzzed and vanished.

"What the . . . ?" she said. "Screen enable."

It failed to obey.

Light fixtures flickered and died. Collins's many images cast shadows across the room.

Ajunwa glowered at them. "There's no way you have this level of control."

"I'm afraid your term in office is up," he said. "Guards, you know what to do."

The secretary-general's two bodyguards reached into their suit coats and produced particle handguns. One guard aimed her weapon at the secretary-general.

Guard number two pointed his gun at Brooke and Marie.

Stiffening, the secretary-general glared at her former protector, judging her in the face of death.

"Do it," Collins said.

The guard pulled her trigger.

A pulse of light leapt from the gun, impaling Ajunwa through the forehead and passing right through her. It struck the wall, burning a scorch mark.

Ajunwa's figure pixelated and flashed.

"A persona," Collins said. "I should've known."

Brooke silently applauded the secretary-general's cunning while her sister clung to her upper arm.

"Did you really think I'd be here, atop the most enticing of all ground targets, with the Earth under attack?" Ajunwa stabbed a finger at him. "You'll never gain control of this government, not as long as I draw breath."

"It doesn't matter," Collins said. "We always viewed the seizing of power as an added bonus. We've accomplished what was most important." He directed his attention toward the first guard. "Retrieve the chip."

The guard pressed a button on the desk, ejecting the chip. She picked it up and stuffed it into her pocket.

"With the evidence confiscated," Collins said, "you'll have a difficult time driving me from office. And with the codes and phase fighter in our possession, we should be able to reverse-engineer the drive, build more, and augment our ships." His eyes shifted to Brooke and Marie. For a moment, Brooke almost thought she saw a hint of remorse. "For what it's worth, I take no pleasure in the command I'm about to give. But unfortunately, the two of you have become too great a liability. It's nothing personal, only necessary." He looked at the second guard. "Kill them."

The second guard raised his weapon, sighting Marie.

A distant rumbling grew to the roar of an engine. The windows warped, destabilizing Collins's many faces, and the office shook.

Both guards whipped their heads toward the window panes. Brooke knocked the gun out of the closest guard's hand and pulled Marie to the floor.

Heavy particle beams shattered the windows, allowing air to gush inside. Shrapnel and debris showered the office like horizontal rain. The beams tore apart the two guards.

Once the last of the debris had settled, Brooke lifted her head.

The Quasar hovered outside the broken windows.

She looked down at Marie and gasped. Her sister clutched her neck with both hands, eyes wavering in fear while trying to stop the flow of blood. A crimson puddle pooled next to her head.

Brooke stared, transfixed, unsure of what to do. Pangs of guilt forced her to gag when the realization hit her. Her armored body had fallen behind Marie rather than between her sister and the windows, leaving her exposed. *Did shrapnel or a ricochet particle blast hit her?* It didn't matter at this point. Brooke had seen enough combat to judge severity. *Marie, no!*

Marie opened her mouth to speak but choked on regurgitated blood. "Maya . . ." Her soaked fingers relaxed and lost their grip. Then her head tilted to the side, and her eyes widened.

The notion of screaming—of calling out her sister's name—passed through Brooke's mind, but she couldn't process what had happened. Denial seized her. Her twin couldn't be dead. Not Marie. "No," Brooke whispered. *I killed her.* Her throat dried. *Just like Dad.* She couldn't breathe. *And Mom.* The tears wouldn't come. "No, no, no . . ." She wanted to release a guttural shriek, but instead she dropped her forehead to Marie's chest in defeat.

A seeming eternity later, she heard, "It seems not all your plans have worked out as you had hoped."

Lifting her gaze, Brooke found Ajunwa's persona standing near the desk, unfazed by the weapons fire.

Collins's images occupied the few jagged remains of the windows. "There's always a Plan B." He lowered his voice. "I'm sorry about your sister, Brooke, but you can have your niece if you bring me the chip and the phase fighter. How about it?"

Begrudgingly, she nudged her head in his direction. From somewhere deep down, she manifested the strength to rise to her feet. "Okay."

"Out of the question," Ajunwa said. "Please accept my condolences for your loss, Brooke. I hope you don't think me callous, but with the responsibility for thirty-five billion people resting on my shoulders, I must be pragmatic. Putting the phase drive in the Vril's hands isn't worth one little girl's life."

Brooke realized her stare had drifted back to Marie's body. She whimpered and ripped her gaze away.

Somehow, she worked up the nerve to face the secretary-general's persona. "I won't let the last remaining member of my family die." To Collins, she said, "You've got a deal." She located what remained of the first guard on the floor, knelt down next to her, and retrieved the chip from her pocket.

"Excellent. Shift to Triton, then. I'll be waiting." His images disappeared.

The ominous sound of rushing air filled the office.

Brooke inserted the chip back into her forearm and stole one final glance at Marie's body. *I made you a promise, Miko, and I intend to keep it, even if it costs me everything.* She sprinted for the Quasar.

Its nose edged inside the building.

"Stop at once, Major," Ajunwa yelled. "That spacecraft is government property. You have no right to take it."

With one heel planted on the nose of the phase fighter, Brooke said, "I'm sorry." She grabbed the edge of the cockpit and jumped inside. "If she was your child, would you not do the same?" Grabbing her helmet, she plopped down in her seat. The canopy lowered.

"If you leave here," Ajunwa shouted, "you're done. You'll never fly again."

Brooke considered the woman's words while donning her helmet. Hesitation seized her, but only for a nanosecond.

The Quasar pulled away from the stratoscraper and soared out over the Atlantic Ocean.

Once the gravgel had consumed her, she oriented the phase fighter's nose toward the sky. Plumes of plasma exhaust punched a crater-sized depression into the water, launching the Quasar up and away from the Earth.

**Thirty-seven—Virago**
**Neptunian System, April 2248 AD**

Out beyond the bridge viewports, and high above Neptune's swirling blue clouds, white-hot fusion exhausts flared. The last remaining pyramid carrier rocketed away from Triton, following a trajectory leading out of the solar system.

Collins observed the pyramid's departure from the bridge of the *Illuminatus*, an enhanced but unregistered UN spacecraft carrier. The stealth ship and others like it allowed members of the Vril to pass undetected between the inner and outer system colonies. Its weaponry and speed also outclassed the capabilities of the pyramids. The Vril had withheld the most advanced technology developed from crashed Roswell ship and the others long before it.

The resident of the UN Security Council—still, he figured, and for some time to come—clasped his hands behind his back. He drew in a breath and let it out, fogging the viewport.

Thoughts of the future warmed him. The Vril had ensured human unification, and continued vigilance by the society would ensure mankind never fought amongst itself again. The pyramid shrinking into the distance carried the last of their cloned race, having vacated Triton, Pluto, and every Kuiper belt colony. Soon, humanity would venture out to Neptune and discover the wonders left behind by "the

Greys." Meanwhile, the pyramid would scout the stars and implement the next phase of the great plan. At subluminal velocities, the ship would require centuries to reach its destination. But once Collins secured the phase drive, the Vril could reverse engineer it. Superluminal carriers could then catch up to the pyramid, install the drive, and shorten its journey.

Phase one of his ancestors' plan had, at long last, reached its conclusion.

Now, the more critical phase could begin. He could only pray it gave mankind a fighting chance against the true peril lurking somewhere out there.

"Sir," said an officer perched on a floating seat in front of her console. Like her superior, the young woman wore the standard-issue UN Aerospace Defense navy blazer with black pants and boots. "You asked to be informed when the phase fighter approached to within one hour of Triton, sir."

*Finally*. Collins rubbed his palms together, but it failed to allay his trepidation. *Everything is about to go my way, so why do I feel uneasy?*

The Quasar had emerged from hyperspace at the edge of the Neptunian system hours ago. Now, it approached at max fusion thrust.

"Are we in position?" he asked.

Another officer said, "Yes sir. We're maintaining an orbit fifty thousand kilometers above Neptune."

"Very good." After retreating from the viewport, Collins settled into the central captain's chair and dipped a finger in the armrest's screen. "Bring the girl to the bridge."

♦

Childhood memories haunted Brooke. In her mind, she watched her thirteen-year-old twin's jaw drop. Fingernails dug deep into her arm, forcing her to wince. She tightened her stomach muscles as the roller coaster plummeted over the edge of Olympus Mons. Marie's shrill squeals pierced her eardrums.

Such times would never come again.

The fact she'd caused her sister's death grated every nerve. *I did it again.*

Brooke came within a mental twitch of unloading every one of the Quasar's weapons.

*<I'm receiving a signal on an encrypted frequency, ma'am.>*

*Huh?* Brooke sniffled and blinked, coming out of her reverie. *Sorry.* She pressed her grief to the back of her mind. *Someone's trying to contact us?*

*<The signal appears to have originated near Neptune, ma'am, not Triton.>*

*Neptune? She checked her mental displays. I don't see anything there.*

*<Neither do I, ma'am. Nevertheless, I've confirmed the point of origin.>*

She altered course. *Okay, we play it like we discussed.* Her dry throat wouldn't swallow. *No matter what happens . . .*

*<Affirmative, ma'am. At this juncture, my programming requires me to inform you of the negligible chances of success. However, in the time we've spent together, I've learned my outcome assessment algorithms neglect key variables, such as human ingenuity and determination. Therefore, I've chosen to disregard mathematical probabilities in favor of a concept I'm only beginning to understand. I believe we'll succeed.>*

Brooke manifested the closest thing to a smile she could muster.

A screen popped into her mind's eye. The image it offered jolted her grief into fury.

Collins sat with Maya on his lap.

Her niece's pale face drooped. Bruises covered her arms.

"Thank you for joining us, Major." Collins placed a hand on Maya's shoulder. "You'll be happy to know that, except for a few initial tantrums, this little one has behaved herself."

"Shut up," Brooke hissed.

Maya's head perked up. "Auntie?"

"Yes, it's me, Maya. I'm here to take you home."

"Once Auntie gives me the special plane she's flying," Collins said, "you'll be able go with her."

*<Three spacecraft carriers dead ahead, ma'am.>*

A second mind-screen appeared to the right of Maya's image. Three sleek ships resembling UN spacecraft carriers pockmarked the blue bands in the background. Carriers two and three each held position a thousand kilometers distant from the middle carrier, Collins's apparent flagship.

"Tell me, how will Maya and I return to Earth or Callisto once I hand over the Quasar? Nothing short of a carrier can make the return trip."

"One of these ships will take you back," he said.

"Why don't I believe you?"

"You've not choice but to trust me, Brooke."

She narrowed her gaze. "I think lying to thirty-five billion people puts a slight dent in your credibility. Sorry, but I'm going to have to decline."

"You've no alternative, not if you want your niece back."

"What will you do with her should I refuse?"

He hesitated a second before glaring at her. "You know what'll happen."

"Will you murder an innocent child in front of your bridge crew?" Brooke raised her voice, directing it at the officers manning their posts behind Collins. "How about it, everyone? Care to watch a little girl's execution?" Her abdomen tightened when she saw Maya cringe, but it couldn't be helped. "Perhaps he'll order one of you traitorous cowards to kill her for him. That's why he's brainwashed you all, isn't it?"

The three people in the background halted their duties.

A young officer rushed up behind Collins's seat. "Don't you realize what this man's done for the human race?" He waved a fist in the air.

"As you were, Lieutenant," Collins shouted over his shoulder.

The man lowered his hand and retreated.

Collins studied Maya. "Congratulations, Brooke. You've called my bluff. I've no intention of harming her. Nor would I ever consider it." He closed his eyes and pinched the bridge of his nose. "No, Maya's fate will be worse than death—in your view, at least. Should you fail to hand over the Quasar, she'll remain with me—with the Vril—indefinitely. We'll raise her to champion our cause, for our work has only begun."

"Put Maya in an escape capsule," Brooke said. "Jettison her beyond weapons range of your carriers. I'll pick her up, and we'll be on our way. Otherwise, I'll take her by force."

Collins opened his eyes and lifted his brow. "Would you risk her life in certain suicide?"

"First, I'm going to destroy both your escort ships. Then, after I collect Maya, I'm going to knock Triton clear out of its orbit. That's why you're sitting a safe distance away from the moon, isn't it? You know the power the Quasar possesses."

"This is your final warning, Brooke. Give me the Quasar, or we'll take it from you."

She leaned forward and scowled. "Go to hell."

Collins whipped his head to the side. "Fire on that craft! Hit it before it can shift. Weapons at minimal yield. I want it disabled, not destroyed."

"Hold tight, Maya. I'm coming for you." *Please forgive me if this doesn't work, Marie.* Brooke terminated the screen.

She rolled her fighter. Particle beams whizzed past her canopy.

Hundreds of death rays zeroed in on her. The Quasar zipped about like a mosquito, avoiding the first thirty or forty beams by mere meters, but it couldn't dodge them all.

Beams struck her Quasar but passed straight though it as if it wasn't there.

*Kevin's shield is working, Bob!*

*<It appears so, ma'am. By shifting the immediate volume of space occupied by the YPF-1, we've phased our spacecraft beyond normal space-time. Normal matter and energy cannot interact with us.>*

*Phase drive at full charge?*

*<At one hundred percent, ma'am.>*

Brooke snarled.

The Quasar dove at one of the flanking carriers. When she reached Bob's predetermined coordinates, she engaged the drive, upshifting to hyperspace.

Due to her proximity to Neptune, the Quasar re-emerged into normal space kilometers away from her planned reentry point, although the offset proved negligible.

Her aft displays showed a raging, solar flare-like eddy. The flare sliced through the stealth carrier like a stick of butter.

The carrier collapsed in on itself and exploded.

Two minutes later, the other flanking carrier suffered the same fate.

♦

"What the bloody hell's going on out there?" Collins bellowed.

"I'm sorry, sir," his tactical officer reported. "The Quasar . . . it's there, but it's not there. Our ordnance passes right through it."

Collins ran a hand down his face. Had he made the mistake of underestimating Brooke Davis—again?

His attention turned to the fireworks outside the bridge viewports. He'd seen vids of the Quasar's dismantling of the pyramid carriers near Earth, yet it failed to prepare him for the awesome spectacle of annihilation. Hull plating twisted and reshaped in impossible ways. Surges of indistinguishable colors confused his retinas.

The girl sat on his knee, wide eyes gawking at the scene.

Shaking, the *Illuminatus* lurched to one side. Collins reached out and grabbed Maya to keep her from falling. The carrier's rotation halted for a second. He felt his stomach rise and fall. "Get us out of here!"

"Altering course away from Neptune," the navigations officer said.

The ship shuddered again. Collins clung to Maya. It took all his strength to keep from tumbling out of his chair. Screens fuzzed.

Plasma strips flickered.

"Sir, we've lost main power," the operations officer said. "The force field's offline and the Quasar's created another space-time wake!"

*Close enough to disable but not destroy us.* Collins rose to his knees, set the girl down, and lifted himself to his feet.

"Sir—"

A screen displayed the view aft of the *Illuminatus*. The Quasar launched a spread of seekers at the exhaust nozzles of the carrier's antimatter engines.

Multiple impacts slammed Collins and every bridge officer to the deck.

He scrambled to his feet once the quakes subsided. The uninjured officers crawled back to their posts.

Maya lay on the deck, curled up in the fetal position, trembling.

The helm officer worked her controls. Blood trickled down the side of her face from a gash in her forehead. "Sir, main engines are inoperative." She slapped a palm against her console. "We're dead in space, sir, caught in Neptune's gravity well. Thrusters aren't enough to break free. We're falling into the atmosphere." She spun around. "The ship will be crushed in less than thirty minutes."

Every crewmember turned to face him.

The screen on his armrest squawked. Pleas assailed him from all over the ship.

Collins didn't know whether to growl in rage, laugh out loud, or hang his head.

He settled into his chair, straightened his blazer, and clasped his hands in his lap. "Abandon ship."

♦

*Okay, Bob,* Brooke hopped down from the Quasar's cockpit. *I'm counting on you to lead me to Maya.* She primed the charge on her particle rifle.

*<The bridge is located three levels above, relatively speaking, ma'am. Distance to traverse is one hundred twenty-eight meters. The interior layout is identical to a United Nations spacecraft carrier.>*

*That should make things a little easier.* She gazed across the cargo bay at the improvised entryway she had blown in the hull. Drums of water and storage bins slid and tumbled toward the breach. *If anyone bothers you, go ahead and launch. You can come back for me later.*

*<Understood, ma'am.>*

Brooke lunged across the curvature of the rumbling deck plating.

At the hatch leading to the rest of the ship, her flight armor's thermal imaging system detected no heat signatures on the other side.

Her finger tapped the panel on the wall, opening the door.

She ascended ladders, traversed corridors, and halted at an intersection. Two red and orange human shapes approached from around the corner.

With her shoulder pressed to the wall, she took aim and waited.

A male and female officer jogged into view. When they saw the barrel of Brooke's weapon, they skidded to a halt and threw their hands up.

"Don't shoot," the woman said. "We're abandoning ship—not interested in a fight."

The man directed his chin back the way he had come. "He's waiting for you on the bridge. We're not to impede your progress." His mouth remained a thin line.

Brooke scanned their bodies. They appeared unarmed.

She relaxed her rifle.

The two officers tiptoed past her.

Peering back over her shoulder, the woman shouted, "What do you have against the future, anyway?"

Brooke considered blowing her head off but let them sprint away.

After traversing further hallways, hatches, and ladders, she arrived at the entrance to the bridge.

She gripped her rifle tighter and pointed it straight ahead.

The doors sensed her presence and parted.

Collins sat in the middle of the vacated command center, staring at her. She couldn't see Maya, but her visor displays showed an orange and yellow smudge off to the right.

Brooke crept into the bridge, swinging her rifle about. Heat sensors didn't indicate anyone else's presence, but she refused to take chances.

Screens flashed red near every control console. The deck vibrated beneath her feet. Neptune's many shades of blue consumed the viewports, giving her the impression of standing inside a submarine with windows.

Maya sat hugging her knees in the far corner, sniffling.

The girl lifted her chin, and her eyes locked onto Brooke.

With a whimper, Maya sank further into the corner.

*I must look like a monster in my gear.* Brooke sent a mental command to her armor. Once its air pressure equalized with the exterior, her helmet unlatched with a click. She kept her rifle trained on Collins and used the other hand to remove her helmet and fasten it to the hook on her waist.

Her niece sat up straight and blinked. The flood of tears ceased.

"Auntie." She bounded to her feet, scurried across the deck, and latched onto Brooke's armored leg.

She stroked the little girl's hair.

"Heartwarming," Collins said.

"I'm here." Brooke glared at him. "Where's the trap?"

He leaned back in his chair. "No trap. You're free to take the girl and go."

"I don't understand. Don't you want the chip? Or the phase fighter?"

He shrugged. "The chip's pointless with Ajunwa still alive. Moreover, you've doomed my ship and forced my crew to evacuate. I can't reverse engineer the Quasar without help, and I'm sure that ultra-smart matrix of yours would protest if I tried, so what use is it to me? I concede this battle to you, Brooke. My solace comes in knowing I've won the war."

Her finger hovered over the trigger. *Shoot and be done with it.* No matter how justified she felt, though, she refused to kill in cold blood. *Not in front of Maya . . .*

"What're you still doing here?" she asked. "Captain goes down with the ship?"

"Something like that." He eyeballed the armrest screen. "Someone has to ensure everyone gets away safely."

"How selfless."

He leaned forward. "Contrary to what you may believe, Brooke, I've taken every action because I care about something greater than myself. My mother taught me to appreciate everything humankind has accomplished. She raised me with an eye on the future, and she educated me about what was needed to ensure that future. I've devoted my life toward that end. I consider myself privileged to have seen our dream fulfilled. Someday, maybe you'll understand what it means to give yourself to a higher ideal, something more important than your own life."

Brooke peered down at Maya. "In a twisted way, you might have a point. But no utopia justifies what you've done. Call me a pessimist, but I'd rather see the human race destroy itself than live in a fake paradise." She shook her head. "You're nothing but a glorified con artist."

He jumped out of his chair.

Maya squeezed her aunt's leg tighter.

Pulling her hand away from her niece, Brooke leveled her rifle at Collins.

His voice boomed. "You don't get it, do you?" He slashed a finger toward one of the viewports behind her. "They're out there, Major. I'm one of the few people who've seen the records from the Roswell UFO. I know how many millennia the real exobeings' visits to our world date back. You can't begin to fathom their role in our history." He redirected his forefinger at Maya. "Someday, our children are going to have to face them, which is why mankind must direct its resources toward advancing technology and settling the stars." He took a deep breath and reseated himself. "And even that might not be enough."

"Wouldn't it have been easier to tell people about the real threat?"

"Do you truly believe a simple announcement would've reigned in the separatists?"

She stuck out her lower lip. "No, but we'd at least live in a society based on truth."

Collins nearly toppled over, laughing. "Society has never been based on truth. Not in ancient times, not now, and not ever. People need to be protected from the truth." He snorted. "And anyone who tries to expose the truth will be silenced. That's not a threat from me or the Vril. It's sure to be Ajunwa's new unofficial policy."

Brooke heaved in a breath and closed her eyes. "I can't expose this thing no matter how much I want. I'll keep your secret, but not because of threats or for the good of humanity." Brooke looked down at Maya and ran a gloved hand through her hair. The girl's round face, eyes, and smile so resembled her mother's features. "I'll do it because of a promise I made. I hate to admit it, but you're right about one thing. Some things are more important."

The deck quaked, and the carrier lurched to the side. Dropping down on one knee, Brooke pulled Maya closer.

"Atmospheric entry in progress," the carrier's AI announced. "Unable to alter trajectory. External pressure will exceed hull tolerance in seven minutes."

"Best be on your way," Collins said.

She slung her rifle onto her back and scooped Maya up into her arms. After one last glance at Collins, she fled from the bridge.

♦

The entrance to the bridge slid shut behind the insufferable pilot and her niece.

Collins focused his attention on the armrest screen. "Establish a channel to the Dryden Advanced Propulsion Research Center on Earth."

A subordinate's face appeared on the flickering screen. "Sir."

"Have you secured the phase capsule?" Collins asked.

"Yes sir. The monkey's ship is in our possession."

"And my neural backup?"

"We've transferred it as you requested, sir."

"Thank you." He nodded and waved a hand at his screen, turning it off.

Tuning out the sound of metal collapsing all around him, Collins stood and approached the viewport. He took his time smoothing the wrinkles out of his suit coat and adjusting his cufflinks. With head held high, he waited for the churning clouds to consume him.

♦

Brooke sprinted into the cargo bay, cradling Maya in her arms.

Another turbulent jolt knocked her off her feet. Falling, she twisted her back to face the floor, shielding Maya from harm as she rolled. Between the low gravity and her armor, the impact with the deck did little more than jar her.

Barely breaking stride, she hopped to her feet and crossed the remaining distance to the Quasar.

"Bob, get ready to go," she yelled. "And we've got a passenger." She tossed her rifle aside and helped Maya climb onto her back.

With a lunging start, Brooke bounded up to the cockpit. She leapt high enough in the reduced gravity to grip the edge, even with the added weight of her niece. The enhanced strength of her flight armor helped her pull them both up and inside.

Bob's voice echoed from the speakers. <Ready for takeoff, ma'am.>

The canopy retracted while she helped Maya onto her lap. "Let's get go—"

<However, ma'am, it won't be possible to achieve escape velocity under our present circumstances.>

Brooke lowered her helmet down over her head. "What do you—?" She ripped off her headgear, realizing the pointlessness of it. The Quasar didn't have a spacesuit for Maya, meaning the cockpit couldn't fill with gravgel without drowning her. In the absence of the gel, the girl couldn't withstand more than a few gees of acceleration. And if the fighter couldn't accelerate close to max thrust, it couldn't escape Neptune's gravity and atmosphere.

The cargo bay rattled, shaken like a tin can by some mighty giant. The carrier lurched, and its orientation tilted. The Quasar slid along the deck. Maya trembled and clung to her aunt.

Brooke tossed her helmet into the rear compartment. "We'll have to shift, then. Charge the phase drive. Target anywhere beyond Neptune for reentry into normal space-time. We'll shift again to get back home."

<Ma'am, we've depleted the YPF-1's antimatter reserves to less than ten percent. The phase shield caused a substantial energy drain. According to my calculations, we have enough power for a single hyperspace shift to the Jovian system.>

"Then let's head straight to Callisto—"

<However, if we shift from our present position deep inside Neptune's gravity well, ma'am, I cannot guarantee our point of egress. We're inside a gas giant's atmosphere and our destination lies billions of kilometers away.>

"So instead of returning to Callisto, we could end up anywhere in the solar system."

<Correct, ma'am, although that possibility fails to qualify as our primary concern. I compute a significant probability shifting in the presence of this level of gravity, surrounded by atmosphere, inside a spacecraft, will destroy—>

A metallic crunch echoed throughout the cargo bay. Another followed. And another. External pressure squeezed the carrier. Multiple dents bashed in the walls.

"We don't have a choice," Brooke said. "We need to shift now."

<Phase drive charged and ready. When we upshift, I shall overclock my matrix in an effort to stabilize our exit point. Should I be damaged beyond repair . . . I'll miss you, ma'am.>

She choked up. "I'll miss you too, Bob. Thank you. For everything." She wrapped one arm around Maya. "Ready, squirt?"

Her niece nodded.

"Here we go." She keyed the manual sequence into the redundant dash controls. "Upshifting to hyperspace."

The cockpit lost focus, tinting to imperceptible colors.

♦

A Vril satellite hung in high Neptune orbit. Its instruments registered a disturbance in the gas giant's northern hemisphere.

The storm raged unlike any other before it. Clouds churned like a miniature Milky Way. An explosion mushroomed upward from the epicenter, lashing out, erupting like a gaseous volcano.

A flash of light overloaded the satellite's systems. When its cameras regained visual acuity, they revealed a new scar on the planet, a Great Blue Spot.

## Thirty-eight—Expiation
## Base HOPE, Callisto, April 2248 AD

The door to Kevin's quarters chimed.

His eyelids popped open. He jumped in his chair, almost tipping it over backwards.

After regaining his balance, he stood and smoothed his hair. He'd let it grow shaggy during his confinement. "Enter."

General Frederick Douglas stepped into the room.

Kevin grumbled, wondering what Collins had in store for him next.

Douglas strolled over to the window, hands clasped behind his back. Jupiter's brown bands churned behind New Galilei's towers and biodomes. "The secretary-general has relieved the Security Council president of his position. Mr. Collins had no authority to remove you from the FTL project. Nor should he have restricted you to quarters or placed Dr. Yeager in charge. Yeager has been taken into custody and charged with treason."

Kevin stood and folded his arms.

"Madam Secretary would like to apologize in person the next time you return to Earth," Douglas said. "Until then, she requests you resume your work. The war is over, as I'm sure you're aware. We need the phase drive to reach Triton and scour the Greys' Kuiper belt colonies."

"The Greys, huh?" Kevin mumbled. He swiped a finger through the screen hovering above his desk.

The screen played Ajunwa's victory speech. "Through our combined might and willpower, we triumphed against the extrasolar threat," she announced from the podium inside the UN Headquarters press room. "Now, let us build toward a true, unified humanity—the IntraSolar Commonality."

Kevin muted the vid. *If they only knew the truth.* He shook his head. *But it's looking more and more like the truth's going to get buried.*

General Douglas's medal-laden chest expanded. "From the ashes of this conflict, we'll build a new civilization, a truly great one." His baritone rumbled like an idling engine. "People of all nations, ethnicities, and backgrounds have come together at long last." He turned to Kevin, deep brown eyes twinkling. "Your technology will bring us closer, not to mention send us farther."

In Douglas, Kevin saw firsthand evidence of why the truth needed withholding. *As much as I hate to admit it, I can't blame the secretary-general for the closed-lip approach. Revealing the conspiracy would destroy everyone's newfound optimism. The truth might crush mankind's fundamental belief in itself.*

Despite his ethical reservations, Kevin couldn't suppress the giddiness warming his chest. He knew what the future held because he would serve as its chief architect. He'd build phase tunnels to connect every colony in the solar system, minimizing the need for intrasolar spacecraft. It might take a decade or two, he figured, to construct a crewed starship capable of exploring the new horizons of interstellar space. With its petty conflicts set aside, the human race could channel its combined efforts into learning and growing.

Someday, he knew, people would see this moment in history as a beginning. For centuries, scientists had pined for mankind to eschew materialism and belligerence so it might focus on what mattered. Now, at long last, the human race stood on the proverbial doorstep of that tomorrow.

So why did his chest still weigh heavy, even in Callisto's one-eighth gravity?

"General," Kevin asked. "Have you heard anything?"

Douglas shook his head. "There's been no word from Major Davis."

"I see. Thank you."

The general stepped toward the door. "Brooke Davis was one of the most resourceful officers who ever served under me." He stopped as the entrance slid open. "Somehow, I doubt we've seen the last of her." He disappeared out into the corridor.

The door to Kevin's quarters slid shut.

He gazed out the window, reflecting on the man's words. *Wherever you are, Brooke, I hope you're safe. I believe in you. Please come back to me.*

♦

With a heave-ho, Maya plopped down into the slush. "Snow?" She stomped and spun around. "Oh . . . wow." The overpowering sound of gushing water drowned out most of her words. ". . . big . . . spring . . . hard . . . breathe . . ."

Brooke spit out gobs of gravgel and slid down the nose of the totaled Quasar, following Maya's lead.

A concussion blurred Brooke's sight. Searing pain stabbed into her right leg and shot upward. She hissed through clenched teeth and clutched her abdomen.

Her body convulsed and fell. Low gravity and mushy water-ice cushioned the impact.

Lunging footsteps crunched toward her. "Auntie, are you okay?" The roaring muffled Maya's squeaky voice.

Images flashed through Brooke's mind. An explosion erupted all around her. The acid trip through hyperspace. Stars. A small white sphere raced toward her. Then gravgel rushed into the cockpit. She cupped one hand over Maya's mouth and nose.

Brooke held her breath.

The sphere grew until it whited out everything, at which point the Quasar smashed into an uneven surface. Impact force crumpled the fuselage like a piece of foil while it skidded across the landscape. Brooke and Maya tumbled over and over, protected by the gel.

One of the auxiliary control grips stabbed out from the dash. Brooke twisted her body into its path. It took all of her self-control to keep her mouth closed as she grunted in pain.

She clutched the little girl as the Quasar lurched to a stop. The canopy shattered into dust. Maya climbed out, followed by her aunt's tumble.

Now, Brooke lay on the surface of this strange place, moaning.

Maya tugged her shoulder. "Auntie, wake up!"

Brooke blinked hard. Her niece's questioning stare came into focus. The girl stood bending down over her.

With wide-eyed confusion, Brooke stared at the overhanging scene. A geyser taller and wider than any mountain soared high overhead. Up in the sky, a thin blue haze distorted the stars. Cold mist settled onto her cheeks.

She slapped one hand to her chest and inhaled deep. *It's so hard to breathe. Where am I? Should I be able to breathe at all?*

"Why's the snow all red around you?" Maya asked.

Brooke lifted her trembling hand up to her face. Blood ran from her knuckles down her wrist.

She took her time lifting herself up onto one elbow. Pain pierced her chest. Throughout her career, she had grown all-too familiar with the sharp pain accompanying broken ribs.

Black and green spots blotted the ice all around her. *Algae? Reminds me of the stuff bioengineered to withstand the harsh conditions on Mars.*

Bright light from overhead forced her to squint. The illumination and warmth lasted a matter of seconds before shifting to another location.

Brooke scanned the sky. Search lights—no, mirrors—combed the wintry landscape, spreading life-giving heat. Mountains of ice steamed beneath them.

She twisted around, hissing. The mangled wreckage of the phase fighter rose up above her. One mangled wing jutted up toward a hazy sky. Jupiter usurped the background. Lightning crackled in one of its two Great Red Spots like the twinkling of an eye.

The realization of where she had ended up jarred her harder than the crash.

The rumbling of fusion engines rose above the sound of the raging geyser. Two Starthroats appeared over the dipping horizon.

A half-laugh, half-gasp forced its way up from her gut. Broken bones knifed into her sides, but the joy of continued life numbed her to the pain.

"What's so funny, Auntie?"

Brooke pulled Maya into her arms. "We made it, squirt." She squeezed her niece tight, unable to force back the sobs. "We're home."

**To be continued . . .**

The story continues in *Beyond the Horizon*, the second book in Greg Spry's Beyond Saga.

Seventeen years after the events of *Beyond Cloud Nine*, the human race has made great strides toward creating a utopian society. All nations have come together under one government, the IntraSolar Commonality. But the truth behind how this foundation was established—and the unscrupulous reality of how such an idealistic and fragile balance is maintained—remains buried.

As a poster child for the new evolved mankind, twenty-two-year-old Ensign Maya Davis, graduate of the new Interstellar Expeditionary Force academy, achieves her lifelong dream of exploring the stars. She earns a commission aboard humanity's first deep space exploration vessel, *New Horizons*.

However, when *Horizons* reaches its destination far beyond the sanctity of Earth's solar system, sabotage cripples the ship, killing the senior staff and leaving its junior officers in command. Maya must risk her life to resolve the turmoil aboard, defend *Horizons* from alien attack, and find a way to get the stranded starship home.

Back in the solar system, civilian flight instructor Brooke Davis uncovers the Vril's unbelievable agenda regarding *Horizons's* voyage. With time running out, Brooke races to save her niece and *New Horizons* light years away.

**About the Author**

**Greg Spry** was born in Green Bay, Wisconsin, in 1978. He majored in industrial engineering at the University of Wisconsin—Madison before earning a graduate degree in space systems from the Florida Institute of Technology. As a jack-of-all-trades, he has dabbled in engineering, information technology, computer programming, web design, entrepreneurship, art, and of course, writing. In his free time, he enjoys playing kickball and cheering on the Wisconsin Badgers and Green Bay Packers. He currently resides in the United States. Visit his personal website at www.gregspry.com.

CPSIA information can be obtained at www.ICGtesting.com
Printed in the USA
LVOW11s2329230415

435823LV00002BC/494/P

9 780990 822400